There were three of them. One lay in a drunken stupor on my parents' bed. His clothes were stained with sweat and pitch and blood. Wine purpled his cheeks and soaked his shirt.

The other two lay on the floor—one astride and coupling with the naked body of one of the serving maids; the other positioned over her head, his mouth suckling her pale breast. They were both naked from the waist down.

I looked at the girl and pointed to her hysterically. "You filthy sons of hell, she is not one of your Scotian whores!"

"Are you afraid to die, boy?"

"I show no fear of filth such as you."

He crossed the room and placed himself directly in front of me. I could smell the stench of murder upon him and see the history of violence in his face . . .

THE LION &
THE CROSS

Joan Lesley Hamilton

BALLANTINE BOOKS • NEW YORK

Library of Congress Catalog Card Number: 78-69659

ISBN 0-345-28632-4

This edition published by arrangement with
Doubleday & Co., Inc.

Manufactured in the United States of America

First Ballantine Books Edition: June 1981

This book is dedicated to Charles. His love and prodding made it happen. And to Isa. Her faith in me made me realize that it might be done. And to the memory of my father, John Leslie Hamilton, descendant of Ulstermen and Republicans, who taught me to be proud of the Irish in me.

CONTENTS

PROLOGUE

"I am Padraic, a sinner, most unlearned, the least of all the faithful, and utterly despised by many."

Yet, in this the hour of my severest testing, knowing that the High King has sent his henchmen into the dawn wood to seek me out and slay me, I know in my heart that Destiny has led me back to Eire, and so I am not afraid.

Destiny? Yes. At last I have acknowledged it. And His name. Though once I mocked them both. For reasons which I shall never know, God has sought me out. From across the far seas. From within the soul of my youth. He has signed His mark upon me in blood and now He roars within me as a lion. He roams my conscience as a restless, prodding wind. He has worked miracles for my sake. He has given me the Sight. He has granted me the Power.

It is by His grace that the druids fear me as a sorcerer. They call me an enchanter, a magician who can command the spirits of the Otherworld. Yes. It is all true. But the Power is not mine to be summoned at whim. Were it otherwise, I would never have been taken as a slave to Eire, nor would there have been war upon the peaceful hills of Dalaradia, nor would I be here now, shivering in the forest, a hunted man. I would be at Tara, seat of Laoghaire, who is now High King over all of Eire. Like the clever, whispering male ghosts which the Gael call fershee, I would wrap myself in the fabled cloak of invisibility and take myself fast and far across the miles. With the sacred Hill of Slane at my back, I would hover like a shadow in the great banquet hall of the High King, eavesdropping upon those who now plot to destroy me.

Yet Tara is many a long mile away and, for now at least, God has brought me here to be sheltered by the forests of the Mountain of Mists. My youth was spent here. Memories of it rise in me now like dawn across an old and ancient plain. It was here that I, a Briton captive, was to learn the ways of the Gael. It was here that God first blessed me with His Power and then blighted me with His wrath. A thousand, thousand years away it seems now, for the Sight has been dimmed within me, and the Power is a mere breath stirring softly in the fallen leaves which are my memories of Yesterday. The dragons still elude me. The dragon Future. The dragon Unknown. They had led me back to Eire and still they are not content to rest. They lead me on, haunting me with the prophecies of long-dead seers, mocking me with memories of flame and stone and magic.

Magic? Oh yes. Do not scoff. There *is* magic. I have seen it worked in the shadow of the standing stone, and in the gray eyes of a man who could see beyond Tomorrow. The druids know it well. They practice it even now, at Tara and Emain Macha and such of their holy places as Dun Ailinne and Cashel. But theirs is a magic born out of Darkness. The Power which is born through me is the Power of the God of Light who came to me in the Long Ago, when I was a boy who knew him not, even though He moved upon my dreams and called out to me from the soft and pliable fabric of my youth.

Youth? I am nearly forty now. An old man. And still I follow the dragons, though at last I am wise enough not to ask why. The way and the reason shall be made known in God's good time. Meanwhile, I am content to follow, knowing that my future has somehow been written in my past and that the road upon which I walk has been laid for me . . . long before I was ever born.

The road. I must speak of the road. It began for me in Briton, on a day ripe with summer. I was a boy then, sixteen and as arrogant and willful as any Gael. I had gone out upon the sea cliffs of my homeland with my childhood friend Claudius. Our talk was of taking up the sword and of becoming warriors for the sake of our people. The hot, sweet rising of young manhood was within us. I did not know that even as I spoke of battle, my life as a servant of God had begun.

Who am I, O Lord, and to what has Thou called me . . .

Saint Patrick—from his *Confession*

BOOK I

FROM THE WESTERN SEA

... My father was Calpornius, a deacon, son of
Potitus, a priest, of the village of Bannavem Taburniae; he had a country seat nearby and there I was
taken captive.

Saint Patrick—from his *Confession*

1

ROMANA called to me. A distant sound. I chose not to
hear it.

The sun was high, not yellow or orange or red, but
white with the noon. The heat of it seemed to be reaching
across Time to touch me, to encompass me. It was life
and I stood beneath it, my face upturned.

"Magonus!" Again my sister's voice.

My eyes had been closed. Now I opened them. The
sea was before me, as calm as a lough. I could look across
the miles and follow the curve of the hills which formed
the lips of the bay. Green they were and as shaggy as ponies in winter coat.

Behind me, the mounded hillsides of my father's summer estate bolted against the sky. Before me, the cliffs
dropped steep-away to the spuming surf. The world ended
there. It slurred away with the suck of the tide. Once,
guarded by the barges of Imperial Rome, ships of many
nations had sailed to safe harbors along the Briton shore.
Now only sea birds, wayward insects, and leaping fish

dared to break the surface of the Western Sea. Silence reigned there now, and the wind. And the barbarians.

It was the Year of Our Lord, Four Hundred and Ten. It was the beginning of that period of history which men would later call the Dark Ages. But we who lived then knew only the moment which was ours in Time. Our world was changing but, we reasoned, so had the world always changed for Man; and so would it always change. The eagle which had conquered the land of my fathers had been called home to Rome. We Britons, living at the very rim of the Empire, had been cast adrift into a hostile sea. The legions had been withdrawn. The barracks stood empty. The great Roman fortresses and roadways had already begun to show signs of decay. Our villages and villas stood unguarded, like so many flocks of sheep whose shepherds had abandoned them.

"Magonus!" Again Romana's voice, more imperative now, growing closer.

It sparked anger within me. By all of the suffering gods of antiquity, could the woman not see that I had deliberately come out upon the cliffs so that Claudius and I might speak privately together? No doubt she was coming to fetch me in for supper, as though I were a child whom she could coddle and bully as she pleased. Lord, save the world from the ministrations and meddlings of older sisters!

"Claudius! Magonus!" Another voice now, a child's call. Romana evidently had little Clodia in tow.

Claudius, seated beside me on an outcropping of stone, stirred and sighed at the call of his own sister. He, Clodia, and their widowed father were guests at my family's villa this day. "We must go back to the house," he said. "No doubt the noonday meal is ready. Your grandfather will wish us to be present for the blessing."

I cast him a deprecating glower. "My grandfather may be a priest, but he is also a senile old fool who slobbers in his soup and cuts wind into his dining cushions. His very presence sours the meal. And what do I care for his meaningless blessing? Both they and he sicken me. By all that is reasonable, Claudius, I cannot bring myself to go back to the house and continue on as though nothing has happened. If what you've said is true, if Scotian raiding ships were indeed sighted but three days' ride from this shore, then we are all in mortal danger. But I tell you that my parents will never believe it. Not they. They insist that the days of peace and plenty shall go on forever. God! How can they not see the truth?"

Claudius shrugged and shook his head. "Perhaps because they cannot bear to see it."

His words seemed to send invisible clouds running out before the sun. I felt cold with fear, yet within me there seemed to be a fever rising. "The legions will never return to Briton. We have been left to fend for ourselves. The edict which forbade us to bear arms has been lifted. Yet what have we done to protect ourselves? Offered up Masses to God! By the milk of Mother Mary, is your father the only man in all of west Briton who is able to see the way which we must follow?"

"Many of the young men are joining with him."

The fever rose up within my neck and ran across my shoulders, causing me to shiver. "And so shall I. I give you my word."

He was not convinced. "Your parents will never allow you to be trained to the sword, Magonus. You are the grandson of a priest, the son of a presbyter. They expect other things of you, my friend."

"I shall do *my* will. Not theirs. I am no longer a child. I shall learn to fight and to bear arms like a man. God, Claudius! The barbarian Scots have already taken half of Dyfed! Is that to be our lot? To be ruled and enslaved by barbarians?"

A droll smile curled on his lips. "Ahh, but old friend, in time we shall surely convert them to Christ, and then we shall all live blissfully together in peace and harmony."

His statement had been a sarcastic echoing of my parents' philosophy. "Peace!" I spat the word at him. "There is no peace within the heart of a Scot! Only addle wits and imbeciles believe that they hunger for anything save land and captives."

One of his dark brows arched indolently. "Then, two thirds of the population of west Briton must be addled." He rose to his feet and adusted the folds of his scarlet cloak. He was nineteen that summer. Three years older than I. Dark, while I was fair. Tall and muscular, while I was small of frame and as lean as a half-grown pup. I worshiped and emulated him. No brother could have been closer to me or more loved.

I rose to my feet beside him. "Your father will convince them. He *must* convince them."

His brown eyes narrowed. Bitterness shadowed his face. "The elders accuse Licinius of madness. They say that by preaching 'the sword' he advocates heresy."

"Elders! What do they know of the new times? Politicians and priests and pious virgins . . . all proclaiming 'the will of the Lord'!" Anger was a hot saliva within my mouth. I spat it vehemently upon the ground. "I think *that* of them!"

He smiled and put a brotherly hand upon my shoulder. "Leash your temper, Magonus. It is a useless weapon unless properly directed. My father and I are traveling up and down the coast, to all of the villas. We *will* make the people see and understand the threat of the times. We will make them see that Britons must draw together, that we must become a unified people, in arms as well as spirit. We must fortify our towns and forge our men into a cohesive army. If we do not . . . if we stand passive . . . we shall soon be as lambs running before the wolves from the Western Island. One night we shall awaken to the cry of battle horns and to the screams of our defenseless neighbors. The Scots shall have descended upon us from the sea. The smoke from their fires shall taint our nostrils, and the flames of our own destruction shall sear these very skies."

His words set a fire raging within me. There had been talk of raiders ever since I could remember. Yet, until last year, the Romans had always been here to protect us. Now wayfarers were telling of wild men in craggy vessels, of carnage and of murder. True enough, the horror was always someplace else. Further north. Further south. Never here; never even near. At our seaside villa, and in the village of Bannavem Taburniae, where I had been born, all was serene. Bees droned in the sun. Fruit ripened on the boughs. Ale fermented in the vats. Fog drifted in from the sea. Winter brought rain and, occasionally, a soggy snow which dripped from the roofs and collected on trees and shrubs like clumps of insect spittle. Spring warmed the earth and roused the bees. Summer brought the fruit, and the flies, and the scent of barley beer in the making. Regardless of the season, life for me had become a continual round of tedium followed by boredom followed by tedium once again. I often wished, and was filled with shame and a strange, intoxicating sense of eagerness, that the dreaded raiders would come.

"Magonus!" Again Romana's voice.

Again it sparked anger within me. Thoroughly annoyed, I turned to see her approaching up the pathway. Her hair, like mine, was the color of faded wheat. Her eyes, like mine, were blue. At twenty-three, she was compact of form and moved with an aggressively matronlike step. Beside her, Claudius' little sister Clodia, all dark curls and dimples, skipped along chattering gayly. The sight of the child caused me to utter an involuntary groan. She was twelve and fancied that she suffered with true and unending passion for me.

Claudius saw my instant discomfort and laughed. "If the barbarians don't get you first, I'm afraid that Clodia will."

"I'd prefer the barbarians, thank you."

Our sisters reached the top of the bluff and came to stand before us. To my dismay, Clodia ran to me and tried to insert one of her plump, beringed fingers through the crook of my elbow. I growled at her and snatched my arm away.

Glaring at my sister, I demanded to know by what right she interrupted me in my conversation with Claudius.

Her chin went up. My rudeness never failed to prick her anger. I was an only son, the last-born of doting, middle-aged parents. I had learned at an early age that an unpredictable nature held advantages for me. I was rarely punished, and never severely. When I sulked I was coddled rather than ignored. When I chose to be belligerent, which was often enough, I could drive away those whom I chose not to see. I had even mastered the art of repulsing my old tutor Veranius, often causing him to throw up his arms in despair of my nastiness. But Romana was my elder by seven years. She knew my moods and would not indulge them.

"The noonday meal is ready," she informed me coolly.

"Go and eat it then," I replied.

She measured me with knowing eyes. To Claudius she challenged evenly: "Have you also come to consider rudeness to be a Christian virtue? Will you, a guest in our house, keep us waiting at table for you?"

To my amazement, Claudius flushed to his hairline and bowed deferentially. To me he said: "Your sister is right,

Magonus. We do ourselves no honor by keeping others from their meal. We can continue the topic of our conversation as we break bread with your family."

"No," said Romana. "Not if you intend to speak of the sword." She reached out to gather Clodia's little hand protectively into her own. "Ours is a Christian house, Claudius. Your father has already sufficiently upset it with his talk of raiders and of taking up arms against them. At our table we shall discuss doing the will of God . . . not the will of those who seem to savor the thought of spilling their brothers' blood."

"Is the will of God not worked through men, Romana?" he said quietly. "And in truth, I do not believe that even your Christ Jesus would call a heathen, raping Scot his brother."

Her face had grown taut with strain. "Is He no longer your Christ Jesus, Claudius? Have you, like so many of the young men these days, chosen to turn from the God of your fathers?"

"The God of Rome is not the God of my fathers. The God of Rome is the God of those who conquered my ancestors and yours centuries ago. Now that Rome has chosen to abandon us, it seems that the power of her God has left with her. Perhaps it is time for Britons to renew their faith in the old gods, Romana? Or at least, to kindle some small faith in themselves."

His words disturbed her. "There is but one God, Claudius. Without Him we are lost. You must not turn from Him. You must not lose faith."

"Faith . . ." I sneered. "Faith in what? There is no God." I took pleasure in knowing that my statement would sting her.

To my surprise, she did not gasp or pale or call out to heaven to forgive me the enormity of my sin. She fixed me with an icy stare and said contemptuously: "What an arrogant, stupid boy you are, Magonus. Do you think that I am ignorant of your foolish dreams? Do you honestly believe that you, an undisciplined, spoiled schoolboy who has not even the patience or intelligence to master your Latin or your mathematics, could possibly hope to learn the disciplines of manly combat even if our parents would allow it?"

She had openly ridiculed me in front of my friend. My temper flared. For Claudius' sake I controlled it, hoping that he would notice the authority and disdainful composure with which I greeted my sister's censure. "I am sixteen," I informed Romana loftily. "I am a man. I shall be a soldier, not a scholar."

Her glance singed me with her displeasure. "You shall not be a scholar. That much is certain."

Anger suddenly took control of me. I raged out at her. "Nothing is certain these days. Can you not see that? Are you the one virgin in all of west Briton who sleeps peacefully throughout the night, dreaming of your sweet, all-suffering, all-simpering Christ while the world around you is threatened to its very life? Or can it be that you wish to be raped in your bed? Is that what you have secretly hoped for all of these years while professing chastity for the sake of your faith?"

It was Claudius, not Romana, who struck me. A resounding, stinging slap across my cheek. The world went white for me. Righteous indignation burned in my mouth. With a profanity shouted at all three of them, I turned and began to run inland toward the hills.

Did I expect my sister to call me back? Or Claudius to cry out with quick and sincere apology? Yes. I wanted that. But there was silence from them both. It was little Clodia who shouted after me.

"Oh, do come back, Magonus!" she cried. "There are sorcerers and devils dwelling in the hills these days!"

The hills rose with a burst and a gallop. The sky was clouded now, peopled by the gathering white legions of the afternoon. I moved at a lope. I looked neither to my left nor to my right, but down at the earth over which my sandaled feet carried me. Had I glanced behind and below me, I would have seen the sea, all misted and vague; a mere suggestion of blue beneath the opaline shawl of gray which had moved suddenly inland to tentatively explore the headlands. The villa was lost to view behind cloud and grassy ridge. I could not hear Claudius calling to me. Even if I had, I would not have replied.

I trotted on. My breath came in long, even draughts. The air which I sucked into my lungs was clean. It tasted of pollen and smelled of the sea. It filled me like a good wine. I drank it consciously. It ran out through my veins as I lengthened my stride. The surface of my skin began to burn with a thin fire.

I had set a goal for myself. In order to dissipate my anger, I would run until I reached the silent, windless comfort of the upland groves. This was a region which had been distinctly forbidden to me during the past few years. I remembered it from childhood wanderings with Claudius. I would go there now, in open defiance. I would run past the mean, smelly shelters of the few people who lived in the dells and furrows of the knolls. They were rumored to be a surly lot of late, not above waylaying travelers or setting upon young men and women to force them into servitude. But rumor and suspicion stalked the hills of Briton these days like some whispering, invisible dragon. It consumed those who listened to it, rendering them impotent with its imagined terrors. I remembered the hill folk as mere shadows, dirty dark forms hovering within the entrances of their ill-made shelters. I was young. I held no fear of shadows, or of dragons which seemed content to dwell within the mists of men's minds.

I ran on. Already I could smell the dank scent of the hill people's smoky fires. I began to pace myself. The earth leveled out somewhat as I left the last of the hovels behind me. As in my memory, I saw no one; only farm stock and sleepy dogs and a cat stalking a breeze-tossed leaf.

The terrain dropped easily into a gentle stream course where the first of the really tall trees grew. Fragrant with shade, their roots clutched the earth like bony brown fingers. I continued to run, finding immense pleasure in the rhythm of my own heartbeat.

The art of the race was the one sport at which I excelled, though I chose never to compete with other youths since I was unable to bear the thought of possibly losing. I chose, instead, to race against myself. I set my own limits and regulations. The greatest joy of the game was to surpass myself.

I ran uphill now. My heart was singing. I began to lengthen my stride, knowing with pride that, indeed, my body seemed designed for the chase. My muscles, lean and hard, had a spring and agility which training alone could not have achieved. This was a skill to which a man was born. I could lope like a wolf for hours and never tire. I could spring and vault like a deer cornered in a thicket.

Still I ran on, past the lichen-clad outcroppings of stone

which told me that the forest was very near. The grade of the track had increased. My heart's song quickened. My head went back with the strain. My lips pulled away from my teeth. My breath was coming fast. Still I continued to lengthen my stride. Full out. To slow down at this point would be to invite mutiny from my raging body.

The land seemed to melt downward, to be held in place by the many trees whose roots jabbed down into the acid loam. The grasses, green on the hilltops, were yellow beneath the thickening shade. They were longer and grew in bushy patches, rather like brittle clumps of whiskers. Bracken intruded, coarse and high. The track disappeared. Bits and wedges of fallen bark trespassed into my open sandals. The scent of the forest was overpowering; dark and sweet and vaguely astringent. I had never been this far into this portion of the inland wood; and never had I ventured so far from the villa alone. I was beginning to feel giddy with the sense of rebellion accomplished.

By necessity, I slowed my pace to accommodate the slope of the terrain. The trees were close around me now; bulky, low-bending giants in scaling armor. They reached well-muscled arms across the sky to entwine their leafy fingers as though they held a conscious desire to shut away the last traces of daylight.

As I continued to move downward into the darkness of the wood, my breath began to come in irregular gasps. The air seemed close and warm. When I drew it into my lungs, it did not seem to have the ability to sustain me. I found myself pulling in deeper and deeper breaths, holding each one captive, draining it of every morsel of oxygen before I released it. Still, I was beginning to feel distractingly lightheaded. My thighs had begun to burn painfully. My heart was leaping with ill-timed cadence. My head was throbbing. Somewhere within me, the voice of Reason counseled: Turn back, Magonus. But I was young. The young seldom heed the voice of Reason.

So I went on, as though drawn, into the deeper darkness which lay at the base of the hill. I would stop there—there where the daylight was turned into night, where the salt wind from the sea could not penetrate.

A low, huffling bellow brought me up short. I felt the immediate superficial skin-prickling of fear. My breath was still coming in unrewarding gasps. I was feeling the first touches of dizziness. I reached out and sought to

steady myself against the low-reaching branches. I could
feel the blood surging in my veins. Sweat ran in hot rivu-
lets down my face and neck. Yet I was cold. And shivering.

Again the sound. Then the noise of duff being furiously
pawed. And then the realization that, through the throbbing, speckled whiteness of my dizziness and the shadows
of the forest, I was virtually blind. I squinted my eyes.
Sweat ran into them. I reached up to rub it away so that
I might clear my vision.

It was then that the boar charged. I viewed it as though
through gauze. And then, with the excruciating clarity of
one who sees through pain and terror, my vision cleared.
I saw the boar as it came directly at me out of the tangled
branches and knee-high ferns. Its head was down. Its
shiny little eyes were wild. Its snout was wet and running.
Its tusks were yellowed. Its shoulder blades rose as a
black-maned mountain. The sound of its frenzied wheeze
and pounding hooves was a clarion call. Death was charg-
ing me out of the darkness.

I did not have time to decide what I should do. I was
unarmed, clad only in my knee-length belted tunic and
sandals. With the forest close around me, there was nowhere to run.

The boar continued to come straight at me. I stood my
ground. When and how, after my long uphill race against
myself, I managed to summon the strength to vault head
over heels over the back of the boar, I will never know. I
can only surmise that God was with me even then, in that
cursed place, though I knew Him not. I think, too, that it
was His voice which warned me to go back from the
wood; His wisdom which tried to shield me from the
Darkness which awaited me. But, as I have said, I was
still a youth. I believed not in the God of my fathers.

I was suddenly in the air, tumbling forward. The boar
roared beneath me, jabbing upward with its tusks. The
danger continued to charge off, squealing and snuffling
through the wood. I hit the ground, not nearly so gracefully or painlessly as an acrobat would have done. I fell,
arms and legs akimbo, and rolled over and over down the
bramble-studded embankment.

An immense, scraggy root at the base of the hillside
stopped me short of landing in the stream. I went flailing
over the root while its twisted elbow caught me about the

waistline and threw me backward onto the grass. A vast, sickening tide swept through me, exploded in my brain. I looked up, stunned. There were only branches and a sky of leaf green. The green shimmered. It eased into gray. Then it deepened into blackness.

I awoke to the sound of singing and the scent of smoke. Soft, feminine singing in a language which I did not understand or recognize. Smoke from a sleepily burning brazier.

I lay on a bed of rushes. Some of them were still damp from their picking. I was in a crude wickerwork shelter, with no windows and only a hole, over which was draped a ragged cloth, for a door. There was no light within, yet I could tell from the haziness of the darkness that it was still daylight.

There was birdsong to accompany the delicate singing of the woman. There was the wonderful sighing of the wind in the tree-tops. I lay on the pallet and drifted back into sleep for a few moments. Heavy, dreamless sleep. Then I awoke, as suddenly as I had dozed.

I sat up and examined myself. I was still fully clothed, though my tunic was badly tattered and soiled. Amazingly, despite a vague soreness about my ribcage and some minor scrapes on my extremities, I was unhurt. My head did not ache. There was a strange taste in my mouth, as though I might have drunk some medicinal brew. I rubbed my temples. I remembered nothing after my encounter with the boar.

There were barley cakes on a saucer beside me, and a cup of water. The knowledge of my hunger overwhelmed me. I stuffed the stale, crumbling cakes into my mouth and washed them down with the water.

"Are you refreshed then?"

A hand parted the cloth doorway. I had noticed that the singing had stopped. The woman who had been the source of the sound now looked in at me.

I looked up at her and nearly dropped the cup of water. It was not that I had never seen a lovely woman before. My mother was said to be fair, as was my sister. Yet, even in the dimness of the hut, I knew that the figure upon whom I gazed transcended mere beauty.

I hesitate, even now, to use the word "aura," yet surely there was that about her. She was as tall as a man and as straight-backed as the mast of a proud ship. Her hair was brushed back from her forehead and fell about her shoulders in soft waves the color of rust. Where the daylight backlighted it, the hair seemed to shimmer with the halo of flame. She wore the poorest, plainest garment I had ever seen. The sleeves, untrimmed, fell in wrinkles about her slender wrists. The neckline was a tattered slash across her throat, caught at each shoulder by fraying laces. The fabric of the dress was a dismal brown. It hung to her bare feet in one long sweep. The material was so pitifully thin that there was not a contour of her body which was not readily evident to me.

If I had ever doubted that I was a man full grown, the desire which the sight of her kindled within me would have immediately put my mind at ease. It was sudden, seething, baffling, unreasoning desire. It was awesome. When she came into the room I drew back from her, terrified by the emotions which her nearness aroused in me.

She knelt beside the brazier and bent to blow life back into it. With long, pale fingers she picked up a charred stick and began to prod the embers. From where I sat, I could see how the neckline of her dress eased forward, revealing her breasts to me. All white they were, with the nipples smooth and round and the color of her lips.

I swallowed. Audibly. She looked up at me, all the while continuing to prod the embers. As I met her eyes and was caught up into their loveliness, there was not a breath she took which did not light embers within me as well.

"Maponos," she said, her voice accented by a dialect which I could not place. "Oh, but the look on your face, young lad! Are you afraid of me then? You, who have tested the magic boar, should know no fear of woman."

Somehow I managed to find my voice. "My name is Magonus," I corrected.

"No, young lad, you are Maponos the Hunter." Her voice was as sleepy as the brazier had been, as gentle as the wind which stirred the treetops above the hut. "I have seen you put the magic boar to shame. Surely, he was under your spell, or else he would have slain you."

"I work no spells," I said, trying to put forth an image of composure.

Her gray eyes held mine. They were the same color as the smoke which rose dreamily from the brazier. They moved meditatively over my face and body. I felt myself blush. She smiled softly and made a small, secretive little sound of laughter.

"I have watched you while you slept," she said. "You work greater spells than you know." She drew back from the brazier. Her garment pulled up to conceal her breasts. "I have not seen you in the wood before."

"I have not been to this part of the wood before."

She picked up a small, highly ornate container. It was of bronze. Tiny stylized animals and figures had been worked into it. She dipped her fingers into the green salve which it contained and moved closer to me. "This is magic," she assured me as she began to massage the ointment into the abrasions on my arms.

I sat dead still, afraid to move lest she stop and draw away from me. Covertly, I studied her face. It was so very white and fine, with the eyes wide-set beneath a well-defined brow; the nose high-bridged and straight; the lips full; the chin round and easing gracefully back into the softness of her throat. She began to sing, deep in the soft throat, making no words, only melody, as her hands moved over my arms and then found my thighs.

I jumped then, like a spitted toad. My face was blood red with shame. Shame of my innocence. Shame of my confusion. Shame of my desire for her.

She clucked her tongue and put down the container. Her hands rested on her bent knees. "Maponos who pursues the magic boar and leaps in terror at the touch of a woman? Are you so young then? Or does my touch offend you?"

"N-no!" I had not meant to shout. "I am a man grown. My name is not Maponos, and your touch does not offend me."

"Then my rude clothing must cause the offense. Surely it must be that." Her hands went up, swiftly, like delicate birds fluttering. "There now," she said.

Before I could utter a word of protest, she had untied the laces which held her garment in place. It fell in a drab, beige heap about her hips. My bladder almost collapsed at the sight of her. I heard myself catch my breath with wonder and confusion.

Her eyes held on my face. She smiled, holding out her hands to me in invitation. My heart leaped to respond, but my body suddenly, uncontrollably, was scrambling to its feet. I fled from the hut, tripping over the brazier as I went, tossing the cup of water onto the rushes.

I had never felt more a child or more inept. As I burst out of the hut my dizziness returned to me. I fought for balance and vision, lost the battle and went sprawling.

I looked up to see that I was in a glade. The afternoon was beginning to ease toward dusk. The colors were soft. The leafy world around me seemed to have taken on the tones of pond algae: thick yellows and greens with the trunks and branches of trees etched black upon them. The wind did not reach here. It sighed in the topmost canopy of the treetops. The colors swayed with ambient rhythm. The leaves cast graceful, dancing shadows.

The woman had followed me out of the hut. I was too humiliated to face her. I turned my eyes to the ground.

"Maponos . . . Maponos . . ." she cajoled kindly as she came to stand beside me. Her bare toes intruded themselves into the line of my vision. How fair they were. All clean, with the nails long and neatly pared and the moons arching high and as white as chalk.

With a soaring sense of relief, I saw the straggly unhemmed edge of her dress and knew that she had clothed herself again. Slowly, I half turned my face so that I could see her.

She smiled then and bent to put her hand upon my shoulder. So light, so very tentative was her touch that I could sense rather than feel it. "Come," she said, "you must rise to your feet now, with no fear of me, young lad, for I shall do only that which is at your bidding."

Her scent was all around me. It was tenuous and pervasive all at once. It was the perfume of freshly crushed sweet herbs and newly washed hair. It was the essence of smoke and smooth, fragrant skin.

"Perhaps you will find a bath in the stream refreshing?" Her voice had formed a suggestion, not a command.

Yet, instinctively, as I rose to my feet, I drew away from her. A bath in the stream would mean that she would see me naked.

The woman seemed to interpret my thoughts. "I will prepare food for you while you bathe in privacy. The water will make you strong again. After it has touched you, surely you shall fear nothing ever again, for it flows from a magic spring."

I would have rebuked her easy references to the supernatural, but she put her fingertips against my lips. "You shall see," she assured me softly, then turned and went back to the hut.

I was alone in the glade. I walked across the gentle grassy depression which led to the stream. There, in the meager shelter of trees as young as myself, I disrobed hesitantly, looking back toward the hut to make certain that the woman was not watching me. I thought of Claudius and was immediately annoyed with myself. What would he have done had he been in my place? Would he have run from the woman's hovel like a hysterical rabbit? No. Not Claudius. He would have answered her invitation with the full measure of his potency, which, he had assured me often enough, was without end. Claudius would never run from any challenge. Like the Celts of old, should the situation ever demand, I was certain that he would march naked into battle in full defiance of the enemy.

Disgusted with myself and confident at last that the woman was not spying upon me, I waded naked into the stream.

Indeed, I thought then, that the water might well be magic if such foolishness as magic were reality. It was the clearest water I had ever seen. Smooth gray boulders formed a natural couch upon which a man might sit or recline, waist-deep in the cool liquid.

But the water was not cool. As I lowered myself onto the stone, I was amazed to find it warm. I cupped up handfuls of it and splashed it over myself. I made a cup of my hands and drank. The water tasted of minerals, primarily of sulphur. The taste was bitter and unpleasant. I spat it out.

I lay back, allowing the mellow liquid to flow over me. I closed my eyes and listened to the sounds of the wood. It seemed to me later that I must have slept then. The warmth of the water ran over me. The stone was smooth and cushioned my body. The soothing sounds and colors of the forest put me fully at my ease. It was as though these elements had combined and painlessly opened my veins, allowing my blood to flow gently away with the current. The woman sang softly in her hut. The wind was held at bay by the treetops. The water was a balm. I lay my head back against that portion of the stone which formed a pillow and, as though drugged, it seemed as though sleep came to me.

I dreamt of the scent of smoke and then, in my dream I thought, I awoke. A thin vapor hung above the stream, a diaphanous pathway which beckoned and begged to be followed. I rose sleepily and began to walk upstream. The smoke enticed me onward, like a dancing, animate ribbon. It touched my nostrils and went up into them, giving me a sweet aroma which was reminiscent of the woman.

The forest changed. It was a much older wood than the one through which I had come earlier in the day. The clarity of the water took on the darkness of the surrounding trees. There were briers on the bank, thorny and brittle. They reached across the stream and seemed to be scratching out at me with the malevolence of living creatures.

There was the croaking of a bullfrog, then a rising, grating cacophony of them. An eel slimed across my foot and splashed away into the darkness of a deep pool which was hollowed into the bank. The roots of an enormous tree hung down into the water like faded, lifeless arteries.

I paused and looked up. My glance followed the writhing majesty of an ancient oak. I wondered how long it had been since the force of life had left it. Its bark hung in stiff, scaling scabs. Insects had ravaged its heart. Leaves, like memories, clung as remnants: dry, brown, shredded.

My eyes followed the westward-pointing musculature of one of the tree's great branches. Three crows perched on a mighty branch. They were dull-feathered and sickly looking. They made muffled, almost chuckling sounds at me. I was amazed by the sight of them. Each wore a blood-red falcon's hood tied about its scrawny neck. Through eye holes cut into the fabric, they looked down at me and began to chortle madly. They cackled. They pointed at me with their wingtips.

I knew that it was not reasonable, but somehow I sensed that they were laughing at me. I shouted up at them for them to be silent. They laughed all the louder. I reached down, picked up a stone and pitched it up at them. They guffawed raucously. The stone missed them, hit the branch, then bounced back directly at me.

I leaped aside, right into a maze of brambles. The crows' glee rose to a scream of utmost delight. Then, with a ruffling of motley feathers, they took to the sky, flying off toward the west, into the darkness of the approaching night, cawing something back at me which sounded like "Pa-trec . . . Pa-trec . . . Pa-trec . . ."

Cursing under my breath, I freed myself of the brambles and waded up out of the stream onto the bank.

A segment of smoke circled the great oak. Still mumbling oaths against the crows, I followed the circle of smoke and gazed spellbound to the other side of the massive trunk.

To my surprise and delight, I saw a tiny room of green grass and new-leafed shrubbery all lighted by a shaft of sunlight which penetrated the high, exquisite canopy of the treetops. Here, in this world of light and life, the ancient tree still lived. The bark grew tightly against the heartwood. Leaves festooned living, limber branches and waved down at me as though in welcome.

The clearing was as bright as noon, walled all around by the somber darkness of the surrounding forest. At the far end of the clearing the earth rose, a gentle mound, carpeted with bright grass and starred with tiny flowers. From the heart of the mound gushed a tiny, crystalline spring all wreathed in fern. Atop the mound, pointing heavenward, was a smoothly hewn man-tall stone. And at the base of the stone, with her hair falling loose to her knees, knelt the woman.

My body suddenly felt as warm as the stream in which I had recently bathed. Somewhere within me something stirred as softly as dawn.

I stepped forward out of the wood, from darkness into light. I had not forgotten that I was naked. I had simply forgotten to be ashamed of my nakedness. The bright lemon light of the sun touched my skin. I felt a surge of pride well within me: pride of myself, of my youth. I stood tall, back straight. I felt a tensing of thigh and buttocks. I looked down at myself and knew that, as I had told my sister only this noon, I was a man.

The woman's head was bent forward. She heard the sound of the branches parting. She turned. She looked at me with no hint of surprise. She held a small lidded basket within her hands. She put it aside. From within it came muted cooings, as from a dove.

She, too, was without garments. Her body shone as pale and smooth as white enamel. She moved, though she did not rise. She held out her arms to me.

I did not pause. Nor did I bolt and run as I had run from her before. I went to her and knelt beside her, facing her.

She leaned toward me so that her breasts were against my chest. Her head went back and her throat was bared to me, as supplicating and flawless as the neck of a swan. Her body began to sway, to brush back and forth against mine. Slowly she began to lean away from me. She arched her back so that, in my desire to keep her near, I reached out to hold her. My arms went about the small of her back, and still she drew me down, down onto the warm green earth where I lay upon her and listened to her murmuring and knew no shame at all.

Still the daylight lingered. Shadowy now. Weary light. We knelt beside the spring, before the man-tall stone. A fire had been kindled there, small and flickering on a foot-wide offering piece of granite.

We were both still without clothing, though the woman had donned a necklet of gold. It was glass-smooth where it lay against her skin. Raised figures of birds and boars and sheafs of wheat were worked into its outer edge as ornamentation. It did not join at the front like a conventional necklace, but was open at the throat like the torques of the ancient Celts.

She had begun an atonal chant in the language which I had first heard her use when I had awakened within the hut. At length, she turned to me and held out the little woven basket. "For my god," she said. Her right hand went out to rest upon my thigh. "We must give thanks. In the way of my people."

Her touch caused me to shiver with renewed desire for her. I moved to kiss her. She pushed me gently away.

"First we must thank the god."

"I do not believe in gods."

Her head eased to one side. Her eyes were full of mirth, of secrecy, of assurance. "The god of the wood has brought you to me. He has brought you to this place. You are Maponos the Hunter, a god yourself. Your magic has flowed into me. The god has allowed this. He asks only that you make sacrifice to him, so that the magic will be strong."

"I am not a god. I do not believe in magic." I took the little basket from her, out of curiosity. It fit easily into the palms of my hands. It was woven into the shape of a bird. When I took hold of it, I heard the sound of cooing from within.

"You must place it in the fire," she instructed.

My stomach muscles contracted unpleasantly. I was beginning to grow weary of her constant allusions to magic. "There is a living creature within the basket."

She nodded. "It is for the god."

"To be burnt up alive? Surely you do not engage in such stupid, primitive rituals?"

A strange expression crossed her face. "I wish to make sacrifice to my god." Her voice had grown stern. A frown rode her brow. "You have taken what is his. I am the god's own. To lie with me again, you must give homage to the god into whose wood you have come."

"I cannot give homage to something in which I do not believe."

Her frown melted into a smile. She made the sound of a sigh, then a knowing, barely audible laugh. She put her face against mine and blew softly so that I could smell the sweetness of her breath. "I can make you believe," she said. "I can make you believe that you are Maponos who has leapt over Death in the wood. I can make you know that you are immmortal, as I am."

I drew back from her. "I do not believe in immortality."

Her features hardened into a mask of reproach. "Are you like all of the young men today? Do you choose to accept your own corruptibility? Is it only the old and the aging, already begun to decay, who can sense the truth? That, somehow, there must be more to life than this?" With the fingers of her left hand, she pinched up a hummock of skin on her right wrist. An expression of disgust turned her lips down. "You are immortal," she said to the flesh of her hand. "I have willed you so."

There was such vehement longing in her voice that I felt pity for her. Surely, I thought, if there were a way to keep her loveliness alive and vibrant forever, I would pursue it. I told her that, then added, in apology: "But truth is truth, regardless of the will of Man. And I am of a Christian house. My people believe that we are forever damned if we make sacrifice to pagan gods."

"We? Do you include yourself among them?"

I did not recognize the trap, and so fell headlong into it. "I am of their flesh, but not of their faith."

Her lips lifted and worked languidly. The color of her eyes seemed to lighten, even as the smoke which rose from the little altar lightened as it rose into the air. "Will your people ever know of me? Or of what you have done for me and for yourself in this wood? Will you tell them of the pleasure you have found within me? And truly, your sacrifice will only be a gesture to please me, since you have said that you do not believe in gods."

"I do not," I affirmed.

She reached out and ran her hands over my arms and shoulders. She leaned against me and kissed me. Her mouth was open over mine, her tongue prodding like a drowsy viper. "What harm then," she asked breathlessly, "to make token sacrifice to a god in which you do not believe . . . for me? Your people will never know . . ."

The basket felt hot and rough within my hands. I shifted it from palm to palm, wanting to be free of it, to put my hands upon the woman. I returned her kiss. The heat of it filled me. I set the basket aside and drew the woman up against me, roughly, so that she could feel my manhood hard against her.

She tensed, went as rigid as iron. "I shall not yield to you again . . . not until you have done with the god."

So it was done. Thoughtlessly. Impatiently. I picked up the basket and thrust it into the flames. The wicker exploded into fire. I could hear the frantic beating of wings. The cooing became a high-pitched scream of agony. And then the very flames were screaming, devouring.

My desire fled from me with a chill, numbing tremor born somewhere deep within me. I could smell the scent of charred flesh and feathers. The woman made a sound of triumph. She was on her feet. Her arms were lifted in salutation. She was calling out to her diety in words which I did not understand. Then, bare-handed, she bent and wiped the smoldering remains of the basket and its contents off of the sacrificial stone and into the spring. There was a whispering, hissing sound. The woman lifted handfuls of the tainted, steaming water. She splashed them over herself.

Slowly she rose and came to stand before me. Her body glistened. Fragments of cinders clung to her. Her eyes had gone enormously wide. The color of them seemed to have become liquid, to pulse, to throb as though in need of release. Her lips were twitching at the corners. She began to intone the name which was not my name: "Maponos . . . Maponos . . ." and then, terrifyingly, was my name: "Magonus Sucatus Patricius, son of Calpornius, pledged to the Christian God. Now you are pledged to me, by blood and by body."

A darkness had suddenly come into the glade. The shadows became long and cold. A wind, smelling strongly of the sea, intruded chillingly. The woman, who had somehow known all along who I was, who had known and found pleasure in seducing me away from all that my people hoped I might be, was beckoning to me. She spoke my name. She lewdly promised me the pleasures of her body. Yet I was deaf to her words, blind to her movements. I saw only her mocking smile and knew, at last, who and what she was.

She was the one who called herself Morrighan. She was the one known as the whore of the wood. She was Morrighan, whose husband had brought her from the north only to be humiliated by her sexual excesses and growing madness. She was Morrighan, from the island of the Scots, who now lived alone in the solitude of the wood, giving herself to any male who sought her body. In her madness, she asked only tribute to her god, a mystical deity that she had brought with her from across the Western Sea. It was only out of kindness, or a sense of guilt, that her patrons supplied her with food and saw to it, now and again, that the thatch of her roof was patched and mended.

How could I not have known her at first sight? The infamy of her beauty and strange powers of precognition had spread far within the Christian community. Men who, ostensibly, had never known a soul who had lain with her, somehow knew of her insatiable lust. They could describe in minutest detail the fornications which she was said to wantonly commit, especially on the Sabbath.

My hands went up to my lips. The bitter taste which I

had experienced upon awakening within the hut was still
vaguely with me. Had she drugged me? Yes, I thought,
she had deliberately put the sweet venom of desire into
me and I, babe that I was, had drunk deeply and willingly of her potion.

Misery rose in me then, though I could not define it as
such. I felt betrayed, not so much by her duplicity, but
rather by the knowledge that she had given herself to
others before me. Then, as a man senses the movement
of clouds before the sun, I began to know that the emotion which was rising within me was more than the sharp
pain of tattered masculine pride. It was an upwelling of
something tenuously subtle and insidiously overpowering.
It seemed to be a voice trying to take substance within
me. It begged for release. It was not my voice. It was not
being born of my thoughts. It was alien, moving within
me, whispering. It sent my sense of reason shattering in a
thousand directions. It defied encompassment. It reached
out of the depths of my soul to remind me of the ancient
Commandment: "Thou shalt have no other gods before
Me . . ."

I, who had so thoughtlessly thrust the sacrificial dove
into the flames, felt this whispering presence shiver within
the confines of my skin. I knew, with the same instinctive
fear which had come to me when I had sensed the boar
waiting to charge at me out of the wood, that this was
more than mere emotion. This whispering, this presence,
was an awakening power which would take possession of
me if I allowed it the voice it sought.

I looked up at the woman called Morrighan. I saw the
gray depths of her eyes staring at me with a wildness
which seemed to be beckoning me toward her. I did not
move. I was half crouched on the ground, hands flat
against the earth. I looked at her and reasoned to myself: Yes, yes, she has drugged me, given me an herbal
brew which has brought me to a state of cogent insensi-
bility. I met her gaze and saw, beyond the wildness, beyond the depths of swirling gray, a foreverness of cloud,
an immensity of appalling distances. Bleak. Cold. Waiting. For me. My head went down. I shut my eyes against
her.

The voice, which I told myself must be the imagining of
my present state of drug-induced madness, was raging for
release upon my tongue. I damned the voice. I damned

myself, and the woman, and her sorceress's brew. I would
not allow myself to speak. I bit my tongue until it bled,
and the familiar taste of my own red blood washed away
the bitter taste of the herbs.

The voice retreated back within me. I trembled as I
felt it hovering, as a shadow, upon my thoughts. I now
realized fully that what had transpired here had been no
dream. I had, in fact, bathed in the sulphurous waters of
the stream. I had dozed, then awakened. I had followed
the ribbon of smoke to the glade where I had found the
woman by the spring, supplicating her god. I had given
to her that which was irrevocably precious, even though
I had given it no thought at the time: my innocence. I
had gone to her and lain with her and had allowed her to
cajole me into making token sacrifice to that dark and
nameless god of her pagan countrymen.

And now, in my drug-induced state of madness, it
seemed to me that her god had, indeed, claimed me. It
scorched me as the flames upon the altar had scorched
the sacrificial dove. It seared me. Deep within the fibers
of my knowledge, the god of the wood spoke to me,
mocking me.

"You are pledged to me," the god informed me. "By
blood and by body you are pledged to me."

A sigh of despair and shame escaped my lips. No, I
thought with the fury of defiance. I am pledged to *no*
god, for there are no gods! There is only fear and ignorance and the desperate need of Man to find immortality.

Then, in the deepening gray of twilight, far off in the
darkening wood, I heard the cackling of crows. "Pa-trec
. . . Pa-trec . . ." they cawed, and then I heard the voice
of the nameless god take form within me.

It was then that I broke and ran. I, who had scoffed at
gods and magic and the powers of unseen forces, suddenly knew, despite my knowledge of the irrationality of
the moment, that something beyond my comprehension
had touched me, something beyond the soothing bounda-
ries of sanity.

Filled with the horror of the impossibility of what was,
indeed, reality, I raged back with what I thought had to
be the voice of Reason: "I am pledged to no gods! There
are no gods!"

I ran out of the glade, off through the brambles which
lay beyond the half-dead ancient oak. Tripping, with the

laughter of crows in my ears, I went to my knees in the
stream. I had only half-managed to get to my feet when
a man's arm jerked me upright. It was Claudius. His face
was taut with apprehension.

"I have been trying to find you for hours. By the grace
of what god do I find you here, stark naked, running like a
madman?"

"By the grace of no god!" My voice was a shout of utter dejection.

There was the laughter of crows coming from the glade.
I looked back. There, leaning against the great oak, her
hair blown around her body by the wind which gusted out
of the glade, stood Morrighan. She held one of the chortling crows outward on her wrist. The other two perched
on her shoulders.

"Come back, Maponos," she called with a derision
which could only be described as malevolent. "Come
back, my little Christian, and lie with me again. Your
God will not want you any more, even though mine has
told Him how well-pleased he was by your sacrifice."

Claudius' fingers dug into my upper arm. "Is it true?"
His face was ashen. "Have you lain with her?"

I felt my lips twist downward into a sneer. "What matter? What concern of yours? Haven't you lain with her
yourself? How else would you have known where to find
me?"

"I came here years ago," he admitted, "but I never
touched her. I could not. Not after I saw what she was."
His dark eyes held cores of fear and of memories best
kept forgotten. "Magonus, you did not sacrifice to the
god of the wood?"

"There is no god! Of the wood or the heavens!" I sent
the words flailing at him. "We have sworn together, you
and I, that there could be no gods!"

The expression which crossed his features then defied
my understanding. Though he stood dead still, it was as
though he were retreating from me. I looked into his eyes
and knew, though we had been as brothers these many
years, that in this moment he was a stranger to me. I
knew not his deepest thoughts or longings or secret
shames and desires. So are the bonds of most men made,
cemented together with superficialities and deception.
We are strangers to all but ourselves and, even to our-

selves often astounded by the stranger who moves within us.

Slowly Claudius withdrew his arm from me and made the sign of the cross. He bowed his head, as though he could not bear to look at me. "May God forgive me," he said barely audibly, "if, indeed through my fault, I have brought you to this."

How long I walked along in the mindless, morose manner of one who is trapped within his own guilt, I do not know. I had gone back to the place where I had left my clothing, hastily dressed, then had run off into the darkness of the forest. I wished to thoroughly outdistance Claudius. I wished to lose myself within the great trees and somehow never be found again. I wished to forget the whore of the wood, and the stone, and the fire, and the madness which had made me believe that a nameless god had tried to speak through me.

Hunger at last made me turn my steps toward home. I was well out of the forest by then, walking along the crest of the hills. It was very nearly dark. The sun had gone down in a blaze of glory, sending its rays up in a shattering display of red seen through purple clouds. I paused momentarily, wondering what I would say to my parents when I returned home. No doubt Claudius would have returned before me. But would he have told them of my dalliance with the woman called Morrighan?

A headache began to sprout in my head like a weed. My nostrils drew in the scent of smoke. It did not speak to me of burning lamp oil or of cut wood crackling on a hearth or within a stoke hole. It spoke instead of scents which I had never before smelled in concert: of charred stone and melting leather, of hair twisting and turning to powder as it burns, of painted surfaces bubbling as they are subjected to intense heat, of meat being seared, of fat being rendered.

My mind was still trying to define this strange congealment of odors when my eyes widened. I realized that, though I was staring at the sunset, I was facing to the north.

"North?" The word was a whispering question born out of the awareness which was reminding me: Fool, the sun cannot set in the north. And yet there it was, defying the

law of earth and stars. The fire of its ebbing was as bright
as the flame on a newly kindled torch.

It was then that I remembered Claudius' warning:
". . . One night we shall awaken to the cry of battle horns
. . . the Scots shall have descended upon us from the sea.
The smoke of their fires shall taint our nostrils and the
flames of our own destruction shall sear these very skies."

I blinked. It could not be. Not here. Not now. Yet,
even as I thought these thoughts, the acrid smell of smoke
was intruding into my nostrils and I knew: Yes, it has
happened. It has happened here. It has happened now.

There were fires burning like beacons throughout the
hills that night. They were not beacons. They were the
burning villas of our neighbors and the farms of the hill
people.

As I came over the knoll which offered a view down
into the valley where our seaside villa had been built, it
was still barely light enough to afford me a view of the
sea. I could see the brown sails of the raider's ships moving slowly from the north and south. For a scant, rushing
moment, upwelling within me on a current of hope, I
thought wildly that there might still be time for me to
give warning to those of my father's house. Then, as I
looked down toward the villa, I knew that I was too late.
The buildings had been gutted. Strange, high-pitched
bellows rang throughout the hills. I froze where I was,
listening to the sound, to the reverberant bellows of a
horn which could have been taken to be the braying of a
gigantic mule. The sound was like nothing I had ever
heard. It rose and fell, triumphant, lingering, a sound
which shattered all hope which still lingered within me.

I put my hands up over my ears. I collapsed into a
seated position on the grasses of the knoll and I wept.

I stayed there, at the base of a dark outcropping of
ancient stone, until the stars had shifted across the sky
and in the east there blossomed the first faint thinning of
dawn. It was silent in the valley below me. I looked toward the sea. The raider's ships were gone. Slowly, shivering with the morning chill, I rose to my feet and went
home.

They had left nothing of beauty. What they had not
stolen, they had destroyed. Great heaps of clothing and

linen had been placed along the frescoed walls and set ablaze so that the paintings were blackened and blistered beyond recognition or repair. The fruit trees within the courtyard had been cut down. There were the bodies of two elderly servants in the fountain, faces down, where they had been drowned.

I could find no sign of my parents, or of my grandfather, or of Claudius and his visiting family. I walked along the colonnades, looking into each room. Deep gouges and chunks of plaster had been rent out of the walls. The pillars which supported the overhang of the roof had been hacked at and defaced. I heard an ominous creaking above my head. I stepped back to observe that the timbered upper story of the house, where it had been burnt, was slowly collapsing. Charred beams protruded like pieces of fractured bone.

I walked on, looking into what was left of the slaves' quarters. I found them gutted and empty. The kitchen was a quagmire of spilled food, smashed pottery, and broken dishes. I saw fragments of my mother's prized Samian ware, which had been imported from Gaul. The body of one of our serving women lay in a pathetic little knot on the floor in front of the ovens. Her two infant children lay before her, bloodied, with expressions of surprise and terror stamped indelibly on their lifeless little faces. The cook and his wife were also there, huddled in death with the fullers. They must have come here, away from the main section of the house, hoping that, knowing them to be slaves, the raiders would spare them. Their hopes had been in vain. All were dead of wounds which could not have ended their lives mercifully. At the door which led from the kitchen into the passage to the dining room, I discovered the body of my slave Arnos. He lay propped against the wall where he had fallen, his hands still clutching the kitchen knife which was imbedded in his chest. His arms and legs looked as though they had been hacked at with axes. Had it not been for the burn scar on his left calf, I would not have been able to recognize him at all. His head was missing.

I did not cry out, nor did I vomit. I saw what I saw. I knew the truth of it; yet, somehow, it failed to touch me. A strange, half-trembling numbness had taken possession of me. I walked on through the ruin of my home as though through some terrible dream.

Here, this pile of rubble: My mother had spun tales of
the Bible for me here when I had been a child. Here,
this place where the tiles had been crushed and washed
with blood: Claudius had taught me to play marbles here.
And here I had watched the slave women make dye.
And there I had watched the fullers clean our garments,
and had even been allowed to help them stretch the cloth
over the wooden frames so that it might be cleansed by
sulphur fumes. A thousand places. A thousand memories.
All bloodied. All burnt. All shattered.

I walked on, dazed. I stepped over remnants which my
sanity would not allow me to stoop to identify. I came
to the chapel and paused, half expecting to find my grandfather there. I thought I might find him kneeling in the
sanctuary. I reasoned placatingly to myself: Why should
they slay a harmless old man, a priest? Why not simply
leave him at peace with his prayers?

I stood at the entrance, looking in. My grandfather was
not in the chapel. The room was empty, soundless.

It had been a small, relatively simple room with a
vaulted ceiling. The sacred monogram of the Chi-Rho
had been repeated in pattern around the doorway and in
a border at the baseboards. Grandfather Potitus had insisted that the room's decor should direct a man's thoughts
to God, not to admiration of the artistry of Mankind. My
father had commissioned an artist to decorate the walls
with a suitable mural. Grandfather Potitus had sent him
away. Only in the floorwork had the old man allowed any
visual form of ostentation. He had designed the pattern
himself. Three master craftsmen had worked nearly a
year to complete the design.

I did not move. Slowly the numbness which had afflicted me began to thin. Without warning, with an agony
of consciousness, it shattered. It was as though a thousand
candles had been lighted behind my eyes. They seared
my vision. Tears welled and fell as I stood in mute comprehension of the scene which lay before me.

The room had been reduced to a burnt-out core. The
walls had been blackened. The once-exquisite mosaic of
the floor had been deliberately rendered into a mass of
broken, crushed bits and pieces of glass. The altar had
been upturned. The Tabernacle and the altarpieces were
gone. The air stank of soured wine and urine.

I turned away and was violently sick. I vomited until

my ribcage ached and my nose ran and the light behind my eyes began to dim. I wiped my face. Mercifully, the numbness began to return to me. I waited for it, as an exhausted man waits for sleep. It flowed out across my shoulders and down my arms into my hands. I felt it within my thighs as I began to walk. Slowly, room by room, I went through the house. I did not even hear my own footsteps.

Then, on the threshold of what had been my father's and mother's bedroom, I paused. I heard the sound of voices: the low moan of a woman, the drunken snores of a man, masculine laughter, voices deep and sated with pleasure, voices in a language which I did not understand but recognized to be the same which the whore Morrighan had spoken in the wood.

I did not think. I simply reacted. I must have known that the men were raiders. Having so thoroughly ravaged this portion of the coast, they would feel safe enough to dally here awhile while their comrades went scouting for other prey. I must have guessed that the men would be armed and that soon enough their ships would be returning for them. Yet I remember now that I simply, unreasoningly, reached out and shoved in as hard as I could upon the door. It had not been latched. It went flying back.

The scene which met my eyes should have sent me running in blind panic. Instead, I stood stunned to immobility, staring wide-eyed at the great, bearded, filthy men who returned my stare.

There were three of them. One lay in a drunken stupor on my parents' bed. His clothes were stained with sweat and pitch and blood. Wine purpled his cheeks and soaked his shirt.

The other two lay on the floor—one astride and coupling with the naked body of one of our serving maids; the other positioned over her head, his mouth suckling her pale breast. They were both naked from the waist down and, like the man on the bed, were vile with the filth and blood and slime of their own passions.

Leaning against the far wall, well-spitted on the end of a spear, the severed head of my slave Arnos met my gaze with the filmed, blank look of the dead.

The girl made a low, whispering sound and turned her head so that one bruised, torn cheek rested against the floor. I recognized her then. She was Mercia, one of the fullers' daughters. Quiet, reserved, devout, and gentle Mercia, whose auburn hair was the color of kelp beds shining in a summer sea. Mercia of the mermaid's eyes, as green as sea moss. She had recently celebrated her sixteenth birthday. Her parents had informed my grandfather that she had expressed her desire to dedicate her life to Christ. I remembered how disappointed I had been by this news, for I had often looked upon Mercia's slender, early-blossomed form and had wished that she, instead of Claudius' aggressive little sister, would smile upon me.

Now she lay with a muscle twitching painfully in her right foot. Her legs were spread wide to accommodate the great thrusting maleness of the pagan who lay over her. The man, surprised, paused in his business of rape. He gaped back at me over his shoulder. His vast white buttocks, with his hairy testes hanging loose beneath them, was exposed to me.

I did not waste any time. Unarmed as I was, the picture which this raping barbarian presented to me put a weapon of sorts into, if not my hands, at least my foot. I charged him, bellowing my fury as I did so. I brought my foot, toes pulled back, hard into the most vulnerable portion of his male anatomy.

He screamed and went falling forward, rolling off the girl. With his knees pulled against his chest, he lay writhing and cursing in agony.

Save for the twitching of her foot, the girl did not move. But the other man was on his feet, reaching down to his ankles to pull up his trews. As he fumbled with the latchings of his belt, he stared at me with open-mouthed amazement. He said something to me in his language.

I looked at the girl and pointed at her hysterically. "You filthy son of hell, she is not one of your Scotian whores!"

The man had very wide-set, black-lashed eyes. His beard was brittle and black and curled over his face. It would have completely hidden his lips had his mouth not opened. He shouted at me in his heathen tongue.

The man on the bed began to stir. He was having great difficulty focusing his eyes. His face had been badly scratched. Purplish, swollen rents of skin stood up around the sockets of his eyes. I wondered if the ravaged girl had injured him, and found myself hoping fervently that she had.

He belched, sat up, and squinted at his shouting compatriot. He made a query. The black-beard did not bother to reply. He stopped his shouting and measured me with a gaze filled with curiosity. He made a comment, then kicked at his companion who still writhed on the floor beside the girl. He pointed at me. He spoke to me, nodding his black lion's head all the while. Then he laughed, heartily.

The sound of his mirth only served to deepen my rage. I know now that my sanity must surely have left me. Perhaps, had I then shown the good sense to break and run, I might well have escaped. But I knew that I could not leave the girl with them. Even if it was not within my power to protect her, I could not leave her. It had also occurred to me that my family's fate had not yet been accounted for. So I stood there and demanded: "I will know what you have done with my parents, grandfather, and sister."

My statement caused the man to fall to silence, though I knew that he had not understood me. It had been the intensity of my tone which had brought him pause. His brows lifted. An expression of total bewilderment crossed his hairy face. His arms went wide to indicate the devastation which had taken place within the room. He spoke to me then, in a Latin which was even more rustic and broken than my own.

"Are you not afraid to die, boy?"

"I show no fear to filth such as you." The words came without my calling them, in Latin so that he might fully comprehend them. It did not occur to me to wonder how a barbarian such as he had come to have recourse to the tongue of the civilized world. I stood my ground, with my knees locked and my muscles held taut so that they would not reveal the trembling I felt within me.

He crossed the room and placed himself directly in front of me. I could smell the stench of murder upon him. I could see the history of violence written upon his face.

The man whom I had kicked had managed to pull himself into a seated position. He was making noises of pain. His head went up. His brown eyes pierced me with their hatred. Slowly, ponderously, clutching and massaging his loins, he rose to his feet and came to stand beside

the black-beard. The black-beard spoke in his pagan
tongue. The other made a sneer of derision at me.

I spat at him. My saliva pearled on his face and in his
beard. I had no way of knowing that I stood before a
Gaelic lord. I knew only that I saw the great slab of his
sleeved, braceleted arm rise. I saw his mouth open as he
spoke an epithet against me. I caught the stink of his
breath. I do not remember when his raised arm fell. It
struck with murderous rapidity, coming down on me at
that point where my neck and shoulder blade meet. It
could have been an axe or a stone, so powerful was the
blow. I saw an incredible vision of white hot light. I felt
no pain. I collapsed into a darkness which was mercifully
free of dreams or memories.

And so it came to be that they carried me away into
bondage, slung over the shoulder of the black-beard while
the girl walked, roped, behind. I cannot tell you of the
voyage, nor of the faces of the many who were taken into
captivity with us. I can only say that on that day ". . . The
Lord brought over us the wrath of His anger and scat-
tered us among many nations, even unto the utmost part
of the earth, where now my littleness is placed among
strangers" in the land known as Eire.

BOOK II

THE MOUNTAIN OF MISTS

And there the Lord opened the sense of my un-
belief that I might at last remember my sins and be
converted with all my heart to the Lord my God,
who had regard for my abjection, and mercy on my
youth and ignorance, and watched over me before I
knew Him. . . .

Saint Patrick—from his *Confession*

2

THE old man eyed me judiciously. He reached over with
his staff and gave me a merciless poke.

I started. He poked me again and I moved away from
him, snarling.

The sun was rising out of the east, out of the distances
of this land which the Gael called Dalaradia. Light was
eating away at the last remnants of the night. Clouds
formed a gray veneer over the sky. Surely, steadily, the
darkness was thinning. Yet the morning brought no
warmth. It only served to define the flinty landscape and
the tiny, stinging particles of dry snow which had begun
to fall.

"Rise up!" the old man demanded of me. "Rise up and
face the day in the name of Christ so that He may bless
you and make you a little less miserable than you insist
on being."

Dubh, a good-natured young shepherd with woolly
dark hair cropped short lest he forget that he was a slave,
moved beside me. Like the old overseer, Leborchom,
Dubh's attitude seemed to assure me that he had been

ver again hope for freedom. He
his eyes and shook his head, star-
wind at the bleating sheep that
mountainside with all of the intel-
shes.

orchom's Christ are many," said Dubh
y, for he considered the old man to be
no fool   that they are always invisible gifts, isn't
that right, L hom?"

Leborchom adjusted his woolens about his broad
and bony shoulders. "Not at all," he dissented, ignoring
Dubh's sarcasm. "The virtues of a patient man are not invisible, nor is the blessing of a decent disposition. Both of
these are virtues which God has given me, through the
love of His Son."

"Ha!" said Dubh. "You are as patient and decent of
disposition as a rutting ram in a field without ewes."

The old man ignored him. He stepped over the flat,
broken stones of the ground upon which we had made our
camp. He looked down at me thoughtfully. Then, decisively, he made a snort of dislike and gave me another
roust with his staff. "What did'ja say the boy's name was,
Dubh? Sucat or Magot or Padraicus or some such foolishness as that?"

"Aye," agreed Dubh. "A grand Roman name it was."

"Grand indeed!" Leborchom gave me still another prod
with his staff. "You can forget Rome here," he said to me.
"You can forget home and warm hearth and dreams of
being bought back to freedom. Miliucc MacBuain keeps
that which he has bought, or kills it. And you are the lord
Miliucc's property now, never again your own. So better
accept your fate, Magot or Sucat or Padraicus or whatever
in God's good grace your name may be, for you'll be hap-
pier with your lot when you own to it. You are a shepherd now. You will know no other companions save Dubh
and me for many a long month until spring."

Dubh got to his feet. He shivered and pulled his lummon, a ragged blanket of a cloak, tight about him. He
was all of one tone was Dubh, as dark as a sun-browned
mushroom. The laws which governed the island of Eire,
including this far northeastern portion of Dalaradia, decreed that only a man or woman of status might wear
more than one color; and then only according to the varying degrees of rank. The fleece of the rare white sheep

was reserved for the nobility. As a slave, Dubh's un-bleached woolens were of the poorest quality, changing in hue only as much as the natural black-brown shades of the garments allowed.

"I hear 'twas the lord's lady who bought the boy," he informed Leborchom. "She called in her own leech to doctor to him, and had him well tended till he was healed."

The old man's brows stood up with interest. He put a gnarled, high-veined hand up against his lips and studied me. "Is it so now?"

I sat huddled in my lummon, my shaven head pulled back under the rough, dark weave, my knees pulled up against my chest, my hands clasped about my ankles. I refused to look at the overseer. I sat without moving, staring off into the portion of the sky which still held the night captive.

The old man's lips drew up over his teeth into a knot of concentration. He held a cutting of oat bread in his hand. It was thin and elastic. He flapped it before my face as though it were a desiccated piece of hide with which he wanted to beat me. "Here. Eat. Or are'ya too busy plotting another escape? Achh! Why will'ya not speak, lad? How many times must'ya be told that we do not wish to keep'ya manacled like a mad beast? How many times must'ya be warned that none in all Eire will succor an es-caped slave?"

"Except the few mad followers of the one'ya call Christ Jesus." Dubh laughed mildly. "Save your words, Le-borchom. The boy is a foreigner. He does not understand us when we speak."

The old man made a noise of profound disgruntlement. He glared at me. "To think that my sweet Lord died to save the souls of turds such as this! Praise be the glory of such a sacrifice!"

"The boy's been ill for many weeks," admonished Dubh. "His shoulder is only barely healed. Those who cared for him within the ring fortress of the Ri Miliucc claimed that he often cried out in his delirium. They say that he gave his own true name and, for a time, spoke willingly to other Briton slaves. Now he finds refuge within silence. In time, when he begins to understand the tongue of the Gael, he'll be share'n his thoughts with us."

Leborchom made a grunt of dissatisfaction. "Time!" He

cast a knowing glance toward the lowering sky. "The weather does not understand Time!" He bent over and examined me with his small, fiery brown eyes as though I were a strange new plant which had sprung unannounced from the soil. "Sucat?" he addressed me.

I ignored him.

He pulled off a mouthful of the oat bread, chewed it and asked me through the mouthful: "Is it Magot then? Like the little white wormies that grow up out of the garbage?"

My lips made an involuntary contraction of annoyance.

He snapped upright and swung his arms wide. "There! I knew it! Did'ja see that? The little spittle knows well what we say to him!"

The old man was correct. The language of the Gael, as these Scots called themselves, was of the same root as the language of my native Briton. I had been in the land of my captors for nearly four months, long enough to have begun to subconsciously pick up the similarities and to have begun to transcribe the differences. Yet I had no wish to learn their heathen tongue. Learning it would be an admission that I was, indeed, fated to do their will, to bow before their decrees, to be a slave in their bleak, cold, abominable land. I had managed to convince myself that it was only a matter of time before I would be free again. Since I had not discovered my parents' bodies among the murdered slaves of our villa, I was certain that they had somehow escaped. Perhaps Claudius had warned them in time. In any event, as I shivered beneath the Dalaradian sky, for the sake of my sanity, I forced myself to believe that my family was safe within the inland town of Bannavem Taburniae, busy with the work at which all good Christians of Briton would no doubt be laboring: that of raising money with which to ransom their sons and daughters out of bondage.

The old man made a snort of vexation. "Well, if your name is not Magot, and it is not Sucat, then it must be Padraicus. Padraicus? No, no, I can't bear the sound of it. Much too grand for a whelp such as you. We will cut it down to size. Yes. Since you will not give us your true name, we shall have to be after name'n'ya ourselves. Henceforth, you shall be . . . Padraic . . . yes . . . that will do admirably. Padraic: a name of no meaning for a boy of no consequence."

I felt my nostrils expand with exasperation. I pressed my tongue hard against my palate lest I speak out inadvertently against the old man's arrogance, nastiness, and barbed tongue.

He was a Gael. I found him to be as rude and offensive as the sheep which he herded. His bellicose attempts to demonstrate his Christianity did nothing to soften his personality. Wherever he had found his faith in the God of the civilized world, he had found none of the graces which should have accompanied it. His long body was lean, pliable, and as dirty as the oatbread which was his main sustenance. Despite his age, he exuded an almost obscene sense of power and agility.

His eyes pierced me with their scrutiny. His mouth, thin and devoid of lip, like a lizard's mouth, curled into an ambivalent grin. "Padraic. Aye, boy, I've seen your like before. Someone's spoiled'ya till you're as pithy as a bad summer apple. But now the wind of life has begun to blow upon'ya. Aye, blown so hard it has that it's swept'ya out of your safe, high, sheltering tree and left'ya bruised upon the ground. You must roll with your fate now, boy, else the worms find'ya and take'ya into the earth with them."

His words chilled me. I did not want to hear them or acknowledge them, yet I did and shivered with the weight of an unwelcome truth.

"It is told that thousands were taken in the last raids," said Dubh. "Aye, there have not been so many slaves brought home to Eire since the days when the great High King himself, Ard Ri Niall of the Nine Hostages, ruled at Tara."

Leborchom nodded and made a sour face. "And sure now if the new High King, the Ard Ri Dathi, hasn't finally set himself to the task of bringing 'glory' to Eire once again so that his name will shine alone, not overshadowed by the memory of his uncle."

Dubh pulled in a breath, then exhaled it wistfully, savoring the pride which he held in the history of his people. "Do'ya remember those days, Leborchom? I was but a lad then. But when the blood lust of Niall was on the land, it was a proud thing to be a Gael. Sure and it was, and shall be again. With hundreds of captives brought home to Eire, and hundreds more sold off across the seas. Oh but the lesser kings must be basking in the pride of it,

making the forges glow so that none will be accused of
not giving his full share to the Ard Ri at Tara."

A sound burst forth from Leborchom's lips. It was neither laughter nor outcry of protest. It was an explosion of
derision directed at Dubh. "Pride?" He twisted the word
into a profanity. "Full share to the Ard Ri? Since when
have the kings cared a whisker or a braid for the High
King at Tara?"

Dubh's eyes went as round as grapes. Anger sparked
out of the blue of them. "Sure now the Ard Ri is the
source of power of every chief. It is he who unifies the
kings of Eire, who strengthens us under the laws of all the
Gael!"

"Nonsense! Sheep droppings! A Gaelic king fights only
for his own glory! And you, Dubh, enslaved by your own
people, do'ya see the evil of it all? No! You slaver with
misery—not because of the wrongs done to'ya—but because you've been deprived of your right to ride out with
the rest of them; deprived of your privilege of winning
battle glory and making obeisance to the Ard Ri Dathi,
nephew of the great Niall, who was so venerated by his
people that he was slain by the arrow of one of his own
deceitful chiefs! By the blessings of Christ Jesus, Dubh,
what insanity sets clan against clan? What madness calls
the Gael across the seas? From whence comes this soul-
destroying need to do battle?"

Dubh's face was devoid of expression. "You are a
Christian, Leborchom. You know nothing of honor."

The old man threw up his hands. "Honor! Define this
'honor'! How is this 'honor' won? By waging war against
one's neighbors? By pillaging across the seas? By killing?
By maiming? By taking heads? By selling and degrading
hostages, even as you have been sold and degraded?
'Honor'? I say that you care not for 'honor'. I say that
you care only that the blood flows red so that the
seanachies will have meat for the meal of their stories.
Stories of 'honor'? Where is the 'honor' when your corpse
lies propped up in its burial mound and the earth sets
about its task of corrupting you?"

"I do not fear death, old man," Dubh said. "I do not
fear the corruption of my flesh. But what has a man,
Leborchom, if he has not honor among his own people?"

"Peace," replied the old man simply, "and the knowledge that his soul shall someday see God."

"Soul . . ." Dubh worked up a saliva and spat it out upon the ground. "I care *that* for your soul! And as for your peace—sure I have found that: the peace of a slave, with no joy, hope, or honor to be found within it." He came and stood beside me. "The boy here . . . may the gods grant that his people are rich enough to buy him home again."

"If it was the Ri's bride who bought him, his fate is sealed. The king will never part with any possession which might please his Rigan."

"If the boy so pleased the queen, why was he sent away from the rath?"

Leborchom made a laugh of bitter amusement. "Who is to say what is the Rigan's whim and will? They say she has the wild spirit of an autumn wind. But mark me, it pleased her to save the boy's life. The day may dawn on which she will call him to serve her."

"To wash her virgin feet?" sneered Dubh nastily.

"Or to hold a scented torch above her plate at suppertime. Whatever is her pleasure. She has purchased him. And I tell'ya now that the Ri will never sell him, unless it pleases the Rigan."

I pressed my teeth hard against themselves until my jaw began to ache. I did not want to listen to the two of them gossiping like venomous housewives. All along my shoulders, shivers were running like rats scurrying along the masts of a sinking ship. I thought, with despair, that if indeed thousands of captives had been taken, there was little chance of my parents ever locating me, let alone offering ransom, unless I could somehow make my location known to them. And had I not begged my captors to allow me to write to my homeland? And had I not been warned to be content with my new station in life, lest I lose my life entirely?

My breath was coming hard and sharp. I knew that I was on the verge of tears. I despised myself for my weakness.

Dubh knelt beside me. Though I did not look at him, I knew his face well. It was a crooked, pleasant, swarthy face. The nose was short and wide. The blue eyes were set so deeply beneath his dark, craggy, uneven brow that they seemed to shine out like bright beacons glowing within the depths of a cave.

"If'ya can understand me at all, boy, then listen well,"

he said to me earnestly, in the manner of one who sincerely wishes to befriend another. "Leborchom's a crusty old sheep's wind, I'll grant'ya that. But he means well for'ya, boy. Truly, he's seen many a good man wallow in self-pity till their brains went as soft and watery as new cheese. Sure now, boy, what with a broken shoulder and a fever on'ya, it's pure and wondrous magic that brought'ya safely to us. I do not know why'ya were not slain upon the shore of your own land, or thrown into the sea when the raiders saw that'ya were ill to the point of death. My own brother was not spared the blade, nor my father, when Miliucc's people raided our rath in the Long Ago." He paused. Swallowed. Licked his lips. There was pain for him in the recounting of this tale. He reached out and put his large, work-roughened hand upon my wrist. There was strength and concern in his touch. "When all's said and done, boy, it's not so bad for the likes of us. Up here on the Commons, tending the Ri's sheep, sure now there's them that's drawn worse fates. There's them that's dead."

I jerked my wrist from beneath his hand. I did not want to hear the bitter truth which he was offering up to me as consolation. I looked into his face, wanting him to see my anger and disdain of him, yet when I met those blue beacon eyes, I saw solace and compassion within them. I turned away, suddenly ashamed, overwhelmed by self-pity. How could one who had lost hope for himself wish to offer hope to another? How could Dubh, who was without comfort, wish to comfort me?

Tears were welling within me, like water being drawn upward out of a bitter spring. A long-haired gray-and-black sheepdog came over to me and nudged me under my right armpit. Since I had first entered the camp of the shepherds, the dog had treated me like a long-lost relative. He would not stray from my side. By daylight he lingered near me even as my own shadow lingered. At night he curled up against my back as though he sought to keep the wind away from me. As he nuzzled me, shoving his wet nose up under my fingers, his nearness brought a shiver of unbearable loneliness to me. I drew him close, wordlessly accepting his friendship.

As I looked disconsolately out across the distances of Dalaradian sky and mountain, I heard Leborchom say to me:

"God's will shall be done, Padraic. You must yield or He will break'ya. His work is glory and majesty, truth and justice. Acknowledge Him and He shall direct your path. Forsake Him and He shall smite'ya. Ask in His name and He shall give'ya. Follow the course He has set and He shall make'ya into iron, forged by His will to do as He shall command." He set a bowl of gruel beside me. "Eat now, boy. Slave or free, a man must eat to live."

I could not eat. I put my head down upon my knees. Silently, within the muffling shadows of my lummon, I wept.

3

THE mountain upon which we herded our sheep was called Slemish, the Mountain of Mists. A great, bleak mound it was, rising like a lonely island out of the fertile lands which surrounded it. Devoid of trees on its upper slopes, Slemish was scaling and gray of skin, with smudges of grass here and there above treeline and huge, sobering slopes of meadow locked within cloud-shadowed highland valleys.

There were forests on the mountain in those days, vast sprawling phalanxes of green which sent out seedling armies to vanquish unclaimed territories with colonies of oak, yew, rowan, beech, and hazelnut. These were the forests of the Ulaid, the home of the magic fogs, the Faéth Fiada, which mantled the mystical entrances to the kingdoms of the Gaelic Otherworld. Here were said to dwell the gods and ghosts of all Eire, and the Twelve Winds which had been created at the beginning of Time itself: four chief winds, with four lesser winds to serve them, and an additional four to serve the lesser four so that there were Twelve Winds in all, each blowing from its own quarter, each with a color of its own.

On clear days, as we walked upon the cold, wind-lashed seaward slopes of the mountain, with the heather frost-blackened around us and the bracken browned and broken by the season, I could gaze across the distances of hill and forest toward the Western Sea. Sometimes I would stand transfixed, braced against the wind, staring off in the direction of Briton until my eyes began to burn

with tears which were not summoned out of me by the
wind, but by an agony of heart which threatened to consume my very soul.

"Come away, boy," said Dubh as he came to stand beside me. Dubh of the endless tales and multivarious tunes
which he sang to accompany the music which he plucked
and bowed from a small, willow-framed instrument which
he called a timpan. He never tired of trying to cheer me.
He slung his timpan over his shoulder and advised sagely:
"It'll take more than an act of will, Padraic, to bring ran-
some for'ya across the sea at this time of the year. Not
even our raiders venture out into such storms as live upon
the waters now."

I turned away from him, staring out across the rolling
vistas of mountain and plain until my eyes came to rest
upon the ring fortress of my master, the Ri Miliucc Mac-
Buain. It was built so solidly into the hills which formed
the flanks of Slemish that it seemed to be a natural outcropping of stone and turf and timber, made not by men
but by the same forces of nature which had created the
mountain.

"Do'ya remember much about your stay there?" asked
Dubh.

I made no reply.

"Did'ja see the Rigan? They say that she's as fair as
any mortal woman dare be, lest she cause jealousy
among the female gods."

I made no comment. I remembered neither the Ri nor
the Rigan. He was often away from the rath. One week
after my arrival, she had been called to comfort her pregnant sister-in-law at a ring fort in a neighboring district.
Her beauty was legendary, yet the memory of her face
was veiled by the delirium through which I had viewed
her.

Dubh shrugged at my silence and grinned amiably.
"Ahh, lad, I've heard grand tales of the ring fortress of
the Ri Miliucc MacBuain. Did'ja know that it's one of the
few raths in all of Dalaradia to contain a well within its
four encircling ramparts? 'Tis no small wonder it has
never fallen before a siege."

He crouched down beside me, balancing himself on the
balls of his feet while he stared off at the distant rath,
absently rubbing his thighs with his open palms. "They
say that the main house is of wood and finely worked

wicker, washed throughout with multihued lime. They say
that the Ri's banqueting hall is close in size to the fabled
hall at Tara, home of the sovereign king of all Eire, the
Ard Ri Dathi himself. They say that the poles which
support the roof of Miliucc's hall are as smooth and as
white as the thighs of a maid. And it is said that the
height of the hall is like the height of a great cloud, with
birds growing breathless when they perch on the cross-
beams." A smile of begrudging admiration bent his lips
upward. "And the windows are set with a magic substance
imported from across the seas: hard as stone, brittle as
spun honey, as clear as the very air. Have'ya ever heard
the like?"

I sat down beside Dubh on the snow-dusted ground.
Silently I looked down at the ring fort. I remembered
little of the place. Dark rooms. Pain. Steaming poultices
placed upon my injury.

"Now, beyond the ring fort"—Dubh was pointing—
"that's all tribeland that'ya see stretching away. It is divided according to the rank of those who live upon it. The
flaiths, of noble blood and position, keep large portions to
themselves and, like the Ri, let out sections of it to ten-
ant farmers and laborers. They're professional people in
the main: judges, poets, physicians, cow lords, warriors,
and druids of unfailing talent. They live in fine, strong
homes, they do. They entertain royally. They hold much
livestock. Their flesh forks never want for meat. They
have many servants and slaves."

He paused. His left hand came up to his lips as though
he wished to wipe away the expression of wry amusement
which had settled upon them. "And yet, I often think that
they are little more than slaves themselves, bound by the
law to the limits of their rank and station as surely as you
and I are bound. I should not find comfort in that, but
somehow I do." He sighed, a philosopher unhappily re-
signed to a fate not of his choosing. Our eyes met. Held.
His brows came down. Shaggy, weather-bleached. Wind-
stiffened. Then they rose again, straight up from the
bridge of his nose. "You understand every word I've said,
don't'ja?"

A wiser and less quick-tempered youth would have
smiled benignly and made his eyes go wide as indication
of his befuddlement. I was not wise. I scowled and would
have sprung to my feet, but Dubh pulled me down beside

him. His hand was hard and unyielding as it curled about my wrist.

"Keep your tongue then, if that's your will!" All mirth had been swept from his features by a gale of sudden emotion. "But know that I was one of them once!" His free hand went out, pointing below us to the tribelands. "I was not born a slave. My father was a king, a Ri who ruled lands as fair as these. But by the Daghda, boy, a man must accept his fate, mustn't he? What I was, what I had, what I once hoped for—I am no more, I have no more, I can long for no more." He caught his breath and stared at me, shaking his head, thoroughly embarrassed by his display of emotion.

A wind was picking up. A chill wind. A thin, cold wind. Dubh drew his lummon closer about his shoulders. He tilted his head up to the sky. How blue it was, save for a few thin tracings of high, wild-stallion clouds with their tails upturned and frayed by the wind.

"Leborchom is right, Padraic," he said. "We must yield or we will be broken—by his god or mine, or by our own ambition."

Officially, day began in Dalaradia not with sunrise, but when the servant boy who tended the Ri's stable of fine horses let out his charges to whinny at the dawn. Day ended not with the coming of darkness, but when the horses were brought home and the Ri's many cows were safely milked and bedded.

The shepherd's day began when the sheep so decreed. Our animals were kept out upon the hillsides throughout the year, save for that brief springtime period which called us into a common camp. Here the sheep were shorn. Some were slaughtered. The shepherd was given a much-cherished respite from the tedium of his work. But all too soon we were out upon the pastures again, following the greening of the grass. Frost drove us down into the valley. The browning of late summer nudged us high onto the slopes of Slemish, where the grasses remained sweet and richly green long past harvest in the valley below.

So it was that winter had caught us high on the mountain and demanded that we gather the flock together for the trip down into the hills. The ewes were swollen with new life. They did not want to move. They trotted and tripped and bleated and balked. We stopped often to allow them time to rest and graze.

Each day the winter deepened. The frostline lowered. We followed it down into the foothills where the warmer climate kept the rain from turning to sleet. Here, though the earth was cold and wet, new grass was already unfurling like millions of tiny green pennants. The sheep clustered here, content to graze.

The mountain loomed above us, a gray brooding mass crowned by ever-moving clouds which murmured with the sound of thunder. Seaward, fogs and mists formed great lakes of vapor and often set us apart from the world below. When these low-lying clouds parted, we could see the ring fort and its surrounding little clots of houses and buildings. Smoke rose from the smoke holes. We could make out the conical shapes of the Ri's beehives and the long, arterial twistings of muddied roadways and sodden pastures.

Once, on a particularly wet and stormy night, we took shelter from the elements within a sagging shepherd's shelter. A miserable excuse for a dwelling it was. Made up of a careless jumble of beams and rough-edged planks, it stank of age and leaked so copiously that one would have thought that it had been designed to do so. Lying on moldy, sour-smelling pallets, we called for sleep. It evaded us. In the darkness of the hovel's interior, the sound of a thousand drips invaded the night.

Then the dogs began to bark. I propped myself up onto my elbows. Beyond the darkness of our shelter, above the frenzied barking of the dogs, I could hear the sound of a horse's hooves making contact with the muddied earth. The gray and black dog, lying against my side, began to growl.

Dubh got to his feet and reached for his staff. The sound of a man's voice, garbled by wind and falling rain, came to us. Dubh tensed, testing the weight of his staff as a soldier balances a spear before battle. "Only madmen and thieves are out upon the hills in weather such as this," he said as slowly. Hesitantly, he went out into the night.

A moment later he returned, beaming from ear to ear as he held open the hide door for the man who scowled behind him. The stranger was sodden to the skin through all of his heavy, dark clothing. As he entered, the scent of fresh-cooked meat entered with him.

I found myself staring at him expectantly. I met bloodshot blue eyes which glared out of a corpulent, hostile face.

"I come from the Rigan Cairenn," he announced dourly, sniffling and obviously not at all pleased to have been chosen for this errand. He bent down. From the folds of his drenched garments he brought forth a small cauldron. It was wrapped in oiled hides to keep its contents warm and dry throughout the cold, wet ride up into the hills. "She said that she'd seen a light on the hillsides. A shepherd's camp, she fancied. On a fearful night such as this she said they should have some comfort."

He gave us a withering look, which was meant to inform us that he did not share the good queen's view. Begrudgingly, with his short, seamed lips pursed all the while, he unwrapped the cauldron, which contained a thick, hearty stirabout made of gruel, vegetables, and large chunks of meat. From bags which he had slung across his shoulders, he brought forth small wedges of golden cheese and packets which contained honey cakes. There were apples, a cask of dark bitter ale, and two loaves of good wheaten bread such as I had not seen since I had been taken into bondage. From around his waist he untied a scroll of greasy fabric. Unwrapping it, he tossed it and its contents onto the soiled floor so that we might see in the dim firelight of the room that it contained slabs of oily fresh bacon which we could cook at our leisure.

The scent of food and the sight of the stranger had brought the gray-and-black dog to his feet. He eyed the man. His nostrils quivered at the scent of the food. His tongue came out to lick at the saliva which was beginning to drool from his lolling tongue.

Dubh, salivating like the dog, contemplated the feast which had been spread before us. "By the Daghda," said he, picking up one of the cheeses and holding it up to his nose. His tongue came out to make a flicking reconnaissance of the treasure's texture. "May the Rigan Cairenn be praised for her generous heart." He swooned as he stuffed the cheese into his mouth and began to chew it ecstatically.

"You are welcome to share this meal with us," said Leborchom to the stranger.

The man's mouth turned down with revulsion. With an expression of complete abhorrence upon his disdainful face, he turned and left us without a word.

Anger and humiliation consumed my appetite. I watched Dubh and Leborchom as they fell ravenously to the food. They smacked and slobbered while they ate, licking their chops more greedily than any of the dogs would have done.

Dubh caught my eye and wiped at his mouth with the back of his hand. "Be grateful, lad," he counseled, "it's not often we feast on fare such as this."

I turned away and stirred the embers of the fire. Grateful? For what? Cakes and apples and cheeses made unpalatable by the arrogance with which they had been delivered? I would as soon eat bile!

I could hear the sound of the stranger's horse as it picked its way down from the hillsides through the darkness. I could hear the sound of my companions chewing, sucking, belching, sighing.

"Thanks be to God," I heard Leborchom say through a mouthful of half-chewed bread and apple.

Dubh took a long swallow of ale. He burped, then added: "And to the Rigan Cairenn. Sure and the tales which follow her name like fairy mist must be spun by malevolent spirits."

The weather cleared, then closed, then cleared again according to its own rule of capricious fancy. The rain did not seem to worry the sheep. Their thick wool kept them dry and comparatively warm. They appeared content as long as there was grass to crop and the wind brought them no scent of wolves or lightning.

Our work dictated that we should not all be together at the same time, save when a storm threatened or the flock grew nervous for reasons which were beyond the understanding of any creature not of their own kind.

Yet I was never left alone. Either Dubh or Leborchom would be with me. They slept in shifts, so that always one of them was by my side. At night I was manacled.

One day, finding that I was being observed even when I sought to relieve myself in the bushes, I inadvertently broke the vow of silence which I had made to myself. To my shock and surprise, I heard myself blurt out in Gaelic which was loud, crude and, most probably, barely understandable.

"Can a man not even pass his body wastes without being watched? The dogs have more privacy than I!"

I had spoken to Dubh. If he was amazed that I had, at long last, deigned to speak to him, he showed me no sign of surprise. He met my angry gaze and shrugged.

"The dogs will not run off from us, Padraic. They know their place, and will keep it. If'ya should escape, Leborchom, as overseer, would pay dearly for your loss. When the time is right, you'll be free to be the third arm of our team. The flock is large. There's much work and worry over it. We shall all have more privacy when we know that'ya can be trusted and are surely one of us."

"I shall never be one of you," I shouted at him.

He eyed me speculatively for a moment. Then, sadly, he said: "Aye, Padraic, but'ya shall be."

4

TIME passes slowly for a shepherd. In winter it is a tedium of cold, wind, bleating sheep, clanking bells, and barking dogs. But it is a blessing from God that the seasons change. Winter claimed its full right to temporary dominion over the earth. It sighed and moaned and made of the sky a wet, frigid mantle.

Then, slowly, imperceptibly at first, the winter began to gentle into springtime. The caera, as the Gael call their sheep, wandered out upon the broad plain which lay between Slemish and the sea. With their heads down, they happily cropped the new green as they went. Lambs began to be born to us. The dogs, like peevish parents, became alert and waspish.

There were great wolves within the forests which surrounded the pasturelands of Dalaradia. They haunted the dark wood and raided out onto the plain and open pastureland like armies of skilled, deadly warriors. Dubh and Leborchom made certain that I never ventured far from camp without my heavy hardwood staff and my small rough-edged knife. I was warned never to stray from sight of the dogs or from calling distance of my companions.

Alone. Yes. At last I was alone, for they had come to trust me. Time was indeed passing swiftly. Dubh and Leborchom no longer feared that I would run off from them. Their judgment was well-founded. I had decided to become, at least temporarily, an amenable fellow. Spring was ripening. Soon the Western Sea would be calm. I told myself again and again that soon a ship would come to Eire from Briton, laden with ransom with which to purchase the freedom of those Britons who had been taken captive.

Meanwhile, I worked with Leborchom and Dubh as a part of their team. We were a triad, a three-pronged fork, each tine independent yet fully tuned to the needs and functions of the others. The dogs were extensions of ourselves. They were ever alert, always ready to do our bidding or to respond to the instinct which made them snap at strays or manipulate back into the fold those willful ewes which tried to wander off to give birth alone.

Once, on a misty dawn, as Dubh and I walked upon the clouded hills, we were startled by the sight of three tall stags rising out of the fog like ghost trees. Their ponderous antlers reached out like coraline branches. They stood frozen, taking in the scent of men, dog, and sheep. The black-and-gray sheepdog, who was ever by my side and whom I had fondly come to call Shadow, growled deep in his throat. Though I whispered him to silence, the stags exploded into flight.

Dubh seemed melancholy after that. As the fog began to thin, we sat together on the dry duff which lay beneath a sheltering stand of wide-crowned yews. The sheep grazed before us. They baa-ed and burped contentedly. The lambs stayed close to their mothers, suckling, nudging, dozing on their feet. They had already forgotten the huge kingly beasts which had intruded their majesty into the calm of the morning. But Dubh had not forgotten.

He spoke to me wistfully of the royal sport of the hunt. He told me of how, as a royal youth, he had accompanied his father and the nobles and chiefs of his tribe. They had gone out into the realm of the mactire, the realm of the wolf, for the mactire was a true son of the earth, Ri within his domain and lord over all of the creatures which dwelled within the forests. The hunters trespassed into his realm, stalking him with their great wolf dogs. They hunted the tall stag too, and the brave boar. Sometimes, for pure amusement, they sought broc, the cantankerous, low-bellied badger, or dobor-chu, the water hound which some called otter. They would seek the lithesome, clever fox, or catt the dangerous, enchanted feline or, sometimes, the raptors: the shrilling falcons, the keening kites, and the wondrous golden eagle whose cry was a crescendo of triumph and whose wingspan was so wide that it could block off the light of the sun.

He spoke until the morning was done. When at last he fell silent, the sun had slipped past the noon meridian. We heard the distinct sound of a chariot coming toward us. We were in taut, hilly country, just up from the plain and less than a mile from the ring fortress of the Ri Miliucc MacBuain. We could not see the chariot, for it was still on the flat land. Yet we could discern the shouts of the driver as he commanded his pony. We could make out the clatter of wood straining against metal, the sound of stones flurrying.

Dubh frowned and rose to his feet uneasily. "By the Daghda, what sort of madman would be driving a chariot full-out along a country track? There's no decent chariot road hereabout. No doubt it is some frustrated noble, judging from the royal clatter of the chariot. Bestir yourself, Padraic, we must be certain that none of the Ri's caera have wandered into the idiot's path."

Taking up my staff, I followed Dubh downslope and upslope and downslope once again before we came to pause at the road's edge. It was a narrow, rutted, well-worn track. Drying yellow-green cow patties, in varying stages of freshness and decay, offered indication of its main use: a mere cowpath. There were no stone walls to indicate its peripheries. On one side the grassland simply reached a point where years of foot and hoof traffic had laid the earth bare. On the other, where Dubh and I stood, a steep rain-eroded embankment kept the edge of the track true. Atop this embankment, trees leaned out over the roadway, thrusting their root systems through the decomposing loam and out into the light of day. They protruded from the earth like a mesh of finger bones, holding small stones and snaring larger boulders. As we stood atop the embankment, looking down upon the herdsmen's track, we saw that none of our sheep had strayed this far. We would have turned and walked away had not our combined weight caused a small avalanche of stones to break away from the embankment. We heard the sound of them as they cascaded dustily onto the road. Shadow, who had been at my side, vaulted forward in barking pursuit of the tumbling stones.

We saw the chariot then, driving full-out toward us. The dog saw it too. He forgot the stones, which had settled, forming a small, dusty heap of rubble which would have been no obstacle to the charioteer. Head forward, nose out, the dog began to bark as he took an imperious stance in the middle of the track. It was as though he had, in this moment, decided to appoint himself guardian of all the lands which lay beyond him.

We fully expected the charioteer to run him down. What was one shaggy shepherd's dog to a landed Gaelic flaith? The chariot did not slow. The driver shouted commands and worked the rein expertly. I knew that any attempt on my part to pull the dog to safety would put me beneath the chariot's wheels. With a shout of pure desperation, I called and whistled for the dog to come to me. It was the sound of that whistle, high-pitched and screaming, which caused the charioteer's pony to shy.

Only the most skilled and level-headed driver could have kept the chariot from pitching over. The driver was both. He was in full control of a small, exceptionally well-made one-horse chariot. The pony was young and skittish, sweating and frothing copiously at the bit. She was prancing and rearing in terror. The dog stood his ground before her, crouching down and showing his teeth, snarling like a wolf. With rein held taut, the driver brought his vehicle to a stop and spoke firmly to the whinnying horse in that special tone which horsemen use to reassert their dominance. The pony's ears went back, pivoted. Its eyes were enormous with fear. It danced back a few steps, trying to keep away from the foolish dog which had begun to punctuate its snarls with deep, warning yarfs.

In the clear afternoon sunlight, the metallic ornamentation of the pony's trappings shone with a brilliance which hurt my eyes. The detail-work of the chariot glimmered with the luster of gold. The iron-tired bronzed wheels blazed as though with an inner radiance. Yet it was the driver who drew my attention.

He was unusually tall, as lean and well-made as the finest fighting sword. His perspiring face was flushed. His features were pulled taut by the tension of the moment. I could not tell his age, but he was certainly no youth and must have been all of thirty. His nose was a straight, high-bridged promontory jutting down from the bold, black statement of his eyebrows. A thick, black mustache shadowed his upper lip and curled down alongside his mouth. The ends of it upcurled at the line of his collarbone. From where I stood, I could see the sunlight catch and shatter into prisms which danced along the meticulously arranged masses of his hair. Never in my life had I seen a man so coifed. His hair had been plaited and coiled around his head, then drawn tight against the base of his skull by an exquisite silver clip. From this, one single plait of hair fell like a twisting serpent down his broad back to below his waist. At each side of his head, directly behind and a little back from each temple, a perfectly round ball of gold about the size of a large grape had been fastened into his hair.

Yet for all of the elaborateness of his coif, he was dressed lightly and simply. His powerfully muscled legs were clad in unpretentious linen trews. A short-sleeved knee-length leine, similar to the tunics worn in the Roman world, covered his body. He wore no cloak. His arms were devoid of bracelets. I could see but one ring, intricately wrought of dragon stone and gold, upon his right hand. Only the pale color of his clothing hinted at his high rank.

"Call back your dog." His voice was deep and peremptory. He was no stranger to giving commands.

I met his eyes and was momentarily stunned by what I saw written there. Was it premonition? Perhaps. I shall never know. Yet I remember catching my breath and feeling a slight upwelling of dizziness. Set deeply beneath the well-defined expanse of his forehead, his eyes were as dark and clear as lake waters which lie black and smooth in that tremulous moment of dawn before the sun has shown above the horizon. It is a tenuous moment. The night is gone. The day is yet to be born. The light is perfect. It puts everything into bold relief. Clarifies it. Outlines every form and obliterates every shadow. So were the eyes of this man: dark yet filled with light. Direct. As keen-edged as a striking blade. As cold as the moon. As merciless as the sun.

It was the wisdom born of the instinct of survival which sent me half-falling, half-sliding down the embankment. I went down upon my knees and gripped the dog about the neck. I could feel the eyes of the charioteer upon me. I could hear Dubh babbling away in an almost hysterical Gaelic: sorry, did not expect a chariot, afraid caera on track, sorry, never again, sorry, sorry, forgive.

The man made no reply. He was staring at me. I looked up at him. There was aloof arrogance written boldly across his handsome black Celt's face. Within his eyes I saw the calm assurance of power and the subsiding heat of anger. He was studying me. His heavily lashed lids lowered speculatively. I was being appraised and found amusing. His mouth adjusted itself into a smile which turned his lips downward. It was a smile which hinted at the potential of violence. Still, I met his gaze and held it so that he would know that, slave though I was, I was not a cur who would grovel at his feet.

His long, full mouth relaxed at the sight of my measured but obviously intended defiance. He seemed surprised, pleasantly so. For a moment I thought that he would speak to me, but he was content to pinion me with his eyes, as the raptor glares down at the captive mouse it is about to consume.

I felt rage rise within me. It roared behind my ears. I continued to glare up at the stranger. He was infinitely tall, infinitely magnificent, infinitely magnamimous. Loathing of him filled me and threatened to overcome my sense of judgment. He saw the hatred move upon my face and took a moment to savor his total disdain of it. Then, with a clicking of his tongue, he snapped the reins and drove on, forcing me to scramble awkwardly backward to escape being caught and mangled by his chariot wheels.

Flat on my buttocks, cursing and cuffing the still-barking dog, I turned to see Dubh sliding down the embankment.

He took a worried stance beside me. "Are'ya mad, boy? Trying to face him down? By the Daghda, Padraic, I never thought'ya a fool until now."

I got to my feet, angrily releasing the dog and wiping the dust from my trews. "And I never thought you to be a sniveling coward."

"Did'ja not know him, boy?"

"Nor do I wish to."

A long, convulsive shiver ran the length of Dubh's body. Sweat had broken out across his forehead. It pearled his cheekbones and upper lip. "Mark this moment, Padraic, so that'ya may never forget the face of Death. 'Twas the Ri himself, Padraic. Miliucc MacBuain. His wealth makes him as powerful as any of the five great kings of the five great provinces of Eire. And I swear to'ya, boy, by the sun and moon, water and air, day and night, land and sea, that where he goes Death shall follow, for of late it is told that he keeps no law save that which pleases him and, may the gods have mercy on us, he holds within his hands all of the dark powers of the druids."

5

THE season deepened. The landscape began to succumb to verdancy. The pasturelands spread out between the forests like vast green blankets laid out to freshen in the springtime sun. Within the forests new ferns were uncurling. Buds were swelling and exploding into bloom and fragrance. Tender new leaves, pale and trembling, absorbed color and vitality from the ever-lingering sun. The clouds of winter were gone. Now the sky was awash with fair-weather mists, with great rafts of benign clouds which drifted continuously toward Slemish from the sea, wrapping themselves languidly about the summit, where they lingered like wraithing spirits waiting to be dispelled by the night.

The lambs began to grow strong. Days passed. Weeks passed. The time came for the shearing of the sheep. We moved out onto the heart of the plain to make a special camp. Other shepherds joined us, driving ahead of them the huge flocks belonging to the lesser lords of the Ri Miliucc MacBuain's tuath, his district of sovereignty. The shepherd's camp blossomed upon the plain like a great and raucous flower. Holding pens were built to contain those animals which were to be culled from the flocks and slaughtered. From the village, which stood outside the fortified rath, came butchers and shearers and leeches to see to the accumulated ills of those who had been out upon their respective pastures for months which had seemed to be without end.

During the daylight hours, women came to the camp. Women with keen eyes who would judge the fleece and gather up the wool; women who would cook our meals and, by the Ri's decree, lessen the burden of the time we would be spending in this crowded and teeming camp.

Young and old, tall and short, fat and thin, the women would take the fleece to their homes, where they would degrease, scour, card, and transform it into thread. But while they were in the camp, they made it flagrantly clear that they would enjoy their measure of the season and would share the full bounty of their exuberance with us. They were hard workers all, and sterner taskmasters than the overseers. But they laughed easily and sang the songs which were traditional for the woolgathering. All but two, who were as grouchy and homely as bee-stung sows, taunted and teased and flirted outrageously as they brought out wicker carts filled with good fresh food for both slave and bondsman. All who worked ate. And, after the day's work, drank dark, mouth-puckering, un-aged ale. It numbed the mind and made laughter come readily to the tongue.

I was overwhelmed by my new surroundings. It was good to see women again, though I had never known such women as these. They flustered me. I was quick to blush when in their presence. Leborchom advised me to stay well away from them. It was not always possible, nor, I must admit, desirable. The older women seemed to have an insatiable desire to mother me. The younger women demonstrated no such maternal instincts, but openly professed insatiable desires which, to a boy far from home and fresh from long, lonely months upon a bleak and wintry mountain, were highly intoxicating. Yet, despite their gaiety and impious tongues, there was an underlying sadness and unspoken desperation about them. They were bondswomen sent out to please us. I knew that. Watching them, I was reminded of caged birds suddenly released into a large room where they could enjoy full flight. The space, though larger, was still confining. They could not fly too high, lest they break their wings. But fly they would. And did, in high, mad, defiant circles.

"Why so glum, Roman boy? Or are all high-born Britons so gloomy?"

I looked into eyes as brown as new-turned loam. The girl was as young and soft-fleshed as morning. She came and stood close before me, fragrant with the scent of perspiration only recently dried by the late-afternoon breeze. Her hands sought mine. Warm hands, with palms hard and calloused from years of work. I saw the rising of her ample breasts beneath the loose-fitting fabric of her dark, coarse leine. She caught my eyes midway in the path which they followed and stepped closer to me.

Did I touch her? Yes. And kiss her? Yes. She yielded to me and filled me with a desire which burned within me like noon upon a summer field.

And then Dubh was behind me, his hands upon my shoulders. He pulled me away from the girl with a ferocity which stunned me. He slapped her, hard across both cheeks. She shrieked and stumbled back, raising up her arms to ward off his blows.

I lunged at him, but he was ready for me. He tripped me and kicked me out of his way.

He stood over the girl. "Whore!"

His accusation startled me. I stared at her wide-eyed and blinking, suddenly sickened by memories of another afternoon, of soft and gentle winds, of fragrant woman flesh and of the passion which had led me to lie with the one who was called Morrighan.

But this girl was not Morrighan. She was merely a terrified slave. She broke into sobs and wailed a denial at Dubh.

"Have'ya forgotten that'ya have a husband in the village?" he demanded of her.

She sniffled and wiped her tears. "You're a madman, Dubh, and will come to no good for it!"

"Mad is it?" he snarled. "And is it out of madness that I remember you, but two springs back, swearing to cherish Tulchinne as husband?"

"To cherish him, yes! And that I do. But for the sake of reason, Dubh, I can be wife to no man! I am a slave to Banna the beekeeper. I must lie with him at his pleasure, and also with any man to whom he wishes to give me."

"Banna is not here to force'ya to pleasure slaves! What'ya do you do of your own free whim and will. You bring dishonor to Tulchinne, a good and honest man."

Her face had flushed red with anger. "Tulchinne is crippled with illness and, for a woman's needs, a man no more. Yes! I act on my own whim and will, for I must find my few small pleasures when and where I may. I am a slave, Dubh. I care not for honor; it is a virtue which is not within the province of slaves. In time, if'ya are not a complete fool, you will come to understand."

"Never."

"Then, may the gods have mercy on'ya."

I shall never forget the look which crossed his face then. It was the expression of a man in agony. His features had gone as taut as hide being stretched across the face of a drum. "Whore . . ." he said again.

The girl shook her head. "Your pride shall be the death of'ya, Dubh."

The days passed. The work went on.

I had been shaken by Dubh's confrontation with the girl, and so chose to put off any further advances by the bondswomen. I summoned up my old rudeness and was gratified when even the matrons began to refer to me as "the Roman snob." I was free to jog with Shadow along the peripheries of the camp, or to seek out quiet places where I might sit alone during my free time, pondering the changing shapes of the clouds and envisioning the ship which must soon come to Eire with ransom for such Briton slaves as I.

I saw little of Dubh in the days which followed, and was grateful. Since we had first come to the camp of the shearers, he had seemed distracted, as though waiting for someone. When whoever it was failed to appear, his temperament had become variable—in light one moment, in shadow the next. Bursts of temper, as he had exhibited to the bondsgirl, were common. He drank himself into a stupor each night.

Then, late one afternoon, he came to fetch me from my solitude. His face was radiant. Though his eyes were alight with a glow nurtured by drink, there was no hostility within them, only laughter.

"Come on along, lad," said he. "Tonight I am to play seanachie."

"Seanachie?"

"Historian! Storyteller!"

He was not alone. He had his arms slung across the

shoulders of two equally intoxicated young men. I had not seen them in the camp before. They beamed, and the three of them did a little jig before me. Quick, lively, intricate footwork, with foot crossing foot and the ankle going slack, then tightening just when it seemed as though it must crack beneath the dancer's weight.

"Sure now, did'ja not know that Dubh is the finest storyteller of them all—outside of a royal court," said one of the young men, stifling a belch.

"And inside too!" corrected Dubh. He undraped himself from his companion's shoulders and beckoned me with a wink and a grin. "Come on along, lad. I'm inspired tonight."

"You're drunk," I told him.

He winked again. "And so should *you* be, my boy. But no matter, come on along."

He held out his hand to me. I took it.

The fire had been built high. A large group of men was clustered around it. They were a rough and diverse lot, these shepherds and shearers and butchers, yet they buffeted me with their good humor and welcomed me to their ranks.

"Before Dubh begins, tell us a tale of Briton, lad," suggested one of the shearers.

"Aye," encouraged another, "for 'tis my own homeland and I have been gone from it now for fourteen long years."

Never before had the dimensions of my own ignorance and arrogance been so painfully apparent to me. There was I, son of a decurion, a citizen of Rome, raised in a Briton villa with turos and slaves and servants to coddle me, with the wealth of my people's culture to broaden the scope of my intellect, and what had I to show for it? Only the realization that I had totally succeeded in my role as the errant student.

"Go on, lad, tell them a tale of Briton. Sure now, I've been so long away I feel like a Gael myself. But you are high-born, not like the likes of such as me who was a slave to my own people. Tell them, Padraic, so that they may know that not only the Gael is a prideful race."

I looked at the man across the flames, completely at a loss for words. "Errr aaa . . ." I said.

"Spin us a fable of your gods," prodded one of the shepherds.

"Ummmm . . ."

"A story of war and battle?"

"Ahhh . . ."

How my tutor Veranius would have clasped his hands and laughed! How quickly would Romana have wheedled a finger and proclaimed: "I told you so!"

"Have your people no history, then, Padraic?"

I shook my head lamely and mumbled out some poorly remembered data, some bits of information concerning Roman roads and emperors and dates of conquest. The shepherds and shearers and butchers sat forward, eagerly awaiting that which I was incapable of presenting to them. At length, a long-nosed man with rotted teeth shook his head and waved me to silence.

"Dubh, show the boy how it is done."

And so I first heard Dubh tell the tales which he had heard told by the royal seanachies of his father's house. He was a born teller of tales. He had the ability to quicken his listener's conscience, to spur our ambitions, to awaken our forgotten fears and yearnings. He gave us more than mere words. He breathed the tales out alive, in all of their dimensions, in all of their light and shadow, with every nuance and battle cry whispered and shouted from the very depths of his soul.

He brought to us the tales of Eire's ancient kings, of royal battles and cattle raids, and of strangely mortal gods which lived beneath the earth. He gave us magic and mystery, sagas and sorcery. He gave us the epic tales of the Red Branch Knights of King Conor MacNessa. He gave us the blood-chilling legends of the amazon queen Maeve. He gave us Deirdre of the Sorrows. He gave us Cuchulainn, Commander of the Red Branch Knights, the god-man who was immortalized for his skill as a hounds-man and warrior.

He gave us Manannan McLir, the three-legged god of the sea, who had once lived a mortal life on a distant island. He gave us the Daghda, the Good God, the Ruad Rofhessa, the lord of perfect knowledge. The Daghda's understanding of science and mathematics had made of him an all-powerful magician. He was wise and kind, but not above poisoning his adversaries. He had a wife known by three names: Breg, Meng, and Meabel—Lie,

Guile, and Disgrace. His daughter, Brigit, was the Gaelic goddess of wisdom and poetry. His sons were great and feared magicians who dwelled in glistening crystal castles beneath the earth.

"For that is where all of the ancient godfolk, the Tuatha De Danann, now dwell, for it was the time of the fulfillment of the first of the two great prophecies of the ancient Gael. A new people came to Eire from across the sea. Fierce they were. Great in their battle frenzy. They caused the kings and queens of the Tuatha de Danann to flee into the hills. But the conquerors were not an unjust race. It was decreed that Eire would be divided equally: The conquerors would occupy all of the land above the ground, and the Tuatha De Danann would dwell forevermore beneath the earth."

He paused here and lowered his voice, as though he feared that the ghosts of the past might hear him. "But they are not content. On the night of the great feast of Samain, it is said that they rise up and walk about the earth. The mystical doors which lead down into the shees are thrown open. The magic fogs lift. Out of Relig na Rig, the burial place of kings, fly terrible birds led by a keening vulture whose very breath withers the crops in the fields and causes grazing animals to die upon the spot. A brave man, who fears not for his life, may scour the hills on Samain night. He may find an open shee and peer down through it into the Otherworld itself. He may even enter and walk about. But by the first light of dawn he must be safe away, for if he is not, the demons of the air will descend and sing to him the songs of Death. The magic mists, the Faéth Fiada, will have come down to the earth again. He will be lost in them. Then the banshees, the female ghosts, will ensnare him, and the fershees, the male ghosts, will gnaw away at his courage until they have made a madman of him. By the light of the growing dawn, he will emerge from the Otherword and will fall upon the earth, watching as the Tuatha De Danann return to their realm beneath the ground, carrying the king's great candle before them to light their way into the darkness. By the time the sun has risen, the poor foolish mortal who has looked into the Otherworld can only babble like a dying brook about the things which he has seen. And what sane man can understand the language of a brook?"

" 'Tis true, 'tis true," sighed one of the butchers. "But tell us, Dubh, of the second of the great prophecies of the ancient Gael."

Dubh replied quietly, reverently:

" 'Adzehead will come over a furious sea;
His mantle head-holed, his staff crook-headed
His altar in the east of his house
All of his household shall answer
So be it, so be it!' "

The butcher raised a questioning brow. "What does it mean?"

Dubh shrugged. "No man knows, my friend, for it has yet to be fulfilled."

When Dubh finished his tales, sleep did not come easily to his listeners. When at last we claimed it, our slumber resounded with the clash of battle, with the frustrations of unrequited love, with the valorous integrity of morally pristine warriors who dared to stand alone against the dark and miscreant powers of wicked conjurers.

I do not know how long I slept. I dreamt of the wind, but it was not the wind at all; it was the wailing of long-dead gods, the sighing of ghostly music; the singing of the bronze harp of Ane, the melodious laughter of the magic harp of Craiphtine.

And then it was more. It became enmeshed with memory and I jerked into wakefulness, straining to hear what I thought to be the cawing of crows.

There was no moon. Stars swirled against the black cape of infinity. Then, not in my dream, shattering the silence of the night, I heard:

"Pa-trec . . . Pa-trec . . . Pa-trec . . ."

A sound borne up out of yesterday. My eyes strained to penetrate the darkness. It seemed to me that I had never seen a night so black. Yet, rising on the blackness, a deeper darkness. Three winged forms, perceivable against the stars, swooshed toward me, dipping their wings as though in greeting, laughing, then moving away until they grew so small that they merged with the blackness beyond the stars. Only their voices lingered, mere shadows of sound, calling to me as they had called to me so long ago in the woods of Briton: "Pa-trec . . . Pa-trec . . . Pa-trec . . ."

Dubh stirred beside me. "What is it, boy?"

I could not speak.

He prodded me. "Padraic . . . ?"

Padraic.

The sound of that name seemed to explode within me. It was the same sound which the crows were calling. Pa-trec . . . Padraic . . . the same sound.

The night seemed suddenly cold. I shivered and pulled my woolen lummon up about my shoulders. I told myself that I was a fool, that my imagination was being contaminated by the superstitious nature of the Gaelic riffraff with whom I was being forced to live. I drew my hood up over my head and lay down again.

"I thought I heard crows calling," I said to Dubh, "but it must have been only a dream. I hear nothing now."

He made the smacking sounds which sleepy men make when they have been awakened and are on the verge of drifting back into sleep. He snuggled beneath his bedding.

"Crows, eh?" he said through a yawn. "A bad omen for someone, boy. But not for the likes of us. Omens are for kings and flaiths and holy men. Go back to sleep."

I tried. I succeeded. The crows did not return. Yet it seemed to me that other winged shapes moved upon my dreams. Softly. Transiently. Surging in, murmuring words which I could not understand, then running out as a pale tide which I could not hold. And in their wake, a light such as I had never seen. It seemed to grow out of itself, innascible, luminous beyond description. It moved. It flowed. It encompassed me and yet remained aloof from me. It was as though someone, or something, called me toward it.

Within the dream, I saw myself walking as though caught up within the heart of a great and pulsing crystal. As I moved forward, each step I took revealed to me new and wondrous facets of the radiance which surrounded me. Ahead, the light seemed to be taking on substance, to have revealed a central core: a towering, three-trunked pillar of fire from which a corona emanated as though being born out of the sun itself.

I was blinded by its radiance. Within the dream, I saw myself fall to my knees. I saw my forehead go down and press against my thighs. The essence of the light filled me with an all-pervasive balm of serenity. Slowly, my conscious thoughts began to thin and diffuse. The dream dissolved. I slipped into the deepest, warmest, most peaceful sleep that I have ever known.

It was to be the last day of the shearing. The morning dawned pink and clear. I awoke before Dubh, roused by the sound of hoofbeats. Sitting up in my dew-dampened bedding, with Shadow stretching beside me, I looked across the camp.

Things were just beginning to stir. A few fires had been made and were already smoking. Smells of food and soiled humanity rose as a tandem mist with the vapors of the morning. I could see the ring fortress of the Ri rising on its hill below the southern flank of Slemish. Washed by the morning ground mists, its gray walls were transposed into mauve and silver. It seemed an enchanted place, something seen in a child's daydream. The sense of peace which had come to me in last night's dream still lingered about the peripheries of my consciousness. I felt warm, blissfully secure within my meager bedding.

I watched as a four-wheeled oxcart moved slowly toward the ring fortress. The driver sat up front on a high wooden seat, wrapped like a corpse in a heavy brown hooded cloak. The cart itself was filled with six men. Two of them stood very straight, with weapons evident even in the dim light of dawn. The other four were stooped into the posture of those who are unutterably weary. Even from my distant vantage point, I could see that their hands were manacled. Their clothes were in in tatters. There was blood on one man's tunic. His head was bent. Behind the cart, bound by their necks and leashed to the stakes of the cart like hounds, two other weary, dirty men walked.

The feeling of peace left me. I knew that I looked upon captives. I was suddenly aware of my own situation. With the approach of summer, the Western Sea had no doubt grown calm. Raiders were once again crossing it to work their depredations upon the Briton shore. Why, then, had there been no word from my home? Could it be that if a ship bearing ransom had left for the island of the Gael that it had been met and pirated by Gaelic raiders before it ever reached the sight of land?

"Get away from me, I tell'ya!" A voice disturbed my

solemn musings. I looked up to see a skinny middle-aged shepherd arguing with an elderly hag who had wandered into the camp. He was backing away from her, stammering in terror: "Get away from me, I tell'ya. I need none of your cures!"

She continued to advance toward him. "But I tell'ya that the yarrow and the daisy will cure the pink eye for'ya! Always the yarrow and the daisy, but the blossoms must be mixed with the milk from the breast of a woman who has just birthed a daughter and then added to the blossoms of the flower of The Little Bright Eye, with just a grain or so of White Copperas. 'Twill work for'ya, man, if you'll but let me try it."

He cursed her. Loudly. Profoundly. She made a shriek of dismay, backed away and cursed him in kind, screaming at him in a croak which scratched and twisted upward out of her vocal cords. "May your affected eye rot in its socket! May your manhood shrivel and suffer drought!" From somewhere within the folds of her dark lummon, she pulled a black feather. She lifted it and let it fall before the shepherd. It was an omen of death. He gasped with fear and ran from her, leaving her to guffaw as she bent to retrieve the feather.

She made an amazing picture. A tiny, crooked woman with a misshapen spine, a bandaged hand, and a filthy, unraveling basket clutched to her belly. She leaned on a tall gnarled staff and teetered against it like a frail, grotesque sapling. She must have sensed my stare, for she turned to fix me with huge, bulging, rheumy eyes.

As she came toward me, I was revolted by the sight of her face. It was exceedingly pale and bloated, washed with the greenish pallor of severe illness. She was toothless. Her lips were an inverted, swollen seam tucked up beneath a broad, sunken nose. There were supperating growths on her eyelids. Her forehead was marred by a vast, scabby, white-edged sore through which tiny pocks of blood had welled and clotted.

"Have I a cure for'ya, lad?" said she to me as she hobbled around me, facing into the rising sun until she had completed three circuits. She paused then, panting, leaning on her staff. " 'Tis true what they say. There's special magic in the cures of a leper."

I was appalled by the desecration which the disease had worked on her face. "I need no cures," I told her.

She inclined her head toward me, lowering her grue-some brow. "All men need cures. Herbs to heal the body. Words to poultice the soul." Her pussy lids flickered. She tottered against her staff.

"Go away!" I heard myself shout, panic-stricken by the thought that she might fall down upon me and touch me with her unclean flesh. Instinctively, I retreated into my bedding.

Shadow, who had been sleeping by my side, let off a bark. The sound woke Dubh. He sat upright. His face was rumpled. From the squint to his eyes, I knew that the ale he had consumed last night would plague him well into the new day. When his vision finally cleared, I saw revulsion move on his face like a visible cloud.

"Be gone, poor creature," he said to the hag, summoning up courage to gentle his tone. "Can't you see that this is but a shepherd's camp? There's no comfort for'ya here. Make'ya off to the ring fort. By law they must offer'ya sustenance there."

The woman's head strained forward on her neck. She stared at Dubh as though appraising him had suddenly become the sole purpose of her existence. "Aye . . ." The word was a hiss. The swollen lid of her left eye half-closed. From beneath it flicked a membrane, white and mucose as the nictitating eyelid of a bird.

Dubh flinched visibly when he saw it. "Go," he said to her.

"Aye, and that I shall, young man. There is nothing I can do for you. Your disease is loneliness. Your blemish is despair. Had I a cure for these, surely I would use it to cure myself."

I heard myself exhale a relieved and tremulous laugh as she walked away from us. "Poor old hag, her disease eats away at her brain."

Dubh's face was white. "Only a fool laughs at the expense of a leper. May the gods protect us both against the spells of such as she."

"I do not believe in spells."

His brow settled into a frown. "Then'ya are an ignorant lad, Padraic."

I was irked by his tone. It ignited the spark of antagonism within me. "I am a Roman," I replied disdainfully, knowing full well that the statement implied wisdom and culture beyond the ken of any Gael.

His eyes narrowed. "A Roman . . ." He contemplated me for a moment before he went on. "And 'tis the Romans who rule the world now, is it not?"

"For a thousand years," I affirmed haughtily.

He cast a sardonic glance about the camp. "Is it so now? Strange, but I see no Romans here. I see only slaves and overseers, captives and humble folk. Why have the Romans not come, Padraic? Why have they not come with all of the might of their great Caesars to wrest their stolen people from the hands of us heathen, superstitious Gael?"

Even as he spoke the words, I knew what he was going to say. My heart began to pound. I felt the blood surging away from my head, dizzying me as it went. My hands had grown cold, as though ice sheathed my fingers.

"The Romans do not come, Padraic," informed Dubh, "because Rome is finished. No one has wanted to tell you, but for days we have known it. The city has been breached. The might of the Empire and its 'invincible' armies has been cracked and shattered. Your parents will never send for'ya. You'll be lucky if they are still alive. The coast of Briton is wide open to our raiders and colonists. You'll be a slave in Eire forever now. Aye. Forever."

Forever.

The word reverberated through my mind with the dull, resonant echoing of a lid being placed irrevocably upon a coffin. All through the morning, as I went about my work, I felt the oppressive weight of it lying like lead upon my gut and heartbeat.

It was nearly noon when Leborchom came to me and put his hand upon me. "Dubh has told you?"

I wheeled. "Why was I not informed of the truth before this?"

He stood like a rock before me, unflinching, his lizard's mouth set. "Because you've clung to your hope of ransom like a drowning man. I've prayed for'ya, Padraic. I've asked God to give'ya the strength and humility to bear that which is His will for'ya. I've prayed that'ya may know the peace of Christ."

"I can know no peace as a slave!" My voice broke with anguish.

"There can be no peace—no freedom—for slave or

king, save that peace and freedom be won through the grace of God."

My hands went up to wipe at the air as though I could erase his words from it. "Spare me the doctrine, old man. I am the grandson of a priest, the son of a decurion. What good did their faith do them? What peace did it bring to them? They gave their lives to God, and how were they rewarded? Did their prayers keep the raiders from destroying their home? Did their prayers save me from being sold into bondage? My grandfather, holy man though he was, may well be dead and decayed back into dust, murdered by the hands of those who probably never even heard of his God!"

He put out his hands and lay them upon my shoulders. "But God has heard of them, Padraic."

I stepped away from him, twisting free of his touch. "Then, why has this God not struck them down for the gravity of their sins? Why do only His followers seem to be singled out for His 'grace' of suffering? Spare me your philosophy. It is so much pious excrement to me. If there are gods which rule the lives of men, then it seems to me that they prefer a diet of gentle, passive, Christian folk. Thank you, but I do not care to be eaten. I will not spend the rest of my life as a slave, lord only to hounds and sheep. I will not passively accept such a fate. I was born for better and shall find better."

"Then, you must escape from Eire."

The words, spoken so matter-of-factly caught me off guard. "How?" I asked incredulously.

His right hand went up to his mouth. His fingers played with his lips, squeezing them as though they were two pieces of soft clay. "You must pray for guidance," he said meditatively.

I spat out a sound of derision. "Then, surely I shall be here forever!"

"If it is God's will that you shall be a free man, His will shall be done." His expression was one of unflinching conviction. His hand went down from his mouth. The tip of his tongue came out to moisten the corners of his lips. As it moved, a slight smile twitched in its wake. "But I warn'ya again, there is not a freeman in all of Eire who'll willingly give aid to an escaped slave—unless, of course, you managed to find 'gentle, passive, Christian folk' to take'ya in, and they would do so, even though they knew that they risked their very lives."

Defiance moved within me. "I shall ask nothing of any man, be he Christian or pagan."

Leborchom shook his head. "Your hair has been shorn so that you'll be recognized as a slave, no matter where'ya go."

I ran my palms across my close-cropped skull. "I shall grow my hair."

"How? The Ri's men will see that'ya keep it shorn according to the law."

I knew the truth when I heard it. We were constantly checked upon by riders who came out from the ring fortress. They came, ostensibly, to see to our health and to keep us supplied with food. Yet, their brusque, imperious manner informed us that their primary function was to keep us at heel. Once each month, they observed us as we cut our hair. Still, I mumbled stubbornly: "I will find a way."

"If it be God's will."

He left me then, reminding me that the day was young and that there was much to be done. I stood staring after him, hating him, shivering with the desire to bolt and run. How easy it would be to simply turn on my heels and flee the camp. No one would notice me. Everyone was busy at the thousand tasks of the day. It would be easy. By the time anyone noticed my absence, I would be safely hidden in the inland woods, resting, biding my time, living upon the wild foods of the forest while I made my plans of escape from the island.

But if I fled, Leborchom, as my overseer, would surely suffer at the hands of the Ri's men. He would be beaten, perhaps even maimed or killed. Yet he had encouraged me to go. Why had he not reminded me, as Dubh did time and time again, that his life might depend upon my actions?

Closing my eyes, I felt tears well within them. They stung me like acid. The dog Shadow was beside me. I bent down and ran my fingers through his long, matted neck hair "Oh, good friend," I sighed to the dog, "how long must I wait for my freedom?"

It was late in the day when I at last finished my work and sought the solitude of a stand of hazelnut trees which grew just beyond the perimeters of the camp. When I reached the trees, I heard the sound of voices: male, harsh, held low, insistent. I had come to the edge of the grove. The voices stopped. I heard whispering. Then someone called my name. Hesitantly, I entered the little wood.

Dubh and the two young men with whom he had danced the little jig were seated on a bank above a small, brackish pond. The two young men were brothers. Twins. Red-haired and freckled, with strong young bodies which tended to stoutness. Whatever their conversation with Dubh had been, it stopped abruptly upon my arrival. They rose to their feet simultaneously, as though both were bound to the same nervous system. They wiped leaves and grass from their buttocks and explained that they must be on their way.

I stood facing Dubh. He sat cross-legged and solemn. With a nod of his head, he indicated that I should join him. I told him that I had come to the grove to be alone with my thoughts.

"Why?" he asked. "So they may prick'ya to despair?"

I walked around the weed-choked pond and sat down beside him.

"And what brings you so far from the encampment, Dubh? Have you and the twins a stash of ale?"

He cocked an eyebrow at me. "Rodui and Fordui followed me here to talk me out of my plans to escape."

I was certain that he jested. "And did they succeed?"

"Aye, they did."

I put down my hand and stirred the surface of the pond water. "And where does it go from here? Does it stay and stagnate? Or does it somehow find its way to the sea?"

"Would'ya go with it, Padraic?" He flicked at an insect which had mired itself in the hairs of his bare forearm.

"Have you never tried to escape, Dubh?"

"Oh, yes. Once. In the Long Ago. When I was a boy of few years and little knowledge of the ways of men. I was caught. My back was laid open by the whip. I was forced to watch while the one who was then my overseer was castrated. He was a young man. Three days later, he hung himself."

I thought of Leborchom. I thought of the distances of land and sea which separated me from my homeland. I folded my arms across my knees and put my head down. "There must be a way . . . without hurting others . . . there must be a way . . ."

He shrugged his dissent. "The bonds of conscience are of a cruel metal. They bind a man as tightly as any chain. But, even if I could escape, I know that I'd find no life as a freeman. The Ri's men would hunt me down. And, even if I could escape them, where would I go? I am kin-wrecked. The Wood of Focluth, which was my home, is now ruled by strangers. Perhaps, if Miliucc were a more benevolent king, freedom might someday be mine. There are many Gaelic Ris who deign to give a slave a place within the tribe after he has served loyally for seven years. Not that there is ever any hope of restored rank, but a man might live freely within the tuath, earning a livelihood by his labors, legally taking a wife, raising sons and daughters which he may call his own, swearing fealty to his Ri in time of battle need. But Miliucc? He has fought many a battle. His sword has made slaves out of many a flaith and many a prince. He dares not be gentle with his slaves, for fear that once made freemen we would draw together and nourish thoughts of vengeance against him." Again he shrugged. "So you must learn to be practical, Padraic," he advised bitterly. "Is not Miliucc generous to those of us who do his work? Are we not fed and clothed? At the time of the shearing, are we not allowed to roam about at will? Tonight, the last night of the encampment, we will be royally feted. There will be good food and drink. There will be entertainment: jugglers, jesters, musicians, and willing maids to take pleasure upon. How much more could a man want?"

My features clotted with anger. "I am fed and cared for as the dogs are fed and cared for. The day which finds me grateful for that will be the day upon which I will deserve no more than that—a cur's portion. Have you come to that, Dubh? Have you been in bondage so long that you have forgotten what it was like to be free?"

My words had found their mark. "What would'ya have me do?" he asked wearily. "I must be reconciled to my fate or else bring pain to others." His hand closed about a small rotten nut, one of dozens which lay about us, cast off by the tall hazel trees. He lifted the little brown orb and pitched it into the pond. It lay on the surface of the water for a moment, bobbing like a curagh. Then, slowly, it sank bubbling to the bottom. "To Tir Tairnigri with you," said Dubh to the nut, "for, by the Daghda, 'tis a land I'll never see."

"Tir Tairnigri?"

"Aye. The Land of Promises. 'Tis walled all around by the good hazelnut trees, just as is this little glade. There's a magic well there. It is fed by the spring of Segais. When nuts fall into that well they cause magic bubbles to rise —the bubbles of pure magical inspiration. These bubbles are eaten by the great salmon which lives in the well. The wisest creature in all the world is the salmon of Segais. A man who captures this fish, ahh Padraic, he would grow as wise as the salmon—wise enough to best any situation, wise enough to free himself from bondage and take all of his loved ones with him."

"Another of your stories!"

"No. 'Tis true. Many a man has sought the salmon of Segais—and has sought the Land of Promise, for there it is springtime forever, one long perfect day wherein there is neither illness nor deformity, but only youth and beauty."

"My people have such a place. They call it Heaven. But Heaven or Tir Tairnigri, it's all foolishness; legends created by men who are ill at ease with the knowledge of their own mortality."

Dubh smoothed the grass free of nuts and lay down on his belly. He bent his arms and propped his chin on his upturned fists. "This Heaven, have there been Britons returned from there to tell of it?"

I laughed. "No Britons. Only a man called Jesus, who claimed to be the Son of God."

"Which god?"

"My people believe that there is only one."

"That is what I have heard. But tell me, other than this Jesus, have there been no mortal men traveling to Heaven and back again?"

"Only in their dreams."

He read the skepticism of my tone and admonished me. "There is magic in dreams, Padraic. And power. And prophecy. A wise man does not ignore his dreams."

"You sound like my grandfather," I said with a sneer.

"Was he a druid? A diviner of dreams?"

"He could divine nothing save the weather through his

aging bones. He was a priest, a naive old fool. Nothing more."

"Cannot Christian priests work magic then? Have they not the Sight?"

"The ability to predict the future? Oh, they would have us believe that, all right. Often enough they have promised me doom and damnation. But in truth they can work no magic. Their faith is dark and juiceless, devoid of joy, snagged in events which transpired hundreds of years ago, rootbound in sin and sacrifice and endless acts of contrition."

"Yet, Leborchom has spoken to me of miracles. He has told me of a magical spirit which speaks the word of your god through living men. He has told me that Christian law has come to your people out of antiquity, from a time in the Long Ago when your god made known his will with a finger of fire and appeared to a prophet as a flame in a bush which burned and yet was not consumed."

I made a face of disgust. No doubt such tales would appeal to the childish mind of the Gael. "So the old ram's been trying to convert you."

"We have been on the mountain together for many years, Leborchom and I. We share our thoughts. He believes in the promise of the one he calls Lord Jesus, just as I believe in the tales which the seanachies and druids tell. I do not know how Leborchom came to the god of Christians. But I do know that the gods of Eire have brought me to accept the fact that there are powers in this world which are beyond the ken of mortals such as you and I. Our gods *have* walked among us, Padraic. My gods. Your god. Can we, who know so little of our own world, and nothing at all about the Otherworld, deny the wisdom of seers and prophets?"

I rubbed the flat of my hand along the ground. It was rich and mounded with hazel mast. My fingers disturbed the blanket of decomposing nuts and leaves. I caught the scent of mold. The decaying nuts were rough beneath my palm. Finding the feel of them unpleasant, I moved my hand onto my thigh and rubbed it on the cloth of my trews. "Why is it, Dubh, that the stories which come to us of heavenly places and of gods walking the earth are always stories born in the Long Ago. Always the gods *once* walked. Always the Age of Miracles was *yesterday*. Perhaps, if I could find but one man who had actually seen, within his lifetime, a god or a miracle, then perhaps I could believe."

"I have seen."

He had spoken so matter-of-factly that I did not take him seriously. "And what did you see?" I drawled facetiously.

"The ravens flocking. Great, black tides of them. In a dream it was. I was a boy. I was still living with the sons of the neighboring chieftains in the Boys' House, where we were being tutored in star wisdom and the arts of combat and in the ways of cutting the ogham word inscriptions into the green stalks of the willow. But I was not like the other boys. Like you, I'd lost my faith in dreams and magic and the divinations which were drawn out in the colored sands of the seers. Yet the dream did come to me. It came on the night before I was to take valor; before I was to be tested as a man and a warrior. The ravens flew within me. An old hag walked before them. With her were two flame-haired sisters. One of them was maimed and twisted. There was blood on her hooded mantle. There was killing madness in her eyes. The other was a fair maid. As tall as a man she was, and as beautiful as freedom, with her breasts bared to me as enticement. A cask of water she carried, and she called out to me from my dream: 'Come, lad, open the doors of your father's house so that I may bathe his limbs for him. He must be cleansed for battle.' Then she turned the cask down and allowed the water to spill out; but it was not water. It was blood."

Dubh's face was wet with sweat. He sat up and wiped it away. "There is a legend among the Gael that before a battle the gods grow restless. Some of them choose sides and rise up out of the earth so that they might appear as warning to those mortals who have been predestined to die in battle. The three women of my dream were the three forms of the one great goddess of war, the Phantom Queen. To lie with her is to assure one's victory. But to allow her to bathe one's limbs, that is a statement of resignation to one's own death. It is an old legend. As a boy I knew it well enough. The three women were the Three Furies, the three faces of the Phantom Queen: Badhbh, Nemhain, and Macha, portents of battle frenzy, madness, and death. Yet, even when the three figures stood together and merged into the one, with the ravens standing on her

extended arms, I said to my dreaming self: 'Tis but a
dream brought on by too heavy a meal. I'd eaten roast
badger, and it has never agreed with me. So, when I
awoke, I told no one of the dream, for I knew that it
would be taken most seriously. The day of my taking
valor was sure to have been postponed while wise men
gathered to pour out and contemplate the red and white
sands of divination. And so it is that my father and
brother and most of the boys within the Boys' House are
dead or enslaved. That very day the raiders of the Ri
Miliucc MacBuain swept down upon us. We were not
prepared to do battle with them . . . because I was a foolish boy who chose not to heed the warning of the gods
. . . of the Phantom Queen . . . of the one who is called
the Morrighan."

Memories came down upon me with a surge of actual
physical pain. Morrighan, with the three crows perched
on her extended arms. Morrighan, flame-haired, as tall as
a man, standing at the base of the great oak. Morrighan,
the gray depths of her eyes staring at me with a wildness
and emptiness which seemed to be beckoning me toward
her; an emptiness which was somehow filled with dark
mists of gray, a foreverness of cloud, an immensity of appalling distances. Bleak. Cold. Like the winter mists of
Slemish. Waiting. For me.

"Padraic, what is it, boy? Sure now, you look as though
you've seen an apparition risen from the shees!"

I heard Dubh's voice. I could not answer. I stared
ahead, my eyes open wide, blind to the moment, filled
with visions of yesterday. I saw the predawn sky to which
I had awakened the previous night. A moonless sky.
Black beyond all imagining, yet seared by the distant light
of ten thousand suns. And on the blackness, three dark
birds winging, crying my name as they had cried it out of
the woods of Briton before ever I had been taken as a
slave to Eire, before ever Leborchom had called me
Padraic. "Pa-trec . . ." they had cried. "Pa-trec . . . Padraic . . . Padraic . . ."

I saw the ruined villa.
I saw flames.
I saw death.
I saw the faces of the raiders.
I heard laughter.
Not of raiders or of birds or of dreams. Laughter of a

red-haired woman. "You are pledged to me, by blood and by body, you are pledged to me." To the Morrighan. To Eire. To Dalaradia. To the people of the Western Sea.

"No," I said. "It cannot be!"

I felt Dubh's fingers curl about my shoulders as he began to shake me. The recently healed wound in my shoulder sparked with pain. I blinked. I stared at Dubh.

"What is it, boy? By the Daghda, Padraic, what's wrong with'ya?"

"She knew . . ."

"She? Who . . . ?"

"The Morrighan." My voice sounded strange to my ears. It was broken, a barely audible whisper trembling with incredulity. "Merciful God in Heaven, Dubh, I have seen her, too . . ."

6

I was still a youth. A mere boy. I had not yet gone to live within the great ring fortress. I had not yet seen the dark and evil standing stone which was in the mountain glen. I had not yet dared to challenge the will of the Ri Miliucc MacBuain. I had not yet fallen under the spell of still another woman. I had not yet witnessed the savagery and warfare which were soon to be loosed upon the peaceful hills of Dalaradia. Yet, in that moment in the hazelnut grove with Dubh, I was forced to acknowledge the fact that there were indeed forces moving upon this earth which are beyond the understanding of men. I, who had been touched by the hand of prophecy, had looked into an enchantress' eyes and had tried to ignore what I had seen written within them. But somehow those eyes had followed me across the miles, across the distances of time and storm-tossed seas. Yet my arrogance and defiance of truth lay across me as a mantle of darkness. I did not want to believe in God or gods, in promises of prophecy. I was as a stone lying imbedded in a mire—blind to the wisdom which was my heritage as a Christian, stubborn and unyielding as the most prideful seed of Adam. In time, and sooner than I could have then imagined, the mystical Spirit of God would flow into me—not as a balm, not as a soothing unguent which would bring a passive faith to my soul, but as a flaming brand which would mark me forever in His name.

We left the camp of the shearing behind us and began to graze the flock along the hillsides once again. I was not the same boy. I moped. I brooded. My mind was filled with dark memories, with questions which disturbed and plagued me, questions for which I could find no answers.

Dubh, too, had changed. He preferred to work alone. It was as though his spirit had been poisoned by some terrible disappointment. He would not speak of it. Only Leborchom was cheerful. He greeted each day with aggressive prayers of thanksgiving. Crude, homespun, punctuated with gross misquotations of Scripture, nevertheless his prayers reminded me of my lost homeland and served to contribute to my deepening despondency.

I kept to myself. Through days and hours and weeks of an ever-ripening summer. Then, one early afternoon, when in the valley below us fruit was fattening on the boughs and seeds were sprouting in the gardens, I heard a shout of glee come rioting out of Dubh's mouth.

"Padraic! Padraic! Come on along, lad!"

I looked up from the flock to see him waving to me, flinging his arms up and down, beckoning and bellowing with explosive jubilation.

"Can't'ya not hear?" he called.

I listened, turning my head first to the left and then to the right. I heard the distant mooing of cows, the voices of men, women, and children. Loud voices. Merry voices. Highlighted with laughter. Growing closer and closer. I got to my feet, perplexed and curious.

" 'Tis the people!" shouted Dubh.

"What people?"

"The Ri Miliucc's people. They come a'booleying!"

"A what?"

"A'booleying, ya dimwit! Come on along!"

"What about the caera?"

"The old man and the dogs will mind the caera. Come on along!"

And so I learned that it was a tradition for the villagers to pack pad and parcel and come up into the hills to spend the summer. With their gardens planted, and a few slaves and bondservants left behind to tend them, the majority of the villagers migrated up into the pleasant dells and cool forests. Here they settled into temporary camps which they called booleys. They brought their milk cows with them, and their best dispositions. They would spend their time tending the first tender months of summer with leisure, trying to forget that autumn must inevitably come, and with it the heavy toil of harvest.

As I came up the slope toward Dubh, I saw that he was not alone. A girl had come to stand beside him. She was a woman grown, plump and robust as a heifer. Her face was ablaze with freckles, as many as there are stars on a summer night. Her youth and good health made her as pretty as she would ever be; yet, when she smiled at me, her smile was warm and welcoming enough to have turned the darkest night into brightest day. She was small beside Dubh. He reached out to her. She came easily into his arms and yielded to his embrace.

I gaped. Then I saw Rodui and Fordui, the twins, rounding the top of the little hill. They stopped beside Dubh and the girl, took one look at the expression on my face and broke into peels of laughter.

" 'Tis our sister Darerca," Fordui informed me.

"Don't gape so, lad," chuckled Rodui as he came to stand beside me. "It's for want of Darerca that Dubh's been pining these past weeks. Did'ja not know that they are man and wife?"

The villagers set up their camp amidst a broken forest of tall trees. There was a stream nearby, with a small waterfall in which the boys cavorted like otters. New shelters went up. Old ones, left standing from past booleys, were swept and aired. Blankets snapped in the sunlight. Young girls tended hastily made fires. Dogs barked. Babies cried. Men unloaded carts. A child's pet goose squawked and strained to be free of its tether.

Leborchome came to investigate the source of the noise. With a thoroughly jaundiced eye, he informed us that we would have to move the flock into higher pastures the very next day. His fingers played with his lips as he appraised Dubh and Darerca. He looked at me, then back at Dubh, fixing us both with a stern scowl. "And you two, I don't suppose it'd be asking too much if I expect ya back at your duties by the light of dawn?"

Dubh grabbed Leborchom and danced him around and

around. "May the gods of Eire bless'ya, ya old sheep's wind!"

Leborchom pushed him away and readjusted his clothing about his bony frame. "I am already blessed, thank'ya, by the only God who is over us all."

The villagers, in the main, were a kind and sympathetic lot. The women seemed anxious to make certain that Dubh and I consumed a full summer's portion of food at one sitting—after they saw to it that we had thoroughly washed ourselves in the stream. The men were friendly. Darerca's master, an elderly miller, offered to teach me to play the game of chess. I had never been interested in mastering the game when in Briton, but the old man presented the challenge well, and soon enough I was fascinated. He kept me so well plied with ale that, after a while, I could not keep the moves straight in my head. The miller was amused. I was happily oblivious to the fool which too much drink had made of me, and as for Dubh and Darerca, after we had shared a meal, I saw them not during the whole of the day or during the long night.

I found my way back to camp alone and thoroughly intoxicated. Shadow, guiding me as though I were a blind man, barked his greeting to Leborchom and the other dogs. The old man eyed me, shook his head, then cast a disparaging glance out into the night.

"And when may we expect Lord Dubh?"

"By the light of dawn." My words were slurred. My head had begun to ache. "Why should he come before? Did you not know that he and that girl are wed?"

"According to whose law?"

"The law of Eire, I imagine."

"They may have made vows to one another, boy, but their union is sanctioned by neither God nor Ri."

"They are not Christians. They do not need the sanction of God."

"We will not quibble over that. But they do need the sanction of the Ri. Without his blessing, the girl is still legally the property of her master. He may do with her as is his want: Sell her, give her as a gift to a passing friend or, if his juices still flow, lie with her himself."

The words almost sobered me. "But Ersa seems a good man. He has allowed the marriage. Why would he not honor it?"

Leborchom let out air through his nostrils. He rolled his eyes heavenward as though in supplication. "He has allowed the 'marriage' to pacify the girl, so that she'll not trouble him during the long months when he is not a'booleying. No doubt it was Dubh, with all of his 'honor,' who devised such a scheme. Marriage! Between slaves without consent of the Ri! Foolishness. Dangerous foolishness if'ya ask me. But Dubh is a strapping youth, and Ersa the miller is no fool. If Dubh should get the girl with child, think of the fine babe that'd be born of such a union. By the laws of Eire, the child would be Ersa's, born into bondage to do his will."

"But it would be Dubh's child."

"No more than the girl is his wife."

I slept poorly that night. Singing and laughter from the booley punctuated the darkness. The sheep grew restless. It took both Leborchom and me to keep them controlled. By the time the stars began to plunge toward morning, things had quieted enough to grant both sheep and shepherds a semblance of sleep.

I woke at dawn. I felt ill. Dubh had not yet returned. The morning came up sluggishly through a sky banded by clouds. The light of it was pale and yellow. I viewed it biliously. My head throbbed, courtesy of Ersa's copious supply of ale. The sheep seemed passive. They had spread out and were grazing. I took Shadow and walked from the camp. I stopped atop a knoll, gazing down upon the sheep, the camp, and the silent booley where all were now asleep. After spreading my lummon upon the dew-dampened ground, I sat down, put my head upon my knees and dozed. Shadow would watch the flock for me. He had drunk no ale in the booley.

It was nearly noon when I awoke. I was startled to find the sun so high. Dubh, looking rested and at ease, was sitting beside me.

"Darerca's fixed the noon meal. Go on and eat. I'll tend the caera for a while."

My head felt as though it would drop from my neck and land in my lap. I looked at Dubh, saw two of him, felt nauseated, then put my head down again with a moan. With my usual lack of tact, I mumbled: "Leborchom says that Darerca is not your wife. He says that you never petitioned the Ri to wed her."

"Oh, but I did. Yet it seems that kings do not pay much heed to the petitions of slaves."

"Then, you're not married."

"Ersa has allowed us to be together. Darerca shall be with me now, all the rest of the summer, until harvest. I have Ersa's word."

I rubbed my temples in an attempt to stop the hammering within them. "If she is your wife, it should be your right to have her by your side throughout the year, not just during the summer when there is no work for her in the village."

Anger flared briefly in Dubh's eyes. His lips contracted. "Ya have an adder's tongue, Padraic. Ya know as well as I that as a slave I have no rights."

I knew that my words had stung him. I had not intended that. "I only meant . . ."

He interrupted me, shaking his head. "Ya must learn to think and act as a slave, Padraic, if'ya are to find any happiness at all."

My head went up. "And you, Dubh, who might once have been a lord, have you found happiness without the honor which was due you as your birthright?"

"By all the gods, boy, ya know that I have not. In the shearer's camp, when Darerca did not come to me as she had promised, I nearly went mad for want and worry. The day by the pond, when'ya found me with the twins, 'twas only their prudence which kept me from running off to find her. They advised me that their master was ill and that Darerca was tending him. They promised that she'd join me in the high pastures. And now that she's indeed with me, I can only bless old Ersa for his good heart and his generosity. I'm as happy as I can ever hope to be, Padraic. Do not prick my heart with hopes of what can never be."

I thought of Ersa. He had seemed an amiable enough man, yet I remembered his face as a long, shrewd wedge. His eyes were keen. His mouth was sagacious. It occurred to me then that perhaps he had deliberately plied me with ale so that he could find his pleasure in humiliating me. "Can you trust Ersa, Dubh?" I asked, unable to put off my suspicions.

Our eyes met. Mine were sullen and dark with misgivings. His were filled with irony and the soft gentleness of the loving husband.

"I must trust him, Padraic. I have no choice."

It is the fate of a slave to know no human rights at all. Yet, during the weeks which followed, it seemed to me as though I were free. Summer has a way of working on the brain like a good warm wine. My memory allowed itself the luxury of forgetfulness.

The hills and unfettered distances of Dalaradia unfolded around me like bolts of endless cloth, unfurling in long, peaceful shadows and warm, radiant colors. True, I was a slave bound to watch the wandering of the sheep, yet with Dubh, Leborchom, Darerca, and the dogs to help me, it was easy work. In truth, it seemed no work at all.

I moved beneath the tender sun of Eire unchained. Leborchom would tend his portion of the flock, Dubh and Darerca another. I kept to myself, responsible for my own small segment of the flock.

With winter gone, the land of my captivity had succumbed to the full potential of its beauty. It had become, even to the jaundiced eye of a slave, a land of incomparable loveliness. The very air seemed to take on the texture of velvet. It caressed the skin. It brought to the nostrils the wonderful amalgamation of aromas which constitutes the good sweet scent of a fertile island set within temperate seas: scent of surf and stone, of pastureland and forest, of sheep and rutted cow tracks, of salt spray blown inland with the smell of seaweed; scent of bog and moorland, of broad smooth-shouldered mountains upon the heights of which a man, or a boy, might find the Light and the wisdom to guide his life out of the Darkness.

It was then, during that first summer, in that brief golden period which preceded the tragedies which were soon to come, that the Light of God's love was being kindled within me. A tiny flame at first. A distant flame. Born out of my dreams, it obliterated the laughter of crows and the remembered grayness of an enchantress' eyes. A lambent light, it glowed persistently within the confines of my soul. It lingered always on the fringes of my consciousness. And sometimes, when I slept, I would tense with an awareness of its presence, for beyond the

Light, beyond that wondrous Light, I could hear the soft murmuring of words which I could not understand. They would surge within me like the distant whispering of the summer surf. Wave after wave of words, with the Light intertwined like the wings of a thousand angels enmeshed in flight. Then I would awake, confused yet filled with an utterable sense of peace, trembling with awareness of an unacknowledged reality: God was with me, though I knew Him not. As surely as the sun is with the earth, even though it may be obscured by cloud, He was with me.

And then, slowly, the sense of peace and harmony with the world began to ebb away from me. We had taken the sheep high onto the mountain, deep into the highlands where the clouds gather like convocations of gossiping spirits. Here, though the earth lay naked beneath our feet and the grass was confined to limited areas of soil, the new growth was rich and sweet and deeply green. The caera feasted. Dubh and Darerca made love. Leborchom prayed. And I?

I wandered alone with Shadow by my side. I felt as though I were searching for something. For what? I could not have said. Yet I know now that among the Gael there are certain men who are born with the Inner Vision, the Power, which allows them to know when a change is about to occur in their lives. I am not a seer, though there have been times when I have been allowed to glimpse, ever so vaguely, beyond Tomorrow. And there have been times when I have stood, tense as a man balanced at the edge of an abyss, knowing that I must go forward regardless of consequence, forward into the Unknown even if the path must lead me into danger and darkness and despair. So it was then on the mountain of Slemish. I stood at the edge of the abyss. I sensed it. I could not turn away.

The nights were long on the mountain. The stars turned above us: huge, cold, trembling suns. The moon would come up brazen, acquiesce through its phases, then disappear into the dawn.

As the weeks wore on, Dubh exhausted his repertoire of stories and songs of Gaelic history and legend. Darerca tried to entertain us with her own version of the tales, but Dubh never tired of teasing her, and she would invariably end convulsed in giggles. Leborchom chose the nights to keep his watch over the sheep. So, in due time, Dubh and Darerca insisted that I must play the seanachie. They agreed that I was terrible in the role, but insisted that I try.

At first, I gave them what I remembered of the classics: Theseus and the Minotaur, the gods of Olympus, portions of *The Iliad,* bits and pieces from *The Odyssey.* I told the tales badly, not only because I felt ill at ease as a storyteller, but because I did not remember them well enough to invest them with any detail or insight. So I turned to the Bible stories which I had learned as a child.

I gave them tales which I thought I had forgotten. I gave them Adam and Eve in the Garden. I gave them Cain and Abel. I gave them Noah and the Flood. I gave them slaves and kings and heroes. I gave them love and lust and sacrifice. I gave them the God who had touched His chosen people and had directed their destiny. I gave them Moses and Pharaoh, Joshua and Jericho, Sodom and Gomorrah, Lot and his daughters, Sara and Abimelech, David and Goliath. How easily the stories flowed from my lips. I had suddenly, unexplainably, remembered them all. The names. The places. The sequences. As I spoke, I grew amazed at myself and at my sudden ability to reach my listeners. And reach them I did, for when I finally finished, Dubh nodded his head and said: "Told like a true seanachie, Padraic. Tomorrow night, ya must tell us more stories of your gods."

"They are not stories of gods. They are stories of men of God."

He shrugged. "I do not see the difference."

"The people in the Bible tales are made of flesh and blood, as are you and I. It was their faith in God which strengthened them. It was their faith which sometimes made them appear to have been gods themselves."

He frowned. "Sure now, Padraic, your Moses was a god. He parted an entire sea!"

"God parted the sea. Moses led his people through."

The next night came up dark and moonless. "Tell us tales about the one whom Leborchom calls Lord Jesus," Darerca requested.

It seemed as though the sky lay sighing above me, heavy with the benign knowledge of history. Beneath its vastness, the works and plans and dreams of all Mankind had been played. Against the velvet of its night, a star had risen. Long ago, yet remembered still. A great star, rising out of the east. A guiding star. A sign unto all nations. And in the fields, shepherds stood watching their flocks even as we now watched the flocks of the Ri Miliucc MacBuain. Shepherds. I began my tale with them. And as I spoke, it was as though another spoke through me, so that I became a listener and a wonderer. It seemed as though, somehow, I sat outside of myself.

I told them of the virgin birth and of the fulfillment of prophecy. I told them of the boy, growing to manhood as all boys grow, yet turning from boyhood to follow His God. I gave them Christ the man, the teacher who trod the dusty earth of a far land in sandaled feet and crude homespun garments. I gave them the sun-baked earth of Nazareth and Bethlehem and Jerusalem, and the blue shining waters of the Galilee where fishermen worked their nets and then left their nets so that they might become fishers of men, following in the wake of the one whom people had begun to call The Messiah.

How real these people seemed to me as I spoke, how vulnerable and trusting within their flesh, with the blood of their mortality pulsing in their veins, and the hope of eternity with God burning in their hearts as they saw their Lord on the way to His Calvary. And the Man Himself, the one who was called Jesus. No simpering, eyeball-rolling martyr He. But alive with enthusiasm, possessed of a charismatic virility which was as compelling as sunlight. And then, at the very end, afraid within the mortal confines of His body. The Lamb of God, the Light of hope, how weary He had been, how bloodied, how infinitely forgiving unto His last breath.

I saw the weeping mother. I saw the hand which thrust the spear. I tasted the gall. I saw the great darkness fall upon the face of the world. And then I saw the tomb. I saw the stone rolled away even as the angel said: "Behold! He is risen!"

It was dawn before the last words were spoken. Dubh and Darerca lay fully awake, close in each other's arms. Dubh met my gaze. He smiled at me. Gently. Peacefully. Darerca's eyes shone with tears.

"Oh, Padraic, is it a true tale?" she asked. "For if it

is, then surely all men should rejoice and hold faith in their salvation."

I grew suddenly cold. I crossed my arms over my chest and pressed my hands against my shoulders. Within me, a plummeting sense of loneliness, of despondency. I met Darerca's questioning gaze and shook my head, like a terminally ill man reluctantly drawing out of a dream which has promised him health and longevity. I felt sick and weary with confusion. "I don't know . . ."

"Padraic . . ." Leborchom's voice.

I looked up. How long he had been in the camp, I do not know. He was seated atop a pile of bedding, a gaunt-faced patriarch in his tattered lummon. Slowly he got to his feet. Leaning on his staff, he reached out his hand and beckoned to me.

"Come with me, boy. There is something which'ya must see."

I do not know how far we walked. I followed Leborchom across the face of the mountain and into the light of the rising sun. We went downhill, following a broken, twisted escarpment of ancient stone until we reached a steep incline. Here we descended into a dark, shrub-choked ravine.

The dawn had not yet reached this place. There was barely enough light to see by. We walked on, carefully picking our way until the bottom of the ravine widened into a natural amphitheater. The walls of the mountain rose nearly vertically on all sides. We could go no farther.

Ahead of us, against the cliffs, stood an enormous tree. It was dead, centuries old. Its branches were splayed outward like the arms of some twisted demon supplicating eternity to bring it back to life. Insects and birds had written their undecipherable graffiti into its trunk. Its dried, lifeless roots lay across the mound of earth which had once nourished them, veining it, lifting it, distorting it. No seedlings had sprouted here. Only a few grasses. Small, pale, sallow. Yet out of the mound of earth, between us and the tree, there rose a stone. Tall. Slender. Blotched with lichen. Smooth and gray, with angular inscriptions etched into it and two like-sized indentations at its base.

"You must choose, Padraic." Leborchom's voice was

low. It was barely more than a whisper, yet it was a challenge.

I could not take my eyes from the stone. "Choose?"

"Between Good and Evil. Between the Darkness and the Light. I watched'ya tonight, boy. When'ya told the Gospel, sure and the Lord Christ Jesus was with'ya, though'ya knew Him not. He spoke through'ya, boy, uniting us in His love. Now'ya must reach out your hand to Him or surely'ya shall be lost forever."

His words sounded hollow, the naive babblings of an old man who had seen Death in his future and was blindly reaching out for the Christian alternative. "Why should I choose to follow a God who has allowed me to become a slave? He is the God of my fathers, but where is His country, Leborchom? Where is He sovereign? Where is His peace? Where is His salvation?"

"The things'ya ask for are not of this earth, boy. Life is pain, Padraic. It moves to death. The future promises the grave—to both slave and king alike. But when the Spirit moves within'ya, as It did within you tonight, surely its coming proves that there is more for us than the mere legacy of flesh and blood and darkness? You were blessed tonight, boy. You were touched by the power of the Holy Spirit. Did'ja not feel it?"

A dawn wind was rising. It made a shh-ing sound as it entered the ravine and blew into the amphitheater. The grasses bent, trembled. The dead branches of the great tree creaked and made the sounds of stress. I shivered. I stared at the stone, unable to look away from it. "Why have you brought me to this place?"

Leborchom walked forward to the edge of the earth mound. He turned to face me. "This is a shee, Padraic. An entrance into the Otherworld."

I wanted to turn and flee back up the ravine and out into the light of the growing day. But I could not move. I stood transfixed, staring at the stone.

"They are not myths, the tales which Dubh tells of the mystical people of the Tuatha De Danann," said Leborchom. "Long ago, when this tree still lived, they came here to bury their kings, to worship and make sacrifice to their gods. They came here as conquerors, to dispossess and, eventually, to be dispossessed, for that is the fate of all conquerors. Now, like this tree, they are dead. But their gods live on."

He gave a kick to the soil of the ancient barrow. "Do'ya believe that they are here, Padraic? In the earth, waiting to rise up and haunt us? Or do'ya imagine that this is merely soil, the covering of a grave, no more, no less? Do'ya think that if a man should put a spade to this mound he would find only caverns and corpses, dead men and women buried 'midst the refuse of their history? Think as'ya may. But the gods do live, Padraic. Aye, they do. They rule Eire even more strongly than they did in the days of the Tuatha De Danann. If not from the shees, if not from the Otherworld, then surely from the throne of every living pagan Ri."

He rubbed his foot back and forth over the earth until he had loosened the soil. He bent. He lay his hand upon the earth. "Once there was life here. The druids came to worship the billa, the great holy tree. It was living then, miraculously they must have thought, for little light penetrates to this place. Yet the tree lived, misshapen though it was. It reached for the sun. The life blood of the earth rose up within it, nurturing it. So they came, the druids who worship the earth. They reverenced the tree as a symbol of the cycle of life. They brought forth their young men and women to be mated here, beneath the tree, before their watchful eyes. They brought forth their sacrifices. The blood of animals and living human victims was mingled with the sperm of kings to be put upon the phallic stone as offering to the gods of the earth. Kings were consecrated here. You can see the two worn places in the stone wherein they placed their feet. Bull feasts were held and dreams were dreamt and divined. But then the tree died. How frightened the people must have been, for there could have been no omen of more terrible portent. They abandoned this place. The druids of this day have forgotten it. But I have found it. I, a Christian, following a lost ewe, have found it; and tonight, watching'ya, at last I know why."

I was staring at the tree, at the stone, at the mound of earth. My mouth was dry. My heart was pounding. "Long ago . . . in my homeland . . . I stood before such a stone . . ."

"And knew its intent?"

The wind was rising, murmuring like a trapped spirit as it moved against the walls of the mountain. Far above, sunlight was beginning to touch the meadows. A single

shaft of light was deflected downward. It touched the
barrow. It touched the tree, the stone, the old man. It
touched me.

The palms of my hands were suddenly hot. I could hear
the screams of the burning bird trapped within the sacrificial wicker basket. My nostrils were filled with the scent
of charred reed and flesh. Flooding my vision, images of
scenes I had never witnessed were caught in the wind,
clarified by the sunlight. They seared my consciousness.

Figures in white robes.

An enormous dark stone, wailing, carved into the shape
of a man.

Trees etched as black hieroglyphics against a night sky
turned red by leaping bonfires.

The sound of a child crying in terror.

A woman's hysterical laughter.

A blade as sharp and gleaming as a crescent moon.

Blood. Dark. Running out of white flesh.

Then moaning.

Chanting.

Sound of men murmuring, a sound like river water in
late summer: deep, sure, dark beneath the night sky.

The stone, growing, swelling, catching the light of dawn.
The stone, its shadow spreading out upon a land which
stretched burnt and bleak beneath the growing daylight.
A land which met a rocky coast. The shadow of the stone
spreading out across the surf. Out across the ocean swells,
nine waves distant and beyond. Out across the sea to an
island rising green and tall. And there it turned the green
hills black beneath its spreading form. Black, impenetra-
bly black. And beneath the darkness a people crouched
and prayed, lifted up their hands and called for the Light.

And the Light came. It spread out and over the shadow
of darkness. It obliterated the image of the great stone. It
spread quickly, with an intensity which was nearly blinding. It illuminated the faces of the pople who stood beneath it. Strangers all. Save one: a young man, blue-eyed,
wheat-toned hair cropped short, shadow of a yellow beard
bristling on his jaw and chin, his body lean and hard, clad
in the single-toned garments of a slave.

"I've found this place for you, Padraic," Leborchom
said. He touched my shoulder. "Here, boy, in this place
where men once communed with their gods, you must
choose between the gods of Darkness and the God of

Light. Here, in this place where the gods of the old way have begun to die, you must choose."

Clouds had begun to intrude into the sky. The shaft of dawn light ebbed. The warmth of it was gone. I heard the shh-ing of the wind. Or was it more than the wind?

Leborchom took a small wad of oil-soaked cloth out of the hide pouch which he carried at his waist. He had brought the necessary makings for the beginning of a flame. He went to the stone. He knelt. With a piece of broken branch, he jabbed a small indentation into the earth at the base of the stone. He placed the cloth within it. I watched him make a fire.

"They rule in darkness, the kings of Eire," he said, then bent his head and prayed aloud: "But 'The Lord reigneth; let the earth rejoice; let the multitude of isles be glad . . . A fire goeth before Him, and burneth up His adversaries round about.' "

His eyes went to me. They were bright with the assurance of his faith. They reflected the light of the little fire which he had kindled.

The little fire swayed fitfully in a sudden gust of wind. It needed additional fuel if it was to survive. The ground was covered with broken twigs and branches and bits of bark from the dead and decaying tree. Without willing myself to do so, I retrieved a handful of this refuse. I went to the stone. I bent. Carefully, lest I snuff out the flame, I put it around the burning cloth. It was a gesture made wholly without conscious thought. Yet, as the little fire gasped and rekindled its energy, there flowed through my body the most wondrous feeling of peace.

Then, suddenly, the little flame jumped and sparked. I was reminded of another fire, of small and hungry flames which burned on an altar dedicated to the name of another god. It seemed to me then that I could hear the cries of the sacrificial dove. Once again my nostrils were assaulted by the acrid scent of burning flesh and wicker.

The wind moved across my shoulders. It chilled me with its cold, silken hands. I shivered. Within my head, throbbing, pulsing, rising to taunt me, the voice of the god of the wood rose out of Yesterday to remind me: You are pledged to me, by blood and by body, you are pledged to me.

My fingers went up to my temples and pressed in upon them in a vain attempt to relieve the pain which was growing within my head. It stabbed me, as sharp and incandescent as a white-hot blade. I gasped.

Leborchom, kneeling beside me, made the sign of the cross. His head went up, eyes wide, nostrils distended.

"Listen . . ." he whispered. "The voices . . ."

Now, there are those who have mocked me for what I am about to describe. And there are those who have come to God because of it. You will believe, or you will not believe. I can only tell you what I know to be the truth.

From out of the very bowels of the earth, the Morrighan rose like a raven, surrounded by roiling, diaphanous, screaming specters. The air was fouled by the scent of them. Sulphurous, pungent with the breath of Death and Darkness, she swirled around and within us, blotting out reality with a pain as pure and malevolent as the forces of Evil which had spawned her.

It was to be the moment of our deaths. We knew that. We had defied the gods of Eire and would be destroyed for our blasphemy. The wind blew hot and hard, heavy with the scent of vomit and decay. We were prostrated by it. All around us, leave and twigs and bits of earth went scurrying and eddying until the air became so dusty that we could not see.

I lay flat upon the earth, consumed by wind and sound and pain. Yet I felt the old man's hand as it closed about my shoulder. He lay close beside me, shouting to me above the wind and the voices.

"The stone . . ." he cried. "We must destroy the stone . . ."

It rose above us, a megalith nearly twice my height and more than a dozen times my girth. Obscured by the stirrings of the wind and by the foul, flowing mists which now boiled around us, it was like a great, obscene finger jabbing defiantly toward Heaven. Its weight was the weight of Evil. Squinting through the whirling dust and fog, I shouted to Leborchom that it would take at least twenty men and a team of horses to dislodge it from the earth.

"It must be done!" He was curling upward against the wind. His hand, calloused to the consistency of bone, gripped me and prodded me to rise.

It took nearly all of my strength to get to my feet. The wind buffeted me. The voices shrieked in my ears. Yet, with Leborchom beside me, I put my hands against the stone, half expecting a bolt of lightning, called down by the curse of some ancient druid, to break out of the sky to strike me dead. Instead, the sound of the wind rose to an imperative wail of mind-shattering intensity.

"Now!" cried Leborchom. "In the name of Christ!"

We leaned against the stone, exerting all of our combined power against it. I felt the rough granite unyielding against my palms. I strained against it. It resisted.

"Again!" Leborchom's voice was a command. "In the name of Christ, boy, else we both be lost forever! Speak out His name!"

I felt the wind against me, burning me, searing me. It was as though I were being burnt alive by flames which I could not see. Was it the pain which made me scream out the supplication? I do not know. But cry out I did, a great shout that was a prayer, a mighty prayer, torn out of the very heart of my dying soul.

"God of my fathers, help me! Christ be with me! Now!"

Once again I put my weight against the stone. Within me I felt a swelling, totally unnatural sensation of power surge through me. I pushed against the stone and it went tottering back, hitting the ancient tree as it fell. I thought I heard a scream of pain as it shattered and crashed upon the earth, broken into a thousand irredeemable pieces.

The wind was gone, as though it had never been, and with it the mists and the specters and the Morrighan. I stood in stunned silence, staring at the ground.

There, despite the roaring wind which had blown across it, despite the dust which had not yet fully settled to the ground, the little flame which Leborchom and I had kindled still burned.

I fell to my knees. My right hand went up and slowly made the sign of the cross. In that moment, the faith of my fathers was mine.

It has been written that only a blind man given sight can fully appreciate the wonder of light and color, and that only those who have suffered despondency can ever fully know the buoyancy of joy. My newly born faith was as strong and as pure and as uplifting as sunlight. God had revealed His Power to me. Surely now I was blessed. Surely now it would be only a matter of time before my days of slavery were ended.

Dubh teased me mercilessly, for was I not the same lad who had mocked him for his belief in the Otherworld? Leborchom prayed with me. Darerca found time to stray from Dubh so that she might sit beside me, for she was filled with queries concerning the religion and the God of my people.

Time. It slipped away like an eel. Days. Nights. Summer's fragrant hours. Then, early one morning, before the sun had yet risen, I awoke shivering within my bedding.

I sat up and rubbed the sleep from my eyes. Not far away, Dubh slept, breathing deeply and rhythmically, a series of bumps and mounds beneath his blankets. Beside him, Darerca was sitting up, wrapped tightly in her cloak against the morning chill. Her suntanned, freckled face was lifted to the clouds.

" 'Tis a sad morning, Padraic," she said as she looked at me with a wan smile. She indicated my blankets with a nod of her head.

There, like a snail's shining trail, the mark of the coming winter was written in frost upon the dark wool.

"The harvest must be brought in now," she said. "Down in the booley camp they'll be making ready to return to the village. They'll be needing me." Her lips twitched into a half-hearted smile which was not a smile at all. It was a tear, an acquiescence to a fate over which she held no control. She reached out and placed a tender hand upon Dubh's shoulder. As he stirred beneath her touch, she said: "Up with'ya now, man. It's time I was going home."

They left camp that morning. Dubh assured us that he would return in no more than two days. It was cold all afternoon. When night came to darken the earth, it brought with it a chill wind which whistled bleakly across the mountain. Yet, the wind mocked up, for the following morning dawned free of frost. Soft summer clouds came rolling lazily in from the sea.

The days passed quickly. Warm days, with only the great black night sky to tell us in the language of its stars that the seasons were indeed turning. On the morning of the third day, we awoke expecting to find Dubh curled up beside us. But the days continued to slip away and

Dubh did not return. We found ourselves listening for the music of his timpan or the sound of his lilting songs. In the evenings we watched the dogs for any signs of restlessness that would tell us they heard him coming up the mountain to us.

On the morning of the eighth day of his absence, we awoke to frost once again. The sky was striated with thin, high clouds of ice.

"The time has come to take the sheep to lower pastures," Leborchom informed me. Then, with a tone which was oblique in its attempt not to show concern, he said: "Go in search of Dubh, Padraic. We need him now, and he has been too long away."

I took Shadow with me and began to make my way down the mountain. I retraced our route through the high pastures, leisurely following the cropped grass and sheep droppings until I came to the place where the booley camp had been made. How silent and lifeless it seemed, with the empty shelters and the little stream running cold and alone. The sun was high. I could see the distant ring fort and the village. I estimated that I could be at the base of the mountain well before dusk. Unencumbered by sheep and the old man, I was filled with the buoyancy of imagined freedom. I lifted my voice and called Dubh's name. My voice called back to me out of the distances of Dalaradia. I smiled. With the optimism of youth brimming in my soul, I imagined that I would find Dubh taking his ease at Ersa's cottage. The old miller was reputed to be a generous host, notoriously kind to even his slaves and bondservants. I gave Shadow's ears a fondling.

"Come on along, dog. Soon Darerca shall fix us a sound meal, and I shall scold Dubh for staying so long away."

We went down the mountain at a jog. It was well before sunset when I slipped a tether about Shadow's neck. It did not take me long to find the round house of Ersa the miller. I walked eagerly toward it, smelling the good smells of a village at suppertime. My stomach growled as I walked up the well-swept garden pathway to the house and called Dubh's name.

The silence which greeted me gave me a sense of foreboding which I chose to ignore. I knocked at the door, waitd, then knocked again. A woman, carrying a basket filled with fresh root vegetables, paused to stare at me. I gave her a ready nod of greeting. She looked quickly away and hurried her pace.

When Darerca at last opened the door, she greeted me as one would greet Death. She stared at me, her eyes red-rimmed, her face pale and taut with apprehension. "Why do'ya seek Dubh here?"

"It has been eight days since he left the camp. The old man grows both worried and vexed."

She stepped back and bade me enter the house. It was a simple abode. One large clean room in which the family lived, slept, and ate. There were sleeping compartments arranged along the walls, with wooden partitions allowing for privacy. A fireplace occupied the center of the room, with two day couches set near it. Oatbread, set to dry, hung across the rafters like strips of beef. Rushes were strewn across the floor. Darerca walked backward over them, her skirts making a rustling sound. She did not take her eyes from my face as she seated herself on one of the couches. She was trembling. She picked up a pillow and clutched it to her bosom.

Her manner completely unnerved me. The silence in the room was shattering. I looked about. "Where is Ersa?"

"He has gone to be entertained by a fat widow." It was Rodui's voice. He stood behind me, framed in the open doorway. His clothes and hair were dusted with the flour which he had been milling. "What brings'ya here, Padraic?"

"I have come to fetch Dubh back to the flock."

The color bled from his face. His glance flew to his sister. "By the gods, girl, have they killed him then?"

Her arms tightened about the pillow. "They promised that they would send a leech to tend him." There was panic in her voice. A wildness and desperation shone within her eyes.

"They?" My word hung in the air.

"Our good master's sons." Rodui's broad mouth twisted the word viciously.

I was confused and made no attempt to hide the fact. "Where is Dubh?"

Rodui closed the door. "Ersa's sons returned from their wanderings. They sought out my sister for their pleasure. When they learned that she was on the mountain with Dubh, they rode out to find her. They beat Dubh into submission and then, for amusement, they lay with Darerca before his eyes."

The words numbed me. I could not speak. I stared at the girl.

Her pale face flushed. "It's not as though I were a free woman, Padraic." Her voice was very low. "Ersa's sons have lain with me before. It was they who kept me from coming to the shearer's camp. Such is their right. It is not as though I found pleasure in it. But Dubh, would he listen to reason? He would not. Had he not flown into a rage, had he let them have their way, they would not have hurt him."

If she had slapped me, I could not have been more stunned. "He is your husband . . ." I exhaled my disbelief of her words and attitude. Then painfully, I remembered the young girl in the shearer's camp and Dubh standing over her, shaking with contained fury.

"Husband!" Darerca cried. "Are'ya another fool then? Oh, now, Padraic, do not look at me like that. I have loved Dubh as truly as any wife could love. But I have never been able to speak truth to him. His false sense of 'honor' would not allow it. He still thinks he is a lord. Husband? He is a slave, as I am a slave. Why, he behaved as though he were equal to Ersa's sons. I tried to gentle him, to explain that by law he must stand aside for them. But there was killing madness in his eyes. Even when I told him that I carried his child, and for the sake of that he should do my bidding, he would not listen. He cried out like a wounded animal." A tremor went through her. Her hands went up to her face. She began to weep. "Oh, Padraic, and true it is that he fought like a lord, but he had no weapons . . . none but his pride and his anger. When it was done, they swore to me that they would send a leech to tend him. He was so badly beaten."

I do not know if I spoke. I only know that I turned and ran from the house. I saw nothing, I heard nothing until I felt Rodui's hand upon my forearm and heard his wheezing breath and voice.

"Hold up, boy. Darerca told me that they were in the wood by the booley camp when Ersa's sons overtook them."

It was dark. I was back upon the mountain. I could feel the blood pounding in my head. The moon was rising, illuminating the slope of the mountain with a thin, white light.

"We must wait till morning," panted Rodui. "It'll be impossible to find him in the dark."

I cast a glance toward the moon. How far away it seemed, that round, shining, impassive face in the sky. I stood, sucking in deep breaths. "By the time we reach the booley, there will be light enough to see by."

We went on. Wordlessly. The moon climbed. Its light upon the earth became blue and bright. When we reached the place where the booley camp had been, stones and trees and boulders were casting long shadows. I could make out the texture of the earth.

We entered the wood. We could hear the sound of the rushing stream and the cascading waterfall. We slowed our pace. We began to call Dubh's name. A rabbit flushed from the shrubbery. Shadow took chase. We followed him.

It was the sound of the limb, bent with Dubh's weight, which led us to him. I think we both knew what we would see even before we found the tree. It was a hazelnut, tall and well-formed, as perfect a tree as those which are said to grow by the spring of Segais in the land called Tir Tairnigri. It had a broad crown and firm outreaching branches. He had evidently climbed high, so that when he fell he would be safe from the ravages of wolves and wild pigs. There was blood upon the bark, as tracing of his climb. He must have been hanging there for many days. Birds, insects, and rodents had rendered his face unrecognirable to us.

The people of Eire lived by the law, a vast and all-encompassing system of justice which had come to them out of their most ancient history. Brehon Laws, the Laws of the Judges, there was not a man or woman, slave or free, who was not bound by the intricacies of these judicial traditions.

The law touched us all, in life as well as death. A clansman became king, according to the law. He was inaugurated according to the law, and ruled according to the law. The great feasts and festivals of Eire, during which no man could strike another lest he be put to death, were staged according to the law. A man and woman courted, wed, and brought forth their children according to the law. The fate of orphans and widows, bondservants and foster children was determined according to the law. Hospitals were kept, houses were raised and completed according to the law. Physicians and conjurers, cupbearers and lampooners, charioteers and harpers practiced their trades according to the law. So also were weapons made and seams sewn and garments dyed. The Ri and his Rigan might wear seven colors at once, according to the law. High-born ladies were coifed, according to the law. Slave women suffered the humiliations of their station according to the law. Society was structured, girded, and made strong according to the law.

So it was that, according to the law, the miller Ersa made full recompense to the Ri Miliucc MacBuain for the death of a valuable slave. No judges had to be summoned to decide the case. No warrants had to be served. Though the slave Dubh had taken his own life by hanging, his death was a direct result of the drunken and unjudicious actions of the miller's sons, a pair of lecherous wastrels who had already fled the scene. Suicide was not uncommon among shepherds. Still, Ersa acknowledged that the fault was his own. He verbally expressed his regrets and personally made the long trip to the slave market on the inland tip of Lough Larne to purchase a suitable replacement.

Summer bled away. Slowly. Day by day. Each hour filled me with the anguish of a growing discontent. As surely as autumn's frost had touched the highlands of Slemish, so winter chilled my soul. I had not realized how much I had come to care for Dubh. I no longer dreamt the wonderful dreams in which the Light of the Lord brought me peace and a sense of harmony with the world. I no longer prayed. I had not lost my faith in God, but I believed, with all of the vanity of youth, that He had betrayed me.

Leborchom prayed for Dubh's soul. Day and night. Night and day. He offered up a resounding litany, a constant plea. When he was not praying, he was berating me, demanding to know by what right I dared to sit in judgment upon the wisdom of the Lord.

"Did'ja not see His Power upon the mountain? How many miracles must He work for'ya before your faith in Him will be secured?"

Within me, a twisting of pain and remorse. "Power . . . over demons and apparitions . . . yes, I have seen that.

But if He is a God of mercy, why can He not grant it? Dubh was a good man. There was no need for his death."

Leborchom's head moved slowly with dissent. "Dubh is dead because of the sin of pride . . . his pride and the pride of those who enslaved him. He is dead because the old gods still reign in Eire. He is dead because the religion of the Gael seeks justice but has no understanding of mercy, humility, or forgiveness. Someday the word of God shall come to this island. When that day comes, there shall be no kings or slaves in Eire. There shall only be brothers and sisters in Christ. There shall be peace then. Only then. We must pray for the advent of that day, Padraic. You and I and all of the Christians who now worship in fear and submission to the power of the Ris."

I did not pray. I could not pray. I remembered Dubh. I missed him. I mourned his death.

7

THE harvest was gathered. Within the forests, summer green had long since yielded to the amber and gold of autumn. The moon of the hunter rose high into the November sky. Orion reigned over the nights, his jeweled belt marking the apex of the heavens. The first rains of winter danced on the surface of ponds and streams. The days grew short. Snow came. Then it was spring again.

I was eighteen. I was no longer the lanky, sinewy youth who had kicked open the door of his fate on that day, two long years before, when the raiders from Eire had come to the Briton shore. I had changed. Though I had gained little in height, my physique had broadened and hardened. The smooth oval of my face had lengthened, defining the angularity of my features, sharpening the look of my eyes and drawing emphasis to the stern set of my lips. My hair, still cropped short as my lack of status demanded, was bleached by the elements to the color of dried corn. Along my forearms, calves, and chest there was a thin sea of curling, yellow-white hair. Once each week, when Leborchom sat down to lather and shave his beard, I joined him.

It was a fair spring day, cool yet filled with the promise

of summer. I saw the figure of a man, red-headed and stocky, coming up the hillside toward me. I stood up and waited until he was close enough to identify. He kept his eyes upon me as he approached. He held out his hand to me. "Padraic . . ."

Though he had gained considerable weight, he had not changed. I spoke his name: "Rodui."

He nodded his head. His Adam's apple slid up and down the length of his broad neck. He appraised me, taking in the one-toned garments which were mine: The sturdy leather shoes tied by thongs across my instep, my tattered, undyed leine, the patched lummon, the rough-textured trews which protected my legs against the impetuosity of the Gaelic wind. "Ya've grown to your manhood, Padraic."

I made no comment. I had not seen him since we had cut Dubh from the tree and had brought his body back to the village. His presence brought all of the old painful memories back. I asked coolly: "What is your business here?"

"Darerca has come to the time of her travail. The child is slow to be born. She has been three days at her labor. She's asked me to fetch'ya to her."

"Why?"

"She's sore afraid for her life, Padraic."

"Then call a leech to tend her."

"She's beyond the help of man or woman now. She's asked for'ya to bring her comfort. Leborchom has given'ya the leave to come with me."

My mouth was filled with the saffron taste of bitterness. "Were it not for Darerca, Dubh would still be alive. I cannot find it within myself to offer her consolation."

"She carries Dubh's child."

"Surely there is no way to prove that."

His eyes narrowed. I stepped back, expecting him to strike me. He stood perfectly still, trembling as the storm of his rage swept through him. Then, fighting for control, he said: "It's the women who suffer most within the bonds of slavery. Their humiliation is the greatest. We've been born into bondage—Darerca, Fordui, and I. We know no other life. You and Dubh, born free, could never understand us. Yet it is a sad thing, because born free, or born slave, it's Fate which has chosen us . . . to live as we must live, to bear what we must bear. And you, Padraic, have'ya grown into such a bitter and unsympathetic man, that'ya cannot even suffer to bring comfort to the dying?"

We walked down from the hills together. We did not speak. He left me to ponder my thoughts.

The miller's house was dark. If Ersa was within it, I did not see him. People whom I did not know stood up, whispered, then moved past me. They spoke to Rodui. They spoke to me. I do not remember what they said. I had a vague impression of aromas heavy with the oils of rendered herbs, humid with the dank scent of damp linens. It was a moment before my eyes grew accustomed to the darkness. Then I saw Darerca lying upon one of the sleeping couches. Her body was swollen with life. Her face was turned toward me. Her eyes were unnaturally bright.

She exhaled a swoon of gladness to see me. "Ahhh, Padraic, sure and I knew you'd come."

"I can do nothing for you, Darerca."

"Oh, but'ya can, Padraic, ya can. The healing stones have been placed at my feet. I've been bathed and cupped and probed a thousand times, yet all has been for naught, and now they must cut the child from me. I'll not be afraid, after ya've prayed with me."

"It is Leborchom you want."

"No, dear friend, 'tis you alone can give me courage."

As I looked down at her, I saw not her face but Dubh's. I saw him clearly, alive and vibrant, his blue beacon eyes laughing out at me. Then, cruelly, as always happened, memory brought me the sight of him as he had been in death. I closed my eyes against the unbidden specter, and against the girl, for she had been the cause of it.

She reached out and closed her fingers about my wrist. "Ever since that night on the mountain, when'ya told the story of Lord Jesus, when your God spoke through you, I've believed in Him . . . and in you . . ."

"God did not speak through me." The denial was tremulous.

"Oh, but He did, Padraic. Surely we all heard Him. Leborchum has sworn to us that'ya are a holy youth."

Somewhere within me, something turned and twisted and stung, like a viper injecting the venom of confusion into me. "What does the old man know?"

"He knows what he has seen." Her hands tightened

about my wrists. "I am weary of angry, vengeful gods, Padraic. I would be a follower of Lord Jesus. I would be baptized in His name. If I am to die, so be it then, but let me die as a Christian." Her fingers suddenly curled violently into my wrists. She gasped. Her eyes distended with agony. A vein throbbed hideously at her temple. "Pray with me, Padraic," she pleaded.

I could not help but pity her as she clung to me, screaming, while the contraction hardened her distended belly. I thought, with an agony of spirit as strong as the physical agony which was rendering Darerca weaker and weaker with each new contraction, that the God whom she sought must also be weak, subservient to a greater Power: to the god which had tried to take control of my tongue in the wood of Briton, to the god who ruled the lives of men and made of the earth a crucible of anguish and death. Oh, yes, I had felt the other Power: the God of my fathers, the Spirit which had allowed me to over-throw the runic stone in the mountain glen. But what was one stone? What a pitiful defiance that seemed now—a meaningless repudiation. I had kindled the flame, the statement of Christian faith, and still the gods of the Otherworld mocked me. I was still a slave. Dubh was dead. Darerca was dying. The God of my fathers was powerless to help me.

Darerca's hands relaxed. She exhaled a long sigh, which was a moan of gratitude for the momentary respite from pain.

"I cannot baptize you, Darerca," I said.

"Surely'ya can. You are yourself baptized, the son of holy men. The power to christen is in the hands of every Christian. You've told me that yourself when'ya spoke of the faith of your people."

"Their faith is not mine."

Her face contorted with sudden anger. "Why? Because the Lord does not rule the world as'ya would have it ruled?"

My temper flared. "Because He is merely another Power . . . another Force which manipulates and makes a mockery of the lives of men. There are no gentle gods, Darerca."

Her expression softened. She still held my hands within her own. Firmly, decisively, she released my left hand and lay my right palm down across her belly. I tried to draw away, but she held me tightly, fiercely. Another wave of pain was beginning. I could see it tightening her features. I could feel it beneath my palm. It was a hardening of her flesh, a surging. It moved mercilessly. The entire surface of her abdomen became taut and inflexible. Then I felt something stir beneath the hardened wall of muscle. Something bulged and strained upward against my palm. The child! Alive within her womb, fighting to be born. I felt the unmistakable thrust of a tiny heel. I jerked my hand away and stepped back, awed and amazed.

Even through her pain, Darerca laughed. "Ahh, Padraic, can it be that'ya do not see the glory of it? Surely, the world is bitter with the failure and cruelty of men, not of God."

"He has made us what we are."

"No, Padraic, we have chosen that."

Impatience made me frown.

She shook her head. "I'm but an ignorant woman, Padraic, but did'ja not feel my baby move? From the moment of the quickening, I have known that God was with me. For out of me . . . who has never had a life of my own . . . a new life made from the love which Dubh gave ta me. It *is* Dubh's child, Padraic. The time of its coming tells me that it was conceived at the beginning of that last sweet summer when I knew no other man. God has given me this gift . . . this love . . . this mercy . . ."

"And by the laws of Eire, Ersa can take it away from you."

"Has Fordui not told'ya? Ersa has taken me ta wife. Out of guilt or love or pity, I do not know. But he's made a free woman of me, Padraic. When Dubh's child is born, the child will be free as well. Sure and there's proof of God's miraculous grace!"

The words failed to touch me. I looked at her face and saw the pallor of it, and the sunken darkness around her eyes. I thought: You shall die, and your child, Dubh's child, shall die with you.

Someone had come to stand behind me. A hand was laid on my shoulder. "You must go now. She's been too long at her labor. The child must be taken now, while it still lives."

Darerca's head jerked back on her pillow as another

contraction seized her. "Baptize me, Padraic, and my child!" she cried aloud, gripping my hand.

I turned to see the grim face of the leech. "The work must be done now," he said, "if the child is to survive."

I tried to back away from the couch. Darerca let out a sob of protest. Her nails dug into the flesh of my palm. I did not have to look at it to know that she had drawn blood. I told her half-heartedly that I must go, that I would pray for her as best I could. Others had come into the room. I saw the leech's assistant, the tray of blades, the leather restraints, the bandages, the basins which would receive the blood and in which, if it survived, the infant would be bathed. Someone pried Darerca's fingers free of my hand. I was pushed away.

Darerca strained and struggled. Her eyes were wild. "Padraic . . . !" Her voice was shrill, like the terrified cry of a dove caught in a net, sensing its fate, screaming against it. "Padraic . . ."

The dove. It was as though a hand had slapped me. The room was suddenly spinning. My mind was awhirl with memory. The cawing of crows. The swooping of ravens. The cry of a dove.

"The dove . . ." How could it be that I had paid no heed to it before? I had seen only the dark wings of ravens, swooping, cawing; and yet the dove had also called to me, cried out to me.

Padraic . . . Pa-trec . . .

Was it Vision? Was it possession? I only know that in that moment I was somehow changed, transported beyond and within myself. It was as though I walked within that wondrous crystal of my dreams, with the light drawing me onward and the voices surging and whispering around me. The dove flew ahead of me. I followed it. Behind me lay the Darkness and the screaming, angry cawings of crows and specters, and memories of shadows, and a misted netherworld which I had come close to claiming as my own. What happened next, I do not fully remember. Others told me later.

With a strength which was not mine, I shoved my way back to Darerca's side. I shouted for water to be brought to me. Aamzed by my sudden resolution, they did as I bade them do. I leaned across Darerca. Tenderly, I whispered for her to be still. She stared at me wordlessly as I took her face within my hands. Something passed between us. A Force. A visible Power, the others told me later. But I think that it was more . . . I think that it was the greatest Power, the greatest Force upon this earth. It was the Power of God's love and of God's mercy.

I wet my right hand in the water which had been brought to me. Slowly I lifted it and traced the sign of the cross upon Darerca's forehead, staining her flesh with water and the blood which flowed freely from the wound in my palm. I blessed her then, and though I did not remember the words or the ritual of holy baptism, they were mine. They poured forth from me as naturally as the waters of a river seek out the sea, and when at last I was still, bent over her in prayer, the miracle occurred.

A great and violent contraction took control of her. To the amazement of all within the room, the leech cried out: "The child comes!"

The babe was born as easily as dawn. A fine, fat babe with skin spangled with freckles, as many as there are stars on a summer night, and on his matted, bloodied little head, thick black curls like those of a young shepherd who had once walked with me upon the slopes of Slemish.

"Dubh's son . . ." Darerca sighed wearily.

I nodded my head and smiled upon the child. "Aye . . . Dubh's son . . ."

I was out upon the hills for yet another year. In a single day I said a hundred prayers, and almost as many in the dark of a single night. I would rise before daylight, through snow, through frost, through rain, and I felt no harm. The Spirit of God was with me.

Then, with the dawning of yet another spring, I took Shadow in pursuit of a wandering ewe. We followed her across the hills into the shade of a narrow, brambley wood. It was there that Destiny caught me once again. Treed me. Terrified me. And sent me running and clambering for my life.

BOOK III

THE RING FORTRESS

But if indeed it had been given to me as it was given to others, then I would not be silent because of my desire of thanksgiving . . .

Saint Patrick—from his Confession

8

THE sound of the hounds did not frighten me at first. If I had ever seen such dogs before, it would have been as a child when I had been taken to view the circus in the amphitheater of the great fortress of Isca Silurum. So long ago. I did not remember.

When they broke out of the shrubbery, five of them running in poor pack form, I thought that I had finally succumbed to shepherd's madness. They seemed to be nearly as tall as mules. They were shaggy and long-limbed, and I was certain that I saw blood in their eyes.

Up the nearest tree I went. The huge hounds leaped and bayed beneath me. I saw their lolling tongues and their great sharp teeth even as the limb to which I clung cracked beneath me. With a shout of complete horror, I rode the torn limb down to the ground. My scream, accompanying the loud crack of the branch, put the dogs off. They went scattering, yowling, yipping, yap-yapping.

Their retreat was only temporary. They came wheeling back, stopping short of the maze of fallen branches, making noises of confusion as I, a solitary animate object, emerged upward out of the leaves and twigs. I shouted "Back!" at them. I waved my arms and stamped my feet at them. I even howled at them. They cocked their ears. They began to whistle and whine to one another. They could have eaten me then and there for their breakfast, yet they stood at bay.

For the moment. Then they came for me. Not at a run. Not with blood lust in their eyes. Something in my howling must have appealed to them. They approached with heads down, ears back, tails wagging with the tentative movement which dogs make when they wish to extend their friendship but are not certain that it will be accepted. They surrounded me, sniffing, snorting, lifting forepaws. One of the rubbed against me and I collapsed beneath her weight. She lay over onto my lap, legs extended upward, throat exposed to me in a posture of total submission. Amazed, I reached out and gingerly scratched her grizzled chest. The others pressed closer, sending out pounds and pounds of happy tongues to sign their friendship all over me.

"By the gods, it is not possible!" A voice like that of an avenging angel.

Through the dogs, I looked up to see the man who was about to alter the course of my life. There, wallowing amidst the hounds, embracing them with rapturous gratitude for the fact that they had not eaten me, I stared dazedly at the vast, hulking, masked form of Bruthne, onetime warrior, master of the Ri Miliucc MacBuain's wolfhounds.

"Rise up, young man!" he demanded.

I staggered to my feet against the weight of the dogs. Leborchom, altered to my plight by Shadow, was running toward me. When he saw me amidst the dogs, with the huge houndsman glowering at me, he cried aloud.

"Call back your coursers! The youth was only tracking a wayward sheep. Have'ya no mercy?"

"Mercy?" Bruthne's stentorian voice sounded as though it bubbled out of a deep and cavernous well. "It will be a mercy to me if he will tell me how he has elicited such adoration from the worst, most vicious lot of pups it has ever been my misfortune to train!"

"Pups?" I shouted out a declaration of the impossible.

"Six months of trouble," affirmed the houndsman.

"What is your name, youth? And how come you to such a way with the wolf dogs?"

"I am called Padraic, I am a shepherd. I do not know why your dogs have taken a fancy to me."

"Shepherd, you say? By the memory of the great god of houndsmen, Cuchulainn, you'll be a shepherd no longer!"

And so it was that I became a houndsman and went to live within the ring fortress of the Ri Miliucc MacBuain. I was given a pallet within the kennel. Three months passed. With Bruthne to teach me, I quickly learned the ways of the wolf dogs and of the smaller scenting hounds. The Ri and his court were away from the tuath. They had gone to attend the great fair of Lugnasad, leaving a full three months early so that the Ri might visit with the lords and chiefs of the surrounding tuaths and thus fulfill his multivarious royal social and legal obligations to them.

All was peaceful. I had been given new clothes, still all of one tone but of a considerably better weave even though the trews still itched against the soft flesh of my inner thighs and the leine fit to tightly across my shoulders. I had adjusted happily to the clothes and to my new environs and routine. Bruthne was proving to be an amiable, if somewhat tacit master. He had explained to me that my job would be to gentle and bring to heel the five "pups" which had befriended me upon the mountain. "Teach them to run in good pack form, to sight and take down a cold unwounded stag, and mayhap the Ri may be so grateful that he might even decide to grant you freedom as your reward. These are no ordinary hounds, young man. No, by Cuchulainn, they are not."

The thought of freedom was intoxicating. Each day I made a special effort to rise a full two hours before dawn so that I might offer up prayers of hope and thanksgiving before I set to my chores.

Bruthne observed me stoically. "To which god do'ya pray, Padraic?"

"To the God who came to me upon the Mountain of Mists. To the God of my fathers who has ruled all worlds since the beginning of Time. He is the Power and the Light. Beyond Him, there are only the forces of Darkness and Evil. I know. He has allowed me to be touched by them."

"Haven't we all." Irony weighted his words. He had been a king's champion once. Around his neck he wore the golden collar which had been awarded to him, years before, when he had proved himself to be an exemplary battle hero. He was aging now, yet he was still a massive man, indisputably virile despite the fact that he wore a brimless woolen cap to cover the shame of his baldness. His ample gray beard was square-cut. His mustache was worn tightly braided with the ends wrapped in slim strands of leather. He had been handsome once, and more than a bit of a rake with the ladies, but he kept himself as much as he could these days, for he had been hideously disfigured in his last battle. His nose had been lopped off. All that remained of it had been resewn into a grotesque patchwork of scar tissue. His nostrils were two uneven holes surrounded by thick, shining, purplish flesh. They no longer served him. He breathed through his mouth and, when he was forced to mingle with others, wore a hide mask to cover the upper portion of his face. He had allowed me to view his uncovered face only once, to put to rest the questions in my eyes. Now he stared at me through his mask and asked with more than a small shading of skepticism: "And does this god of yours answer prayers quickly then?"

"If it is His will."

He made a grunt of dissatisfaction. "Whims and fancy, that's what a man must contend with when he asks favors of the gods."

"There is but one true God."

He smiled and shrugged. "Well, then, Padraic, best ask him to keep the Ri well-satisfied at the fair until these wretched pups of his are made into decent coursers. I'd not dare to predict the extent of his ire if they are not ready to run out in pack when he returns."

All was quiet within the kennel. The great dogs and the little hounds had been bedded for the night. The stalls had been cleaned. The doors which opened out onto the enclosed green had been shut tight against the cool night air. I walked down the central corridor, checking each stall, listening to the sound of birds roosting in the rafters above, thinking to myself that there were many men and women dwelling in Eire who did not live as well as did the hounds of the Ri Miliucc MacBuain. They were his fame and fortune. Dealers and hunters came from all over the civilized world to purchase dogs from him

"Padraic . . . ?" The child Egan's voice was as the pipe of a flute when it is blown off key. He was new to the kennel, there only one week. A pale boy of seven, he had been brought in to sleep with a litter of pups which Bruthne was weaning. Egan would be raised with the pups. He would be taught how to care for them and to command them. The dogs had already been promised to an Egyptian fancier of hounds. In two years, when they were grown and trained, they would be shipped to his kennel. Egan would accompany them as their caretaker, making certain that they were kept clean and well-fed during the long journey. I shivered to think of such a small boy making such a perilous trip alone. What would happen to him once he reached Egypt? Would he be retained as a houndsman within the Egyptian kennels, or would he be cast adrift into the tides of the greater North African destiny? There was no way for me to know. I prayed for him daily.

"What is it, Egan? Why are you not asleep with your pups?" I paused and looked into his stall. He was backed up against the far wall, as white-faced as a spirit. The puppies slept all together in a warm mound on a clean, straw-covered pallet which was built up off of the ground so that no draft of cold air could chill them. Egan pointed to the opposite wall where a small lizard peeked out from between two sagging boards.

"A monster . . ." he whimpered. "Sure 'tis an offspring of the terrible sea fish which lives in the lake near Emain Macha."

" 'Tis only a wee rush lizard, boy."

He stared at the creature. "No. 'Tis a magic serpent which shall grow in the night and eat me."

"I have been told that there are no serpents in all of Eire . . . magic or otherwise."

"Oh, but Padraic, there are monsters which live in the deep lakes. 'Tis said they have hairy manes and appetites for fair maidens."

"Are you a maiden?"

"N-no."

"And have you ever seen such a creature?"

"Aye," said the child, pointing to where the lizard had been. "Just then, but now it has vanished."

"No doubt in fear of you."

He stared up at me with mournful eyes. "I do not think that anything or anybody shall ever be afraid of me, Padraic."

I went to him to offer comfort. I settled him onto his pallet amidst the mound of pups. I handed him his blanket and watched while he pulled it up to his chin. "I think, Egan, that if there are indeed great monsters which haunt the lakes of Eire, perhaps the true place of their dwelling is here . . ." I touched my temples with my right index finger.

"Figments . . . ?" The question quivered with doubt.

"A wee lizard is but a wee lizard, Egan, unless we allow the forces of Darkness to make a specter of it for us. The power of Evil cannot harm us . . . not unless we consent to it, unless we invite it up out of the Otherworld. Surely, boy, is there not enough cruelty and pain alive within the hearts of men? Must we conjure monsters to add to the burden? I'll tell you this, Egan, that since I've made my peace with God, I've heard no word from sheevras or specters . . . not even a whisper." I sat down and ruffled his hair. "Do you believe me, boy?"

He drew close against me. His lips were quivering. "The people in the village say that you've come face to face with the spirits of the shees. Is it true, Padraic?"

"Aye."

"Did you call them up out of the Otherworld?"

"I think perhaps I did . . . through my lack of faith . . . through . . ." His question demanded an answer which I had not yet found.

"Were you not afraid, Padraic?"

I put my arm around him, relieved by the opportunity to pursue another tack. "Afraid . . . aye . . . of the unknown . . . of the future . . . two terrible dragons indeed. But all men must face them. And I'll tell you, boy, that often I find myself wondering: Why has God brought me here? For what purpose has He shown me His Power and His anger and the grace of His infinite love? Yet, though I still do not understand, I am content. Since I have put my life into His hands, He has rewarded me. When the hounds are trained, God will see me safely home again . . . I will be a free man . . . my prayers shall at last have been answered. Bruthne has practically promised it."

He sighed, openly confused. "I do not know very much about the gods."

"There is only one true God, boy. Pray to Him and He shall make you strong so that you shall grow to your manhood unafraid."

He pondered over this as he snuggled under his blanket and lay his head upon my lap. "Tell me one of your stories, Padraic.

I leaned back against the wall. Every night, since Egan had first come, I had sought him out when my work was done. He was like a pup himself, being weaned even as the pups within his charge were being weaned. Only days before, he had been at his mother's side. Now he was alone, sold off from home and kindred. I could not help but compare his fate with my own. As Dubh had gone out of his way to befriend me, so also did I go out of my way to comfort Egan. I stood by him against the barbed tongue of Draigenn, Bruthne's cocky sixteen-year-old assistant houndsman. I saw to it that he received his fair share of meals. I saw to it that he dressed himself properly against the morning chill. I saw to it that, at night, when he shivered with fear and loneliness within his stall, with none but the pups to keep him company, that I was always ready to sit by his side, telling him tales of encouragement from the Bible until he fell asleep.

Was it my conscious desire to convert him to the faith of my fathers? No. I had not yet imagined myself in the role of the proselytizer. I had found the peace of Christ. God had touched my life and I had been forced to acknowledge Him. I had come to realize that it had been no careless fluke of Fate which had wrenched me so cruelly out of Briton. I had been placed into a pagan land so that I might suffer at the hands of those who knew not His Word. I had been shown the Darkness so that I might readily perceive the value of His Light. To what end? I was not certain. I knew only that I must share the grace of His love and His promise to others. I could not be silent.

Whenever the opportunity arose, I spoke of God and of the risen Christ to anyone who would listen. To Bruthne, to Egan, to Draigenn, to those who made deliveries at the kennel, to those whom we met when working the dogs within the woods, and to the villagers when I was sent out on various errands within the community.

Though I had not wished it, I had begun to earn quite a reputation for myself. The people of the Ri Miliucc MacBuain called me Seanachie. They liked my tales. They fancied the way I told them, even though they laughed at my poor usage of their complicated language and found much reason to make fun of the concept of a god of love. Once, when I had gone out to pick up the new collars which Bruthne had ordered for the hounds (fine, thick leather bands studded with metal spikes to ward away the evil spirits which are said to bring madness to dogs), the leather worker had smirked and smiled all at once, commenting:

"Why do'ya need these? From what I've heard tell of'ya, just a touch of your hand and the power of healing is yours." He had lowered his brow and warned me then: "Take heed, Padraic. It's not wise of'ya to spread your stories of the Christian god to just anyone who happens to come along the roads. There are those in Eire who do not think well of Christians. Aye, your Jesus has been called rabble-rouser . . . and worse. Do'ya not know that there are places where the worship of Christ has been forbidden by the druids? Mark me, you must learn to hold your tongue. Keep your faith to yourself if'ya value your life."

Egan had fallen asleep. As I tucked his blanket about him, I looked up to see Draigenn's belligerent green eyes upon me. His round, pugnacious face was surrounded by lank, unevenly trimmed brown hair. He cast me a withering glance. Draigenn loathed me. Though I had not wished it, I had usurped his role in the kennel.

"Bruthne wants to see'ya." As usual, his voice was curdled by his hatred of me.

Bruthne's quarters were at the far end of the kennel. As master houndsman, he had a room to himself. It was a large room, with an oven to warm it, for it was also the room in which the dog breads were baked.

He bade me close the door and take a place on one of the two benches which were his only pieces of furniture. He was stitching a tether. He did not look up at me.

"Sit down, Padraic." He adjusted his mask. "I've received news that the Ri Miliucc shall return within the week."

"So soon?"

"Aye, sooner than I expected. The hounds which were given to him as a gift by the Red Ri Sencha must be ready when he returns. I have promised him that."

"The five pups in my care?" My brows stood up with disbelief. They were ten months old and had yet to run successfully in a pack. "They are only now beginning to lean proper form," I protested.

Bruthne kept his eyes to his work. "The Ri has been long away from the rath, Padraic. 'Twas at the fair that he met Sencha. There was some trouble there . . . some gossip . . . but I'll not discuss that. Whatever the cause, the dogs came up in the dispute. The Red Ri is anxious to see his 'gift' perform on a hunt."

I did not understand and told him so. "Why can this Red Ri not put off his visit? You have told me yourself that many a good hound has been ruined by too eager a trainer."

Bruthne set his work upon his knees. "The pups were deliberately ruined before they were ever sent to us, Padriac. They were not a 'gift.' They were a challenge, a gauntlet thrown. There's been a muted antagonism between the Ri Sencha and the Ri Miliucc for several years. Once they were as brothers. But no more. The cause of the rivalry? I've my suspicions, but the Ri'd have my tongue if I voiced them. In any event, one wonders what it must come to in the end. Whatever you do, and however you do it, the dogs must be ready by the time the Ri Miliucc returns. We will work on nothing else until that day."

"Within the week? It is not possible."

"We must *make* it possible."

"But surely the Ri would understand if—"

"The Ri understands nothing these days! Once I knew the man. As the gods of Eire are witness, I've loved and served him since he was a boy and I was airé echta, king's champion, to his father. But these days, though I love the man and would give my life for him, I do not know what is in his heart. Sometimes I think that even his own shadow must rise up in despair of him." He exhaled a sigh of frustration, picked up the tether and began to stitch again with nervous deliberation. "The dogs *must* be ready, Padraic. For your sake and mine, the dogs *must* be ready."

9

THEY came with pennants flying and royal colors blazing. They came in chariots of such beauty that I stood back in amazement. They came with horns sounding fanfare and horses of the armed king's guard caparisoned in gold and scarlet, silver and emerald, with harness mounts jeweled and enameled.

The parade of the returning nobles of the Ri's court had no doubt been assembled for the benefit of the people of the tuath. They could not possibly have ridden in such haughty splendor all of the way from the great fair of Lugnasad.

Slave and freeman, common worker, and high-born aristocrat, all who had not been to the fair, gathered to welcome home the Ri and the Rigan and to feast their eyes on the wealth and power which was being displayed for them in the parade.

The royal couple rode alone in the king's canopied chariot. The Ri himself held the reins. His special guard, headed by a giant man named MacCairthinn, rode close on each side of the chariot, grim and resolute with swords and axes held at ready. Just to the right of the chariot, and slightly ahead of it, the Ri's champion rode a short-bodied brown horse as he glowered menacingly at all who looked upon the king.

They entered the ring fortress through the four encircling ramparts, with the common people cheering and the posted guardsmen stepping aside to grant them passage. At last they paused before the great house where four royal guardsmen, with shields and ivory-hilted swords held upright, bowed low before them. The enormous door of the house was ceremoniously opened. The house steward, resplendent in a fleecy mantle, swept out of the house in a most dignified manner. Bearing his staff of office, he paused beside the cairthe, the white standing stone which honored the gods of Eire. It had been placed reverently on its foundation before the house had been constructed. Lifting his staff, the steward bid the Ri and the Rigan a mighty and royal welcome. There was a resounding echo of his words from the assembled company.

I could not see the Rigan. She sat well back within the shadow of the canopy, which was of purple and gold, completely sewn and patterned with feathers. I saw only the bend of a slim knee beneath the folds of a shimmering purple cloak all edged with miniver.

The Ri rose and swung himself out of the chariot. He handed the reins to the elaborately helmeted soldier who was his chief charioteer. As the man removed his helmet and bowed before his king, I looked upon the Ri and felt an unpleasant tightening of my stomach muscles.

Though he had grown a beard, he had not changed. He was still a visage of darkness. He looked out upon the assemblage with his face impassive, his eyes as dark and keen as a striking blade. He was magnificent. I could not deny that. His hair was even more elaborately coifed than it had been on that day when Dubh and I had crossed his path upon the herdsman's track. Shining balls of red glass set into golden ornaments sparkled like fierce tiny eyes against the shining blackness of his coiled and braided tresses. At his shoulder, holding fast the folds of his black cloak, was the largest, most elegantly wrought brooch I had ever seen. It was of gold, with bits of dark carnelian gleaming out of it like pieces of polished, congealed blood.

He threw back his cloak with an impatient gesture. I saw the wine-colored fabric of his leine, embroidered with black silken thread at the hemline. His legs were clad in long, tight-fitting trews which were the same color as the leine. Black embroidery-work defined the powerful musculature of his thighs and calves. His boots and gloves were of the finest black leather, trimmed with the sleek fur of black sea lions. He wore a ring on each of his fingers and bracelets coiled up his arms like golden serpents.

As he relinquished the reins to the charioteer, he walked around the chariot and stood, extending his arms up to his Rigan.

The Rigan. The thoughtful young bride who had, long ago, seen an injured youth upon the slave block and had purchased him out of pity so that he might be nursed back to health by her own servants. The compassionate queen who had seen a light upon the hills and had sent a rider out to poor shepherds so that they might have good food to warm them against the storm.

Even before she stepped from the chariot, I knew that

I loved her. Slowly, in the manner of a frail child, she
put out her hand so that the Ri might steady her. She
half rose to her feet, leaning forward. The hood of her
cloak fell back, revealing the wonder of her golden hair.
No. It was not golden. Gold is a brash and pretentious
color. Gold is conscious of its rank. The hair of the Rigan
Cairenn was the Gaelic ideal. It was the tone of pollen
drifting in a sunlit wind. It was as pale, shining, and fine
as an angel's hair must be. She wore it parted simply in
the middle of her small head, drawn up from the perfect
oval of her face and held in place by two tiny silver
combs. It fell across her back as a silken cape, without
braid or coil or jewels to hinder it. As she placed her
hand into the hand of her lord, she looked out and over
the faces of the assembled people of the tuath.

I saw then that she was as young and exquisite as the
maidens for which schoolboys pine in their dreams. I
caught my breath. Egan, sitting atop my shoulders with
his legs locked beneath my armpits, murmured in awe:
"Oh . . . never was there so fair a queen . . ."

Bruthne, standing masked beside us, cast the boy a
jaundiced scowl. "And she still flaunts the virgin's coif."

His words meant nothing to me. I had eyes and heart
only for the Rigan Cairenn. I was infatuated beyond re-
prieve.

She seemed to hesitate a moment before she committed
herself to the man who was her husband. He spoke to her
then. Softly. In a low tone which she alone could hear.
Her lips contracted. The color seeped from her face. She
gave a tremulous smile to the crowd. They shouted her
name. They waved and declared their delight in her yet
there was an unmistakable hesitancy to the tone of their
adulation, as though somehow she had disappointed them.

She went into Miliucc's waiting arms then, as taut as a
reed before it snaps in a gale. His hands closed about her
waist. He lifted her out and away from the chariot. He
put her gently upon her feet. He embraced her. The
crowd roared approval.

As his arms went about her, I saw not a man at all,
but a dark cloud caressing a rainbow, robbing it of color
and brilliance. When he released her, I shivered with
relief. May God forgive me, but in that moment jealousy
overwhelmed me. I hated the Ri with an intensity which
no true Christian should ever know.

He stood back from her as a group of her ladies-in-waiting descended out of an enormous covered four-wheeled chariot. They surrounded the Rigan, doting upon her. A tall young woman in a green cloak adjusted the queen's hood back up about her buttery hair. The Ri stood aside. Without a word to him, the Rigan walked forward into the great house. Her ladies-in-waiting followed. The woman in the green cloak was the last to enter. As she walked past the Ri, he looked down at her. Briefly, tentatively, she lifted her eyes to the man who was her king. Their eyes met. Held. Then she lowered her face and hurried by him into the great house. I followed her with my eyes. There had been something distractingly familiar about her.

The Ri stood very still for a moment, lost in thought, melancholy. The steward came forward. There were words between the two. The Ri put up his hands. He addressed us all. A formal greeting. He stayed only a moment longer, just long enough to graciously accept the adulation of his people. Then he, too, walked into the great house. The steward went after him. The guardsmen closed the door. The parade began to disassemble noisily.

"Come along," said Bruthne, heading back to the kennel.

I fell into stride beside him. "When do you think he will wish to see the dogs?"

The lower portion of his face was taut and downturned. "What matter? They are not ready."

It has been said that a true leader of men never forgets a face. So it is that they influence their fellows to act in their behalf. Not through force. But by appealing to the vanity of their followers.

Among the Gael there is a strong belief that a true and just king will always know his people. He will know their names, even though he may have met them only once. He will know their histories and be sensitive to their needs and desires. It is believed that when such a king rules, all will be well with the land. There will be peace. The crops will grow tall. The harvest will be bountiful. Earth and sky shall function for the benefit of king and country. But when a king is not just and true, though his people will follow him as the law demands, the very order of the elements will betray him. He shall forget the names of his warriors so that they will grow ashamed of themselves for not being worthy to stand out in the memory of their Ri. Such men will lose their virility. In battle they will show no self-confidence. Standing guard they will not be steadfast. The strength of the tuath will ebb away. The members of the king's court will grow restless. Crops will fail in the fields. The harvest will rot in the granaries during months of perpetual rain. The people will go hungry. In time, the king will die. The gods will take him. A villain will slay him. Or, despondent, he will take his own life.

As I stacked freshly baked dog breads onto their appointed shelves, the sun rose high into the afternoon sky. Throughout the tuath, summer bathed the earth with sweet sunshine. Already the harvest was being gathered. A fat, fruitful harvest. The beehives were swollen with honey. From beyond the ramparts of the ring fort, I heard the distinct singing of a meadowlark. All signs bespoke the fact that in this portion of the land of Eire, a just and true king ruled.

I was so engrossed in my work that I did not hear them enter. When I heard his voice, I spun around, completely startled.

"Is this the lad, Bruthne? I know him. Yes, it was on the mountain with the sheep dog . . . I remember the day well."

I looked up to see the Ri Miliucc MacBuain standing beside Bruthne. The Ri had changed out of his royal finery. He wore a simple bleached linen leine with matching trews. He affected no jewelry, save one ring of dragon stone and gold. His hair was damp from recent washing. It was combed back from his face and caught at the nape of his neck by a cloth band. He stood with one powerful arm draped casually across Bruthne's shoulder. He was smiling at me. Warmly. Expansively.

"Do you not remember me, young man? I was breaking in a new chariot pony along a dismal track. You were with another lad. An older lad. I almost ran down your dog. By the gods of all Eire, Bruthne, you should have seen the dog. A mere shepherd's hound, but it fancied itself to be a lion." His brow came down. "And speaking of lions, old friend, have lions been made of the lilies which Sencha sent to me disguised as hounds?"

Bruthne shifted his weight uneasily. He cleared his

throat and indicated me with a snap of his head. "Padraic here has done wonders with them. But, my lord, Cuchulainn himself would find himself vexed by such hounds."

Miliucc withdrew his arm from Bruthne's shoulder. "There was never a dog born that you could not train. By the gods, Bruthne, when the Red Ri Sencha comes to this tuath, he shall see that I have made good in my vow to turn his curs into coursers."

Was it arrogance or simple stupidity which made me feel free to intrude into the conversation? The Ri's words angered me. His smile and unexpected congeniality had put me off guard. I gave voice to my thoughts, forgetting that the man to whom I addressed my words was not only my master, but sovereign lord of the tuath as well.

"It is Bruthne and I who are the houndsmen," I informed him pointedly. "If the dogs are made into successful coursers, it will be because of our skill, labor, and patience. You will have had nothing to do with it."

Bruthne caught his breath. His lips blanched. I met the Ri's startled gaze and saw something flash deep within his dark eyes. He was smiling again. Not the warm, easy smile which had softened his features only moments before. It was the smile he had worn when I had first seen him on the mountain. Once again he was the raptor observing the captive mouse.

"Tell me, then, Padraic," he said slowly, disemboweling me with his stare, "how long must I wait before my hounds are ready to be shown to the Ri Sencha?"

I had blundered into the quicksand of his ire. I sensed that I dare not retreat. I stood very straight. I tried not to flinch under his scrutiny. "Bruthne has taught me that a hound cannot be forced into feats of bravery. If the pups which were given to you by the Red Ri are to be made into decent coursers, they must be handled patiently. They have the instinct. When first I saw them, they would attack a man but would quiver in fright at the sound of doves nesting in the rafters of the kennel. Bruthne and I have gentled them. We have taught them to take small game, rabbits and the like. But lock them alone in a dark stall and they still howl in terror of their own fleas. When you are ready to ask them to sight after boar or wolf or stag, you will be asking them to risk their lives for you. In time, they may well have the heart for that—if it is not asked of them too soon, and if it is asked only out of love and trust and with gentle command. As things stand now, should you set them to a good and dangerous prey, they will cower and wilt like cropped cabbages in the noonday sun."

Miliucc leveled his gaze at me. "I need dogs with the heart of Bran in them. Can you give me such, Padraic?"

Bran, the magical hound of Gaelic legend. It was said of Bran that she could run down as many as three stags in a single day, killing each with a single thrust of her powerful jaws. Such a dog was not made. It was born. I looked at the Ri Miliucc and said honestly: "I cannot work miracles. I can only do that which is God's will and within His Providence."

The darkness within his eyes lightened. He seemed infinitely amused. "Which god?"

"The one God. The God who is over us all."

"The Christian god?"

"Aye. The God of all worlds since the beginning of Time."

"So it is true. You are a follower of the one who died on the cross. Have you not been informed, Padraic, that Christianity is a forbidden cult in many parts of Eire?"

"I have been informed."

"And yet you do not hesitate to speak of your god in my presence?"

"I am a Christian. I shall exalt the Lord my God everywhere I go."

"Even if I should forbid it?"

I did not hesitate. I kept my eyes upon his face and replied: "Even if you should forbid it."

Unexpectedly, he laughed. He reached out and gave Bruthne a resounding and friendly slap upon the back. "Do you hear that? The boy refuses to suck my breast! By the gods of all Eire, Bruthne, I admire your choice of apprentices. The boy is right. I have been too long away from the hounds. From this day on, they shall know me as their master." His smile was totally disarming. "And you, Padraic, you shall be ready at dawn tomorrow. I will see for myself how well you perform as a houndsman."

Bruthne's face, where it showed below the mask, was devoid of color. He was, quite literally, sagging with relief over the Ri's change of mood. "We shall be ready, my lord," he said.

"No, old friend. You may stay abed tomorrow. It is this young man who shall accompany me." He drew his lips into a contemplative pucker. "Perhaps he will bring his god along with us, eh? If the hounds are as difficult as you infer, we may well have need of a miracle or two before the day is done."

"God will be with us," I said, resenting his sarcasm. "Whether you wish His presence or not."

All signs of amusement vanished from his face. His dark eyes narrowed as he measured me. "That is good, Padraic. You will need your god, for tomorrow I shall teach you how a slave must behave before his king."

He struck me then, with the back of his hand, so swiftly that I did not see the blow until it had been rendered and I found myself sprawled upon the straw-covered floor with the world spinning around me.

10

THE Ri arrived at the kennel each morning at dawn. We took the dogs out, just he and I and two of his body-guards. He did not strike me again. I was careful not to give him cause. Still nurturing the hope of freedom being won through my success with the dogs, I behaved as the perfect, silent kennel hand. Meanwhile, it became obvious to me that the Ri was pacing me even as he paced the hounds.

"You have speed," he observed one morning as we trotted along beside the dogs on an open country track which ran across the hills.

I replied, judiciously I thought: "When I was a boy, it was said of me that I was quick as the silver which cannot be held in a man's palm."

One dark brow rose speculatively. "Prove it," he challenged evenly.

I was confident that I could easily outrun him. With as many as thirty winters upon him, I was certain that his bones must be brittle with age. His height would make him clumsy. His lean musculature bespoke a meager diet. I did not see that with age he would have experience, that his height would give him a longer stride than my own, and that his lean frame betrayed not a poor diet, but the harsh and disciplined regimen of a warrior king who kept himself always physically ready for battle.

We raced. He set me a heady course. As I began to tire, he goaded me on until, at last, I tripped over my own shadow and collapsed upon the ground, thoroughly humiliated. As I lay panting and sweating, with my flesh afire from overexertion, he laughed and stood over me like a lathered stallion.

"Well run, Padraic," he conceded. "But perhaps the quicksilver in your blood has been mixed with a bit of Briton lead?"

He offered me his hand. I disdained it.

Days passed. He gave me chance and chance again to best him. Try as I might, though I rose long before dawn so that I might condition myself for a victory over him, though I jogged in place and sprinted secretly on the kennel green, I could not outrun him. As the days merged into weeks, I found that my loathing of him was being tempered by a begrudging respect.

Nearly a full month had gone by before I was first summoned by the Rigan. The hand of Destiny touched me with her summons. If I felt its weight, all sense of premonition was overshadowed by the quick flowering of curiosity and anticipation.

I shall never forget my first sight of the interior of the great house. It was everything and more than Dubh had said it would be. It was enormous, with ceilings so high that I had to crane my head back to appreciate them. The scent of freshly laid rushes, spiced and crushed with sweet herbs and flowers, rose from the oft-swept earthen floor. As I was led up the stairs to the Rigan's chamber, I caught a glimpse of the banquet hall with its acres of tables.

This was no barbarian's mean abode with rooms dark, dreary, and dank with musty smells. Glass shone in the windows. A richly hued selection of tapestries adorned the walls. Each massive crossbeam and girder was painted and carved with amazing designs which incorporated curling vines, furling flowers, beasts of the wood and gods of the clan. I found myself pausing at every step, turning on my heels, gaping in amazement at the beauty which surrounded me. The messenger prodded me on, impatient with my gawking.

At last I was led up into the grianan, the queen's chamber. The messenger disappeared behind me and closed the door. Never in my life had I seen such a room. Its opulence overwhelmed me. It was round, bright and cheerful, with tinted glass allowing views out over hills and clouded sky. Lush cascades of blue and silver curtains hung by the windows. The posts which supported the roof had been meticulously carved with intricate designs. The ceiling was a canopy completely tufted with feathers of white and blue.

I would have taken more time to survey the intricacies of this usually forbidden female domain, but my attention was drawn by the woman who stood in the center of it on a rug of white pelts.

She was small and slender in a blue floor-length leine of iridescent fabric. A girdle of woven silver and little blue beads and pearls encircled her slim hips. Her hair fell loose, a shining waterfall which cascaded down her back to her knees. Although her cheeks and lips were rouged with ruam, her eyes were untouched by artifice of any kind. Her brows had not been plucked. Her lashes had not been stained black with berry juice. Her eyes stared at me out of her delicately boned face. They were as large as moons. The irises shone like polished blue gemstones. She seemed unreal, a woman of perfect beauty. And yet a child, with the firm round breasts and soft sleek flesh of a budding girl.

"So this is the houndsman who so intrigues and amuses the Ri . . . the Christian whom the people call Seanachie . . . the one named Padraic?" The voice of the Rigan Cairenn was soft and slow and measured. She smiled at me. The warmth of that smile seemed to flood upward into her eyes so that the blue of them softened into that special tone which forms as blue shadows upon snow on a sunlit day.

"I am Padraic." How thick my voice sounded. How unsure. Once again, the beauty of a woman sent my heart soaring. Not with lust. Not with desire. With reverence. With awe. With the searing passion of devotion.

"I have heard it said that your tongue is as clever and soothing as any of our Gaelic storytellers," said the Rigan. "Is it true what I have heard of you, Padraic?"

"Such has been said, my lady, though the stories which

I tell are not stories. They are truths. They are history. They are the teachings of the people of God."

Her delicate brows arched. "I am weary to my very heart of the tales which are told by the Ri's seanachies. I must find some new interest to cheer me, or else I fear I shall die of boredom. Will your tales cheer me?"

"It has been promised that God shall bring salvation to all those who seek His truth. I, who have borne witness to His Power, cannot doubt His Word."

"Salvation?" She looked down at herself, perplexed. "I am not yet eighteen." She turned and appraised herself critically in the long mirror of bronze which stood against the wall behind her. "Does my mirror lie? I see no need of salvage."

"My God speaks of the salvation of the soul, my lady. Surely, even He could not improve upon the loveliness which was made when He created you."

She turned to face me. "Your god created me?" She laughed. It was a light, pirouetting sound. "I was born here in Eire. How could your Roman god have made me?"

"My God is the maker of all the world. We . . . you and I . . . and His children."

She seemed aghast and amused by the notion. Her hands went up and folded across her breasts. "You and I? Brother and sister? A slave and a queen? Impossible! Preposterous!" She turned back to the mirror, leaning close to it as she began to brush her eyebrows with quick, upward movements of her fingertips. "Are your tales only of your god, then?"

"They are of His people."

"Of love and battle and conquest?"

"And of God's . . ."

She cut me off in midsentence. "Enough talk of gods. I do not like the gods. They both weary and offend me. But do tell me, Padraic, how fares the Ri with the hounds which were given to him by the Red Ri Sencha?"

"The hounds improve daily, my lady."

A frown pressed outward at her lips, then collapsed as she turned and dazzled me with her smile. "The people tell tales of you, Padraic. The strangest and most intriguing tales. It has been whispered that you possess the Power. Even within the rath, it is being said that only a magician could work magic such as you do with the dogs. Are you a magician, Padraic?"

"I have been brought to know the Power of God."

She did not like my reply. "Are you a magician, Padraic?"

"No," I said honestly. "I enjoy my work with the hounds. It is as simple as that. Patience and love have been known to work what some men would call magic, on beasts as well as men."

It was as though my words had chilled her. She shivered and crossed her arms over her bosom again. Beneath the bright red of the ruam, her lips went gray. She stared at me, measuring me from beneath a furrowed brow. Slowly, thoughtfully, she crossed the room to where a chess game had been set up on a table of inlaid woods. Toying with the king, she looked back at me.

"Does the Ri confide in you, Padraic?"

Before I could reply, she shook her head bitterly. "Of course he does not. Not to a slave, not to any man save the druid Néladóir." She drew in a breath. "Néladóir . . ." Her lips worked with obvious hatred. She put back her head then and exhaled loudly, as though she wished to clear her thoughts of all memory of the man. "Have I not seen you before, Padraic? Your face is somehow familiar to me."

As she walked back to the mirror and stood looking at her reflection, I explained to her that she had purchased me and had seen me nursed back to health by her own servants and physicians. "I owe my life to you, my lady, for surely the mercy of God was worked through you upon me."

The memory pleased her. She beamed at me out of the mirror. "Of course! I had completely forgotten! You have no idea how much you touched my heart. In truth, you reminded me of me. I was a hostage once, you know. Well-treated, of course, not like a slave, but a hostage most of my life." Her smile had faded. "Surely, sometimes I think that I am a hostage still. Oh, yes, you have grown to your manhood, Padraic, even as I have become a woman. But the child in both of us has died . . . and we are still captives."

She stared bleakly at her reflection, then reached out to touch her image tentatively with extended fingers. "Had I the Power . . . the Power which the druids claim to possess . . . I would fly away from this place; I would ride away on the night winds to a destiny of my own choosing." She pressed against the bronze until her fingers were flat against it, splayed out like bars of flesh across the mirrored image of her face. "Slave or hostage, houndsman or queen, we are both captives, Padraic . . . of a life which will soon enough see us to our graves."

She wheeled then, wrapping her arms about herself as she looked at me and smiled wanly, like a confused and desperate child. "Do you know no happy, careless tales with which to cheer your Rigan, Padraic?"

"Many tales, my lady, but none so fine as the truth which promises a life for us beyond the grave. It is the believe of Christians that if we hold to God's truths and Commandments, we shall never die."

"Nonsense! The Gael too believe in the Otherworld, but never has a man returned from it to assure us of its glories. It is nonsense."

"Christ, the Son of God, born of a virgin, risen from the dead in fulfillment of prophecy, has promised us that it is not nonsense."

"And how do you know that this Christ has not lied to you . . . have you met with him and sipped ale together?"

"He has walked among us in the Long Ago. The miracle of His resurrection was witnessed. The glory of His name and promise is proclaimed throughout the world."

"Really? And do you believe such a story?"

"The Power of God has touched me, my lady. Before my very eyes, the God of my fathers has worked miracles."

She laughed at me. "You are a delightful fool, Padraic."

As she crossed the room and came toward me, I stood the mute wonder of her beauty. She was like an angel of the Lord, shimmering in the sunlight which filtered through the glass of the windows.

"In truth, Padraic, you are young and honest and alive, and your presence alone brings me joy." She stopped before me. I could smell the delicate scent of roses upon her. "Will you serve me, Padraic? Will you come to me each evening when you have finished with the Ri's hounds? Will you be my personal seanachie and filidh? I would have you tell me your Christian tales of immortal people . . . providing that you make them happy tales."

I bowed my head and dropped to one knee. "It will

give me unending pleasure to share with you my joy in the Lord and to bring to you a knowledge of the history of His people."

She bade me rise then, and, as I did, I looked into her face so that she might see my earnest desire to please. It was then, for the first time, that I saw that her beauty was not without flaw. A tiny dot of red, rising like a clot of blood on the cooked albumen of an egg, marred the white of her right eye just above the tear duct. I closed my eyes, unexplainably disturbed to have found this small imperfection in her.

Each evening, after I had seen to the hounds and had eaten my supper, I cleaned myself, donned fresh garments and went to the Rigan Cairenn. I was in love. Not the warm, flowing, consuming ache of passion. The tide which stirred me touched my soul, not my body. When Draigenn made his venomous slurs, I cared not. When Bruthne cast a gloomy eye my way and reminded me that my first duty was my attendance to the Ri's hounds, I smiled benignly and agreed with only half of my heart. I was in a state of euphoria. I saw the face of the Rigan everywhere. I heard her voice. I was reminded of her fragrance. Each night, before I drifted to sleep upon my pallet, I prayed for her. I took her with me into my dreams. Not as wife or bride or mistress, as a shining goddess to be cherished and protected. She became for me a living, golden deity for whom I would have gladly given my life. May God forgive me for being blinded by her. May Christ forgive me for refusing to see her as she was. The days passed slowly. The nights sped away. I no longer yearned for freedom. I no longer thought of home or kindred. I lived only for the evenings in the grianan. I lived only to serve and bring pleasure to the Rigan Cairenn.

A new chest of clothes was delivered to me. A gift from the Rigan. When I looked upon the garments, I found a knot burning within my vocal cords and tears stinging into my eyes. They were dark, of one tone, as befitted my lack of rank. But so fine a weave! For the first time in three years, I donned a pair of trews which did not itch or cause skin irritation. There were undergarments of smooth linen. The brown leine was of the finest wool, as soft as velvet. There was a brass-studded belt of new leather. A short, four-cornered cloak the color of rich loam, lined with a glossy material of a slightly paler hue, came with a simple but elegantly wrought pin with which to secure it at the shoulder. New boots, trimmed with rabbit fur, were as soft and well-made as any of the footwear I had worn as a boy in Briton.

As I dressed and made ready to go to the grianan, I tried to ignore Bruthne, who scowled at me begrudgingly I thought. Fastening the pin, I would have walked by him without a word, but he caught me by the wrist and made me face him.

"You are no stranger to such apparel . . ."

I told him that I was not and that, indeed, through the kindness of the Rigan, God was smiling upon me with reminiscences of home and of the rank which had been mine in Briton society.

Draigenn, skulking jealously in the shadows, observed me with smirking lips and venom-filled eyes.

Bruthne's hand tightened about my wrist. "Padraic . . . be wary . . ."

"Of what?"

"Do not allow this kindness on the part of the Rigan— if indeed it is a kindness—to stir your heart too deeply. Remember always that a man's dreams, if they are spun out of the fabric of What Can Never Be, can become a winding shroud. Be wary, boy."

I saw Dubh's face and shut my eyes against the memory of his death. "I must go to the Rigan," I said impatiently, turning my wrist within Bruthne's grasp until he was forced to release me.

A derisive snicker and vicious cadence of mimicry escaped from Draigenn's lips.

I turned to face him. "Have you something to say to me?"

He feigned an innocence which had not been his since his days in swaddling rags. "Me? Speak to one so finely clothed? Why, 'tis like a flaith you are, fair Padraic. Would that my tail . . . er . . . tales . . . should so pleasure the queen."

His words shocked and enraged me. I demanded that he retract them. He did, but with such mocking self-effacement that, had Bruthne not forcefully sent me on my way, I would surely have struck him.

By the time I reached the grianan, I had forgotten the

malicious youth and the implication which had lurked,
dark and insidious, within his words. I spent a thoroughly
enjoyable evening with the queen. I spoke late into the
night, telling tales from the Old Testament which she
punctuated with questions and impious probings. At
length, after we had partaken of honeycakes and mead,
the Rigan dismissed her yawning maids. We were alone.
She worked upon her embroidery while I told her the saga
of the Exodus. She fell asleep before Moses had descended from the barren heights of Sinai.

I sat very still, content to observe her. Her hands, with
the long, meticulously manicured nails painted crimson,
were lax on her lap. Her hair lay softly against the shimmering blue of her leine. Her face was serene. I could
see the tiny lavender veins which ran through her eyelids.
I thought: She is as pure and angelic as a saint. With an
exhalation of joy at being in her presence, I slipped from
the stool upon which I sat and went on my knees before
her. Lacing my fingers together, I bowed my head and
thanked God for having sent me to serve her. In that moment, so profound was my love for her, had she awakened and offered me my freedom, I would have refused
it.

I do not know how long I knelt immersed in prayer.
My thoughts flowed outward into the night. I was as warm
and secure as a babe in its nursing chamber.

Then, suddenly, my prayer was shattered. My soul
came flying back to the confines of my body. I looked
about, distracted. The room was quiet. The Rigan slept.
And yet . . .

I looked toward the door. It was closed. Or had it just
been closed? Had I heard it move against its hinges? Had
I seen a shadow against the dark hall beyond the grianan?
A chill went up my back. Was I being watched? Spied
upon? I looked back toward the sleeping queen. She did
not stir.

I rose to my feet, gathered up my cloak, put it on, and
went out of the room quietly. In the antechamber, a lady-
in-waiting sat upon one of the two benches which were
on either side of the door. Another woman stood back in
the shadows. I could not see her face.

I informed both women that the Rigan slept and that
I would take my leave. Then, pointedly, I asked them if

either of them had been within the grianan while I had been at prayer.

The woman on the bench chuckled. She had a face which held her years well, except when she smiled, which she did. It was a thoroughly amused and knowing smile, one that sent all of her features plummeting inward around her nose in a collapsing of musculature which was quite unpleasant. "No one enters the Rigan's chamber without invitation," she informed me, then added with a conspiratorial wink: "Not even the Ri . . . and he is never invited!" She chuckled again, then yawned a wide, gaping yawn which revealed all of her well-worn teeth. "Good night, young man." The words were clearly a dismissal.

I went past her and began to descend the steps. Halfway down, I was again overcome by the sensation of being watched. I turned and looked back. Against the torchlight of the antechamber, the figure of a woman was silhouetted above me in the stairwell. She was tall. All detail of her face and form was claimed by shadow. I could make out the color and texture of her hooded cloak, for the torchlight backlighted it, defining the curve of her head and shoulders. The fabric of the cloak was green, the color of the velvet moss which grows on the north-facing side of trees within the heart of the darkest forests. Overlying the green, like tree shadows, I saw swirling black Celtic designs embroidered in silken thread. It was an unusually beautiful garment. I had seen it before, on one of the Rigan's ladies-in-waiting on the day when the royal couple had returned from Lugnasad.

"Magonus . . . ?" The woman's voice formed a question. "Magonus!" A statement, a whisper barely audible as she descended the stairs and came toward me.

The sound of my name brought a trembling wave of confusion rushing through me. With the light behind her, she held the advantage. She stopped, one step above me, reached up and folded back the hood of her cloak.

Though it was dark in the stairwell, with shadows of blue and gray upon the benighted walls, I saw her face. On the soft rising of her right cheek there was the thick-fleshed mark of a small scar. I knew her at once.

I could not speak. Memories were blurring my vision. Memories of home, of the ruined villa, of the desecrated chapel, of the bloodied bedroom where the head of my slave Arnos, impaled upon a spear, had stared at me with the unblinking sightlessness of the dead while two great and filthy men worked violence upon a young girl whose cheek was torn and bleeding.

My hand went up and gently traced the line of the scar which was not long enough or wide enough to mar the gentle loveliness of her features. She was no longer a girl. She was a woman. I spoke her name with tremulous disbelief.

"Mercia . . . ?"

She nodded her affirmation and would have spoken, but we were suddenly interrupted by the voice of a heavy-set serving maid who had begun to ascend the steps which led up to the grianan.

"There you are, girl!" she said, exhaling a sigh of relief at having found the object of her search. "The Ri has asked for you again," she announced with a sour tone of disapproval. "Go on. I shall take your place here."

Mercia took my hand. We went down the stairs together, passing the disgruntled maid as she heaved her girth up to the Rigan's antechamber. At the base of the stairwell, we paused. Mercia looked at me intensely.

"It was I who watched you in the grianan, Magonus. The other maid was dozing and so did not see me. When the Ri's court returned from the fair of Lugnasad, I thought I saw you in the crowd, but I could not believe that you were still alive—let alone here, living within the rath. Nor could I believe that Magonus Sucatus Patricius, who was the despair of his parents because of his lack of faith, could have become Padraic, the one known as the Christian seanachie. The common people say you have the Power. Is it true?"

"God has been with me, Mercia."

She drew in a breath, a sigh. Her hands went out and rested gently upon my forearms. "I must go now. I dare not stay longer. But someone must speak to you, Magonus. Someone must warn you. Long ago you risked your life . . . you sacrificed your freedom in an attempt to help me. Now I must help you." Quickly, obviously afraid of being overheard, she looked about, to make certain that we were alone. Assured that no one was about, she leaned close to me. "Be wise, Magonus. Beware of the Rigan. Because of her attentions, you have won dangerous enemies within the Ri's court."

11

THERE had been a meeting of the flaiths of the tuath. Some of them had traveled far to sit at council with their Ri. Now they were in need of merriment and exercise.

A Gaelic lord needs little excuse to play the host. Miliucc MacBuain was no exception. The sun had come up round and true. The mists of early morning lay sweet upon the fragrant hills. Birds sang in the trees. What better reason to ride out into the countryside for a day of hawking? The flaiths chose their mounts from among the Ri's finest steeds. Carts were filled with sumptuous food and drink. Ladies of the court, intoxicated upon breakfast wines, were mounted upon gentle mares so that they might ride out and observe for themselves the skill of their respective lords, the magnificent rapaciousness of the hawks, and the blood of gentle doves raining from the sky.

They brought their eager mounts to rein before the kennel. The falconers were with them. The ladies were giggling amongst themselves. Bruthne and I had been grooming the hounds out on the kennel green. We looked up as the Ri proclaimed, with a sweep of his gloved hand: "Ahh, here's my Christian. Look well upon him, my friends, for if Sencha's spies bring him word of the magic which this lad works upon my hounds, surely Sencha shall have his druids put the death curse upon the youth's head."

"Sencha is not the only man to wish the youth an early death," observed a stunningly dressed flaith with a rogue's eye. "Is this not the same lad about whom the druids of your court are fuming?"

"Indeed," assented the Ri, smiling drolly. "Can you not recognize a threat to the gods of Eire when you see one?"

"You should not jest, my lord," objected one of the ladies respectfully. "There are those who say that the youth possesses the Power. Indeed, people say that his god waits upon his command."

The Ri's lips worked as he suppressed a laugh. "A god of slaves!"

One of the women, flagrantly drunk, dressed all in red

and gold and darkest blue, eyed me in a brazenly speculative manner. "He's the Christian, the seanachie, isn't he?"

"So I've heard rumored, though he's learned to keep
his tongue when in my presence," replied the Ri.

She tittered. "But not so with the Rigan. And no small
wonder, if you ask me. They are about of the same age.
Ahh, would that I might entertain so young and fair a
youth in my grianan." She pointed an impudently wagging index finger at the Ri. "Beware, Miliucc, that she
seeks no more than his stories to pleasure her."

I snapped to my feet and only Bruthne's hand, slapped
hard upon my thigh, warned me to keep my protest left
unspoken. I glared at the woman and prayed that her
horse would bolt and send her flying to land amidst the
dog leavings of the kennel yard.

The rogue-eyed flaith, evidently the woman's husband,
cast her a withering and totally sobering stare. "You have
drunk too deeply at table this morning, woman. Apologize to the Ri and then hold your fool tongue, else you offend your own lord beyond any possible hope of forgiveness."

She harrumphed and muttered her apology. Miliucc
made no comment. I dared not face him. The heat which
had flooded into my face informed me that I was in the
full flower of a blush. I kept my head turned down until
the horses were away and Bruthne and I were alone.
Then, for the second time, I heard:

"Beware of the Rigan."

Startled, I looked up to meet Bruthne's troubled glance.
He had risen and stood beside me, his broad mouth taut
with worry.

"How dare you speak against the queen?"

"Against her? No. I do not do that, Padraic. Would a
man speak against wind or storm or tide? The forces of
the elements are not understood by such as I. Nor is the
Rigan. But it is as the druids foretold. She has been nothing but trouble to the Ri ever since she came to the rath.
Serve her as you must. But beware, Padraic. Be alert
for danger. With Cairenn, there is always the threat of
storm."

Had he impugned the nature of Christ Jesus I would
not have been more incensed. My temper flared against
him. "She has shown me nothing but gentleness and concern and kindness."

His lips worked over his teeth as the muscle body of a mollusk writhes within its shell when it is prodded. "So she's already begun to spin her web about you . . . all sweet and silver gold as she . . . but be forewarned, boy, so that you may recognize the shroud in time."

Anger congealed in my stomach like a sour stew. "I will hear no more words against her, Bruthne. I am not a boy. I am a man, and I am no virgin lamb who can easily be manipulated by women who would use me or assume me to be a fool."

If he was amused, he was kind enough not to say so. "Of course, you are as old and as wise and as experienced as Time itself. But let a friend share his concern for you. Beware of the spells of women, Padraic. May the gods of Eire protect you if you are not."

"There is but one God," I reminded him hotly.

"So you always say. One god, eh? That would explain it then, if the god were a woman . . . aye . . . a bitch god in eternal heat, with all of the males slavering after her and, failing to reach her, turning in frustration upon one another."

Never in my life had I heard such a blasphemy. I made the sign of the cross against it and would not speak to Bruthne for the remainder of the day.

That night my dreams besieged me. I dreamt of the sea, of home and of laughter and of the soft yellow of the Briton sun. I dreamt of youth and of freedom. I dreamt of a handscape unscathed by violence. I dreamt of a boy with hair the color of wheat: an innocent with eyes aflame with the impatience of youth. I saw the boy so clearly. He ran along the familiar beach of home, ran with the joyous abandon of a wild creature: leaping, loping as though consciously trying to escape his own mortality. He would be mist. He would be sea. He would be sky. He would be wind, confined by neither flesh nor Time. And then a great wave rose up out of the sea. It swept the boy away, rolled him in choking waters of darkness and confusion. I awoke, drenched with perspiration. I stared up into the darkness. The light of morning was beginning to intrude. Bruthne was calling my name.

The Ri had brought his most trusted flaiths to the kennel. They wished to see the Red Ri's hounds and the Christian seanachie at work. As Bruthne and I readied

the dogs and leashed them into the cart in which they
would be driven out into the hills, Bruthne leaned close
to me and advised: "They've been up all night with their
ale. Be a lamb, Padraic. Buckle down your arrogance and
ask your god to muzzle your temper. When the flaiths run
out in pack, with their Ri to show them sport, they can be
an impetuous lot. Do not judge them, lad. And do not be
fool enough to blunder into the path of their animosity or
make of yourself a subject for their merriment."

We went out into the hills. The flaiths consumed their
morning meal as they rode, washing it down with ale.
They showed no ill effects from the previous night's de-
bauch, of which they bragged. The morning chill seemed
to prick their appetites and sharpen their senses.

They treated me well. After the dogs were worked, I
found myself being cuffed and cajoled in an almost brotherly fashion.

"You've got them running out sweet as honey, boy."

"Ahh, Miliucc, I'd sell my darling wife to see Sencha's
face when he loses this bet!"

At noon, a canopied four-wheeled chariot was driven
out to us. It was filled with garrulous young women, not
the flaiths' wives. Each had a lunch basket and a blanket.
They were all mildly intoxicated and obviously eager to
be seduced. The flaiths, losing all interest in hunting with
hounds, made off with the maids into various sections of
the wood, anxious to pursue another sport. I was left with
the Ri and the driver of the dog cart. A few moments
later, from our shaded spot atop a little knoll, we heard
the clatter of chariot wheels. Along the well-kept road
which led out from the ring fort, we saw a small covered
vehicle approaching.

The Ri tensed with anticipation. Without saying a word
he descended the hill and stood waiting by the roadside.
The chariot drew to a stop beside him. A woman
emerged, fresh and lovely in a soft peach-colored leine,
her auburn hair plaited and coiled and shining in the
sunlight. She took the Ri's extended hands. They embraced, held close together in a lover's joining. Then
they parted. The woman turned and reached back into
the chariot for her cloak. As she withdrew it and folded
it across her arm, I saw that it was the color of velvet
green moss, with the rising of black embroidery running
across it like shadow patterns on a forest floor.

"Mercia . . ." I whispered her name as I watched her
walk with the Ri across a stretch of flowered meadow
toward a stand of tall, sheltering yews.

Slowly, the afternoon conceded to dusk. I spent the
entire time alone with the driver of the cart, who contentedly snored the day away while I found myself
wrathfully contemplating the Ri's duplicity and woefully
ruminating over the cruel twist of fate which had singled
out poor Mercia to be the helpless victim of an adulter-
ous king.

The shadows were growing long when the flaiths began
to filter back to the knoll. They did not bring their ladies
with them. The big chariot, filled with heavy-eyed, satisfied, drunken women, returned to the rath. At dusk, we
heard the sound of the smaller chariot leaving the hills. It
was nearly completely dark by the time the Ri came to
take his place at the head of the company so that we, too,
might return to the ring fort.

As we approached the outer fortication, the Ri brought
his horse to a trot beside the cart where I sat, brooding
silently, beside the driver.

"Will you go to the Rigan tonight, Padraic?"

I cast him a baleful glower. "I go to the Rigan every
night, at her command."

He nodded. "I assume that it is not necessary for me to
remind you to exercise discretion . . . to forget that to
which you have been witness?"

I did not intend to speak, yet I blurted: "The girl whom
you dishonor . . . whom you force to lie with you as a
whore . . . she is a Christian."

The words surprised him. "What do you know of Mercia?"

I saw no reason to lie. If he disdained Christians, as he
claimed, perhaps he would seek another maid to pleasure
him. "She was once a slave within my father's house. Had
your raiders not taken her, she would have dedicated herself to Christ. My grandfather had already given her his
blessing."

Anger sparked within his eyes. "The past is dead for
both of you."

"Is it?" I asked, daring to disagree with him. "Or is it
better said that a man is the summation of his years and
that all of his yesterdays dwell within him?" I was remembering my dream of the previous night. The dream of the

boy who had been me. Long ago. So long ago. I thought that I had forgotten him. But I had not. He would not allow me to forget.

The Ri's mouth twisted down. "When you are with the Rigan tonight, be a wise lad with a short memory and a silent tongue. If you are not, you may not live long enough to appreciate the 'summation' of your years."

"You need not threaten. I will say nothing ever to cause my lady pain." Accusation curdled the words like rennet working in a pudding.

"Your lady?" He laughed. A bitter laugh. A laugh heavy with deprecation. "By the gods, Padraic, are you a blind man as well as an impudent fool?" With a violent jerk back on the reins, he wheeled his mount around and rode back to join his flaiths.

It was fully dark by the time the hounds were fed and bedded. Bruthne informed me that the Rigan had sent a messenger to ascertain the reasons for my tardiness. Hurriedly, I cleaned myself, dressed, and gulped a meal of cold stirabout. For the first time since she had called me to serve her, I had no desire for her company. I was afraid that I should not be able to face her without blurting out my knowledge of the Ri's deception.

As I walked across the compound toward the great house, I was physically and emotionally fatigued. How could I possibly find a tale to cheer her when it was I who needed cheering.

The night was cool, spiced with the distinct promise of an autumn wind. The moon was rising above the walls of the ring fortress. The wind moved restlessly in the leaves of the apple trees. Along the topmost edge of the timbered inner rampart, a domestic cat sat and surveyed the night, twitching its tail. High above, a night bird arched and shrilled.

I saw the dark robed figure of the druid coming toward me out of the shadows of the apple trees. Had he been waiting for me? I do not know, for I had often seen him coming and going from the great hall to his own quarters, which were at the far side of the orchard. He was the Ri's chief priest, a man reputed to be a conjurer and soothsayer of great power. He had been the Ri's tutor; now he was his most trusted adviser and interpreter of dreams. He paused before me. He wore the sacred golden

lunula upon his breast. The moonlight seemed to sense
a kindred form within the crescent, for it transposed the
metal to silver; flat, cold, gleaming, reflecting its light upward into the druid's gray eyes; eyes which fixed me
with the appraisal of one who has learned to anticipate
the worst from his fellow men.

"Néladóir." I spoke his name, half greeting, half question. We had not met before.

"You go to the Rigan . . ." He twisted the words into
a statement of contempt. His hands moved and folded
across his midsection. His fingers laced, drumming nervously up and down over his knuckles. I saw that he wore
wore a ring which was exactly like the one ring which the
Ri always wore: a sweep of golden sea wave with the
seven planets set in dragon stone beneath the wave crest.
When he spoke, his voice was redolent with warning. "If
there is to be an eclipse, it shall not be of your doing . . .
its coming was foretold . . . long before you were ever
born."

I cast a glance toward the moon. It was in its proper
phase, still on the rise, unmarred by earth shadow. The
druid's words made no sense to me. "I must go," I said,
anxious to be away from his dark countenance.

"Your god will bring blood to Eire." His voice was the
voice of one who had made an art of presenting grim
forebodings. He stood very still. His features were clearly
defined by the moonlight. I was struck by his resemblance
to the Ri. "I have seen Death in the magic wheel . . . I
have heard it promised in the voice of the kite of Cloon-O
. . . I have dreamt of the roar of the Waves of Eire . . . I
have heard the moaning of the royal shields . . ."

I had not lived in Eire long enough to appreciate the
scope of druidic influence. Standing there, facing the accusing form, I understood only that rumor had come to
me that the druids of the Ri's court, spurred by Néladóir,
had been angered by my visitations to the Rigan.

"Do you threaten me, Néladóir?"

"I have warned the Ri about my dreams. I have cau-
tioned him against you and the subversion of your god."

"My God cannot subvert that which is already His."

His brows came together over the bridge of his raptor's
nose. He stared at me, analyzed me. His eyes dissected
me. They seemed to pierce me to my very soul. I felt
the cold, skin-prickling of anxiety rise on my neck. Once

before I had seen such eyes. Gray eyes. Fathomless eyes. The eyes of the enchantress Morrighan. Without willing myself to do so, I made the sign of the cross.

Néladóir's head swung upward on his neck, the head of a serpent recognizing its prey. "So it is true . . . those who possess the Power recognize it in others."

"There is no Power save through the grace of God."

"Yes . . ." The word was sinuous. "And the Power of the gods is worked through men . . ." He smiled then. Completely without malice, he informed me: "I have advised the Ri to have you slain."

"Padraic." A serving maid's voice intruded into our conversation.

Without giving me an opportunity to comment, Néladóir turned and hurried off toward the great house.

The maid had put her hand upon my arm, pressing urgently. Her eyes were wide and earnest with concern. "You must come quickly, Padraic. The Rigan has heard evil gossip concerning the Ri. She is waiting for you to cheer her. May the gods be with you if you cannot."

The maid had not exaggerated. I had never seen the Rigan so disturbed. Though she would not admit to the cause of her grim humor, she verbally abused her maids and disdained my every word. The night went on interminably. At length the maids were sent away, but not before two of them had been slapped.

The Rigan sulked in her chair. She demanded that I tell her tales of the vengeance of the Lord. Instead, I gave her Joseph and his brothers so that she might know of His infinite mercy. She listened without interest, sipping wine.

I spoke until my voice was hoarse and my throat was dry. Finally, the Rigan's head sagged and her breathing became deep and relaxed. I heard the lonely voice of a wolf bay out into the moonlit night. The Rigan did not stir. Sleep had claimed her.

I felt drained to my very spirit. My limbs, buttocks, and back ached with the need to move about. I rose to my feet and wearily walked to one of the long, slender windows of the grianan. Again the wolf cried out. Beyond the ring fortress, the mactire roamed his kingdom.

I rested my hands upon the wide sill. I could see the round silver face of the moon riding against the night.

It was already easing toward its rest. Within its fading light, I could see the hills and the lean, dark shadows of the forests. I could see the flocks of sheep clustered in little clumps upon the flanks of Slemish. For the first time since I had come to live within the ring fort, I yearned to be beyond its ramparts as a shepherd again, with faithful Shadow beside me, and Dubh to guide me across the pastures while Leborchom lifted up his crude, homespun prayers to God.

My eyes were fixed upon the moon, upon those gray-ringed ancient eyes, upon the long mouth, upon the pock-marked cheeks. It seemed to me then that God himself smiled down at me out of that face. Patiently. Serenely.

I was suddenly filled with a sense of warm and wondrous peace. I knew that soon the sun would rise. The mactire would seek the solace of his lair. And I? I could not go back into Time. I could not be a shepherd again, nor could I be a boy upon the Briton shore. I could only go forward according to a will greater than my own. He who had saved my life upon the Briton shore, He who had saved my soul upon the Mountain of Mists, had His purpose for me. When the hounds were run before the Red Ri Sencha, I would have my freedom as reward. For now, I found my hope and comfort in that. Despite the whims and threats of the Ri and his druids, God had not left me to drown in confusion.

Slowly, lost in thought, I gathered up my cloak and left the grianan. As I closed the door, the serving maid whose duty it was to await her queen's command, rose from her bench and advised me grimly: "You have been summoned to the Ri's chamber, Padraic. You must go to him now, at once."

His was the room of a warrior. Sternly appointed, devoid of ostentation, the walls were whitewashed. A display of weaponry provided the only form of what one could have called decor.

He sat in a massive chair before the hearth. His unclad legs were stretched out before him. He wore a simple saffron leine such as any common man might wear. His arms were bare. For the first time I saw, tattooed deeply and precisely into his biceps, the mark of his ancient Pictish lineage. The great chair in which he sat was softened by several thicknesses of dark, sleek fur. Behind him, at the far end of the room, the curtains of his bedstead were parted to reveal a wide expanse of unmade bed. The pillows were covered with bleached linen. The sheets, of the same fabric, were thrown back as though someone had hastily risen.

There were little couches built into the walls, arranged in such a way that, if need arose, a group of men might sit upon them and address their lord while he was still abed. The Ri instructed me to take my place upon one of them, then changed his mind and commanded me to come and stand before him.

Though my eyes had begun to burn with need of rest, I obeyed and stood resentfully before him as he made a slow appraisal of me.

"Tell me, Padraic," he asked, "what is it about your tales which so entrances my Cairenn that the lights in her grianan burn until the moon is nearly ready to abdicate to the dawn? Or is it, as rumor insists, the man and not the seanachie which pleasures the queen?"

My eyes met his. For a moment, brief and totally disconcerting, I imagined that I saw not the Ri's eyes at all, but the eyes of the druid Néladóir. I blinked and the impression vanished. "I tell the history of the people of God, as God gives me to tell it," I replied.

His lips moved. Into a smile? A frown of amusement? An expression of disdain? I could not tell. I could not read him. I could only react to him, adversely as always.

"And how does your god give you these tales, Padraic? Does he whisper them into your ears? Does he take possession of your slave's tongue and, by so doing, seduce my wife from my bed while attempting to win her to the ways of Christians?"

"I learned the tales as a boy in Briton, even as you have learned the history of your own people and gods."

"But the Rigan claims to have grown weary of Gaelic history. I think, perhaps, you take advantage of her weariness. Would you bring dissent into my house, Padraic? For this is what my druids and seanachies say of you . . . among other things which, in truth, are even more damning."

"Your druids and seanachies have no cause to speak ill of me, or of the Rigan. I tell her the tales of my people . . . as God gives me to tell them . . . as she commands me to tell them."

"In my tuath, I command both the Rigan and your god. Do you dispute that?"

I could smell the scent of danger within the room. A dark, hungry cat, crouching, waiting to hurl itself upon me. I dared not speak.

The Ri prodded: "Your silence answers for you, Padraic."

I felt trapped. "The Ri has taught me, through the pain of his blow, how disputation by a slave is rewarded."

"Would your god dispute my rule, Padraic?"

"He has no need to dispute it. Not here. Not now. Not upon this earth."

He was not satisfied. "But you infer that he will dispute me?"

"On the day when all men are called to Judgment, so too shall you be judged. It has been written. It shall come to pass. Along with all of Mankind, with flaiths and millers and workers of stone, along with slaves and freemen, women and children, Gael and Briton, Egyptian and Greek, you shall be judged."

He was obviously annoyed. "What vanity is bred in the hearts of you Christians! How come you here, from your 'civilized' lands, and dare to claim that only your god Jehovah is just and judge over all? Oh, yes, do not gape, my boy. I know the name of your god, for like many a highborn Gael, as a youth I traveled far from Eire and have seen many lands, including those in which your god is worshiped. Did you imagine that you were the first Christian I have ever met or disdained? And do you think that I am unaware of the fact that even now, as I speak, in small pockets like the pus which rises and leavens within the sores of a man stricken by plague, Christians are meeting throughout Eire in secret little clots and pustules? But by the gods of Eire, I shall not have it here. As long as I rule this tuath, the gods of Eire shall also rule. Do you dispute that, Padraic?"

"I do not. By God's will, you are Ri."

"God's will! Not the will of your god, boy." He stared moodily into the flames. "The very order of the world beyond this island is crumbling. Your god . . . the old gods of the continent . . . their conflicting philosophies war and sweep across the earth, confusing the people, obliterating their pride in their history and their culture. But in Eire

. . . our traditions, our gods, our laws, they survive intact. Even your own great Caesars feared to attack us. Why? Because our gods are with us: gods of the earth, gods of flesh and blood, of pride and strength, gods which warriors can understand; gods of potency, goddesses whose fertility is the fertility of the earth itself. We need no passive Christ to lead us to submission to the powers of a vacillating and dying world. Néladóir is right. The worship of Christ is sedition. By encouraging you, a Christian, to spread your doctrine within the very walls of my rath, she has gone too far. As long as I am Ri, there can be no Christian queen beside me."

"The Rigan has expressed no wish to become a Christian."

"When she discovers how thoroughly the thought galls me, she will request it. Now she is content to taunt me with the prospect."

"Yet the lady Mercia . . ."

I had trespassed into forbidden territory. "The lady Mercia does not speak to me of her god." A frown of sullen introspection moved upon his face as he lifted up his right hand and gestured with it. "You must understand, Padraic, that I hold no rancor toward you. You are what you are: a man of your own country and of your own faith. We have made a slave of you. You did not request your station. And you have served me well, despite your damnable god. But what you do not understand is this: The Rigan has made a pawn of you in a game which has gone on much too long. It is a dangerous game, Padraic, especially for pawns. They are expendable."

I stood very still. The scent of danger filled my nostrils. The shadow of the cat, the sense of foreboding, turned my hands cold.

Without looking at me, the Ri said: "Tomorrow night you shall be summoned to the great hall. You will tell the tales of your god before Néladóir and his druids, before Corpre and his royal seanachies. I trust, Padraic, that you will demonstrate to them that you are no threat to my court."

Out of the shadows, without warning, the cat pounced upon my back. I caught my breath, aghast. "Am I to be judged then? For what crime? I have obeyed the command of the Rigan. If you do not wish me to attend her, command me to stay away. You are sovereign. I will obey you in all things . . . unless you should ask me to violate the Commandments of the Lord my God."

He shook his head. "The game . . . the game . . . I do not wish to alienate the Rigan over it, my boy . . . only to dissuade her from pursuing it too actively. If she finds pleasure in your tales, should I deprive her of that pleasure? No. I wish only to pacify the druids, to lay to rest the outrageous myths which are hovering around you like apparitions risen from the shees. You are a houndsman, a most able houndsman, and that is indeed a rare gift . . . one which I greatly value. Yet my druids have dreamed dark dreams, Padraic. Only this evening Néladóir came to me again with more of his dire prognostications. I must assuage his fears. And without doubt, Padraic, I must quell the rumors which circulate about you within the rath. By the gods, boy, they say that you have the Power . . . that fire waits upon your command, and wind, and storm, and that you can heal and bring forth dead babes alive. It is outrageous! It is ridiculous. Look at you, a puny lad at that!"

The beast of fear was gnawing at my gut. I felt it pawing within my heart. I felt it marauding within my veins. I saw the druid's eyes before me. Gray eyes, as cold and nebulous as winter mist. I saw the whore Morrighan's eyes. Gray. Bleak. Encompassing distances too vast for mortal men to conjure.

The Ri lifted up his right hand and held it out so that he could observe his ring. The golden wave crest shimmered in the firelight. The tiny jeweled planets took on the color of the flames. "Néladóir claims to possess the Inner Vision. He fears the future because he has seen it, or so he says. He fears prophecy. He fears that what has been foretold shall indeed come to pass." He stretched his long legs and turned up his toes so that the fire could warm the soles of his bare feet. "Do you believe in prophecy, Padraic?"

I was trembling. "I have witnessed the truth of it."

He raised a skeptical brow. "Have you now?" He exhaled his lack of belief. "Long ago, it was prophecied by the people of antiquity that someday a man would come to Eire over a furious sea. His mantle would be headholed, his staff crook-headed. His altar would be in the east of his house and all of Eire would bow before his god, saying: So be it, so be it. Have you heard this prophecy, Padraic?"

I remembered the night before the fire in the shepherd's camp, with the shearers and butchers all gathered round while Dubh told the tales and quoted prophecy to them. "I have heard it."

"Tell me, when you came to Eire, was there a storm upon the sea?"

I caught the tack of his thought and was startled. "I do not know. I was unconscious."

He looked at me with a laconic furrowing of his brow. "Does not the supreme altar of the Christian god lie to the east of Eire in Rome? And do not the priests of the Christian god carry crook-headed staffs called crosiers? And do they not wear the simple head-holed mantles of the common people?"

"I am not a priest."

"But you are a Christian . . . and you cannot deny that you have come to us from across the seas!"

"Eire is an island! Everyone who comes here must come from across the seas!"

He roared with sudden laughter. "Such is the wisdom of prophets!"

"You do not . . . you cannot . . . believe that I . . . am . . ."

"By the gods, my boy, I do not. But Néladóir is correct when he points to the facts: You are a Christian . . . you have come from across the seas . . . and you do spread the doctrine of your god wherever you go, even into the grianan of the Rigan herself."

"At her command."

"The druids claim that you have bewitched her. Néladóir has informed me that tonight he confronted you and observed for himself that you are indeed possessed of the Power. He contends that you are a sorcerer and will bring blood and death to Eire through your god."

The statement was so outrageous that I could only gape.

He studied me. Slowly. Carefully. Then he smiled. I read genuine affection for me in his dark eyes and was thoroughly startled by it.

"Play the fool tomorrow night, Padraic," he advised me paternally. "I value your 'magic' as a houndsman."

12

THEY were drunk. Not riotously. Not outrageously. They were forthrightly drunk. Happily drunk. They sat at the main tables, each according to his rank, sipping and back-slapping and succumbing to loud conversation.

It was a small gathering by Gaelic standards. The shield hooks behind each lord's seat were nearly empty, for only a few of the flaiths were present. The meal had already been served and eaten. Musicians and jesters performed. A little bandy-legged man, attired in the outlandish garb of the court fool, pranced about the room with all of the rows and rows of bells which had been sewn onto his shoes and clothing jingling and tinkling.

I stood fascinated by the scene. The women sat at a table of their own. They were as intoxicated as their lords. Each wore a little half-mask over the upper portion of her face: delightful, gay, feathered whimsies. As with the lords, they were seated according to their rank all along the inner edge of the table so that no one sat opposite the other. The Rigan was not present, nor had I expected her to be. I had been informed that since the banquet which had feted her marriage to the Ri, she had not joined him at the royal tables.

I recognized most of the flaiths. They flaunted the colors of their rank. They were the Ri's closest friends, tribal chiefs of ancient and honored lineages who often came to dine with him. The Ri's physician was present, as was the commander of his fighting forces, a gray-haired man with the solid physique of a hardened fighter. I had often seen him training his men on the fairgrounds, which lay just beyond the outer fortifications of the rath.

Behind the Ri, the king's candle burned. It was a huge pillar of wax, as tall as a man and as thick as a warrior's thigh. Its rough wick spat and sparked. All along the walls, oil lamps burned in iron holders, and at various places along the length of the tables, small beeswax candles shimmered in multibranched candelabras.

At the far end of the room, the royal harper plucked and chorded while he stifled yawns and stared blankly. Not far from him, a cluster of young men stood listening

attentively to a most remarkably dressed individual. Like
the court fool, he carried a wand, but his was very long
and made of finest gold. Tiny golden bells, each with a
varying tone, trembled and tinkled as he used the wand
to thrust and parry the fine points of his conversation. He
was short for a Gael, yet he was somehow long-boned and
big of joint, with too much flesh upon him and very little
muscle. His face sagged and shivered as he spoke. His
nose was enormous, cleft at its vast tip. It was the ugli-
est nose I have ever seen on a man, not withstanding
Bruthne's disfigurement. Swollen with excess cartilage, it
rather resembled an erected penis standing out, pink and
veined, over the man's fat, soft, and thoroughly petulant
lips. His forehead was high and domed, tufted with hair
the color and thickness of mist. His ears were the ears of
an ape, with the lobes hanging loose and swinging freely
as he spoke. He was, physically, a thoroughly amazing
specimen. Yet it was not his incredible appearance which
first caught my eye; it was his long and flowing mantle. It
was made entirely of the feathered skins of some wondrous white birds. It was this robe, this downy cape of
utmost luxury, which informed me that the man was
Corpre, the Ri's personal historian and poet. Only a
seanachie and filidh of great rank was permitted to wear
such a cloak.

Behind him, like a sleek and handsome cat in his black
druid's robes, with his black hair falling freely about his
shoulders, stood Néladóir. Around him, like worshiping
fledgling bats, hovered his assistant necromancers, sooth-
sayers, and neophytes.

I had been led into the great hall by two servants.
Standing close on each side of me, they cried out in unison: "The slave, Padraic, by the Ri's command."

All eyes went to me. There was silence. Not immediate.
It took a moment to settle. I heard a belch or two. A
woman's high-pitched laughter reached a crescendo, then
faded, like the scream of someone falling from a cliff. The
assemblage stirred on their seats and observed me expectantly, as though I were some sort of new and intriguing
entertainment which had been brought before them to
brighten the long night.

The Ri rose. "Ahh. Good. Welcome, my boy. Come
and stand before us, Padraic." As he indicated me with
an outstretched arm, he also bade Néladóir and Corpre

to come forward. His manner was one of utmost congeniality. "Now, Corpre, Néladóir, here is the youth who is the subject of your concern." To his guests he declared: "I ask you, my friends, to look upon this youth and tell me: Does his countenance suggest any manner of threat to me or the members of this court?"

There was a general stirring. Someone, a woman, questioned: "Is he not the one whom the common people believe to be a wizard?"

"But not wizard enough to free himself from bondage," said Miliucc.

The druid and the filidh approached the Ri. Corpre seemed confused. Néladóir was clearly angry.

"My lord," the druid protested with an amicability which was quivering with strain, "this is not the proper place or company for such a council."

"It is exactly the place," disagreed the Ri in a light and careless tone which revealed to all present that he considered the situation to be of little import or gravity. "Padraic is my slave. He is one of my most valued houndsmen. He is a harmless youth with a gift of storytelling which has made him popular among the common folk. His tales are unusual. The people like the boy. It is no fault of his that they spread idle gossip about powers which he does not claim to possess. And can he be blamed because the Rigan, having heard word of his foreign stories, has called him to share them with her?" The friendliness of his tone ebbed somewhat. "If, indeed, the youth is a threat to this court, you . . . the most trusted members of this court . . . should have the opportunity to see him and to judge him for yourselves. As Ri, I must inform you that the situation has begun to greatly annoy me. I depend upon Padraic, and upon Padraic alone, to help me to answer the Red Ri Sencha's challenge to me. To no other man do Sencha's hounds respond as well . . . not even to me. So I hold no fear of the dreams which Néladóir has dreamt concerning the youth."

A whisper was exhaled from all present. The Gael do not take their dreams lightly, especially when the dreams are dreamt by druids.

The Ri heard the exhalation and reminded firmly: "Dreams are easily misread, my friends."

"That they may be," agreed Néladóir, bowing before

the Ri, bending his knee as a gesture of respect and submission. "But always they must be read carefully . . .
judged with complete dedication, never lightly."

"As we have done. Together. And always your inter-
pretation is different and darker than my own."

"My lord . . ." The druid's voice was very low; imploring. "Why have you done this? The matter must be discussed in proper and lawful council, before the judges,
Miliucc, not before a gathering of sotted . . ."

"Enough!" The Ri's tone had acquired an unmistakable bite. "It is my judgment that the matter does not
require the calling of council. Tell the assembly of your
dreams, Néladóir. Allow them to judge for themselves if
the youth is the threat which you imagine him to be."

The druid tensed like a man in pain. "What madness
is this? My divinations are not to be discussed with those
who have no understanding of the Power!"

The Ri nodded his assent. "Then let all present know
that you have discharged your duties well. You have discussed your dreams with me. As your sovereign, I have
chosen to assure you that the dreams have no relation to
the youth at all. Padraic is no threat to my household. He
is an asset."

Néladóir rose to his feet in fury. "Has it come to this?
Can it be that to assure the winning of Sencha's challenge, you would deliberately ignore prophecy?" He
wheeled and pointed an accusing finger at me. "And you,
do you deny that you attempt to subvert the Rigan to
your god of Christians?"

I felt the eyes of everyone within the room upon me.
Remembering Néladóir's confessed advice to the Ri, I
knew that, though it was against my nature, I must
choose my words carefully. "I am a slave," I said hum-
bly, bowing from the waist, staring at my toes. "I am
bound to obey my queen's command. Would the learned
druid suggest that I do otherwise?"

Néladóir drew back his finger and arm as though my
words had sent a shock of pain into them. Cradling his
hand against his chest, he warned me: "Do not bandy
words with me, lest I curse your tongue and you find it
withered and useless within your insolent mouth!"

Corpre lifted up his wand and shook it so that all of
the little bells tinkled in fierce, high-pitched unison. "Let
us have no threats," he cried in the voice of a peace-

maker. "I do not know of dreams, but I do know the law. The youth, as he himself professes, is a mere slave. At best he is a prattler without lawful learning. My most unskilled apprentice bard has had seven years of training. Most respectfully, my lord, my objections to the youth are not raised against him . . . but in defense of the law and of my own reputation. The Rigan has chosen to set a dangerous precedent. By calling upon such an unworthy individual to serve as her personal seanachie and filidh, she has struck me a cruel and undeserved blow. Any of my bards . . . the least talented of them . . . are more qualified to please the queen. Yet she spurns them and admits an unskilled foreigner, a slave, a shepherd, a houndsman, to entertain her! Surely, my lord, I am shamed before all of my class."

Miliucc smiled. He was used to dealing with bruised egos. "Good Corpre, in all of Erie there is no one of your class . . . save the chief filidh of the Ard Ri Dathi himself . . . who is held in greater esteem. You combine the art of the historian with the art of the poet. There is not a man or woman within this hall who would deny your value or your talents."

Corpre was not pacified. He straightened and puffed himself up within his feathered garments like a scrawny bird preparing to stand against a gale. "The Rigan denies it, my lord."

The Ri gave the filidh a knowing look which begged for sympathy, "And would you deny the Rigan her small pleasures, Corpre?"

The man's obscene nose had become engorged with blood. "Only if she continues to enjoy her pleasures at the expense of the law. It has been decreed who shall serve as seanachie. It has been decreed how long a man must study before he may call himself a filidh. Do not allow the law to be broken, my lord, else the land be broken with it."

The Ri leveled his gaze at me. He summoned me further forward. "Do you claim to be a poet, Padraic?"

"I do not."

"And would you have it said of you that you are a historian for the Gaelic race?"

"I have little knowledge of the history of the Gael."

He put up his hands. "There. Neither poet nor historian. Now, my boy, what about his business of magic. Is it true that you are a magician? Is it true that by your Power you can command the Spirits of the Otherworld?"

Within me, memories rose: of wind and of flame, of a shattered stone and of the cry of a newborn child. "No, my lord," I replied. "That Power is God's."

The Ri's features tightened with reproach toward me. I suddenly remembered his words of the previous night: "Play the fool tomorrow night, Padraic. I value your 'magic' as a houndsman." I stared at him and saw warning clearly written in his eyes.

"Are you a magician, Padraic?" he pressed.

With sudden insight, I realized that to both of us the word was synonymous with trickster or charlatan. "No, I am not that," I said forthrightly.

He was obviously relieved. He rested the palms of his hands upon the table. "Then the matter is closed." He turned his full attention toward the assemblage. "Padraic is my houndsman. He claims no other skills, no Powers. I, the Ri, sovereign of this tuath, allow him to answer to the Rigan's command. If there be further disputation concerning this youth, the dispute shall be with me."

There was silence for a moment. Total. The Ri came out from behind the table. He embraced both Corpre and Néladóir. I was close enough to hear him say quietly to Corpre: "Be patient with the Rigan, good filidh, she'll soon tire of this new game." And to Néladóir: "Trust me, for truly I see no evil in the youth." He kissed each man then, three times on each cheek in the Gaelic fashion. Then he approached me.

He did not embrace me. He did not kiss me. To my complete amazement, he picked me up bodily, swung me over his back, and carried me to the table as though I were a beast taken in a hunt. I heard a roar of laughter and applause rise in the hall as humiliation flooded through me on a wave of rage. As I was placed soundly onto my feet, red-faced I looked around me in bewilderment. The Ri had placed me beside him at the head of the table. He reached out, poured a cup of wine, put it firmly into my hand, then pushed me backward into a chair.

"Now," he declared to me so that all present might hear, "so that you will know of what we speak, we shall demonstrate to you, slave of the Roman god, how a true seanachie and filidh goes about his work. Corpre, a wise word to a foolish lad! Christians are most favorably disposed to commandments of gods and ancient kings. Tell us, then, of good king Cormac and of his words of wisdom to his son."

As the harper began to pluck the strings of his instrument, Corpre, smug and pacified at last, began to speak. Like Dubh, he was a consummate artist. His words were aflame with passion and pathos.

> "I was a listener in the woods,
>   I was a gazer at stars,
>   I was unseeing among secrets,
>   I was silent in a wilderness . . ."

His arms went wide. His wonderful cape flowed out like the wings of a magical bird. He waved his hand. The bells sang the song of cascading icicles.

> ". . . Be not too wise, be not too foolish;
>   Be not too conceited, be not too diffident;
>   Be not too haughty, be not too humble;
>   Be not too talkative, be not too silent;
>   Be not too harsh, be not too feeble.
>   If you be too wise, they will expect too much of you;
>   If you be too foolish, you will be deceived;
>   If you be too conceited, you will be thought vexatious;
>   If you be too humble, you will be thought without honor;
>   If you be too silent, you will not be regarded;
>   If you be too harsh, you will be broken;
>   If you be too feeble, you will be crushed."

He jabbed the wand forward into my face and jingled the bells with prideful ferocity. "Such is but a portion of the wisdom of the great Gaelic king Cormac MacAirt, Christian! How do the teachings of your insipid Christ compare to such as this?"

He had twisted the name of my Lord downward with such dersion that I was impelled to speak my mind. "My Christ is the Son of the Living God. He has promised that at the ending of the days of men, the feeble shall not be crushed. Christ has promised that, when He comes again in glory to judge the living and the dead, His kingdom shall have no end . . . and it shall be the meek who shall inherit that kingdom."

The women laughed first. A burst of good-natured snickers. The flaiths followed suit. Corpre's features expanded around his nose into a smile of total glee. He shook his wand so that the bells jangled hysterically. Miliucc was gracious enough to give my reply a moment of thought before he, too, succumbed to laughter.

"May your god and your Christ have mercy on you, then," he proclaimed, slapping me hard upon my shoulder. "For by the gods of all Eire, Padraic, you are anything but meek!"

As I tried to remain firm and unflinching against the storm of mockery which assaulted me, I was suddenly aware of the druid Néladóir standing white-faced before the table. I had forgotten all about him. Yet, as I gazed at him, I knew that he had not forgotten me. His eyes, as gray as the sea on a foggy morning, held no laughter. They were filled with sadness, with the unspeakable despair of one who has seen beyond Tomorrow and knows that he is impotent to change anything which he has witnessed.

He stepped forward. "The road has been laid." His words were heavy with pain and concern. "Before any of us were ever born, the road was laid. But it is not yet too late, my lord. There is still time to turn back from the course which the Fates have set for us. I know that the Rigan speaks against me, that she disdains my council and would seek to take me from my duties. But do not listen to her, my lord. Death walks upon her words and deeds. Send the youth away, for he is the fruition of a prophecy which shall change the land and all who dwell upon it. Take heed, my lord, if you cannot find it within your heart to have him slain, free him then. Get him back to his own people. Now! Get him away from the Rigan and away from Eire. I tell you, I have heard the kite of Cloon-O. I have heard the roaring of the royal shields. Death has spoken of his coming. Send the boy away, my lord. Send him away now."

Miliucc tensed beside me. "Enough!" The word was an impatient snarl which sent the druid stepping back. "I am weary of prophecies which invariably speak against my will, Néladóir. Do not speak against the Rigan or this youth again, or you will force me to take actions which shall displease us both."

The druid bowed. His body spasmed as he fought violently for control. "So be it, my lord . . . so be it . . ."

When he looked up, his eyes were focused directly upon me. A wave of dizziness went reeling through me. It seemed as though an actual force had come out of his eyes to take possession of me. I tried to look away. I could not. His eyes held mine, locked them to his own.

I shared his vision then. Not clearly, for the Sight was his and I did not want to accept it. It came to me against my will. There was no detail. Yet, within a scant, rushing breath of Time, I saw flames and darkness and heard the cries of mourners. I saw the green hills of Dalaradia darken with a shadow which flowed across them like blood.

I blinked and the vision was gone. The druid was backing away. My dizziness was ebbing. Néladóir turned softly on his heels and strode from the great hall. I felt weak and confused as I watched him go. Once again, as on the Mountain of Mists, I knew that I stood at the edge of some terrible and unavoidable abyss. I sensed it. I knew that I could not turn away.

It was late when I was at last dismissed from the banquet hall. Shaken by my confrontation with the druid and filidh, distracted by the Ri's obvious display of favor toward me, unnerved by the vision which I had shared with Néladóir, I had developed a profound headache. I walked back to the kennel slowly, rubbing my temples, taking in deep breaths of the cool night air. I looked about me. The night was veined with rafts of gray cloud through which the stars shone like eyes. Druid eyes. Executioner's eyes. Eyes without mercy. I turned my face away from them and began to pray.

All was quiet within the kennel. Egan slept beside his pups. The light which often shone late into the night from beneath Bruthne's door was out. As I walked to the stall where my hounds were bedded, to my surprise, I came face to face with Draigenn.

He had been leaning across the stall door. He held a long, pointed stick within one hand. A stripe of fabric had been wrapped tightly just above the sharpened end. The cloth was ripped. In the confining darkness of the kennel, I could smell that it was wet through with dog saliva. Upon seeing me, Draigenn had leaped to the ground. Now he crouched before me, holding the end of the stick with both hands, jabbing out at me with it threateningly. Behind him, within the stall, the hounds cowered and snarled.

It did not take the Power or the Inner Vision to know what he had been about. He had been baiting the dogs. My head began to pound with the pressure of my rising anger. I reached out and tried to grab the stick from his hands. He jumped back and swung out with it, slicing the air, bringing it hard across my forearm, numbing my arm to my fingertips.

One does not forget violence. It sits upon the memory as a permanent bruise. As I met Draigenn's eyes, I knew that it was his intention to kill me if he could. He jabbed out at me with the stick again, piercing my shoulder through the fabric of my leine. It was a minor wound, yet enough to prick and draw blood. As I stared at it, he jumped out at me, bring the stick down hard across my neck.

My brains quite literally rattled within my head, but the blow had not been hard enough to thoroughly stun me. I leaned back and kicked out at him. The force of the impact caused us both to fall. Draigenn dropped the stick. Even as he did so, I threw myself upon him. I grabbed him about the throat, choking him until my rage worked to calm me. He lay gasping and sputtering as I released my grip.

"By the gods, what is this?" Bruthne stood beside me with a torch in his hand. Egan had retrieved the stick. He offered it up to the master of hounds. I saw then, as did Bruthne, that the cloth which had been tied about the shaft was a piece of fabric torn from my old woolen shepherd's lummon.

With an exhalation of disgust, Bruthne threw the stick to the ground. He handed the torch to Egan and scooped up Draigenn by his collar. He slapped him then, mercilessly, again and again until the boy shrieked.

"Mercy on me! It was at her command! Bait the hounds, she says to me. Bait them with something of Padraic's so that they'll turn against him and be ruined for the hunt. Mercy on me! I had to do it! I had to!"

"At whose command?" pressed the houndsman.

There was wildness and despair within Draigenn's eyes. "The one with the scar on her cheek . . . the one who wears the green cloak . . ."

It was as though uncounted numbers of insects had suddenly exploded into life within my brain. They swarmed within my skull, flurrying for release. I rose to my feet and flung myself at Draigenn. "Liar!" I screamed as I wrenched him free from Bruthne's grasp and pummeled him to the ground.

Bruthne knocked me off the boy with a mighty swing of his foot. He bent and lifted me by my belt.

"The girl of whom he speaks is a Christian," I gasped, trying to twist free of his grasp. "She would never plot against the Ri."

The houndsman released me with a push which sent me stumbling backward against the stall door. He glared at Draigenn. "The girl in the green cloak, eh? And since when does a mere serving maid possess enough power to entice a man to commit treason against his Ri? And for what reason would she wish to disgrace her lord?"

Draigenn's features had shriveled with terror. "Padriac has spoken the very words: The girl's a Christian. The Ri disgraces her each time he forces her to lie with him. These Christians, all of Eire knows that they worship a chaste and passionless god who forces them to act against the rule of nature and kings. It's a commandment of their god, that they shall not lie with any save their legal spouse."

Bruthne let out a sniff of annoyance. "Legal or illegal, Christian or no, she goes to Miliucc willingly enough. The serving maid has had no part in this. Now I'll have truth from you, boy, or I'll finish you here and now as reward for the treason which you'd work against my Ri."

Draigenn was not bright enough or brave enough to continue his deception. He withered beneath the houndsman's threat. "I've done what I've done by command of the Rigan."

The blood seemed to rush downward out of my veins. It welled within my feet. For a moment I thought I would faint.

"Why implicate the serving maid?" pressed Bruthne.

"Also at the Rigan's command." Draigenn bowed his head as he began to cry. "She wishes the girl dead. At any cost."

Bruthne was not satisfied. "A serving maid, even a girl favored by the Ri, is dispatched easily enough by a clever and well-paid assassin's hand. Why would the Rigan choose such a bumbling dolt as you to work such a scheme?"

"I'm no assassin of women!" the boy protested. "It's the Rigan's desire to publicly humiliate the Ri in his contest with Sencha. By discrediting Padraic as a houndsman, the Ri's judgment of men will be proven faulty. Yet the Rigan feared that her plot might be discovered. She feared that the druids would trace it to her. So, what better irony said she, than to lay it at the feet of the serving maid. After all, it's not so unusual for a man's mistress to turn against him. And then the Ri himself would be forced, by law, to have the girl slain. In the confusion that'd follow, I'd be spirited off to a place of safety within the court of the Red Ri Sencha. The Rigan promised. She said I'd be a free man for my part in it."

Bruthne's mouth had grown taut with controlled rage. "If the Rigan would keep her promise, would be a wife to the Ri, he'd never have sought a mistress. Now he cherishes the girl. He would never allow harm to come to her."

"If treason could be proved against her, the brehons would demand that she be tried in open court. The law would demand her death."

"And you . . ." The houndsman's voice was sibilant with loathing. "You would have been the one to bear witness against her . . . you . . . a sniveling sneak and liar who has not even the guts in him to perform such a puny and malevolent intrigue as this. Tell me, Driagenn, how long have you been at this stinking task?"

Draigenn's nose had begun to run. He snuffled at it with the back of his hand. "It was first begun this night. Only this night"

Bruthne gave him a brutal bash with the side of his foot. "Out of my sight. Out of the rath with you."

Draigenn drew himself into a kneeling position. "I cannot leave the rath . . . not unless you inform the guards to call in the ban hounds."

"I will not inform the guards." Bruthne's voice was flat and cold.

Draigenn was aghast. "I cannot go out beyond the

ramparts without leave. The hounds will attack and slay me."

"They or I," replied the houndsman. "The choice is yours."

The boy's lips quivered. Clutching his bruised thigh, he rose to his feet. "I shall go to the Rigan. I shall tell her of your threats."

"Good," said Bruthne. "I am certain that she'll be delighted to know how you have confided her scheme to us."

Draigenn's shoulders twitched and rounded upward. His head went down. He stared at us out of eyes made feverish with desperation. "Your knowledge of the conspiracy compromises you . . . all three of you . . ."

Bruthne gave this a moment of thought before he reminded: "True enough. Our lives are in jeopardy. But you, the instrument through which the treason was to be worked, shall surely not be allowed to live to tell of the queen's duplicity. If the Rigan learns of your failure tonight, and of our knowledge of it . . . all of us shall die, Draigenn. All of us."

"But if Sencha arrives and the hounds perform well, I shall be slain for my failure to ruin them for the hunt. The Rigan has sworn that to me."

"Pity." Bruthne's sarcasm could not have been misread.

The words sobered the boy. His eyes had gone enormously round. "Then I must go to the Ri. Yes. Yes, I shall." He was speaking quickly now, spinning himself a tenuous web on which he might climb to safety. "I shall tell him the truth . . . aye . . . all of it. It is time he saw the truth: that he would take a viper to bed. The druids despise her. The flaiths whisper amongst themselves of their pity for the Ri who has wed himself to a maid who would ever taunt him with a virginity which she would take safely with her to her grave. In truth, she is a vicious bitch, and I would be serving my lord well by speaking truth of her to him."

Bruthne nodded. "To protect her honor and his own pride, he has twice fought in defense of her name. He has spurned the advice of his druids and of his council. Do not doubt for a moment, Draigenn, that he would cut the throat of any man, woman, or boy who might threaten to speak against her."

The truth of the houndsman's words brought the

spasming of dread to Draigenn's features. "Then, what must I do?"

The houndsman measured the shivering youth with hostile eyes. "You have not fared well in this game, Draigenn. The Rigan has covered her moves well, as she has always done. But you? You are in check. Leave the rath now. While it is still dark. If you are clever enough, you might still manage to pass by the guardsmen unseen."

A sob of agony broke out of Draigenn as he lurched forward and grasped Bruthne about his knees. "But the hounds . . . they shall tear me to pieces!"

The houndsman kicked him roughly away. "Out of my sight, before I kill you myself, and with pleasure, for your attempt to bring dishonor to my Ri."

"But what else could I do? Protect the Ri's good name and be slain by the Rigan?"

"It must have pleased you to act in her behalf," accused Bruthne knowingly, "when you discovered that, in doing so, you placed the life of Padraic in certain danger."

Draigenn suddenly shrieked and crawled to me, hugging me piteously about my ankles. "You're a Christian . . . you've said that your god is a god of compassion . . . tell him, Padraic, tell him to help me . . ."

Bruthne gave me no opportunity to speak. He picked Draigenn up by the scruff of his neck and shoved him toward the kennel entrance. "Go," he demanded. "Go now."

Draigenn, shivering like a man caught naked within a storm, looked back at us. "All right. I shall go. But you'd best pray that I'm not caught. For if I am, I shall implicate you in whatever way I can. This I swear to you!"

Bruthne tensed as the boy turned and walked out into the night. "Wait here," he said to me in words which were a command. "I had better see Draigenn safely beyond the ramparts."

I did not guess his intent. As God is my witness, I did not.

Draigenn was found dead the next morning. "Poor young lad," exclaimed the kitchen maid who brought us the news. "He was evidently trying to steal apples from the Ri's orchard when he slipped and fell and broke his neck. I don't suppose, though, that we'll ever be knowing what caused the marks on his throat . . . as though he'd

been strangled. But, I ask you, who'd be after murdering
a poor kennel lad?"

"Who, indeed?" echoed Bruthne, but he did not meet
my eyes.

13

THE sequence of events which followed flows through my
memory as leaves drifting in a silty stream.

The Red Ri arrived, uninvited and unannounced, one
week after Draigenn's death. I clearly remember the confusion which followed. The Ri Miliucc MacBuain's gaming arenas were hastily readied for the contests which
were always a part of royal visits. I can see the guest
houses being hurriedly cleaned and aired. I can see the
colorful, squabbling parade of the Red Ri's entourage as
it entered the ring fort beneath his swirling red banner.
They were a clamorous, unelegant, pretentious lot; reflec-
tions of their lord: brawling, bragging, intoxicated upon
their own bravado. With them came Sencha's black-faced
lampooners, his master harper, his chief filidh, his high-
est ranking seanachie, two of his druids, his most trusted
physician, his hairdresser, two bodyguards, a huge hairy
strong man, assorted foot soldiers, and the five eldest of
his thirteen sons by two former wives, now deceased. He
had brought his present wife, Étain, Miliucc's sister, and
their infant son. From his stables he had brought his finest mount, and from his kennel he had brought his keen-
est hounds. He had brought gifts: a string of twelve fine
ponies, three female slaves, two milk cows, a cage filled
with well-fattened fowl, and a four-wheeled cart loaded
above its rim with haphazardly bundled presents specifi-
cally for the Rigan.

"By the gods," Bruthne observed, "one would swear
that the lord Sencha's come courting."

Memories.

Like leaves. Twisting. Turning. Some of them have
fallen to the bottom of the river of Time and I shall never
be able to recall them. Others drift in that dark and silted
stream of Yesterday, so that I can perceive their presence
but can no longer fully grasp their images. And others
are caught forever at the surface of my memory. They

spin slowly, painfully, forever alive within the light of my consciousness.

The pale figure of Étain. Proud, raven-haired Étain. I shall ever see her walking alone beneath the apple trees in the dark, silent hours which preceded those last few peaceful dawns. She did not know that I, kneeling at prayer beneath the sheltering crowns of those same fruitful trees, watched her and knew that she wept.

The games. I remember the color and the spectacle of the arena, where I was sometimes allowed to sit with Bruthne and Egan, watching the Red Ri's sons and the Ri Miliucc's flaiths engaged in friendly but hard-pressed clash of arms.

"When will they test the hounds?" I asked Bruthne.

"After all other contests are finished."

I remember the nights in the grianan. They were no longer pleasant nights for me. If the Rigan suspected that I had been involved in any foul play concerning Draigenn's death, she gave me no hint of her suspicions. Yet she sensed a change in me and openly castigated me for it, demanding to know why I had grown sullen and introspective. I dared not speak. I dared not inform her that, through Draigenn, she had shattered my love, my trust, my implicit faith in her and, by so doing, she had made me know that once again a woman had used me for a fool.

On the night of the Red Ri Sencha's arrival, I was called to entertain the Rigan and her guest, the Rigan Étain. It was a night which spoke to us of the coming autumn. Sodden banks of cloud chilled the summer wind. The Rigan Étain sat with her newborn son at her breast. How honey-sweet the Rigan Cairenn had been at first, doting on the new mother, consoling her for her past three miscarriages, recalling with utmost sympathy the stillbirth of her daughter. Then, smiling, her words had turned into a flow of acid, cruelly stinging the visiting queen with rumors pertaining to her ill health and Sencha's dissatisfaction with her inability to sustain her pregnancies.

Étain's features tightened. "Your words have truth to defend them, Cairenn," she replied graciously. "Yet at least I have born a child, and a son, and no one can say of me that I have not been a true wife to my lord."

The implication was clear. The Rigan Cairenn flared

into quick and defensive anger. "Of what do you accuse me? You, who are responsible for seducing me into a union which I never wanted. The gods know how I curse the day which brought us together at Lugnasad years ago. I was a virgin child. Yet a marriage was made for me because you carried back to your cursed brother all of my girlish confidences."

Étain's eyes narrowed. "You told me then that not in all of Eire was there a lord to win your heart . . . until you looked upon my brother. And you did look upon him, Cairenn. You taunted him with your restless innocence and whispered to me of your longing for him. When his heart was yours, you turned away, but not until you were wife to him. The marriage was made, Cairenn, because you wanted it."

The Rigan blinked. She was not used to disputation. "I wanted? In all of my life I have never had anything as I have wanted it. As a child, my own father sent me from my home to live as hostage. I was sent to dwell with strangers, against my will, to be abused or treated kindly according to their whim. *Theirs.* Never mine."

Étain sighed. She had evidently heard these words before. "And never was there a hostage treated more royally, or more totally spoiled by a doting Ri who loved you as a daughter. As for your father, you cannot revenge yourself upon him through Miliucc . . . or through my lord Sencha." Adjusting the folds or her infant's coverlet, she advised: "The games have gone on long enough, Cairenn. The people, once sympathetic to your youth and beauty, grow impatient with you. It is time for you to be a wife to my brother. You were a child when the marriage vows were made, and before all the tuath he made it known that he would not force his right upon you. He has been patient for nearly four years, Cairenn. You shame him before his people. He is not a eunuch. Nor are you a child. Virgin though you may be, you are not an innocent. You well know what you are doing. But do you realize what the outcome must be if you do not yield in time?"

The Rigan Cairenn's smile trembled as she fought to control it. "Outcome? Games? Why, Étain, I fear that you have taken on the suspicious nature of a battle lord."

Étain exhaled a weary sigh. "Be wife to my brother," she repeated earnestly. "Now, before it is too late. Now, before you bring warfare to the land by setting Ri against Ri and clan against clan. Now, while they cross swords in friendly combat, sit beside my brother at banquet, Cairenn. Coil up your hair and rest your arm upon his so that all assembled, including my own lord, may know that you are at last truly and completely the Rigan of Miliucc MacBuain. Sencha would not dispute such a statement. He would not dishonor you."

"As he dishonors you?"

Étain did not flinch. "Would you go with him, Cairenn, if you succeed in maneuvering him into openly offering suit?"

"And be a second wife? Never."

"Then let him be. Give yourself to my brother, as is your duty. He will put aside his mistress then. Bear him a child and you will have his love forever, as will you also have the love of the people who now look upon you with disdain."

I had been standing back against the draperies, near the narrow window which offered a view of Slemish. The women had forgotten my presence, or else, since I was a slave, they assumed that I, like any other serviceable piece of furniture, was deaf to their conversation. I watched, stunned and sickened, as the Rigan Cairenn leveled her gaze maliciously at Étain.

"I have his love now," she declared viciously. "He cherishes me! If he did not, he would long ago have cast me out or forced himself into me. And I have your lord's love as well. Oh, yes. Ever since I came to sit with you at the birthing of your first child . . . one of the many which you deliver up dead . . . he has loved me. He could not keep his eyes or his hand from wandering to me. All of your household knew of his attentions. And again, this year, at the fair of Lugnasad, he flaunted his love for me until you were ashamed to show yourself and until my own Ri came near to challenging him over his obvious improperties."

"Love? You have no understanding of the word, Cairenn," said Étain quietly. "You are not loved. You are desired. You are not cherished. You are coveted. Sencha is a man of deep and fleeting passions. I know that he lies with other women, younger women, more beautiful women. Yet he sleeps with me, Cairenn, and lays his head upon my breast and spins his dreams to me. I am more

than his wife. I am his friend. Sencha and I shall grow
old together. He is a good man, though he is often a rash
and foolish one. If he were to take you to his bed this
very night, nothing would change between us. For what
could you possibly give him that would lastingly pleasure
him? Your beauty will fade, as has mine. A virgin's blood
is shed in one hot night, Cairenn. And, in truth, I doubt
if you would even willingly give him that."

The Rigan's eyes filled with wild, unbridled defiance.
"No," she proclaimed with an expression of revulsion,
turning down her lips, "I would not. Not to any man!"

14

DEEP within the earth beneath the ring fortress, there was
a passage. One reached it through a door which was not
a door at all. It was a stone set to slide aside when it was
maneuvered into the proper position. Beyond the stone,
the passage led into the earth. It smelled as a grave must
smell after it has been long sealed off from the light and
breath of the living world. Narrow, low-ceilinged, torch-
lit, the passage had been dug to assure the royal family's
escape if ever the ring fort fell before a siege. Only certain chosen members of the Ri's most trusted guards
knew of the secret which lay beyond the stone. One such
man was MacCairthinn. He was a Christian.

On a night not long after the arrival of the Red Ri
Sencha, I returned from the grianan to the kennel earlier
than usual. The Rigan had been busy examining some
of Sencha's gifts to her: bolts of luxurious fabrics. For an
hour or more, at her command, I told my stories of the
Holy Word while no one listened save the cricket which
resided somewhere within the woodwork. A seamstress
arrived with a bevy of assistants. Together with the
queen, they began to unfurl the yards and yards of cloth
so that they might examine it. At length I fell to silence.
No one noticed. The Rigan chattered happily away to the
seamstresses, holding fabric up to herself, arranging it
about her figure, studying her image in the mirror. It was
as though I had become an animate extension of the
stool. They did not care about me. They did not even
mind gossiping in front of me, for a piece of wood cannot

repeat gossip or find amusement in women's gibberish. I grew ill at ease and thoroughly resentful of their attitude toward me. I cleared my throat. Once. Twice. A third time. The Rigan turned to stare at me blankly. I asked for her permission to return to the kennel. My feelings must have shone out of my eyes, for she laughed and dismissed me with a wave of her hands.

"We did not mean to offend your sense of usefulness, Padraic. Of course. Run and tend your hounds. I must tend to woman's business so that my garments will be certain to please the Ri."

I gathered up my cloak and moped out of the grianan, wondering which Ri she had in mind.

It was a moonless night. As I approached the kennel, a woman's voice called out to me from the far end of the green.

"Magonus . . ." Barely more than a whisper.

It was Mercia. I could see her, a dark silhouette tensely etched against the night. I went to her and would have spoken, but her fingers went up against my lips.

"Praise God," she whispered, urgency steeling her words. "I feared that the Rigan might keep you half the night. But now you are here and we must go now. There is no time for questions."

"Go? Where?"

The pressure of her fingers muffled my questions.

"You will know soon enough. For now, we must keep silence at all costs. There is danger for us in this, Magonus. Follow me now, and quietly."

I hesitated, listening to the raucous laughter which emanated from the great house. The Ri and his visitors were evidently well on their way to thorough intoxication. Lights blazed from every window. Voices rose and fell.

"Magonus, we must go now or not at all."

I looked at Mercia. I could barely see her in the darkness. She was merely a shadow swathed in a dark cloak.

"Trust me," she said. "Follow me. Quickly."

I did not question her further. Instinctively, I knew that she would never seek to bring me to harm. I dogged her steps. We moved lightly so that our footfall would rouse no sound. When we passed the well, ducking down a narrow corridor, we paused at last beside a vine-covered section of old and ill-kept wall. There were others here. I

could not make out their faces. Overcome by curiosity, I
started to speak but was immediately "shhh-ed" by them.

No one spoke. In the darkness, I saw the burly form of
the giant, the king's guard MacCairthinn, and was startled. He was one of those men who seemed to have been
born of another species, with vast hands and feet and features. Even among the tallest of the Gael, he would be as
readily identifiable as a mountain standing upon a plain.
In the darkness, he was like an enormous cloud, bending,
sighing as he bent his weight and height against an obstacle which I could not see.

There was the grinding sound of a stone being moved.
A sigh of relief from the giant. Then, a moment later, led
forward by Mercia, I found myself descending into the
earth by means of a narrow-stepped stairway. The others,
mere breaths and sighs in the blackness, followed close
behind me. Above us, I heard the sound of the stone
moving again. Then there was total darkness. Behind us,
a light flared. The giant had set a torch to flame.

The shadows assumed identity. There was Umall, one
of the royal cooks; his young and pretty daughter,
Mairead; two bondswomen; and the giant. I looked from
face to face, confused, feeling the complete stranger. Then
Mairead stepped forward shyly and embraced me in the
Gaelic manner. The others followed suit.

Mercia smiled at my confusion. "We are Christians,
Magonus," she explained.

"Tonight we shall partake of the Lord's Supper,"
added Umall.

"A Mass?" I pressed, incredulous.

"Aye," affirmed the cook.

"But how? There are no priests in Eire."

"There is one," said Mairead, "taken as a slave in the
last raids . . . and brought here to us by the certain grace
of God."

"Come," prompted Mercia, taking my hand. "We cannot dally here. We must all be safely back in our beds
before dawn."

MacCairthinn frowned as he looked at her with concern. "I mean no disrespect, my lady, but what if the Ri
should call for you before then?"

"He drinks with Sencha. They will have to match each
other cup for cup before the night is done. No doubt they
are both already half unconscious."

The giant nodded. "Then we must go on."

He walked ahead of us, bending low beneath the meager height of the passage, holding the torch so that we might see our way. We followed the light into the realm of worms and roots. Here and there, water leached through the earth, staining it, drip-dripping emptily. When next we paused, MacCairthinn snuffed out the torch. Again we were in total darkness. Again I heard the sound of grinding stone, the sound of earth showering downward. Water dripped onto my head from one of the countless ground wellings. Shielding my eyes from falling soil and water, I looked up as MacCairthinn's strong hands pushed aside the stone. The light of heaven invaded our mole's domain. Drawing my cloak close about me, I followed Mercia up a flight of steps into the fresh, clear wind of the late summer night.

We walked across the dark hills. We used no torch to light our path. Compared to the darkness of the unlighted passage, the night was brilliant. Though there was no moon, we had no trouble seeing our way. The world seemed blue. The night was afire with stars. We moved in silence. Before long, I recognized the sweet, sharp scent of the rising earth. I knew that I was back upon Slemish, walking upward across the shoulders of the Mountain of Mists.

Others began to join us. Groups of two and three, merging into silent gatherings of six and seven. Cloaked. Anonymous. Faces downturned. Footsteps light and cautious on the earth. An occasional pausing, hands uniting in silent greeting. Then moving again, as silently as shadows.

I stopped when we entered the ravine. The others, except Mercia, moved on ahead.

"What is it?" she asked, sensing my reluctance to go on.

I could feel the walls of the mountain close about me. "I know this place . . ."

Her fingers curled about mine. "It is only a little way now. We must go on, Magonus."

I followed her.

Even before we reached the amphitheater, the image of the tree began to take form behind my eyes. Had I been a blind man I would have seen it, just as clearly as I can see it today, sensing its presence through my skin and blood and heartbeat. There was a trembling tide of anticipation rising within me. The amphitheater widened out before me. I saw the others gathered there, before the great tree, before the ruined stone where the little fire which Leborchom and I had kindled so long ago still burned.

Mercia dropped to her knees and made the sign of the cross. As she rose, she watched me, waiting for me to genuflect. When I did not, she seemed surprised. "Once this was a pagan shrine, Magonus. Now it is a holy place. Can it be that you have not heard of it? Do you not know that the will of God was worked here, through a holy youth who toppled the heathen stone and ignited the fire of God's Power? It was a miracle. Look. Even now the wind blows and seeks to snuff out the flame. Yet the will of God prevails. The sacred fire burns. It will not be extinguished."

The wind seemed to enter my head and roar within it. "Who told you such a tale?"

Mercia rose to her feet. "It has come down the mountain to us, in a hundred ways and from countless mouths. They say that an old shepherd has guarded the flame, has kept it kindled in the hope of this night . . . when a true priest of God would lead us all to Communion with our blessed Lord. I thought that surely, after all of your years upon Slemish, you must have known of the place . . . perhaps even known the old man and the identity of the holy youth . . . how else would such a youth as you have come to the knowledge of the God of your fathers . . ." She paused and stared at me, doubting the validity of the question she next asked even before it was spoken. "I have even wondered . . . if . . . you might be the one of whom they speak . . . the stories that are told of you . . . they seem so . . . so . . . but no . . . it is obvious they confuse you with someone else . . . with the other youth whose name is never mentioned lest the druids seek him out . . ."

I strained to see Leborchom among these who were gathering before the tree. He was not there. "Where is this old shepherd?" I asked her.

"Tending his flock," said a man from behind me. "I have brought him the Holy Eucharist. It is best for him, and for the youth who has brought God's blessings to this place, to remain anonymous . . . for now."

As I turned to look upon the man, there seemed to be a soft gentling of the shadows of the night. Illusion? Perhaps. It was as though an opaque bird had flown before the stars and hung aloft, a winged kite, frozen upon the wind. The man was young, perhaps only a few years older than I. His face had been tempered by the elements. Yet the eyes, clear, honest, and startlingly forthright, told me that his soul remained unscathed by earth and Time. He wore the garb of a slave, a shepherd's clothes, though he bore no stink of sheep. His fair hair, paler than my own, was closely cropped. He carried a tall, gnarled staff.

"May the peace of Christ be with you, brother," he said to me.

To my amazement, he spoke in the language of Briton. How sweet it was to hear the familiar words of home. In the rath, I never heard them spoken, save by Mercia, and I rarely saw her or dared to converse openly with her. I found myself blurting to the stranger: "Have you been long away from Briton? From what district do you come? Do you know the house of Patricius?"

He smiled at my exuberance. "I am called Victoricus," he replied as he embraced me, firmly kissing me on my cheeks in the Gaelic fashion. "In truth, our house is one."

I did not understand his meaning. He stepped back from me, openly measuring me with an expression of affirmation which made me feel that he knew me better than I knew myself. I felt uncomfortable before his scrutiny. "You *are* from Briton?" I pressed him.

He nodded, assenting not to my question but to some inner probing of his own. "Our house *is* one, Padraic," he repeated.

It occurred to me that he should not have known my name. Others were pressing close about us, speaking to him, reaching out to touch him. He lifted up his arms, addressing us all.

"My brothers and sisters, let us worship the Lord!"

It seemed to me that he still spoke in the language of my people, yet everyone present, Gael and foreign slave alike, seemed to understand him perfectly. Silence fell instantaneously. He nodded, pleased. He lowered his arms and handed his staff to me. I often think now that when I accepted it from him I should have felt some sort of shock of recognition. The wood should have soothed my palms. Its contact with my flesh should have been a balm to my heart. But there was no reaction from me. No sense of precognition.

He directed his attention fully to those assembled before him. Again he raised his arms. His head turned up to the night as he cried out the ancient psalm. He did not chant it. He did not make of it a grim mumbling. He lifted his voice in joyous song, in an alleluia.

"Create clean hearts within us, O God,
    and a steadfast spirit renew within us.
Cast us not out from your presence,
    and your holy spirit take not from us."

He spoke The Creed then, as it was spoken then, as it is spoken now, as it shall be spoken until the end of Man's reign upon the earth; the profession of Christian faith; the pure and wondrous statement of doctrine and salvation. And as he spoke, so did we speak; out of one heart in Christ; in one tongue; in one lasting and eternal knowledge of fellowship.

"We believe in one God, the Father Almighty,
    Maker of heaven and earth,
And of all things visible and invisible.

And in one Lord Jesus Christ,
The only begotten Son of God,
Begotten of his Father before all worlds:
God of God, Light of Light,
Very God of very God,
Begotten not made,
Being of one substance with the Father,
By whom all things were made . . ."

The words flowed from us as a spring is born up pure and innocent out of the earth. When at last we said "Amen," the Sacred Mysteries were celebrated. The Body of Christ was broken out of the small loaves which the women had secretly made and brought with them. The Blood was poured from a new flask into a wooden chalice, carved by a woodsman, and never before stained by any save the consecrated wine of this night. As had been commanded by the Son of Man five hundred years before any of us had been born, we shared the Body

he first. You must promise that
i again."
le."
ercia. And your immortal soul."

you slain. She has already plotted
in a conspiracy of treason against

p. Fear paled her features. Then,
d tranquillity, she said: "God's will

"
with weary eyes. "Is it not?"

smiled. "Why, Magonus? Because you

d walked away from me then. I stood
, angered and frustrated and battered by
lequacies of my youth. Memories of vio-
and human degradation caused me to
e dead of my family's villa. I remembered
Mercia and the weight of Dubh's body
eath within my arms. I saw the years and
d the endless hours of my captivity, and,
a voice soured by confusion, I exhaled the
ich Man has asked of infinity since the first
his comprehension of the world.

instant, as when a man imagines that he sees
ping within the heart of flames, I thought I
vhat? . . . a great and brooding plain . . . and a
wn into the image of Man . . . a stone that
it into the night . . . and then . . . nothing . . .
ss . . . and a voice, softly mocking: "Tell me,
u came to Eire, was there a storm upon the sea?"
raic . . . !" Umall the cook took me roughly by
n. "We must return to the rath. Now. Look, the
re falling toward dawn!"

ep evaded me. I lay upon my pallet, eyes closed
ng for first light. Then, finally, I slept. Dreams cam
e. Of Mercia. Of Victoricus. Of the flame and c
shattered stone and of the twisted corpse which ha
been a living tree. I dreamt of the Rigan, and i

and the Blood of Christ and embraced one another in silent communion with Him beneath the witness of God's Heaven. In the place where the gods of Eire had once been worshiped, the God of my fathers touched the Gael. He filled us all with a knowledge of His presence. He filled us all with the wonder and the promise of His love.

As they had come, in groups of two and three, so they filtered away into the night to return to their homes across the far hills and within the distant valleys. Darerca was with them, accompanied by her twin brothers and her tiny son. My heart leaped when I saw her, but as I started toward her, warning flashed in her eyes and she turned her face tightly down against her chin. As she hurried away into the night, pretending not to know me, I was perplexed and offended.

Victoricus came close to me. "The hour grows late. The time has not yet come when Eire may worship the Lord beneath the light of day."

I stared off after Darerca and the twins, lost in memories of Yesterday.

"It is best for us to keep our anonymity for the present," he said.

"When will you come to us again?" Mercia asked him.

He shook his head. "There are many souls dwelling upon this island. Many have not yet heard the Word. There are those who would be baptized. There are many who would confess their sins and share in Holy Communion with Christ. I must go to them."

MacCairthinn had come to tower over us. "But there's great danger to you," he warned darkly. "There are many wolves dwelling upon the hills of Eire . . . wolves who walk upon two legs and carry daggers at their belts . . . thieves and druids who would happily offer you up as living sacrifice to the gods of greed and darkness."

"I have come many a long mile, good MacCairthinn," assured Victoricus. "I have learned to watch for wolves."

The giant's worry was not eased. "I will go with you. I will be your strong man," he volunteered.

"You?" Umall the cook was aghast. "As inconspicuous as a horse in the soup pot! With such as you clomping along behind him, sure he would be captured. And wouldn't the druids slaver at the chance to accuse a Christian of treason against the Ris of Eire!"

The words brought me out of my reverie. I cast a surreptitious glance at Mercia. Her face was serene. She had no knowledge of the Rigan's wish to see her dead.

"I do not fear the Ris of Eire," insisted MacCairthinn. "Christ is with me. As a boy I walked these hills and hunted them, until there is not a shadow beneath any phase of the moon which is a stranger to me." From his great height, he dropped to one knee and bent his head before Victoricus. "Allow me to serve my Lord God through you. Allow me to be your champion . . . and His."

Victoricus bade the giant rise. "In time, MacCairthinn, another will walk these hills in the name of Christ. You must wait for him. You will know him when he comes. You shall be his champion and God shall shield you both from harm, for His name's sake. For now, remain here as a witness for Christ. As for me, good brother, you need not fear for my life. God is with me. I am with God."

He had spoken prophecy. We heard it and knew it not.

He turned to me then. He studied me for a moment, then reached out and laid both of his hands, palms down, upon my shoulders. "The Way has been difficult for you. So shall it continue to be. But God is with you. Never doubt Him. Follow your dreams and we shall meet again. I promise you that."

He allowed me no time to pursue his words with questions. I had held his staff for him during the celebration of the Mass. He took it from me now. It was nearly as tall as he, as gnarled with age as he was straight in his apparent youth.

"You must go now," he advised," casting a knowing glance at the sky. "The hour grows late."

We left him alone beneath the great and twisted tree. We followed MacCairthinn into the night, walking downhill as quickly as we dared. I took Mercia's arm and fell into step beside her. She sensed my need to speak with her and paused.

"Once," I said, "at the base of the steps leading to the grianan, you warned me to beware of the Rigan." She could not have misunderstood the urgency of my tone. "Now I must warn you. You must not go to the Ri again."

She tensed. "I am not free to ignore his command."

"Feign illness."

"I cannot."

"You must promise
you shall not go to the R
"You ask the impossi
"You risk your life, N
"Perhaps."
"The Rigan will hav
to involve your name
the Ri."

Her head went
slowly, with straine
be done."
"It is not His wil
She measured m
"It cannot be."
She sighed and
say so?"
She turned a
staring after her
the obvious ina
lence and pai
shiver. I saw t
the rape of
slumped in d
the miles an
suddenly, in
question wh
dawning of
"Why?"
For an
images le
saw . . .
stone, h
wailed o
brightne
when y
"Pa
the ar
stars a

Sl
wait
to n
the
on

s
w
bot

"
preci

The
ness to
as well
gin of Cl
as a whore

She twist
was not Go
which you w
long ago when

Her words s
Mercia, you mus

"Free will?" H
tempt to control he
advice for those w
either of us, servan
free will? By sweet
ask to become what I
the mocking turn of Fa
the man who is my mast

Her admission stunned

My naiveté touched he
Magonus. Those who have

A dark, fleeting image o
behind my eyes. I saw his do
eyes, the glass beads shining
pieces of congealed blood. "He
her.

"As were you once. Have you f
"Long ago. In another world."

"Yes," she assented, with a gentle
tone. "But this is another world for
do not pretend to understand it. Or my

The others, already far ahead of us,
Cairthinn's arm go up as indication tha
hurry and follow him.

"We must go," said Mercia.

my dream I said to her: "Why will you not find comfort in the teaching of my Lord? Why will you not listen to me?"

And in the dream she spoke to me, not with her voice but with the voice of the druid: "I cannot listen. I must follow the road. As it was laid for us both . . . long before we were ever born . . ."

It seemed to me that we stood together, the Rigan and I, high on a battlement. We faced out over a dark sea. A wind rose around us. I reached out to hold the Rigan safe against me, but she disdained my help and gave herself freely to the wind. In horror, I watched as she was swept away. I called her name but there was no answer. There was only the wind and the dark sea and the rising violence of a storm. Far below me, I saw a ship fighting for its life upon the sea. And far off through the darkness, there was a tiny light . . . small and trembling . . . like the flame which Leborchom and I had kindled so long ago upon the Mountain of Mists.

Holy youth . . .
   Holy youth . . .
Voices called to me within the fiber of my dreams. Yet surely, I thought, they could not be calling to me. Was there ever a less holy youth than I?

Yet they called. Accused. Flailed.

Holy youth . . .
   Holy youth . . .
Pa-trec . . .
   Pa-trec . . .
"Padraic! Up with you, lad! Wake up now!" Bruthne was shaking me.

I awoke in a daze. The kennel doors had been flung wide. Dawn lay gray upon the earth, misty and cold. Birdsong was trapped within the clouds. It echoed hollowly.

"Up with you now," commanded Bruthne. "Today we run the hounds before the Red Ri Sencha."

15

I did not see the gold. I did not see the scarlet. I did not see the running out of vermilion rivers upon serrated plates of bronze. I did not see the leaves of the late-summer forest, leaves already burnished by the promise of their impending deaths. I did not see the yellowed, brittled grasses or the bracken tipped with rust. I saw only the mist. The world around me was silent, hushed by the clouds which lay upon the earth.

The regal hunting party moved slowly, as silently as it is possible for men and beasts to move. Now and again I heard the hushed voice of a man, the slobbering suck of a hound's breath as it strained against its tether. Then Bruthne's voice, the barest scrape of a whisper: "Hold!"

The great stag stood directly before us. Sleek, heavy-bellied with summer's browse, he lifted his antlered head and drew in the taste of the air through his black, wet nostrils. When at last he broke, he acted upon the instinct which had served him well for many seasons of life. He leaped away from us in an explosion of power.

"Now!" My own voice. A shout. A command. "Release the coursers!"

The five hounds shot forward as living arrows. They held their heads high, sighting, not scenting their prey. They did not swerve. They did not falter. Draigenn had failed in his ill-fated attempt to ruin them for the hunt. The months of careful, patient training now showed their reward.

The stag was taken. The hunting horns bayed out like triumphant wolves. Blood poured out upon the earth. Hot. Red. Did the stag cry out as Death ran to meet him? It seemed to me that he did, that he screamed with outrage and terror when his throat was opened and his belly was ripped. Or was it my own cry? Was it a reflection within me of his agony? It is said that dogs become an extension of the hunter. And I, as trainer and hunter, might well have momentarily been assaulted by my soul reminding me of the inevitability of my own death as the dogs brought down the stag. For is this not the instinct which drives a man to the kill? Does he not wish to triumph, no matter how briefly, over the forces which control his destiny? As the world will someday claim him, so will he also claim the creatures of the world at his whim and will. It is a demonstration of his power, of his strength, of his fearlessness. It is his statement of indomitability to a world in which, but for the grace of God, nothing is indomitable save the merciless, passionless onslaught of Time.

I shivered and sweated as I worked with Bruthne to tether the dogs. When we were done, the master houndsman handed his splaying knife to me. I looked at him, overcome by the honor which he paid me through this gesture. He had acknowledged, before the Ri, before Sencha and all of the assembled hunters, that I had been the master of the pack.

Shaking with the elation of the kill, I bowed my head and accepted the knife. As custom demanded, I knelt before the Ri and, with the blade lain out across my palm, I offered it up to my king.

His spear had finished the stag. He stood before me, still wiping the dark blood from his finely worked weapon.

"The kill is yours, Miliucc MacBuain," I acknowledged.

He smiled. Not at me. At Sencha. The challenge had been met and won. He had worked many hours to assure it. Now he would savor his victory. "I will grant to Sencha the portions of honor," he said, "for were it not for his generous gift, surely the kill would not have been possible." His statement had been a haughty and obvious parody of humility.

Sencha roared. Laughter came easily to him. The sound was slightly soured by an unexpected defeat, but it was good-natured enough. Sencha, at least superficially, knew how to lose graciously. "Your houndsmen are sorcerers!" he proclaimed jovially. "Is there a man present who does not know that no mere mortal could make meat out of the gruel which I sent to you disguised as hounds? I tell you, many a time I swore to my flaiths: If Miliucc can make those curs run in pack, I'll grant he'll be the finest houndsman in all Eire." He threw out his arms in all-encompassing admittance of defeat. "By the gods, the challenge has been well met. I acknowledge your victory, Miliucc."

"Not mine alone, old friend. Rise up, Padraic. Allow

Sencha to see the sorcerer who has worked with me to make this day's kill possible."

I stood and forthrightly met Sencha's approving gaze. He was a massive man. Not tall, but wide, with a swelling musculature which surged restlessly over his bones like the twitching flesh of an ill-serviced bull. He wore an armored tunic, seven oxhides thick. It had been pounded and polished until it shone like metal. His leine was a flaming red, as were his trews. His multicolored short hunting brat was a cape all embroidered with designs depicting a hunting scene. It was held in place by a gaudy brooch which sagged of its own weight. His hair, though meticulously coifed at the outset of the hunt, had become disarranged. It stood out away from his corpulent, flushed face like spikes of starched fire. It was not unusual for Gaelic lords to tint their hair so that they might achieve the golden tresses which were the Gaelic ideal. But Sencha's mane had suffered for his vanity. The limewater rinses had made the natural red shafts of his hair brittle and dry. They no longer held the dyes well. As I looked at him, I saw a lord with hair three distinct colors: bright red at the roots, orange for the main portion, and yellow at the tips.

He fixed me with eyes which were so deep a green as to be almost black, with flecks of yellow in them like fish droppings floating in turgid harbor waters. "What will you have for the lad?" he asked Miliucc.

I almost choked.

"I am not free to sell him," replied the Ri. "He was purchased by the Rigan."

"Then, I shall make an offer to her."

"I doubt if she will part with the youth."

Sencha raised his head, chin out, brows arched. "Then, I shall buy the queen and have the lad in the bargain!" He laughed. A blatant, thoroughly unroyal snort. Could he have failed to see the anger spark within Miliucc's eyes? Perhaps. He was a back-slapping, cocksure lout of a man, sensual and filled with gutter humor to the core. Yet there was an open-faced sincerity about him which made him likable despite his garrulous crudeness. He walked to Milucc and embraced him. "Wine!" he demanded of his host. "I must raise a toast of concession to the victor!"

The wine was brought forth. It was drunk. The Red Ri

Sencha lifted his voice and led us all in a rousing hunting song which rapidly deteriorated, under his enthusiastic direction, into a lilting, lecherous rhyme concerning wandering warriors and nubile female forest spirits dallying amidst the sheltering woodlands. His imagination knew no bounds. His sense of humor was as prodigious as it was lewd. The men shouted their approval. Only the Ri Miliucc MacBuain seemed tense and strained. He joined in the song, lest he offend the visiting Ri. Yet anger lived within his eyes: heavy, restless, ill at ease within its dark constraints.

Though the victory was in truth partly mine, I did not expect to be called to join in the victor's celebration. I had returned to the kennel and was bathing when the invitation came from the great hall.

Bruthne was astounded. "A great honor is being given you, lad. Without doubt, the Ri will ask you to chose a reward for yourself. Name your heart's desire . . . your freedom . . . and it shall surely be yours."

Freedom! Even as the word soared within me, I began to shiver within the tepid, soapy water of my bath. The heated warming stones had cooled, as had my momentary sense of release. Freedom! For this I had dreamed and prayed for nearly four long years. Yet memory jabbed me. Prodded me. Freedom might well be potentially mine. But could I take it now?

I rose from the oaken tub, my mind boiling, my body shivering. Bruthne splashed a bucket of clean, cool water on me. I trembled violently as he handed me a drying blanket. I wrapped myself within it and began to absently rub moisture from my skin. My eyes were burning. Not from a residue of soap. With tears. Within my mouth, the hot, sour saliva of fear began to swell and thicken.

Bruthne was staring at me, curious and confused by the grim and resolute expression of desolation which must have been evident upon my face. "What is it, Padraic? Is this not the moment for which you have hoped?"

"It is."

"Then why so glum? Or can you not bear the thought of parting company with me?"

He rarely jested. He stood before me, grinning widely beneath his mask, waiting for my comment.

I gave him none. Instead, I asked thoughtfully: "By law must he grant any request I might make of him?"

He shrugged. "If it be your heart's desire, providing that it is within the province of reason."

I nodded, numb to my very soul. "Then I shall ask the Ri to grant the release from bondage of the woman who is called Mercia."

"His mistress?"

"Her life is in danger here. I will ask for her freedom . . . and for my own, so that I may see her safely home to Briton."

He withdrew from me as though I had breathed the specter of plague upon him. "By all the gods of Eire . . . it is true what they say of you Christians . . . you are mad!"

It was a royal celebration. The Ri Miliucc MacBuain had set the glory of his court before the eyes of Sencha. There was music. There were lampooners and jesters. Corpre and his seanachies were there to recount the sagas, in a more ribald and explicitly violent manner than usual, for this was a gathering of hunters and warriors. There were no women present, save for the slave women who circulated with platters of food and refilled the containers of ale and imported wines.

I was brought into the great hall and introduced formally to the assembled flaiths. They drunkenly cheered me for my work with the hounds. Sencha raised a toast to me. I was given a seat at the far end of the table, beside a flaith of minimal rank. My presence obviously offended him, though he dared not protest to the Ri. My attempts to converse with him were met with disdain. Whenever he felt the need to belch, he deliberately leaned close to me and did so in my face. I did not complain. I was given food and drink and tried to ignore the humiliations to which the serving women were subjected. I watched the Ri and thought: When he is ready he shall call me forth. May it be God's will that, before the night is done, I shall be a free man with Mercia beside me.

The night went on. I was too apprehensive to eat. I drank instead, to quell my fears and bolster my courage.

Hours passed. The Ri forgot me.

The flaith beside me passed into a drunken stupor. The harper fell asleep and slumped over his instrument. All along the great table, the lords bent their heads and snored into their armpits.

Only Miliucc and Sencha remained fully awake. Now and again they called upon a serving maid to refresh them with bowls of chilled water into which they would plunge their hands and wrists so that their blood would be cooled and spark the ice of wakefulness into their veins. Towels were brought, wet and cold, with which they wiped their faces and necks. It was an extension of the continuing game of challenge which they played with one another. The victor would be the last to succumb to slumber. Sencha's champion and his five grown sons, nodding and blinking in warm, drunken satisfaction, made periodic attempts to stay awake so that they might monitor the game and bring no dishonor to themselves in the eyes of their lord and sire.

What followed was inevitable. I know that now. Yet it does not erase the horror of it. Wine and ale, working together upon a proud man's mind, can become a bitter and dangerously antagonistic venom.

Sencha burped into his beard and proclaimed with a slurred tongue: "I meant what I proposed in the wood. I will have the young houndsman. Name your price. I shall pay it gladly. And Cairenn will offer no restraint once she knows who has taken the lad."

"Will she not?" Miliucc had grown pensive. He was scowling into his chalice. "Cairenn is happiest when offering restraints. Besides, I have other plans for the boy."

Sencha wiped his mouth with the back of his hand. "Restraints to you. Promises to me. That brings us to it. Aye. And squarely." He drew in a breath and nodded, smacking his lips. "Name your price. For the lad and for your queen."

Miliucc looked up, not certain that he had heard the other correctly. "What . . . ?"

"For your queen, man! All of Dalaradia knows that she does not yet share your bed. By the gods, Miliucc, if you cannot use her, let at least a friend . . . a brother-in-law . . . find pleasure in her before she withers and grows old from neglect."

Miliucc stared.

Sencha went on, pointedly, in a friendly manner. "We are old friends, you and I. We shared our youth in the Boys' House and came to take valor together. But be reasonable, Miliucc. Is this mistress of yours merely an ornament to protect the image of your manhood? The girl has yet to conceive, and the Rigan has yet to be shafted. And I shall make no more pretense, to dishonor either of us. I desire your wife, lord. Aye. I would have her."

Miliucc had drunk much. Too much. Yet the words had come close to sobering him, as they did me, instantly.

Sencha belched and wiped his mouth again. "Surely, old friend, you are a warrior and proven in the field . . . but you would be the first to agree that a man without sons in unfulfilled, and that a man without issue at all . . . well . . . there must be doubt that he is a man. And Cairenn . . . the thought of her virgin still . . . god, man, my loins grow hard when I think of it. And the Rigan, she has looked at me and encouraged my desire. Aye. Make no mistake about that."

Softly, like a poisoned mist, the words had seeped through the webs and fogs of those who drowsed and snored upon the tables. One by one, heads began to go up, bleary-eyed but curious. They were like so many dull-witted, drowsy sharks swimming surely and steadily, guided by an awakening, instinctive voraciousness toward a distant and only vaguely defined prey.

Miliucc did not speak. He did not look at Sencha. He stared down at his hands. Beside him, Sencha's oldest son had gone as taut as a man in pain.

"My father is drunk," he said to the Ri. The words were not an apology, merely a cautious reminder of fact.

"We are all drunk," observed Sencha.

"Aye," agreed the son. "But, my father, perhaps your tongue grows injudicious?"

"Bah!" declared Sencha. "Miliucc and I need not sheathe our words or our intentions! Now, old friend," he leaned close to Miliucc and smiled the confident smile of an experienced tradesman. "Why keep a mount if you do not intend to ride it? If the fair Cairenn were mine, there would be a son for each year, and milk in her sweet breasts enough for them and me to suckle."

The silence which descended then was the silence which pursues the dead into their graves. There was not a flaith at table who was not fully awake.

I saw the color ebb from Miliucc's lips even as the darkness deepened within his eyes. He did not move. He said, concisely and with complete control: "Your potency has proven but one truth of you, Sencha—that the issue of your seed is from the testes of a pig . . . for a pig you are, my lord, a blundering, stupid, graciousless pig."

Sencha's eyes went as round as fish eggs. If his dry, brittle hair had not already been standing out as though starched, it would have done so now. His five sons muttered their outrage. Sencha waved them to silence as he rose to his feet and flung his chalice to the floor. "I would rather have it said of me that I was a boar, than have it implied that I was a gelded stallion! But then, there need be no further implications made, if you would allow us to ask your queen if she be virgin still."

The vein of anger had risen along Miliucc's right temple.

"Call her into the hall!" demanded Sencha. "Let her choose between us!"

Miliucc's hand closed about the stem of his chalice. I saw his fingers tighten about the silver, saw the blood running out of them and the flesh whitening. "I do not bring my Rigan into the presence of swine," he said evenly.

Sencha's eldest son's eyes, like his father's, had gone enormously round. His youth and rage blazed out at Miliucc. He snapped to his feet to stand beside his sire. "Swine are we? We have laid aside our arms, Miliucc MacBuain. Let us put them on again, and you yours, and we shall see who shall run off into dishonor squealing!"

"I do not do battle with swine," replied Miliucc. "It is my custom to slaughter them."

I was suddenly aware of the fact that Mliucc's guardsmen had placed themselves around the room, shields up, spears crossed before their chests. A command had been given. Somehow I had missed it.

Sencha and his sons whirled around to see the armed men. Other than Sencha's champion, the Red Ri had brought none of his own guardsmen into the hall. The red-haired lord took in the scene and swung his head back around to face Miliucc.

"What is this treachery?" He was sober now. He shook his head to clear it of any fuzz of alcohol which might remain. "A battle is it? Is that what you want? A battle man to man, if you are a man. The Rigan Cairenn shall be the prize. We shall wave the right of Truth of Combat, for, by the gods, I cannot wait the five days required by law before I fight you!"

I looked up toward the grianan. It was built in such a way that the queen and her ladies might, if they wished, look down into the great hall without having to venture from their woman's domain. I wondered if the Rigan watched, if she cringed in terror and dismay, for surely she must know that she was the cause of this.

Two armed men had come to stand beside each of Sencha's sons and his champion. Their faces were tense with the assurance and resolution of men who are ready to kill at a moment's notice.

"Escort the piglets to their quarters while I deal wiith the boar," commanded Miliucc. "And set a guard to any of Sencha's people who are outside of the hall."

The sons of the Red Ri, young men all, made to resist. There was a brief scuffle. The Red Ri's champion lifted up a carving knife only to have his own arm sliced with it. Overpowered, he and the sons of Sencha were escorted forcefully out of the hall.

Their father watched them go. He was breathing nervously, pulling in noisy snorts of temper. There was a new expression on his face now. It had replaced the flaring of his anger. It was fear. It was confusion. He glared at Miliucc. "A battle then, Miliucc MacBuain. Man to man. Leave my sons out of it, since you have none of your own to stand beside you."

He was not a wise man, this Sencha. He was a passionate savage who fancied himself cunning. He was completely insensitive to the motivations of men wiser and more intelligent than he. He had made a fatal error in judgment. He had seen, correctly, that Miliucc MacBuain was no impulsive barbarian. But he had failed to recognize in the calm, dark handsomeness of the Pict the arrogance of the Gaelic race, the pride of them, the passion of them, and the potential of murder done for just cause within them. He saw all that now, saw it clearly in the black, steady hatred which he had caused to swell within Miliucc's eyes.

I looked at my master and was appalled by the sight of him. A strained, quivering smile twitched at the corners of his lips. "A battle man to man?" He twisted Sencha's words into a question. "But you have impugned that I am not a man. Here. At my table. Drinking my ale. Enjoying the full hospitality of my tuath, you, pig that your are, openly lust after my queen, insult her virtue, and raise question of my manhood." He rose to his feet. "Well . . ." he said, thinking as he spoke, staining the words with the acid of sarcasm, "if I am not a man, Sencha, then we cannot do battle man to man, can we? And if you are a pig, which I assert, you are not worthy of doing battle with a man. But then, you say that you are not a pig . . . you say that you are a boar and that I am a gelded stallion. Perhaps we should make the contest equal in your eyes?"

A roar went up in the hall as the assembly realized his intent. They lifted Sencha up. He cried out in protest and terror as his small mind began to fasten upon the knowledge of what was about to happen to him.

I had never seen bold lust rise within men until that moment. It came on a tide of laughter and resounding shouts of approval. Sencha was clouted and pounded until he lay splayed upon the table before Miliucc. They jerked his trews down about his thighs, exposing the source of his legendary fertility. How pale and flaccid it seemed as they held up a torch so that they might better observe it.

Corpre, shaking violently, had come to stand beside the Ri. "The law!" he reminded desperately. "Do not act without the brehons, my lord. The man has a fool's tongue and a dullard's wit, but the brehons must decide punishment for his offense. The brehons, my lord! They alone must judge him and decide his fate!"

"I am Ri! I need no brehons here!"

Corpre stood back from the specter of vengeance which Miliucc presented to him. "The law, my lord . . . do not disdain the law . . ."

The filidh was pushed aside. I watched in horror as Miliucc drew his dagger. I saw the cold, dull shine of the blade. Then the knife was brought down. Like wine being squirted out of a bladder, there was blood pulsing upward from the place where the Ri Sencha's virility had been. I heard his scream: short, staccato, a pathetic snort of agony, a moan of incredulity. I heard the rising crescendo of triumphant laughter rise in the hall as the Ri Miliucc MacBuain lifted his trophy high, impaled upon the blade.

"Staunch the neuter's wound so that he may live to grow fat and complacent. We wish him no ill in this hall."

I saw a flaith go to the fire and bring forth a brand. I stood and watched as the white-hot metal came down onto Sencha's mutilation. His body made one great leap of agony upon the table and then lay still. The scent of charred flesh and blood and hair rose into the air.

I could stay in the hall no longer. I ran out into the night. In the darkness, leaning against the wall of the great house, I tried desperately not to be sick. A cold sweat stood out on my brow.

God forgive them, I thought, for they know not Your Word or Your promise.

Taking in deep draughts of the night air, at last I felt strong enough to make my way back across the compound to the kennel. The laughter of the Ri's men resounded in the darkness. I could see that, outside each of the guest houses which sheltered Sencha's people, armed guardsmen were stationed with weapons drawn. From one of the houses, I heard a man's voice raised in protest.

"Miliucc MacBuain will regret this day! By the laws of Eire, there will be war against his house!"

It was then that I heard the sound of a woman's laughter. I turned toward it and found myself staring up toward the lighted windows of the grianan. I could see the figure of a woman, a small, slender woman, etched against the light. Her head was tilted back. I think I knew, even before I walked forward so that I might identify the silhouette, that the laughter came from the throat of a sadist, from the throat of one who I had once loved and cherished. It was the laughter of the Rigan Cairenn.

Once again, as on that day so long ago when I had flung myself into my parents room to discover the raiders, I did not think about what I should do. I ran back to the hall. There were no guardsmen at the doors. They had dispersed within the hall to congratulate their Ri. I went straight up the steps to the grianan. I pushed aside the protesting serving maid as I kicked open the door, entered, and stood glaring at the Rigan.

"Do you know what you have done?" I demanded.

She was startled by the slamming of the door and by the burning hostility within my eyes. She measured me quickly, defensively. Her face assumed the expression of innocence personified. Her hands folded across her breasts. "What I have done?"

"A man has been destroyed!"

"Sencha?" Her hands went out, a light fluttering upward of wrist and fingers to inform me that she considered the matter to be of little importance. "Étain shall be spared further pregnancies." She allowed a smile to come slowly, with full satisfaction. "And Miliucc shall have his wish: Sencha will cease his attentions toward me."

"Do you think that it will stop there? What of the man's sons? His guardsmen? His champion? The members of his court. Do you honestly believe that they will allow the castration of their lord to go unchallenged?"

"Of course not. But their anger, be it justified or not, is of no concern. By dawn they shall all be slain." She went to the mirror. She turned toward it, away from me, and began to smooth her hair. "Now go away, Padraic. Your manner and your naiveté distress me."

The anger which boiled within me was as foul and as hot as vomit. I would not be dismissed as a slave. I went to her. I put my hands upon her shoulders and turned her forcefully toward me.

"There will be war," I said. "Sencha has allies, friends. The living members of his clan will not allow this night to be forgotten. In the name of Christ, I cannot believe that you want this to happen. In the name of Christ, you must stop it!"

"I cannot stop it. It is done."

I must have hurt her with my grip, for her face spasmed as she realized that I was no longer the adoring cur who could be dismissed as easily as a cosseted pet. "Release me." Her command was unstable. I felt pleasure in the knowledge that she was frightened.

In my anger, I had forgotten the serving maid. She had entered the room and had come to her mistress's aid. Pummeling at my back and shoulders with her fists, she screamed at me. Then, without warning, I felt a sharp, thin pain burn upward beneath my ribs. I gasped as I realized that I had been stabbed—and thoroughly. I released the queen and whirled around to wrest a small knife from the hand of the maid. She sobbed and collapsed into a whimpering heap upon the floor.

I was shaking uncontrollably as I fought to control my rage. Along my side, blood began to well at an alarming rate out of the wound the maid had inflicted upon me. I stared at it, then at the Rigan.

She was afraid of me. I could see that. Yet she was Rigan and would not easily yield her command of the moment to me. The blue of her eyes was astounding. Deep. Treacherous. A riptide of emotion ran out of them, surging to form a raging comber which poised to crash upon me out of an alien and totally hostile sea. "You are a dead man . . ." she promised.

"No. Not until I warn the Ri. Not until I inform him of what you have brought upon his house. Someone must speak truth to him. You are his enemy, not his wife. By the name of merciful God, I will not stand by and allow him to compound his sin by working murder upon innocent people. There will be no killing this night . . . not at your whim or for your pleasure . . . on poor dead Draigenn's name, I promise you that."

She was like a serpent then, drawing back from me, neck rigid, nostrils flaring. "So you know . . ."

"And so the Ri shall soon know . . . of your duplicity . . ."

She released a sigh which seemed to have escaped from her very soul. "Miliucc will hear no words against me. He will not listen to you . . . not to any man . . . so speak against me and speak treason . . . speak treason and forfeit your life."

I was suddenly hot. Then cold. Then hot again and suddenly sweating as though I stood before a furnace. My body was ice. Melting. My hand went to my side. Pain lived there, welled red against my palm. I llifted my bloodied palm and stared at it, only half-believing. How bright the room had grown. Intolerably bright. I felt confined, entombed. I must escape it.

"I must go to the Ri . . ." I began to move toward the door.

"Go, then," she prodded, contemptuously. "But I shall have my men upon you before you are halfway across the courtyard. I will have your life, Padraic, as penalty for your misguided loyalty."

How far away the door seemed. I reached out and stumbled toward it.

The Rigan laughed at me. "Do you truly believe that Miliucc would listen to you? You, a slave? When he has repeatedly spurned the advice and the warnings of Néladóir?"

"Néladóir . . ." Even as I spoke his name, I knew what I must do.

His quarters were at the far end of the compound. I knew that I would find him there. Since the night of his confrontation with me in the great hall, he had not left the walls of his own sanctuary. Bruthne had warned me to beware of him, had suggested that he had drawn inward into his own realm of magic potions and incantations. I saw no reason to fear him. Had we not shared a vision? For my sake, and for the sake of the Ri, Néladóir and I must work together.

Another man of equal rank and reputation might have commanded his own lands outside of the ring fort, a minor tuath with guardsmen and slaves to serve him. Yet Néladóir had chosen to remain close to the Ri. I thanked God for this as I made my way across the compound and through the orchard toward his house.

There was a fever upon the guardsmen. With flushed faces and voices strained with tension, they moved in groups of four across the compound, arresting and manacling any of Sencha's people who were not within their allotted quarters. I avoided them, moving within the shadows, fearing that the Rigan would have already put out a command requesting my seizure and immediate imprisonment or death.

I had lost much blood. My growing weakness frightened me. Each step took acute concentration to complete. Clutching the dagger with which the serving maid had stabbed me, I moved forward, fighting the growing desire to simply stop and lie down upon the cool earth. When at last I reached the druid's house, I did not knock against the door. I fell against it. It was not latched. It swung open as I staggered inside.

Néladóir, asleep upon his couch, started up. I must have reflected the violence of the past hour, for he was on his feet in an instant. He would have lighted a lamp, but I signed for him to stop as I reached back and weakly closed the door behind me. I tried to speak. I could not. Slipping the dagger into my belt, I pressed my hand against my wound. The cloth which lay over it was warm and wet with welling blood. Slowly, against my will, I slumped to the floor.

He came to me out of the darkness. With deft fingers

he probed the place of my injury. I winced. The pain put
an edge of coherency onto my tongue.

"I must warn the Ri . . . before God and before the
laws which rule your island with at least a semblance of
justice . . . he was drunk . . . drunken men often act
rashly . . . cruelly . . . perhaps the brehons would not
judge him harshly for, in truth, Sencha provoked him . . .
but it must stop now . . . before murder is worked upon
innocent men. War must not come to the land . . . not at
her whim . . ."

I was breathing heavily. A veil of sleepiness was descending over my thoughts. I licked my lips. They were
dry and feverish. I shook my head and told the druid
what he must hear: of the happenings within the great
hall, of the Rigan's intended treachery against the Ri
through Draigenn and the hounds. The words spilled out
of me. Jumbled. Broken.

"Why do you come to me with this?" he asked.

"Because the Power did not deceive you when you saw
that Death would wear a woman's mantle within this
house. I do not understand my place within your visions,
Néladóir, but I do know that I am too weak to reach the
Ri without you. And the Rigan no doubt has set her
guardsmen to silence me against her. With you beside me,
they dare not touch me. The Ri must be warned. He must
be stopped."

His fingers probed at my side. I had to strain to keep
from crying out.

He exhaled a bitter sigh. "Miliucc will hear no words
against her."

"But he must! At best, the woman is mad. Surely he
cannot love her so much that he will allow her to blind
him against her deceptions?"

"Love?" The word turned to acid on the druid's tongue.
"Miliucc does not love the Rigan. It is the serving maid
who has his heart these days. But Cairenn . . . she is a
thorn caught within the fiber of his manhood. Like the
hounds of Sencha, she is a challenge which must be met
and won. For the sake of his pride." He drew in a breath
of disgust and released it through clenched teeth. "Pride.
It has been the drowning stone of many a good man. My
brother shall be no exception."

"Brother . . . ?"

"Not of the same womb. But of the same seed. Long

ago our father, a man with the Inner Vision, gave us both the druid's ring. Yet Miliucc will not acknowledge prophecy. He defies the stars and the Power. But tonight the great wave of Destiny has swept us up and, by the Power which is mine, I will do what must be done . . . what should have been done when first he defied me and took Cairenn to be his bride."

His eyes burned with purpose. He stared into the darkness, searing it with the passion of his resolve. Then he left me for a moment. I could hear him moving within the depths of the house. When he returned, he held a cup to my lips. "Drink this. It will ease your pain."

He should not have looked at me. He had forgotten his own warning: "Those who have the Power recognize it in others." I met his eyes. I saw the grayness of them—the bleak, boiling distances of cloud. The somber pigment reflected out to me all that he sought to accomplish. I caught my breath with amazement and horror. I had been a fool to trust him. I had been a lamb seeking shelter within the jaws of a wolf. He would not help me to reach the Ri. Instead, he would make of me a corpse upon which he would heap his guilt. I saw it all clearly, as images moving in miniature within his misted eyes. I saw myself lying dead. I saw the druid ascending the steps of grianan. With the dagger which he had taken from me, I saw him confront the Rigan. I saw her eyes. Those wondrous eyes, as blue as snow-shadow on a sunlit day. I saw the tiny imperfection, the miniscule clot of blood which marred the white of her right eye, suddenly explode and spurt forth blood. It welled with the druid's eye, drowning the vision in a floor of red.

I must have screamed. Néladóir's hand came down in a slap across my lips. "Young lad of vision, what you have seen with the Inner Sight shall be a curse upon us both. Yet it must be done. And done quickly. To save my brother from the agony of a greater vision, one which I have not shared with you."

I had barely enough strength to snap my head hard to the left, freeing my lips from his smothering palm. "There will be war."

The words were no threat to him. His fingers were like sharpened bone against my neck. "War is no stranger to the Gael, young lad, nor is it always an unwelcome adversary. The Rigan must be slain. If she is not, in her madness she will destroy the Ri. So it has been prophesied. What I will do, I do for my brother."

"But he must know . . . he must not be allowed to slaughter Sencha's people . . . Cairenn is no longer the issue here . . . innocent men must not be killed to avenge a slur against her name . . ."

"The will of the gods shall be done. With us. Through us. Despite us."

Weariness rose in me, an unwelcome balm. "Have you forgotten the teachings of your own people, Néladóir? That a Ri must wear the mantle of truth and justice. Without it, the very earth shall rise up against him. The Ri must be told of Cairenn's duplicity . . . he must not . . . work . . . unlawful vengeance . . ." The words were flowing out of me quietly, as acquiescently as tidewaters flowing back to the sea. "God . . . help him . . ."

"And you, young lad. And you." Néladóir put the cup to my lips. "Drink," he commanded.

Death poured into my mouth. I had not the strength to resist it.

The killing was done. As dawn colored the horizon, Sencha was brought out to view the dead. They say that he did not speak. He had been stripped naked, with only a bloodied bandage to cover his mutilated loins. His wife and infant son, hostages now, were brought out to complete his humiliation. Yet they say that he stood firm. He did not flinch. His feet were bare upon the earth. He was led out of the ring fortress at the end of a tether looped to the hound's collar which had been placed about his neck. As he began the long walk back to his rath, they say that at first the people of the Ri Miliucc Mac-Buain mocked and jeered him. Then they fell silent. The Red Ri stood tall and resolute. Despite his pain and his nakedness, he walked like a lord, disdainful of those who had sought to bring him to his knees.

They say that Étain did not weep. She stood beside her brother on the outer rampart. "Allow me to go with my lord," she requested, holding her babe close within the fold of her cloak.

"You are free to go," he replied. "But the child remains as hostage. If Sencha attempts to bring retaliatory raids against us, the babe will be slain."

They say that she did not visibly react to her brother's

words. "You have misjudged a man," she said. "But the gods shall not fail to judge you for what you have done this day." She turned and left him then, neither asking nor receiving his permission to do so. He made no move to stop her.

The bodies were taken outside of the ring fortress to be burned. When the pyre was ready, the Ri grimly demanded that the Rigan Cairenn be brought to stand beside him so that she might witness that which had been done in defense of her name.

It was then that they found her body, with her serving maid and one of the house guards beside her. Clutched in the queen's hand, they found the brown cloak which she was known to have given to me. The druid came to them then, in fresh robes of white. He declared that he had just awakened from a dire dream concerning the Rigan and her Christian seanachie.

"It is Padraic who has slain our good and gracious lady!" he keened, eagerly leading the way as the search for me began.

How surprised and secretly vexed he must have been when they discovered naught but the stain of my blood and a pool of my vomit. He had failed in his attempt to kill me. After forcing me to drink his poisonous brew, he had dragged me out of his house and had left me to die within the shadows of the orchard. By the grace of God, I wretched up his sorcerer's brew. Moments later, I was found by the giant MacCairthinn. He carried me to the secret passageway. Mairead, the daughter of Umall the cook, was summoned to tend my wound. There, safe within the cool and sheltering earth, I fought for my life against the armies of fever and infection while the Ri's men searched for me within the rath, throughout the village, and across the hills. That night, under the cover of a moonless darkness, I was moved, unconscious, to safety within the granary of Ersa the miller.

When at last I awoke, I was lying behind a mountain of flour sacks. Darerca was beside me. I was too weak to speak or to drink the thin soup which she offered to me. I slept again. A full day must have passed. When I was again aware of my surroundings, the room was dark and sacks of flour seemed to give off a strange gray light of their own. Rodui was standing beside me, looking down.

"Is it true?" he asked me bluntly. "Did'ja kill the Rigan?"

The question caused me to sigh with a weariness which weighted me to my very soul. So the vision had come to pass. "Néladóir . . ."

"The druid?" He interrupted me with a frown.

I nodded my affirmation. "He slew the queen . . . for reasons which I only begin to understand . . ."

His face had grown stern and pale. "If there's a druid mixed into this pudding, it shall be of wicked leavening for all of us. You must find your strength quickly, Padraic. The village has been searched, but it might well be searched again. An edict has gone out. You are not to be killed on sight. You are to be brought before the Ri so that he may work justice upon you himself. Anyone caught offering refuge to you will forfeit both of his hands, all of his personal possessions, and his place within the tribe. Not a pleasant prospect, for either of us. So heal quickly now, old friend. I can't say that I savor the risk which your presence brings to us."

He left me. I lay quietly, listening to the soft scuttlings of mice, to the whispering sound of their gnawing and squeakings. There was sustenance for them here, and safety, but not for me. There was a bowl of thin gruel beside me, and soft cheese and a pitcher of milk. I ate slowly, knowing that I must draw strength from the food. Long before dawn, I slipped out of the granary. Like the mice beneath the shadows of the flour sacks, I was sheltered by the night as I made my way carefully out of the village, across the plain, and up across the flanks of Slemish.

With the strength of God rising within me, I walked across the familiar hills unseen. There was no moon. Only the creatures of the night observed my progress. Only the lonely owl lifted his voice in a hoot of annoyance at my intrusion into his domain.

16

THE Mountain of Mists sheltered me. I ate as the wild beasts, feeding upon summer's fallen bounty, upon ripe berries and herbs and those roots and plants which Dubh and Leborchom had shown me to be edible. It was not difficult for me to avoid the parties of men which came out from the ring fortress in search of me. Slemish had been my home for three years. I knew the mountain as a child knows its own mother. The Ri's men were strangers here. The mountain did not welcome them, nor did it share its secrets with them.

When did the legend begin to grow up around me? I know only that among the Gael there has long been a belief in a certain myth: that some men, upon witnessing the violence of their fellows, succumb to a magical madness which causes them to flee into the depths of the forests where they dwell forevermore as mystic spirits. It is believed that feathers sprout out of their shoulders and arms, enabling them to fly upon the air as though they were birds. It is believed that they run across the tops of trees and feed upon the clouds.

There was nothing magical or mystical about my life within the forests of Slemish. If I flew, it was only with the fleetness of foot which was born in me, and out of panic when I found myself being spied upon by shepherds or farmers or hunters who might betray my presence to the Ri's men. Once, when a young cowherd saw me bent within the mists of an early morning, I might well have seemed to be grazing upon the ground fog. Had he looked closely, he would have seen that I was merely straddling a freshet and was gathering the good, green, spicy cress which grew within it.

I did not venture near Leborchom's flock. I had no wish to endanger the old man, even though, as the days passed, I longed for his company. I was an outcast. A hunted man. I lived by my wits. I found solace in my prayers. I had no doubt that God was with me and that, through His intervention, my life had been saved. The knowledge of this softened the pain of my confusion. Yet, often in the long nights, I would lie awake, raising my voice to Him, not in prayer, but in question.

"For what purpose, Lord? The years and the miles . . . the dreams and the visions . . . for what purpose . . . ?"

As summer yielded fully to autumn, with the trees around me succumbing to the season, a golden rainfall began to descend around me. One morning, I awoke shivering beneath my blanket of leaves. I lay deep in prayer, looking up toward Heaven through a latticework of bare branches. My prayer ceased. It was as though God had spoken to me. I knew, with sudden clarity of thought and purpose, that now that the forest was becoming sparse of leaf, only the evergreens would be able to offer me shelter. Soon there would be little for me to eat. The mountain would grow cold and bleak. I knew that I must leave it.

So begging God's guidance and strength, I began to descend into the lowlands. I walked around the great mound of Slemish, heading north, far from the lands of the Ri Miliucc MacBuain.

On a clear and cold dawn, I was wrenched out of my sleep by the distinct prick of a spear being jabbed into my belly. I looked up, surprised and instantly awake, to see three sloppy-looking hunters eying me with curious and wily speculation.

"A runaway slave, if we judge him by the cut of his hair," drawled the holder of the spear.

"Aye," agreed the second man. "Perhaps he's the one they've posted reward for?"

"Could well be," assented the third, "but we're a long mile from the tuath of Miliucc MacBuain."

The second man stared at me and furrowed his brow with concentration. "Yet we're not so far from the rath of the Red Ri. He's posted reward for the slave as well."

The holder of the spear guffawed. "Sencha? He's nothing left with which to pay a decent reward. He's sold off half of his lands to raise an army against Miliucc."

"Poor lord . . . poor lord . . ." sighed the second man, shaking his head. "Can'ya imagine it? Havin' your manhood sliced clean away? And without proper judgment? 'Tis no small wonder the Ard Ri at Tara has sent the man his blessings. Sure and Miliucc MacBuain's brought the wrath of all Eire down on his neck. And all for a queen who still causes good men to fight for her, even after she's dead and done with."

The third hunter squeezed his lips between the thumb and index finger of his right hand as he mused contemplatively: "We should not be forgetting that, right and wrong doings put aside, Miliucc MacBuain is still one of the richest lords in Dalaradia. If he's offered reward for this youth . . . ?"

"A fat one it'd be."

"Aye, fat enough to make us lords ourselves for the taking of it."

Quickly, but not quickly enough, I attempted to roll out from under the spear. The man lifted it, then jabbed it down again, as a fisherman does when he fishes in a stream. I felt the jagged, ill-kept blade tear through the flesh of my shoulder, pinning me to the earth. I cried aloud and cursed the man.

The third hunter yowled at the spear thrower and bent down to peer at the damage done to me. "No more of this, idiot! The reward will not be paid unless the slave is brought in alive!"

"Are'ya sure, man?" asked the spear thrower, drawing his weapon out of me with no concern as to the pain he caused me. "I've no pity in my heart for them that murders women."

"The druid slew the queen," I informed them, grasping my torn and bleeding shoulder.

"Druid!" They exhaled the word in dismayed and fearful unison.

The second man stepped back. "I'll have no hand in druid business . . ."

The spear thrower agreed. "Nor I. If we bring back the slave and he accuses a druid . . . oh no, oh no, thank you . . . it's not my intention to be made the subject of evil spells or, worse, to be dragged off into the woods by those who'd disembowel me alive and then tie me to a stake with my own guts."

The third man shook his head. "Use your imagination for better and more profitable purpose, dimwit! The slave'll make no mention of any druid, mark me."

"What's to prevent him?" challenged the other belligerently.

"A man can't speak to accuse . . . if he has no tongue with which to form the words . . ."

Once again, despite the pain in my shoulder, I attempted to roll away from them and get to my feet. They kicked me mercilessly and held me to the ground with their booted toes pushed into my belly while they trussed my feet and hands behind my back. The jostling caused my shoulder to spurt blood. Alarmed, lest their means of treasure bleed to death, they packed the wound with a strip of filthy rag hastily taken from their saddle packs. There was a brief debate over who should remove my tongue, then it was decided, after much arguing, that the spear thrower would do it just before we reached the ring fortress. After all, the shock of such unwelcome surgery might not sit well with me. I might sicken and die from it. They did not want my death. Only my silence.

So they fixed a hearty breakfast and forced me to eat my fill of it. They taunted me the while, and the spear thrower advised me that I had indeed been a fool.

"You picked the wrong direction to run, lad'o. Now me, I'd have gone south straightaway. To a harbor. Aye. Not to Larne, for the Ri's men would surely be looking for'ya there. But further south you might well have found work for yourself as a seaman on a trading ship. They's always glad to have another hand. No questions asked. But you headed north. By the gods, lad'o, that was a fool's journey. Sweet fortune for us, though! Sweet fortune, indeed!"

The meal done, they mounted their horses and, with me trotting behind them, leashed like a hound, began their journey to the lands of the Ri Miliucc MacBuain.

The next morning we were still not within sight of the rath. My shoulder ached and burned with fever. I told them that the wound must be cleansed, but "cleanliness" was an alien word to them and we went on. By noon, the illness of infection had worked deep within me. When I collapsed, they flung me across a horse like a dying stag. I was incoherent when at last they paused and set to the task of removing my tongue. They had already drawn the blade when the spear thrower said: "No purpose in this. We'll be in sight of the rath by nightfall. The lad'll say nothing about anything at all in his condition. Sure if we cut out his tongue, he may not last the hour out. I'll not have brought him all this way only to deliver to the Ri a slab of dead and worthless meat."

So we rode on. By the time we reached the outer rampart, I was unconscious. Later I would be told that my captors claimed ignorance concerning the state of my health, or knowledge of how I had come to my wounding. They were paid their ransom and went hurriedly on their way.

17

No physician was called to tend me. In the midst of my delirium, I heard voices speaking over me.

"His life is in the hands of his god. The Ri has ordered it."

"A fat goose and a milk cow if you'll cauterize the wound."

"A cow, you say?"

"And more. But act quickly, man."

Out of the darkness of my fever, I awoke to light and searing pain. A massive hand lay across my mouth, stifling my scream. I could smell the scent of my own burned and putrid flesh. Then the world went dark again. Mercifully dark. The darkness of oblivion.

Then there were dreams. And voices. And memories. And somehow I knew that I was fighting for my life, though I could not understand why. When at last I called for water, a bilge-faced man brought me a grimy cup and observed me with an incredulous frown.

"I'd not have believed it possible . . . not in a thousand, thousand years. Pity it is, though. You should've been content to die, young man. Aye. Soon enough you'll wish that'cha had."

The following days passed in darkness. My cell was small. There were no windows. I was manacled to the wall in such a position that I could barely move. No thought was given to my comfort. I was not even given a bucket in which to pass my body wastes. Once each day, my manacles were slightly loosened so that I might feed myself out of a bowl filled with rough, unpalatable gruel. It was a diet which cut into my intestines and loosened my bowels. I suffered with constant cramps and diarrhea. I was forced to sit within my own filth. In time, sores broke out upon my flesh, little suppurating pustules which swelled and erupted from the pressures of the poisons which grew within my body. My gums began to recede from my teeth. My beard lenghtened even as the hair of my head began to fall out. Beyond the walls of the ring fortress, winter descended upon the earth. I shivered within my cell. Then, weak beyond endurance, I began to make of my life a litany: "God . . . deliver me from this . . ." Was it a prayer for death? God forgive me. Yes. It was that. Freedom seemed so far away.

Then, one night—or was it morning? or perhaps afternoon—I felt myself being prodded and poked. Within the darkness of my cell, I sensed that I was not alone.

"I tell'ya he's beyond waking." The cellkeeper's voice. Irritable. Held low.

"Then, carry him, you treacherous bastard, and now!"

"But 'tis madness!"

"Madness for you, to have accepted our offerings and then left him like this."

"What'd'ya have me do? Fix him up pretty like a proper pet? I tell'ya, the druids thrice tried'ta have'm poisoned. Thrice! 'Twas only quick thinking on my part saved the lad at all. Said he was too ill'ta eat. Lookin' at'm, the druid believed. Saved both our skins I did."

"No time for words. Pick him up. We must be done with this, and quickly."

"Pick him up? He's foul!"

Someone came very close to me. I felt the weight of an enormous shadow. "Merciful God . . . I'd not have known him . . ." The voice was familiar. I tried to open my eyes, but could not. They had rimed shut with infection and filth. "Loose the youth's chain, man. I'll carry him myself."

The cellkeeper grumbled. A garbled whisper of fear and annoyance. "Madness," he protested. "You've tricked'm so far. But this . . . I tell'ya, the druid'll know. The Ri'll have our heads on a stick!"

I heard the swift, silent movement of men around me. Again I tried to focus my eyes and failed. The weight of the manacles fell away from my ankles and wrists. Someone propped me up and rested me in strong, wide arms.

"And I tell you that no one shall know. As long as we all keep silence. Look at him. And look at the corpse.

Same size and age and coloring. Faces swollen with sickness. Could've been brothers. But enough of words. It's the grace of God that has presented the situation to us. We must not waste it. The exchange must be made now, and quickly."

"He'll know. Him'n his eyes. They sees everything. They knows everything. I tell'ya, Néladóir has the Sight!"

The familiar voice made a growl of anger. "Henceforth, the corpse is Padraic, and Padraic is called by the dead man's name and occupies the dead man's cell. Look at him, man! God himself would barely recognize him."

The cellkeeper rattled phlegm in his throat. "I don't like it. I tell'ya, the druid had the Inner Vision . . . he . . ."

"He wants Padraic dead. That is his 'vision.' You will grant it to him and, mark me, he shall bless you for it. Here now, help me to change him into the dead man's clothes."

The cellkeeper muttered an imprecation. "MacCairthinn, you and your lady walks on dangerous ground."

"When you accepted our gifts . . . the cow and the goose . . . you consented to walk with us. I suggest you not forget."

So I found myself in another cell and in another portion of the prison. It was darker here. A forgotten hold of humanity, festering within the womb of the earth. Yet my cell was reasonably clean. I was given water with which to wash myself. I was given a blanket to ward off the chill of winter. A pitcher of milk was brought to me, along with a small loaf of wheat bread and a bowl of stirabout. I wept at the sight of it, with joy, with ecstasy. I soaked the bread in the milk and sucked it past my bleeding, ulcerated gums. I wolfed down the stirabout, sobbing with pure and unrestrained delight. A few moments later I was violently sick. It would be nearly a full week before my malnourished body would be able to successfully and painlessly digest a normal meal.

Spring came. And passed.

Summer ripened.

The first chill of impending autumn began to crisp the apples on the trees. My gums were healed. My hair had ceased to fall away. My complexion was nearly clear. The cellkeeper paused beside the bars of my cell and tossed an apple my way.

"Live a little longer, you, and'ya may well have lived long enough ta see the light of day again. Aye."

I held the piece of fruit in my hand. I did not bite into it. The man rarely spoke to me.

"And ya'd do well, lad'o, ta remember that'char proper name is Tuathal of Connacht and that'char here for the repeated crime of thievin' from'yer brothers at feast days. Lucky not'ta be dead. And grateful too. Wretched lad. Your own kin set'cha before the brehons as a hopeless felon."

I sensed a warning in his words. "What has happened to Padraic?"

His body seemed to spasm inward. "Dead! Dead in the Long Ago! Druid himself came down'ta see the corpse." He lowered his voice to a sibilant whisper. "Ya do not mention his name. Ya do not mention it again, fer'ya have no cause'ta know it. None! Do'ya understand?"

"No. I do not understand."

He fixed me with a hostile eye. "Now see here, you. We'll be under siege soon enough, if I've read the signs aright, and it don't look good fer us. The well's shown signs of dryin'. The rains was sparse. The harvest was the worst in forty years. I tell'ya, even the mice in the granaries is goin' hungry. The people is beginnin' to whisper against the Ri, sayin' that the gods is angered and offended by what he done unlawful against Sencha. I tell'ya, there's many a good man run off to join up with the Red Ri . . . for the sake of honor and justice says they . . . but'ta be on the winnin' side, says I."

"And Néladóir, what says he to all of this?"

"He sits at the right hand of the Ri, advising him in all things. He had the Power and exercises it. He determines what is law and what is justice." His brow came together over the humped bridge of his nose. "Forget the druid's name, Tuathal of Connacht. Thieves has been known ta be pardoned in time . . . if their keepers puts in a good word for'm now and again . . . if'ya takes my meaning, Tuathal of Connacht."

"And if Sencha should take the rath?"

He almost smiled. "Fer certain ya'd be a free man then, and ya've no idea, lad'o, how glad I'd be ta see'ya far and away from the likes of me."

I awakened to the sound of the Ri's voice in the cell next to mine. I started up. Blinking, listening, at first I was certain that my dreams were tricking me. But the voice was real enough. The Ri was interrogating a high-ranking warrior who had been captured while leading a raid upon a distant village within the tuath. He was speaking quietly, with obvious respect. He offered the warrior no threats. The man remained silent. The Ri went on quietly, persuasively. At length, with a sigh of finality, he reminded the warrior: "You have seen these last days what imprisonment within this rath has meant for you and your men. I can assure you, it has been nothing compared to what you shall face if you insist on remaining loyal to Sencha. I admire the stubbornness of your allegiance. But to die for it, my friend? When you have only to swear fealty to me? Fight by my side. You shall be well rewarded."

"I wish no reward from you." The captive's voice was the voice of one who has faced the inevitability of his own death and accepted it. "When you offended Sencha, you offended the laws of Eire. The Ris are the strongest extensions of those laws. Regardless of Sencha's offense to you and your house, by law your brehons should have judged him. By law he should have had recourse to council. Yet you called no council. You turned your back on the brehons. You defied a system of justice which has taken the learned men of our race a thousand years to perfect. The laws are the fibers which gird the land with peace. Without them there can be no justice for any of us. There is not a Ri in all of Eire who will stand with you, Miliucc MacBuain. It is a true fact, my lord, that it is reward enough for me to know that I die and bring honor to my name by standing in defiance of you."

The silence which descended then did not fall. It congealed. I felt it weight the air until my very breath was still and my heartbeat became labored. I heard the sighing of the Ri's garments as he rose to his feet. The door to the neighboring cell opened and closed. I heard the Ri's footfall along the corridor. Then, to my amazement, I heard my own voice. I had called his name. Or had I? Had the cry come from my lips or from my soul? To this day I am not certain. I only know that his footfall stopped. Silence seemed to swell and thicken within the darkness. He called out to the cellkeeper. I heard them approaching my cell. Heard the cellkeeper chattering in an unnaturally high-pitched voice.

"A thief, lord. Tuathal of Connacht. Sent here more'n a year back now. Wretched lad. Aye. Tuathal of Connacht."

The sound of the key turning in the lock was deep and hard. The door scraped open. Dim, gray light invaded my cell, sought me out against the far wall where I sat upon my cot.

The Ri's shadow fell across the floor and over me. He called for a torch. Still chattering, the cellkeeper brought it to him.

"Just a thief, lord. A thief. From Connacht. Tuathal's the name. Aye. Dragged before the brehons by accusation of his own kin."

The light of the torch found me. So did the eyes of the Ri.

A fire burned upon the hearth. The room was as I remembered it. The Ri sat on the massive chair, his eyes locked upon the flames. He did not look at me as the guards brought me to stand beside him. The men were dismissed. We were alone.

The minutes passed. I waited for him to speak. He stared into the fire as though I did not exist. Then, slowly, he turned to look at me. His face registered no surprise at the sight of the dirty, half-naked, long-haired and bearded prisoner who stood manacled beside him. It was I who was startled by the change in him. He had shaved his beard. His mustache emphasized the extreme gauntness of his face. Even in the warm glow of the firelight, his lips were taut and gray. His once lustrous eyes were as dull as ash. Beneath them the flesh had sunken and grown tight and dark. There were veins of silver intruding into his hair. In the year since I had seen him, he had become an old man.

He measured me with weary eyes, reaching up to press against his brow with the tips of his fingers. "Why are you not dead, Padraic?" he exhaled the question in a voice languid with fatigue.

I was shivering and did not know why. "I am innocent of any crime. God has protected me."

His hands came down and rested upon his thighs. He scrutinized me with contempt. "From the looks of you, your god has not done good work." He pointed to the ugly scar which marred my bare upper arm. "Did my men do that?"

"It was done by those who claimed reward for my capture."

"And the pockmarks upon your face . . . you have been ill?"

"I have been ill fed . . . thank you."

One brow went up. "Still the impudent fool?"

"Not impudent. Truthful. I have been in Hell, at your decree. I have learned that my God is strong even there, for by His grace I have survived the torments of the damned."

He made an exhalation of annoyance. "Your god has had nothing to do with it. You have had two saviors: Bruthne, and a nearsighted cellkeeper who evidently takes such poor care of his charges that he cannot tell one of them from another. You are alive because Bruthne championed you. He is a good and honest man. And a brave one. He risked his life to speak in defense of you. He informed me of how the Rigan tried to work against me through the hounds, and of how she would have seen you humiliated before me and my court. It is not the first time that she has played such games, Padraic. Bruthne convinced me that you had slain her out of loyalty to me in a passion of righteous indignation."

"And so, by your grace, I was left to die of my own accord without further inquiry into the truth?"

"By right of law, you should have been slain."

"By right of law, I should have been allowed to speak . . . to protest the accusations made against me! I am a Christian. I could not have slain the queen."

The statement caused him to shake his head at my insistent naiveté. "And are you not also a man, Padraic, as well as a Christian? The Rigan would have used you as a fool. Bruthne advised me that he had witnessed your quick temper and ready recourse to violence when you attacked the kennel lad Draigenn. He claims that had he not struck you, you would have killed the boy. No, Padraic. Being a Christian does not remove you from your kinship with your fellow man. When the blood is up . . . with gods, without gods, despite gods . . . men work death upon their own kind. It is our way."

"Through the blood of Christ there is another way."

"Is there?" His expression revealed his disdain of my words. "I know only this, Padraic: Once you were trusted within this rath; once I cared for you enough to stand with you against the warnings of my own brother. Only once before did I not heed his word: when I took Cairenn to be my Rigan. And now? As Néladóir foretold: Cairenn has plotted against me, and you have brought blood to the people of my tuath."

"*I* have brought?" My face flushed with indignation. "Avarice and drunken pride have brought blood to your people. How have I had a hand in that? I would have warned you of the Rigan's treachery against you had Néladóir not stopped me."

His eyes were stern and angry. "Néladóir is my brother. He has no cause to work against me."

"It is not his intention to work against you. What he has done he has done out of fear of prophecy. He has the Power. He has seen beyond Tomorrow. In his attempt to defy and avert those things which he has seen with the Inner Vision, he has sown seeds from which surely only death and destruction can flower."

"Dreams! All men dream dreams! But what is a dream? How can a man claim to be bound by that which is, in fact, bound within him? No. I will not hear it! I will not be commanded or manipulated by what others claim to have seen in the future. I will not believe that I am merely a pawn in a play of Fate which no mortal can direct or understand."

"Yet Néladóir has seen the future."

"Néladóir is a wise man who would have others believe that he is a seer. His intellect allows him to read the natures of his fellow men. I accept his wisdom. He sees the world more clearly than I. Yet he is no prophet, for there are no prophets; there are only wise men who too often attempt to use their intellect to subvert and control the minds of others. I will not accept the premise which holds that on the day of my birth the circumstances of my death were already written. I am not a prisoner of Destiny. I am Ri!"

"Because you were born to rule."

He was clearly angry. "And I have held that right by my own hand and will and wisdom. If I have erred in this matter with Sencha, the blame is mine. I will not lay it in the lap of Fortune, nor ascribe it to the machinations of a pathetic and misguided queen. What is done cannot be undone. The dead cannot be brought back from the Otherworld. I am Ri and, as such, I shall best these raiders who harass me like fleas upon the hide of a hound. I will not turn up my throat to the brehons of the Ard Ri at Tara. I will hold what is mine and shall prove my right to rule without dispute."

"And without justice?"

The words stung him. He flinched. "The black goat has been sacrificed, Padraic. The sacred hazel rod has been dipped in its blood and charred in the flames of Sencha's war council. The Red Ri has sent it, the Cran Tara, out to all of the clans, calling them to join with him in battle against me. His couriers have gone out from his rath like heath fires burning beneath the Green Branch of their mission: to inform the Ard Ri that Sencha will accept no restitution from me until first my head is severed from my body and brought to him preserved in camphor oil." A droll smile moved upon his lips. "But the Ard Ri has been generous to me. Since Sencha provoked my actions against him by grievous insult to me and to my Rigan, it has been decreed, through the benevolence of the High King, that only my lands and title shall be forfeit to the Red Ri." The smile turned down, twisted. "My lands and title are my life. Forfeit either, and I forfeit all. So you see, my boy, they have left me no choice. I am not about to part with my head in order to appease Sencha, nor can I abide the decision of the Ard Ri. I must stand against them both. To the death, if need be."

How cold I was. "You cannot stand alone against the might of Eire. The High King will send his allies against you as relentlessly as the sea sends her tides against the shore."

Again he seemed amused. Darkly. "Ahh, Padraic, it seems you do have the tongue of a seanachie. But know that this rath has never fallen before a seige. Time shall be my champion in this battle. Let the tide come against me. I shall be a rock against it. Mark me, the High King will weary of his decision. What will he gain by it, eh? His men will be better spent raiding foreign shores, not devouring the resources of his own people. In time, and I am certain of this, it is I who shall have Sencha the Red's fat head sweetly spiced in camphor oil. Though, by the gods, in truth I do not wish it." The words sobered him. He put back his head and closed his eyes. The subject depressed him. He did not wish to pursue it. He drew in a breath, exhaled it and fell into silence. For a moment it seemed as though he had drifted into sleep. Then his eyes opened and found me again. "In truth, Padraic, we both know that Cairenn gave me little cause to grieve for her. The people believe that justice was served you long ago. It is the truth when I say that I no longer desire your death. And it would please the Rigan to know that you lived."

A piece of wood snapped on the hearth. The sound jarred me even as the Ri's words confused me. "The Rigan . . . ?"

"Has no one told you? In November, the month of marrying, Mercia became my bride."

I stared at him. "It cannot be. She is a Christian."

He laughed at me. "She has disdained your god, my boy. Long ago. Now the people rejoice. She carries my child. With Mercia beside me, peace shall soon bless the land. Néladóir has promised this."

Again a piece of wood snapped upon the hearth. Again the sound jolted me. It should have brought me pause; bought time in which I should have more thoroughly assessed the Ri's mood, evaluated his weary eyes, remembered how quickly his winning smile could vanish. But judiciousness has never been mine. I suddenly remembered the cellkeeper muttering a warning to the huge man who cradled me in his arms: "MacCairthinn, you and your lady walks on dangerous ground." His lady. Merciful God! Of course! MacCairthinn was the Ri's strong man. Who else would "his lady" be but the Rigan. The new Rigan. The Rigan Mercia! Overcome by my amazement, I blurted: "Praise be to merciful Christ, now I understand through whom the graces of God have come to me. . . ."

His laughter vanished. The flesh of his face went taut. "What do you say . . . ?"

I was overwhelmed by the fully human desire to inflict pain upon the one who had been the cause of my suffering. Without thinking about the possible danger which my words might bring to Mercia, MacCairthinn, or any of the others who had worked against the Ri's will to save my life, my head went up and I informed the Ri with triumphant disdain: "It is God's truth that she loves you, Miliucc MacBuain, yet she is still a Christian. While you thought me dead, she knew that I lived. She took pity upon me. Through her faith in the Lord our God, my life was spared. Though you disdain Him, the God of my fathers lives within your house, and it is a Christian woman whom you have taken as your wife."

He rose then. Quickly, without warning, he struck me a great, pounding blow which sent me to my knees before him. His ring had sliced my cheek. I felt the hot salt taste of blood intruding into my mouth. His right leg went back then came forward hard into my gut. The air exploded out of my lungs as I curled forward upon myself, cradling my head between my knees as I fought the dizzying, sickening, nearly overwhelming desire to vomit.

"You . . ." He exhaled his loathing of me. "You have been a blight upon my house . . . upon my lands . . . upon my people. You have sown the seeds of distrust and conspiracy within my house. You and your cursed god have brought ill fortune upon me. Néladóir was right. By ignoring his warning, I have brought the wrath of the gods of Eire upon myself and my people."

There was a sword mounted upon the wall near the fire. He went to it, stared at it, then took it and slid it purposefully from its scabbard. "Padraic . . ." His voice was devoid of expression. "I have not wanted this for you." With both hands curled about the haft, he swung the great blade high. It is your god who has won it for you."

My jaw ached where he had struck me. Pain jabbed upward across my temple. Blood, welling from the ring gash on my cheek, flowed across my lips, into my mouth, and over my beard. The blade hung above me, poised to slash. I had no defense against it. I stared up at the instrument of impending death and dismemberment, wondering why it did not fall. Why did he not strike me? Why did he wait? I saw the blade begin to tremble in his hands. His face was set. His body began to spasm as though with fever.

"I was brought to Eire against my will . . ." The words came quietly, quickly, in breathy exhalations made ponderous by fear. ". . . I have prayed only for deliverance . . . as both shepherd and houndsman I have served you loyally . . . do not kill me . . . only bid me leave your island and I shall gladly go . . ."

The blade went down. He stared at me, incredulous. "Leave Eire? You, who have murdered my wife, and now claim to have conspired with the new Rigan against my will?"

"I conspire with no one. And by the holy name of the God of my fathers, it was Néladóir who slew the Rigan and allowed you, ignorant of his crime, to work murder upon innocent men."

His face contorted with sudden rage. He threw the sword across the room. "I will not hear it! I will not humiliate my brother by once again taking a slave's word against his own. You have betrayed me, Padraic. And if that is not so, then why did you not come to me when you first learned of the Rigan's treachery?"

"I dared not lest you kill me to protect her name."

An expression of infinite sadness touched his face. "Are you so poor a judge of men, Padraic?"

The question seared me to my very heart. He gave me no time to reply. He drew in a breath, held it, then exhaled it slowly.

"You have worked to turn me against my own flesh, against the only man in all of Dalaradia whom I can trust. Even now you seek to plant the seeds of distrust within my heart so that they will blossom against Mercia. Well, I shall not have it. I should have had you slain long ago, when Néladóir first advised it. But emotion is the enemy of reason. I could neither kill you nor see you gone from the rath. You and your vile Christ have repaid my faith in you with treachery against my house." Thoughtfully, he crossed the room and opened the door, summoning the guard who stood just beyond it. "Take this man." The order was issued in monotone. He did not look at me.

Confusion swarmed in my head like bees. "Am I to be slain, then?"

He stared at me expressionlessly. "No. Not by my hand. A shepherd you were when Bruthne found you. A shepherd you shall be again; a captive in a prison of your own making, where no kind and Christian queen shall be allowed to succor you. Sencha's raiders have slain four of my shepherds this past month. Perhaps your death shall be on their hands? If not, so be it. But at least your vicious lies concerning my brother shall be of no harm to him out amidst the grasses and the sheep dung."

A hot, sour saliva filled my mouth. I tried to swallow it and nearly gagged. "I shall escape."

His eyes pinioned me. "Have you forgotten that for every shepherd who flees, another is mutilated as an example to others? I think that you shall not escape, Padraic. I think that your Christian conscience shall manacle you. It is your god, not I, who shall chain you."

The guard pushed me toward the door. Roughly. I resisted. He jammed his elbow forward into my back. I winced with pain. And with the pain, a sparking of anger ignited my temper within me.

"I shall pray for Sencha's victory over you!" I shouted, despising myself, for my voice cracked and tears stung my eyes. I was sobbing, yet I would be heard. "Justice shall be done, Miliucc MacBuain. May the wrath and the fire of Heaven descend upon your house. By the name of the most holy Lord, may it be God's will that I shall not see your face again!"

He could have fulfilled God's will for me then and there. He chose instead to simply turn his back upon me. To the guardsman he said quietly: "Take the man from my sight. I can no longer bear to look upon him."

18

I was a slave shepherd upon the Mountain of Mists for nearly seven months. Loneliness was my meat and bread. Despair was my drink. Prayer was my only sustenance.

I worked with Leborchom again, and in this found my only joy, though illness had made him weak and less obstinate and less able to maintain his share of the work. He dozed often, and had grown forgetful, much to the disgruntlement of my only other companion, a sour young man named Dris. Winter descended, deepened, lengthened into a marathon of wind and rain and mud. Leborchom's illness grew severe, yet he would not have us send for a physician.

"Time," he said. "A man must face his time. Weaning and winnowing. A man must not try to divert the seasons."

I nursed him day and night, ignoring Dris's grumblings against the extra work I made for myself, and for him, since I was not always readily available when trouble arose with the flock. Then, on a midday brightened by the distant silver sun of winter, the old man's wheezing eased and he put up his hand to ward off the light.

"Bright . . . so bright . . ."

I had brought him to rest within one of the sagging shepherds' shelters. Welcoming the sunlight, I had left the hide-door curtain slung back. I drew it shut again at the complaint of the old man. The small dank room was consumed by an almost stifling darkness.

His forearm remained folded across his eyes, held slightly above them. "The light . . . it blinds me . . ."

"I have shut off the light, Leborchom."

"No. Tell him to take it from me. I cannot bear it."

"Hm?"

He sighed, infinitely weary. "That is better." His arm went down to rest, folded above his grizzled white head. He licked his lips, nodding feebly. "Better. Aye. Much. Soothing now. Thank'ya, Lord."

Lord? I looked about the darkness. There was no one. I went to the old man and asked him if I should fetch him water. He stared at me, his eyes very clear and somehow startlingly young within his time-worn face.

"Do not go back to the glen, Padraic. Sencha's men. Sure'n 'tis no longer safe."

"I need not go to the glen for water." I turned, interpreting his words as a request for a cooling drink, but he stopped me with an imperative:

"Padraic!"

I turned back to him. His eyes had gone round with concern. They stared at me, somehow imploring. "Do'ya still see the billa, boy? Oh, ya must not forget it. The voices. The wind. The flame. Remember and know that, despite all that has happened to'ya, there *is* a purpose. For us all. Aye. 'Tis the will of God."

I saw death in his face. I felt it within the room and shivered with its unwelcome weight. "You must rest now, old man."

He nodded. "You're a good lad, Padraic . . . aye . . . you'll bite the mactire back someday . . . that'cha will . . ."

He lingered for several days, and when at last he died, quietly and with no fear, I knew that he had found a solace in death which, as a slave, he had never known in life. Yet I grieved for him and could not be consoled for his loss.

The dog Shadow mourned with me. An old dog now, he too was ill and wheezing and stiff-boned from the damp and unending cold. I did what I could to make his days as pleasant and warm as possible, drawing him close to me in the night, often carrying him in my arms as I followed the flock. Long ago, when I had been a boy desperately alone and in need of a friend, he had sensed my needs and given to me his warmth and his love. Now that he was old, he had a friend in me; an only friend, for surely Dris would have preferred to have bashed in his aged skull with a stone.

The days passed bleakly. On a gray day, stung by wind-driven sleet, I watched Shadow die content beside me. He had had over sixteen years of life. Long years for a dog, and good years, for a sheepdog is not a slave, as is the shepherd. A shepherd's dog is a lord over the flock. Shadow had lived long and well as a lord. So I dug a grave for him, a royal barrow as befitted his station. I placed him upright in it, facing the forests where his enemy, the mactire, roamed. I covered him with stones, large stones, deeply mounding them around him so that no wolf might dishonor him in death.

Winter decimated the flock. And me. Dris was a droll and acid companion, no friend to man nor dogs nor sheep. He disdained my prayers, calling me a madman and a fool for my faith in a god who, he said, had obviously no power at all in the world of men.

When spring finally came, it was wet and miserable; a mere extension of winter. Caera continued to die. Half of the new lambs drowned in the muck and mud of the fields. Seedlings succumbed to mold and decay before they had sprouted. A frost descended to wither the blossoms upon the fruit trees. When shepherds began to gather into the shearer's camp upon the plain, they were a sorry and pitiful lot compared to the great gatherings of men which I had seen and known during my first years on Slemish.

I was not allowed to participate in the great gathering. A guardsman was sent out from the ring fortress to make certain that I stayed away. He kept resentfully by my side during the shearing and left, eagerly, when he saw

Dris returning to the hills with a close-shorn flock and well-fed dogs.

"Bid the Ri good fortune from us," called out Dris insolently as the man, already beyond earshot, urged his mount down the mountain toward the rath. Jabbing an angry finger at the low, brooding sky, he came close to me and glared. "Will the sun never show its face to us again? I tell'ya, it's all the talk there is among the gathering. The Ri's acted against the laws of Eire, and now the very elements rise up to prove the injustice of his rule."

Everywhere within the tuath, people began to grow ill. Word came to us that the new Rigan had miscarried late in her pregnancy and had nearly died. Sencha's raiders alone seemed to be undaunted by the weather. They came at the tuath like bands of wolves: harrying, killing, looting, stealing women and children, then fleeing with them into the hills, where they disappeared as completely as though they had vanished into the shees.

"I tell'ya, the common folk is carin' for'em," said Dris. "They's hide'n from the Ri's men. And as for the likes of us, the time'll soon come when there'll be a choice'ta make. Aye. Stand and fight for the Ri, or join the raiders and the side of justice."

The days passed. The clouds remained with the land. Thunder echoed across the hills. The caera grew restive. With only two men to guard the flock, the work was long and wearying. Yet, I began to endure brief periods of abstinence from all food, hoping to keep my mind clear, to cleanse my soul, and to harden my body so that I might be prepared for the lean days which had to come.

Early one morning, rounding a knoll, we discovered that seven of our flock had been slaughtered in the night. Two of our dogs were dead beside them, their throats cut to silence them.

Dris muttered a profanity. "The raiders take freely of the Ri's stock while his own shepherds and clansmen go hungry. I tell'ya, the gods is on Sencha's side and, by the memory of the Red Branch Knights of the days'a glory, I'd join ranks with'm myself if I could but find'm."

That night my dreams besieged me. I dreamt of the butchered carcasses of the sheep and saw my own corpse, bleeding and gutted, lying beside them. I dreamt of the great tree rising upon the heights of Slemish, and of the tiny flame defying the darkness while silent forms of men and women knelt in prayer. I dreamt of Leborchom and of Mercia, of Umall the cook, of Darerca and her brothers, of the giant MacCairthinn, and of the priest who had called himself Victoricus. I saw myself, beside Leborchom, crying out to the night: "For what purpose? The years and the miles?" And Leborchom said to me out of the dream: "The will of God, my boy. The will of God." And I replied, angry and purposeful in my resentment: "The will of God. It moves within my mind as mists and vapors which only serve to befuddle me. If I am to do His will, I must know His intention for me." Then, as often happens in dreams, Leborchom became the priest. We were walking together in a dark and narrow canyon. He had his arm slung casually across my shoulder. "It is well that you fast," he said to me out of my dream. "Soon you shall go to your own country."

Then, suddenly, I was awake. Had someone called to me? It seemed so. Yet all was silent. Unnaturally so. The night was black and moonless. Clouds hid the stars, promising rain. It was a few moments before I realized that I was alone. Dris was not in the camp.

I called his name. There was no reply. Again I called. Not even the wind answered me. I knew that he had run off to cast his lot with the raiders. He had left me to face my dreams and my destiny alone.

I began to tremble uncontrollably. When the Ri's men came up to bring supplies, they would note Dris's absence and take me off to the ring fortress where, as a warning to others, I would be mutilated as punishment for my failure to keep my partner in check. I rose to my feet, calling Dris's name again and again until the very clouds seemed to mock me and the wind, which was just beginning to rise up from the broad sweep of the plain, whispered to my growing panic: "Run . . . run . . . run away . . . run away . . ."

"I cannot flee!" I cried aloud to the night. "If I do, some poor unfortunate shepherd working on another portion of the mountain shall be punished in my place."

But the wind said: "Fool . . . think . . . think clearly now . . ." And suddenly I was lightheaded. Dris had brought many tales from the great gathering camp. He had said that though a hundred and more men had run off to join with Sencha, there had not been a single retaliatory castration. The Ri Miliucc had few enough loyal men left to serve him. He wished to alienate no man who might be counted upon to raise a sword in defense of the rath.

"Run away . . . run away . . ." Was it the counsel of the wind, or of my own rising hope of freedom, which prodded, goaded? "Run . . . run now . . . run fast and far . . ."

"But where?" And even as I spoke the question, I laughed aloud. The answer had been given long ago. "Merciful God! You have told me where!" The spear thrower who had brought me into imprisonment had told me. "South," he had said. Beyond the port of Larne. South, to a distant harbor where the Ri's men would not be looking for me. South, where I might find passage as a seaman upon a trading vessel.

A ship. Had I not often dreamed of a ship? I had thought it to be the vessel which had brought me to slavery in Eire. But it had not been that. It had been the instrument of my deliverance. I closed my eyes and clasped my hands and collapsed into prayer. Within me it seemed as though a voice was promising: ". . . Your ship is ready."

The words spurred me. The wind seemed to be whispering within me. "Why do you linger here? Run . . . run away . . . run away . . . now . . ." I rose to my feet and hurriedly gathered up my blanket and all of the food which I could comfortably carry. I selected those utensils which would serve me without burdening me. I did not know how far I would have to travel before I came to a safe harbor. I knew only that I must travel quickly so that I might arrive in time to greet the calm summer seas upon which the Gaelic traders did their commerce. I knew that I would travel completely alone, by night, involving no one who might betray me or who might come to grief because of me.

And so it was that I left the man who had been my master for six years. So it was that, at the age of twenty-two, I, Magonus Sucatus Patricius, known to the Gael as Padraic, took flight. ". . . I went in the strength of God who directed my way to my good, and I feared nothing until I came to that ship."

A fine ship. A strong, lean, eager ship. And aboard her, miraculously it seemed to me then, as it does even now, there was a cargo of wolf dogs made wild by their terror of new sights and sounds and the rough handling of the seamen.

I paid the hounds no heed at first. Ragged and footsore, I was intent only upon securing my passage. The captain bluntly refused me. Not once. Twice. Then I took notice of the dogs.

"Have they no kennel hand to gentle them?" I asked.

"The man lies ill ashore and cannot sail with us."

"I am a houndsman. I will go in his place."

He measured me with a thoroughly jaundiced eye and turned back to his duties, not even deigning to comment.

The ship was making ready to sail. I had no time to quibble with the man. Quickly, dodging those who sought to stop me, I managed to leap aboard. Running to the crate which housed the frantic hounds, I thanked God that I was slim enough to slip between the board slats. The hounds had no time to react to my intrusion. With the authority of experience, I took command, gentling them with my tone and touch.

In their attempts to crate the hounds, two of the seamen had been badly bitten. One of these, a hook-nosed man still nursing his bandaged forearm, cried out to the captain: "By Cuchulainn, sir, did'ja see that! The dogs take the youth to be one of their own!"

The captain turned and stared at me. "So be it, then."

The sails were filling with wind. The ship was beginning to move back and away from the shore. I was trembling with joyful disbelief. "I shall serve you loyally until we reach the Briton shore."

The captain's brow rose sardonically. "Terms? *I* make the terms aboard this vessel. Do not doubt that. Or question it again. And we sail not to Briton. We sail to Gaul and beyond."

"Gaul?" In my eagerness to be away from Eire, it had never occurred to me that the ship might have any other destination save the one of my dreamings. Disappointment turned within me as a blade, stabbing me with my own stupidity. "I have no wish to journey to Gaul." The deck suddenly pitched hard beneath my feet. The rigging went taut with the tension of the expanded sails. The ship was sliding away on the water as easily and quickly as a great bird moving upon the air. I began to work my way out of the crate, suddenly desperate to be ashore again.

"Not so quick, friend." The seaman with the bandaged

hand wedged his hip against the crate, effectively blocking my exit from it. "I'll not be snapped at and bit by these hounds of hell when there's one like you'ta handle'm."

"It is not God's purpose for me to stay aboard!"

"And what god is it reveals his purpose to such as you, eh?"

The mockery in his tone angered me. "The One God. The Father Almighty. The Maker of Heaven and Earth. Now for the love of Christ Jesus, let me pass!"

"Christ Jesus is it?" He continued to block my way. His arms went wide. His head sagged downward onto his chest in the manner of one who has been crucified. "This god, eh?" He lolled out his tongue and rolled up his eyes in as outrageous a parody of the death of Christ as was possible for a man to make. The crew roared their approval.

I gripped the slats of the crate and demanded my immediate release.

"In good time," laughed another of the seamen, winking at me. "When the purpose of the gods has been assured."

When at last they let me leave the crate, the ship was standing well out from the harbor. The open sea had gripped her. It ran high and spuming all around. I could see the distant, misted mountains of Eire falling fast away.

It was then that I heard the bird. High above me, it made a soft, repetitious chortling in its throat which could barely be heard above the wind. Yet I heard it and looked up. Perched upon the rigging, where the mast seemed to jab into the flesh of the sky, the form of a dove was unmistakable. It ruffled its white feathers against the wind, changed its position as though seeking surer footing. Finding none, it cried aloud, unfolded its wings and gave itself to the wind. For a moment it remained poised upon the updrafts. Then it banked away, riding the wind back toward the land from which it had come.

BOOK IV

THE HOLY ISLE

The fear of God I had as my guide through Gaul
and Italy and the islands in the Tyrrhene Sea.
"Sayings of St. Patrick"—*Book of Armagh*

19

FOR a full day we beat our way into a blustering summer
gale which seemed intent upon driving us back to Eire. It
came upon us suddenly. The sea drew the color and substance of the clouds into itself. All the world went gray.
The wind roared and menaced us from across the Channel. The great linen mainsail moaned and snapped while
enormous seas shouldered our little vessel, buffeting her
from all directions so that, for a numbing, terrifying spate
of hours during the height of the gale, it seemed as though
we would not be able to keep her from turning broadside
to the waves and capsizing.

Yet, miraculously, dawn of the second day saw us still
afloat. The gale had wearied of its game with us. It had
veered away to the north, leaving us alone upon a rumpled sea with a cloud-streaked sky and a sweet, fair,
even-tempered wind which promised to carry us south-
ward around Land's End, where we would begin our eastward tack along the coast of Gaul.

We knew there would be danger for us in these waters.
From pirates and slavers. Yet, we were such a little ves-

219

sel, with so meager a cargo. The storm was behind us. Exhaustion, relief, and gratitude for survival was a heady, welcome wine which ran within us. If we thought of pirates, it was only briefly, and then with assurance that certainly they would seek more substantial prey.

We offered up praises for our deliverance. I, to the One God, the God of my fathers, who had at last brought me out of bondage and who had placed me upon a journey which must soon lead me home. My comrades gave their thanks to the MacLir, their god of the sea; and to Bel, the god of the sun, father of the Daghda, who was, in turn, father of all the gods. They lifted their arms in joyous acclamation of his power as he rose above them, burning from the sky all remnants of the storm . . .

"To Bel we offer thanksgiving," intoned the captain. "To the face of the god of life. To the golden eye of the great god. To the golden eye of the god of glory."

"Christian! Why do'ya grovel? Rise up and join us!" It was Amorgin, the hook-nosed man who had mocked me when I had first come aboard. "Would'ja blight our luck in the eyes of the gods?"

I had been kneeling apart from them, alone in prayer. I stood up, unsteadily, for the sea was still rough and the deck pitched and rolled beneath my feet. "I pray to the God of my fathers," I said.

The captain looked at me with his measuring eyes. "Pray to the god of your choice, boy; but as a sign of our fellowship and mutual gratitude for having survived the night, join with us in veneration of the MacLir, and do not stand apart beneath the all-judging eye of Bel."

I sincerely meant no offense. I simply spoke the truth. "My God forbids me to join you."

If there was a tightening of the captain's features, it was so controlled that I only thought I saw it. "Bel welcomes all. He is the father of all the gods."

"There is but one true God," I replied, respectfully, wishing him to understand. "He is not Bel. He has no name."

Amorgin gave an amused grunt through his rusty beard. "No name, eh? And how does one address such a god?" He puckered-up his mouth and screwed his eyes half-shut with pretended concentration. "Ach! Of course!" He nodded vigorously, obviously pleased with himself. "Here's how it's done!" He threw back his head, dropped to his knees in an obvious parody of my own manner of prayer, and bleated to the sun: "Hey, You!"

Appreciative laughter broke from the crew. The youngest member, a young man named Crimthann, called out to Amorgin: "No, that's not right. You've forgot this." And he signed the cross, making a mockery of it.

Amorgin marked off a hasty imitation, asking me with a disapproving snicker: "What's this supposed to mean, eh?"

"It is a sign of faith in the triune nature of God."

He blinked. "In what?"

"The Trinity."

"Three gods?"

"One God."

"But'ja just clearly said that he was three!"

"He is the Father, and the Son, Jesus Christ, and the Holy Spirit."

"As I said. Three gods."

"One God."

Amorgin rolled his eyes and, to the others, shook his head, indicating me. "You heard'm. Didn't he say three? A whole bleedin' family?"

"I's never knowed a Christian yet who didn't talk in holy riddles," added Crimthann.

"Aye," assented Amorgin, sagging indolently against the foremast as he gave me a malicious wink. "One is one. One is three. Three is all. Three is one. One is all. One is one." He stood upright and came close to me, cocking his head, staring a challenge. "Now, if that's not a riddle, I'm not standin' here before'ya."

The little trading curragh pitched on a sudden swell. I stepped back from Amorgin, seeking balance and an escape from my rising temper. Amorgin had sought to shame me and had succeeded. Yet my anger was not with him. It was with my own inadequacy with words. If I could not explain the intricacies of my faith, the nature of God, the fault was mine, not the seaman's.

"Go ahead, boy," prodded the captain, quietly amused by the scene before him. "Solve the riddle for us."

I attempted to clear my head with a long, deeply held intake of breath. Long ago, on the Mountain of Mists, Darerca, too, had been mystified and confused by the concept of a triune God. I had sought a way of simple explanation, both for her and for myself. Floundering, staring at the ground, I had found the answer growing at my feet. With memories of that day, I met Amorgin's smirking eyes and said surely: "On the mountains of your island, there is a little tri-leaved plant which grows—"

"Aye!" He interrupted me with bounding enthusiasm. "The shamrock! Do'ya worship that too?"

Again the others laughed, enjoying the entertainment which Amorgin was providing them at my expense.

I disregarded their mirth and went on, anxious to have them understand. "The God of my fathers has set His wisdom throughout all the world. In all things. Great and small. So that even in the littlest of things can men be brought to an understanding of Him. His Power is reflected in the great seas, and His mercy in the sure turning of the seasons. But in the shamrock there is the wonder of His very being."

Amorgin's smirk deepened. "Such a little god!"

I shook my head slowly, not allowing his contemptuous merriment to touch me. "Picture it, Amorgin. There. Growing in the earth. The shamrock. One small stem rising, and through it pours the Source of life. And where the stem divides into three leaves, so also does the Power flow . . . so that each leaf is a living portion of the whole, yet separate, apart unto itself. So it is with the Father . . . three facets to the One God . . . Father, Son, and Holy Spirit. Surely it cannot be so difficult for you to imagine?"

The concept made Amorgin frown. "Ach," he said, wiping at the air, not wanting to understand. I had ruined his game. He glared at me, seeing for the first time that I was not the naive, half-bright runaway who might be baited for his pleasure. He did not see the willing friend in me. He saw instead a man whose ability to reason surpassed his own. His mouth twisted into a sneer as the bile of resentment rose within him. "Mysteries! Wonders! Shamrocks indeed! Ach!"

He turned away from me. Again his hands swept across the air. His mind was reaching, grudgingly restoring his self-image. "I knows only this: For more'n a full day's runnin', since we took this slave and his god'a riddles aboard, we's tasted naught but the cold wrath of the MacLir. And now he spits in the eye of Bel with his talk of foreign gods. Mark me. I smell the stink of danger on'm."

"Enough of that." The captain's voice was stern, reproving. An unmistakable command. "It was you, Amorgin, who turned the decision in favor of keeping him aboard. So now mark me. It is true that we have tasted the scorn of the MacLir. But the Christian has shown his worth as a man among us. We have weathered the storm together. Now the eye of Bel shines for us. The wind is fresh and the journey ahead is long. The gods shall not sail this ship for us. Nor shall I tolerate threats, no matter how muted, from any member of my crew. Discord is a treacherous tide which can put a ship upon a reef more surely than any storm. We are beyond the Ninth Wave, and I am sole arbiter of law and justice. The Christian may pray to his god, so long as he does so discreetly. The gods of all nations *are* gods. Wise men do not dispute the authority or power of even the least of them."

"But the puke will not bend a knee to Bel!" protested Amorgin.

"Bel is the god of the Gael," replied the captain. "He would not have an unbeliever speak his name. The Christian may worship as his own gods decree."

I bowed my head, in deference to the captain's generosity. Then, and as God is my judge I intended no arrogance, though I realize now that he, as captain, could have read my words no other way, I added in what I thought to be a conciliatory tone: "I have but *one* God. What you call Bel and the MacLir are the sun and the sea. They are God's gifts to us all. I *do* respect them, but I cannot venerate them as you do. One does not worship a gift . . . one thanks the giver."

The captain's face rarely registered emotion. His eyes, like the sea at noon, were intensely blue. They offered no insight into the man. He merely measured me and nodded. "This ship sails from Eire. The men with whom you sail have placed their lives into the hands of the gods of Eire. If you do not fear them, then fear me. I am captain. Your life is in my hands. I will hear no more of your god. Take heed of that, Christian, and leash your arrogant tongue, for I do not warn a man twice."

The little trading curragh bit into the wind and skimmed out across the waves like a greedy cormorant. With her belly ribbed with light, lithe bones of hand-hewn ash, her double gunwales of inflexible oak, her skin a hand-stitched, tanned hide made waterproof with wool grease, she smelled of the land from which she had come.

The sun rose above us, eating the clouds from the sky. Only the surface of the sea, still restless with memories of storm, was a constant reminder that, though the weather had turned in our favor, we were still trespassers into an alien realm. Our curragh was but a tiny island in constant jeopardy as long as she was upon the sea.

"Remember that always. Never forget. When'ya trust the sea, when'ya lower your guard against her . . . that's when she'll turn her cruelest tricks . . ."

Comla had befriended me. He was small for a man of Eire. Like the other members of the crew, Crimthann, Flannán, and Amorgin, the skin of his face and hands had been tanned by the sun to the color of cinnamon. His eyes, like hard, black little stones, were barely visible beneath the visors of his leathery lids. His body was as powerful and as judiciously arranged as that of a monkey, with long arms and torso and immense back muscles, with short limbs and bowed calves and prehensile feet which clutched and grabbed like booted hands. Indeed, when I saw him working amidst the rigging, or lying prone along the gunwales, whistling while he dangled half-overboard to check the lashings of the hide tarps, I thought of my youth and of the great fortress of Isca Silurum and of Roman circuses and strange, wonderful wild beasts from distant lands.

Comla laughed when I told him that, and while he taught me the rudiments of a seaman's trade, nodding often with approval as I warmed to the art of sail, he told me that he, together with the captain, had seen the lands of which I spoke. As boys they had gone adventuring together, far from Eire. He had worked many trades in many countries. He did not speak of the lands by name, but called them: The Land of Wool and Grain, or the Land of Salt and Wax, or the Place Where the Sea Lanes Fill with Blood for the Promise of Slaves and Gold.

From his words, I knew that he had seen the great inland water which men called the Black Sea, for he spoke of ships which carried rich cargo in fur and lead and copper, of honey and of giant slaves with golden hair and skin the color of ivory. He spoke of traveling far to the north, where men traded flax and iron, where the summer days made a man forget that there ever was a night, and where an unsuspecting foreigner might be trapped for endless days of waiting for the spring thaw if he did not heed the coming signs of winter. He claimed that in these lands the eye of Bel was erased from the sky for interminable months, that only the thin light of the moon warmed the frozen land, and the people propitiated wondrous gods who danced in the black winter skies as fire for all men to see.

And he said, too, that he served the captain because some men were born to serve, and others to lead. The captain, he said, had an ear tuned to the very pulse of the sea, that he could actually smell the great sea rivers as they shifted, that he could sense the formation of the infamous Death Wind of Crete, which plunged to the sea from the mountains of that island's southern coast. He claimed that once, in a curragh such as the one which now carried us to Gaul, they had been swept out to sea by an errant wind which carried them to what must surely have been Iargalon, the Land Beyond the Sunset. They had passed islands of crystal on their way, and when, in a world surely beyond this world, they had stepped ashore to replenish their supplies, they had found a place of enchantment, for the men and women who greeted them had skin the color of the earth, and hair as dark and sleek as the backs of ravens. They led them to groves within the forests, places where standing stones had been placed to mark the changing of the seasons and where the ogham writing of other Gaelic mariners had been inscribed. They spoke to them in the language of Eire, their words only partially corrupted. They fed them strange fruits and food which was plentiful, for surely this was I'Breasil, the Isle of the Blessed. Yet men must seek their homeland, so, after weeks spent in the Land Beyond the Sunset, they committed themselves again to the sea. Only the grace of the gods and the captain's understanding of the language of the sea brought them safely home again.

"Ach!" proclaimed Comla sagely, remembering. "We've tested the waters of many a sea . . . the Alborán and the Tyrrhene and the Aegean. And once, I tell'ya, the captain saved us all from certain death within the belly of the whirlpool that the Greeks call Charybdis. Aye. He said to us that there was the strong salt smell of Death in the sea, told us that he felt the runnin' of currents which would leave us to the black land Oblivion and beyond. We heard nothin', smelled nothin' . . . not till he forced us to change tack. We heard it then . . . the siren call, risin' and then fallin' away."

He sighed, happy with his memories. "The man has the Sight, the Inner Vision into the heart'a the sea. True it is that a man finds comfort shippin' with'm. He's a stern one, I'll grant'ja. But a fair man. Serv'em well, Christian, and he'll see you're well rewarded."

'I desire only one reward: to return to my homeland and my people."

He shrugged. "A fair enough request."

I voiced my fear to him. "The captain disdains me for my faith in the God of my fathers. I think, when he has delivered the hounds, that he shall leave me ashore in Gaul."

Comla let off a staccato snort through his nostrils. "The only reason you're aboard at all, boy'o, is because'ya refused to suck his breast on that day back in Eire when'ya leaped aboard brazen as a whore and demanded to come along with us."

I ignored his comparison. "He threatened me when I stood in defense of my God."

"He threatened'ja because Amorgin was about'ta pitch'ya into the sea. And for all of your faith in your one god, boy'o, I hold little stock in the fable that is told of Christians being able to walk upon the water."

"My Lord Jesus Christ walked upon the water. He was the Son of God. I am not."

"I'm quite sure that the good captain was aware of that. 'Twas why he felt the time had come to still the babblin' of your tongue before'ya tripped over it and, with Amorgin's assistance, found yourself in the sea." Again he snorted, this time pulling the sound in. "Can it be that'ja have been a slave to the Gael for six long years and not learned that the men of Eire bear no respect for one who will not face us down? Sure and a man's no man to us lest he'll stand for what he believes. We're a stubborn race. Aye. And we admire pride and a bit'a hard-headedness in a man." He lowered a dry, sun-bleached, salt-rimed brow at me. "As for this need'a yours to return to your homeland . . . are'ya so sure, boy'o, that'ja have not found a home among the Gael?"

The question was not to be considered. "My home is not in Eire."

"How can'ya be so certain?"

"I am a Briton. A citizen of Rome."

"Rome is it? Ach, boy'o, has nobody told'ja that the Eagle has flown the nest? Left its siblin's naked and cold. Briton! Do'ya know what our raiders say of the place? They say that the Britons are like lambs cowed before the slaughter, barely bleatin' as they submit to the ax. They say that Rome has neutered the men and made passive vessels of the women."

His words caused anger to blossom, tangling it in memories which rose bloodied within me.

He saw the pain on my face and said, in a tone meant to clam as well as to console: "Now, now, boy'o, I meant to cause no hurt with'ya. I'm merely seein' the makin's of a fine seaman in'ya, and I'm wonderin' can there be much future for'ya in Briton after all these years in Eire?"

I stared at him. "My home is in Briton. Six years have passed since the day I was taken. When I think of my family, specters of flame and death and ruin rise within me. I must lay those fears to rest, Comla. I must know the truth . . . whatever it may be. I must return to my people. It is the hope of seeing them alive again which has sustained me through all of my long years of bondage."

"And if they's dead?"

"Then at least I shall know it . . . and shall stand for their memory."

"Against the Gael?"

It was a thought I had been avoiding. It caused darkness to move within me. Disquieting. Heavy. "If need be . . . perhaps . . . if such is the will of God . . ."

He was silent for a moment, sucking on his lips, shaking his head. Then he nodded, approving. "Stubborn and hard'ja are, boy'o. Aye. Hard-headed and as unyieldin' as any true son of Eire. If more of your people were as you, sure and they'd have our raiders thinkin' twice before they set out for the Briton shore." He sighed, musing with admiration of what he fancied to be the Gael in me. "Your people . . . their village was by the sea . . . ?"

"No. Inland. We had a summer retreat, a villa on the coast. It was there that I was taken captive."

"Our raiders stay pretty well close to the sea. It may

well be the will'a the gods that'ja may find naught but peace and plenty when'ya reach your loved ones."

The frustration of six years rose in me. "If I ever reach them . . ."

"Oh and'ja shall. If'ya mind your manners, and stay out of Amorgin's way, for I've sailed with'm often enough to know that he's got the black streak of madness runnin' in'm. And'ja must keep silent about your god, for he makes an arrogant ass of'ya. And'ja must learn to show a bit'a respect to your mates when we worships our own gods . . ."

"You have my respect, Comla . . . as seamen. But you worship false gods, spirits spawned of a Power which can only lead you into an eternity of Darkness. I would offer you an alternative, yet you turn away. I cannot respect you for that, nor would I be a true friend to you if I kept silent."

His mouth worked over his teeth as he sought to gather patience. Failing, he stabbed my breast with a warning finger. "Boy'o, the gods is for thankin' and the gods is for askin'. Beyond that, they's not to be understood by neither man nor beast. They has their place in this world, and we's got ours. The two don't go together, lest it be at the expense of us mortals. I learned long ago that a wise man keeps the gods at a nice, sweet, safe distance."

"God lives within you, Comla. Open you Inner Eye, man. He can lead you to life everlasting if you will only . . ."

His finger jabbed me to silence. "The captain's warned'ja once, boy'o. Leash your tongue, or Amorgin may yet see'ya walkin' on the water."

"I have told you. Jesus of Nazareth walked upon the water. I am a simple man of faith. I can work no miracles."

He nodded a grim assent. "I'm relieved to hear that, boy'o, for if the captain hears'ya preachin' about your god again . . . 'twill be a long, wet walk to the Briton shore . . ."

Miles. How clearly I remember the miles. Miles of summer sea. And then the smell of land and sea birds reeling in the heavy, misted air off the coast of Gaul.

"Land!" cried Flannán.

The swell lifted us and dropped us, lifted us and

dropped us. Our little vessel seemed to breathe as she lay upon the water, wheezing like a weary whale. For three long days we had been upon the sea. Two days of sunlight had only served to bring up the stink of the curragh's greased hide. Our clothing was now damp instead of sodden. It itched and chafed against our skin. We smelled of sweat and wet wool and fermented oil. We longed for shore and the promised comfort of long, hot soaks in the scented tubs of the bathhouse which awaited in the village ashore.

Yet the captain stood tense, making no move to turn the ship on a landward tack.

"Land, sir!" cried Flannán again. This time his voice held a slight prod to it.

"Aye . . ." The captain's eyes followed the circling birds. His lean, stern face was pinched with speculative concentration.

"And we've made sweet time of it, despite the mercy of the MacLir," injected Amorgin, staring toward shore as though, by the pure power of will, he might bring it closer. "I see the twin promontories and the marsh fog! The village'll be just inland!" He was as restless as the hounds within their crate, shifting his weight from one foot to the other, welcoming the smell of the solid earth, anticipating the pleasures of a night spent ashore.

"The village . . . ?" The captain tested the words. Softly. Treadingly. Then, as though stung by a wasp, his head went up. His brow furrowed. His mouth turned down. "Listen." The word was a command.

We stood silent. All around us the world was filled with the sound of birds and the slosh, slosh of the sea against the curragh's sides. Far off, landward, we could hear the slow, even break of combers along the shoreline.

Amorgin at last broke the silence, impatiently. "I hear nothing."

The captain turned to him. "Exactly. Nothing. The wind blows to us from the land. There is a village there, built to thrive upon the commerce brought to it by such vessels as this. How many times have we beached this curragh there, on the tidal flat below the salt marsh, within sight and smell and sound of it . . . the shouting vendors, the children laughing, the dogs barking and mules braying, and the women hawking hot breads and baths and spiced wine and trinkets? But listen, man! Do you hear it now? Do you hear any sign of humanity at all upon the wind?"

We listened. It was as he said. There was the sound of silence.

And then, as though they had heard our words and wished to confirm our darkest suspicions, the ravens came.

They flew toward us from out of the inland hills. Keening. Black against the blue miles of the ebbing day. They were massed like an advancing army, moving in close formation, wings rising and falling in the strong, slow, rhythmic sweep of flight. For a moment, rising effortlessly on some vagrant updraft of the wind, they hung suspended—a great, black, living banner. Then the wind caught them and swept them down like leaves, swept them out across the sea. They came so close to us that we could see their eyes glinting like polished agate and their sharp beaks hanging open as they cawed and cried. The wind took them past us, lifted them again, carrying them high and away into the west.

"Land birds seeking the sea . . ." The captain's voice was taut. "And no threat of storm . . ."

Comla nodded. "Ravens," he said, and the way he turned the word was a pronouncement of doom.

I felt the cold, steady turning of premonitory dread even as I heard the captain say: "We will lay offshore for the night. Come morning, we shall seek a landing. But not here. There is the smell of Death in the wind."

Ravens. Dreams. Prophecies spun out of the threads of pain and fear and memories not content to remain caught in the dormant tide of Yesterday. The night came down upon us like a shroud, with no light to tell us from the shore that all was safe and welcoming. The captain had been right. Somehow there was danger for us there, from some quarter which we did not know or care to imagine.

We took our turns at watch though in truth none of us slept, so it is difficult for me to understand now, looking back, how we did not hear them come upon us. True enough, there was no moon. The stars were cold and distant. A fog had risen from the inland marshes, the thinnest veil of cloud. The stars shone through it as though through smoke. The air was filled with the astringent scent of the marsh and with another scent, one which my sanity, but surely not my sense of reason, kept me from identifying or associating with the hungry, tearing beaks of ravens.

And then they were upon us. They came at us like wolves, snarling out of the night. I remember. I dare not remember. They came at us like flame. I feel the heat of them. How many were there? I do not know. I can only tell you that they were pirates, and that their language was alien to us. They came in a great wooden ship which, by their own skill, made no sound as it approached us. Suddenly, like spirits materializing into flesh and blood out of air and darkness, they were aboard and the little curragh was pitching wildly with their unwelcome weight, as though she sensed their intentions and wished to throw them into the sea.

More than half of their number remained aboard their own larger vessel. They held torches so that the boarding party might see. They stared down and called lustily, taunting us as they gaffed the curragh and drew her alongside as easily as a fish taken as prize. The men who had boarded us had unsheathed their swords—short swords ready to swipe out and cut at us if we did not yield. They were dark men and crude, ready to do murder for pleasure. In the dancing light of the torches, with the cold, distant, misted stars shining impassively, we knew that these men intended to make slaves or shark meat of us.

I was gaping in shock at them when Amorgin, with no warning, belched a soul-curdling bellow, lowered his rusty head and charged the pirate standing nearest to him. Startled, the man leaped aside to avoid impact, and our little curragh, with its shallow draught and gunwales so near the surface of the sea, slid over onto her side, depositing us all unceremoniously into the sea.

The cold, black water seeped instantly into our heavy garments and bound us in them. I went down into darkness, choking, fighting for the surface. When I found it, it was bedlam, with the pirates on their ship holding their torches high, shouting encouragement to their sodden comrades. Swords slashed. Men cursed and flailed. I heard Amorgin laughing and I remember thinking: Merciful God, he is enjoying this! Then someone grabbed my hair, nearly snapped my spinal column at the neck as he jerked my head brutally back, trying to force me beneath the waves where, surely, he would hold me until

I drowned. Instinctively, with a backward kick, I swung around and, without thinking, slammed my right arm forward. I could not see my assailant. Darkness and flying water stood between us. My forearm made contact with what must have been a nose. I felt it give even as the hand released my hair and the nose's owner raged in agony.

It was then that I heard the terrfied, gulping yelps of the dogs. I turned toward the sound in time to see them, drowning stones within their heavy cage, sinking beneath the water. Though it was not reasonable to be concerned for hounds at such a time, I pitied them and knew that they were, after all, my charges. Elbowing my way past comrades and pirates, I swam to them, diving after the sinking cage into a world of cold, almost total blackness. I could just make out the cage and went after it, feverishly grabbing and running my hands along the bars of wood and hemp until I felt the slatted door. The water around me pulsed and throbbed with sound. I felt pressure thickening within my ears. The door slid back easily enough, I reached in, grabbed the first hound and guided it free; then the second; then the third; then the fourth. They bounded upward past me, running for the surface like great diving water birds. I caught the collar of the fifth and last dog, a huge gray bitch and, together with her, fought my way to the surface.

My comrades had vanished. Drowned? Taken into captivity? Safe away to shore? I had no way of knowing. I knew only that the water around me was still filled with cursing pirates. Torchlight flickered from the pirates' vessel and men leaned out, pointing at me, shouting.

Beyond the ship, all was blackness stretching out to sea and inland toward the distant beach. I released the hound. Again I dove beneath the surface, tearing at the encumbering yardage of my lummon. With its weight gone from me, I stretched out in the water and began to swim. Long, reaching, silent underwater strokes. When next I came up for air, I was well beyond the reach of the pirates' torches. I treaded water in darkness, listening to their shouts and curses. Slowly, fixing my position by the sound of the distant surf, I began to swim again toward the beach.

It seemed hours away. Years away. The water was cold. My right arm ached where I had struck the pirate. I prayed as I swam. For strength. For understanding. For the safety of the seamen with whom I had sailed from Eire. My body felt trapped within a numbing limbo of endless cold and darkness. Yet I swam on. And on. And in time, my arms ever reaching, my limbs ever moving, I began to wish, not for Comla's or Amorgin's sake, but for my own, that I could indeed rise up and walk upon the water like Christ Jesus had done. But it was as I had told Comla. I, who had toppled the standing stone in the mountain glen and who had faced the Powers of the Otherworld, was, when all was said and done, but a simple man of faith. I could work no miracles. I could only pray to the Lord my God for strength to reach the shore.

And the strength was mine. In truth, that itself often seems like a miracle to me, for I do not remember reaching the beach. I know only that I awoke in darkness, shivering, staring into the questioning eyes of Comla.

"By the grace of the gods . . . does the boy'o live?"

"Grace of . . . one . . . God . . ." I spoke the words through a wave of nausea. Strong hands rolled me onto my side and slapped at my back until I vomited a tide of sea water.

It was then that I heard Amorigin's growl of disappointment. "He lives all right . . . the MacLir's spit'm up, puke that he is."

"Aye . . . aye . . . and praise be . . ." Comla's rough hands were rubbing my back, soothing. "Shake the drippin's off'ya now, boy'o. We must be away from the beach quickly and off to the marsh. There's places there a man can hide. Aye. Till we gets our bearin's and sees what's up in the village . . . if there's a village left at all."

I rolled onto my back, propping myself onto my elbows, closing my eyes as I attempted to drive away the throbbing dizziness which hummed within my temples. "The others . . . ?"

"If they's come ashore, we's not seen'm."

Amorgin grunted. "With the Christian along'ta bring us luck, sure'n they's dead and at the bottom of the sea. The MacLir keeps good men. Aye. More's the pity."

I opened my eyes and sought Amorgin's face in the darkness. The sight of it sent the world flaring into light. His eyes had nearly swelled shut. His once hooked nose was twisted, flattened, and engorged with blood.

A surge of pain thrummed in my forearm, and suddenly I knew that it was no pirate who had met the force of my blow in the waters beside the capsized little curragh. It was Amorgin who would have drowned me.

20

THE dawn filled the world with gray light. The treading fingers of morning fog awakened us. Cold. Wet. We lay beneath the thin, broken cover of marsh shrubs and smelled the dank stink of the morning. The air bore the acid stench of old ashes, the offensive sweet taint of putrefying flesh. We lay still, barely daring to breathe.

The fog shut the sun away from us, granting light but no warmth. We lay still, shivering with cold. Listening. Waiting. But nowhere was there a human sound. There was only the distant roll of the surf, the cries of birds and, growing with the morning, the thrum of awakening insect life and the occasional splash of a fish.

There were five of us huddled together upon a moist spit of land, with the marsh all around and the gnarled, salt-blackened shrubs forming a miniature forest in which we sought shelter. How had the others reached that small and stinking shore to lie exhausted and battered beside me? I do not know, for in all of the surrounding acres of marsh ours was not the only high ground. There were other islands within the fen, mere mounds and heaps of sandy loam—all flat as the chests of prepubescent girls, all wooded with stunted vegetation; all rank with the astringent scent of eternal dampness, all inscribed with the tracings of serpents and the tracks of crabs and rodents. Yet, somehow, we had all, save Flannán, floundered here in the darkness, and the hounds had followed us, half-drowned and cowed. Now they lay beside us, whistling with nervous indecision as they sniffed the new and threatening smell of their first day in this unfamiliar and unwelcoming land.

The hours passed. We lay in silence, waiting for the sound of pirates, not daring to speak until we were certain that only the natural predators of the marsh were about to hear our voices.

Slowly the fog thinned. By midmorning the sun was

visible through a humid, mist-stained cloud cover which lay upon the marsh like a vapor conjured from a sorcerer's cauldron. It stank. It was as thick as pudding, as opaque as the membrane which sometimes forms over a blind eye.

We checked each other for wounds. Other than a minor sword gash along the captain's cheek and Amorgin's broken nose, we were amazed to see that we had come through the attack with only bruises.

The captain was the first to speak. He did so with gestures, signing to Crimthann and me that we were to keep our vigil while he, Amorgin, and Comla left us to check out the whereabouts of the pirates. He, Comla, and Crimthann had their small carrying daggers, weapons worn by all seamen who venture into the trade routes. Amorgin had somehow lost his knife in the melee, but had come up with one of the pirate's short swords to replace it. He grinned as he demonstrated the loss of his knife with a quick upward jab of his right hand. He had evidently lodged it permanently into his attacker's gut. Nodding with dark pleasure, he told of the winning of the sword by turning his hairy fists around an imaginary neck.

They went off in three directions, their weapons drawn as they crawled away from us on their bellies like lizards. The captain made for the village. Amorgin headed back and eastward toward the dunes, which would offer him a view over the tidal flat to the sea. Comla proceeded north to the low range of hills, which would afford him a landward scan.

By the movement of the sun, I knew that little more than an hour had passed before they returned to us. Crimthann sat like a stone the entire time, his knife at ready, his wide young face pale and drawn with weariness. Yet he was alert, for his body spasmed and went taut at the slightest sound.

Comla and Amorgin returned almost simultaneously. Walking. Not crawling. We could hear the slosh of their footsteps coming toward us boldly through the marsh. For a moment we cowered, cold and alert with terror, fearing that they were pirates.

Then Amorgin called out to us. "Crimthann! You and

the puke! Rise up now, boy'os! Not a pirate in sight to piss at!"

Relief ran through us, as sweet as spring water on a summer day. We were standing, embracing and back-slapping one another, like schoolboys who have just learned that their tutor has been taken ill on the eve of an exam, when Comla came to us, nodding his affirmation of Amorgin's words.

"Inland the land's as clean as a new-scrubbed table. Like no man had ever set crumbs upon it in all the days of the world." He bent to unlace his shoes. Baring his feet and wringing brown marsh water from his shoes, he shook his head. "Has Flannán showed his face yet?"

"We have not seen him since the curragh turned and put us in the sea," I said.

The seamen exchanged knowing looks.

"Aye, well, then . . ." exhaled Amorgin, "perhaps the captain'll find'm in the village . . . ?"

"There's no village," Comla informed us bleakly. "From the hill I could see. 'Twas like a stain on the land. Scabbed over. A woundin' done long before we come. The captain'll be findin' naught there to please . . ."

Crimthann's face furrowed with incredulity. "Nothin' at all . . . ?"

"Not a house left standin', boy'o. Naught but bones picked clean by the birds. If there's people left alive at all, perhaps they's in the thin wood on the other side of the river. He'll be lookin' for'm there, no doubt. But from what my eyes saw, and from what my guts say . . . no . . . he'll be findin' naught to please . . . naught to please at all, at all . . ."

"But he has a woman there," said Crimthann.

"*Had.*" Amorgin's tone was heavy with finality. He had packed cooling mud upon his battered nose the night before. It had dried and had begun to itch. He picked at it carefully as he spoke. "A sweet morsel she. But if things be as Comla says they be, she'll be gone. Dead. Or slave to some ruttin' bastard long, long away from these parts."

"I saw no women aboard the pirate vessel," I said.

"The village wasn't smote by no pirates, boy'o," Comla told me pointedly. "It was marauders out'a the heart'a the land done that work. Aye. Days ago."

"Barbarians?"

"Aye. Big, yellow-headed folk with a bent to usin' the axe and a queer sort'a short javelin in battle. They's good hands in a fight, for they's land-hungry folk with a pure and glorious love'a challenge. They prowls the earth these days with their great long shields. They drags all their kin in their wake. They settles where they can. Even keeps the peace sometimes, when it suits'm. Rome's made deals with'm now and again, settin'm up in some sort of legal federations. But'ja can't deal with folk like that, not from the vantage point of the wee lambie tryin' to work out livin' arrangements with a starvin' wolf, if'ya takes my meanin'. These people want what Rome's got, and they likes nothing better'n to prove their manhood in battle. Now, a man of Eire, he can understand that. And by understandin', he can deal with'm . . . because he'd never misunderstand what they was. But the Romans? Ach. They've given away their honor and have gone as soft as babes at breast. I've heard tell that more'n half'a the Roman Army is made up of paid mercenaries . . . men hired from the very ranks'a them that wants to eat what's left'a the Empire."

Amorgin had peeled most of the mud from his nose. With the tips of his fingers, he gingerly felt out the extent of his injury as he snarled: "The Gauls put their trust in Rome. And when the barbarians took a notion to put half'a their land to the torch a few years back, what'd Rome do to protect'm? Withdrew its army to protect its own flank!" He worked up a saliva and spat it contemptuously upon the ground. "Ach, if they'd been men of Eire, they'd've been dragged out to the bogs and buried alive as cowards. Rome! It may've been a great power once . . . before it was took over by the god'a Christian pukes!"

I started to speak a protest, but Crimthann shook his head, as though he wished to clear it of a bad dream, and interrupted me in an unnaturally high and rushing flood of words.

"It's always been peaceful here. Aye. A safe part'a Gaul. Too far south and too small a tradin' center for any of the barbarian armies to be botherin' with. The captain said it many a time . . . settle for the smaller profit so long as its secure . . . less risk . . . steady . . . means more take for a man in the long run. Aye. And we've seen'm all here. Greeks'n Picts. Romans'n

Vandals. Suevi and even a Hun or two. Men who wouldn't run with no pack. Businessmen out for their own fortunes in the world. And we've had good times with'm all . . . been drunk together . . . and I had me a girl here . . . a Frisian girl . . . slave to the old hag who runs the bathhouse . . . a good girl . . ." He paused, confused, wide-eyed. "Why would anyone've wanted to burn the village? Them was kindly folk there . . . honest enough if a man kept a sharp eye . . . willin' to offer pleasure for a fair price . . ."

Amorgin put a brotherly arm about Crimthann's slim shoulder. "Pleasure. Sure'n you've said the very word. It was done for pleasure."

Comla frowned. "Pleasure? What sort'a folk takes pleasure in slaughter? From what I seen, there wasn't no battle glory won that day. It was slaughter quickly done."

"It was such a small town . . . there couldn't even'a been much treasure . . ." Crimthann's voice still had the high, quivering strain of one who clings desperately to control. Yet there were tears smarting in his eyes. He was shaking. "Do'ya think they hurt my girl . . . she was a good girl . . ."

Amorgin drew Crimthann close. "Understand, boy'o . . . there are treasures taken in this world that men cannot see. Mark me, for it is like the great wind that blows down from the mountains off the coast of Africa. It's in us all. Aye. Not often felt. But there. A killin' wind, a lustin' wind. It knows neither pity nor shame. And when it rises in a man, it's like a terrible tide, sweepin' him along after a satisfaction sweeter'n darker than that given by the finest wine. There's no stoppin' it. Sure and it's like the banshee wind risin' out'a the Otherworld, suckin' the very soul from a man's head . . . makin' him know the need'ta kill . . . aye . . . and the need'ta take a maid down screamin', ridin' her till sperm and blood run in'ta the earth beneath the all-seein' eye of the gods'a glory . . . and then burnin' all traces of his deeds behind'm . . . so that only the wind will be left'ta tell of them . . ."

Crimthann stared at Amorgin. "They was our friends . . ."

Amorgin's eyes were fixed, unseeing. Spittle shone in the corners of his mouth. "They's no man's friends now . . ." It was as though he were entranced. Slowly sight came back into his eyes and he focused them upon me. Withdrawing his arm from Crimthann's shoulder, he wiped his mouth with the back of his hand.

He smiled then. "They's all dead now. Like the people of the Briton shore. Ask the Christian. He'll tell'ya. Like the folk in the village, his people fell before the banshee wind. How was it on that day, eh, boy'o? How was it when the god'a pukes led his little lambs to the slaughter? Ach! And'ja still follow'm! Can'ya not see that the true gods live with the men of Eire . . . and with the Vandals and the Alans and the Goths . . . and they feast . . . runnin' with the banshee wind . . . roarin' like lions!"

Comla grunted and sat down, rubbing his toes with concentration. "With it, and before it, Amorgin. From the hill I saw how it is. As far as the eye can wander . . . nothin' . . . not farm or pasture left to offer sustenance to a man. Only the wild hills stretchin' away. If we's lions, Amorgin, we'd best be forewarned that there are bigger and hungrier lions afield . . . and they will eat us if they can."

"We must leave this place." The captain's voice startled us. He had returned so quietly that none of us had heard his movement through the marsh or the surrounding shrubbery. We turned to see him standing behind us.

He was a large man, broad-boned, bronzed from the sun. Yet, in that moment, he seemed shrunken, withered somehow into himself. He was pale, like a great tree that has been blighted from within. Outwardly it seems still untouched, yet a man, looking upon it, knows that he has seen Death in it.

"Flannán . . . ?" Chrimthann turned the question.

"Dead. In the estuary. Of wounds inflicted last night."

Silence settled among us, heavier, more stifling than the marsh fog.

"We will go to the north," said the captain at length. "The gods have not completely forsaken us. We still have the hounds. When we reach a harbor, we will be able to use them as barter to assure our passage home."

"It is miles . . . days to the nearest port!" Amorgin reminded.

The captain nodded. "Aye, and so. What would you have us do, Amorgin? Go lusting inland after the barbarians?"

"I . . ."

"You, alone among us, have come away from this well-

armed. Follow your banshee wind if you wish. I shall not
hold you. As for me, I have seen too much of Death this
day . . ."

For twenty-eight days we traveled across the ravaged
earth, keeping well inland of the sea for fear of pirate
slavers. We took what nourishment we could from a land
which had been deliberately scourged by the pagan force
which had preceded us. Nowhere did we find a village
left standing, or pastureland which had not been put to
the torch.

Gaul stretched before us, a desert. The rivers ran foul
with the remnants of carnage. Even the wild grains had
been reduced to stubble. We set snares for whatever
luck might bring, but many of the creatures of the fields
had died of starvation, and the predators of the woods
and hills—foxes, rats, and birds—had become fat and
wise as they fed upon the refuse of battle. As we camped
together in the night, agreeing that even the carcass of a
mouse might sit well on our starving palates, the watching
eyes of creatures who had come to know the taste of human flesh shone from the darkness around our meager
fire.

On the morning of the twenty-ninth day, the captain
cast a jaundiced eye my way. His face, like mine, was
ravaged by fatigue and hunger. "We can no longer hope
to survive on burnt berries and shriveled roots. Tonight,
if we have found no nourishment to sustain us, we will
have to slaughter one of the hounds."

I nodded. The others had muttered about this for days,
but the captain had held off, saying that the dogs were
lean and would offer little meat. He had reminded us
that they were our sole fortune in this world. They were
our boarding pass, if we should ever find a harbor, let
alone a ship with men to sail it.

"You saved the dogs when they might have drowned."
His voice was quiet, restrained by fatigue. "Now it seems
that, by your act, we may all be saved."

"The hounds were my charges," I replied evenly.

His eyes moved over my face, openly assessing me.
"You have stayed with us. Why? I've awakened each
dawn expecting to see you gone."

"You travel to the north. North leads toward my
homeland. I stand a better chance of reaching it if I re-

main with you. How else would I hope to find passage upon a ship save by your recommendation?"

His mouth twitched for want of a smile. "As you have found passage before . . . by the power of your wit and the pure audaciousness of your nerve. But have you not thought, boy, that you may find Briton as you have found Gaul . . . battered and burnt and no refuge for any man?"

"At least I shall have found it, and I shall be a free man among my own people again, by the grace of God."

"God . . ." He exhaled the word with infinite weariness. "After all we have seen? It brings a man to wonder if it is anything more than the whim of the wind which carries us. The dead in all the villages . . . they had their gods . . . they made their sacrifices . . ."

"There is but one God."

"And he slays with impunity those who do not bow before him? And enslaves those who reverence his name? Indeed, my boy, your god *is* a god of riddles."

I drew my faith around me, seeking strength in it. It seemed heavy. It weighted me with doubt. "There is a purpose . . ." I said with a resolve meant to blight my own questions.

He was silent for a moment. Then he said: "Tell me, Christian, you say that your God is great and all-powerful; why, then, do you not pray for us? As you can see, we are suffering from hunger; it is unlikely that we shall ever see a human being again."

"You have warned me to keep silent about my God. But I have prayed. Across all these long miles, every step I have taken has been with prayer."

"Then if your god is all-powerful, why does he not reply? Surely you have asked him for food, for an end to this hapless trek?"

I looked into his face and saw the condescension of a world-weary man who thought me to be a fool. "The Lord my God has promised: 'Ask and it shall be given.' "

"When?"

I felt the knot of aching hunger within my gut. "Soon . . . surely . . . soon . . ."

"It took him six years to see you away from bondage in Eire." He shook his head, bemused, smiling drolly. "We cannot wait six years for our next meal, Christian. Next time you pray, remind your god that we are mere mortals and must meet certain schedules if we are to maintain our earthly existence . . ."

"We." The word jabbed. I started. "Perhaps that is the key. I have asked. I have prayed. But I am a member of a company, and who among you has asked in His name?"

"We do not honor your god. We honor the gods of the Gael."

"You are not in Eire now."

His brows rose speculatively. "That is true."

"The Lord my God is God here . . . since the day that Constantine the Great declared His Truth and His Way. Ask in His name, and perhaps this very day He shall send us food and we shall eat until we are satisfied."

My sudden burst of enthusiasm amused him. Then, slowly, his mood turned and his smile ebbed away. "Tell me, Christian, when we slaughter a hound tonight, a graceful beast which has been a trusting comrade these past days, shall its flesh satisfy you? Will you, who by your own hand rescued it from the sea, claim it as food sent from your god? For if you do, let me remind you that there are five hounds. One for each man. After one hound has been slaughtered, that shall make it four to five . . . that much less chance for you to see the Briton shore, for the hound which we slaughter I shall personally offer up for you. Your boarding pass shall be gone. Will you thank your god for that?"

He had sought to bruise me with his words. He angered me instead. "The Lord my God has brought me out of slavery in Eire. Yes. I thank Him for all things."

"Did not your god bring you to bondage in the first place?"

"So that I might understand the wisdom of His word. Now he leads me home where, by His grace, I shall not see a Gaelic face again."

He countered evenly. "By the grace of the gods of Eire, you shall live to see the Gael take your homeland as their own. It is happening even now. The Gael to the west of you . . . the barbarians to the east, north and south . . ."

Contempt turned my lips into a snarl of disdain. "I see no difference between the Gael and the barbarans."

His brows rose. "We are both people who will stand for what we believe and for what we desire. How will the Christian lambs of Briton, following a passive god, stand against us? How will you stand against us?"

erous riptides of the times. Two days to the
they told us, was a small harbor of sorts. Sea-
aghs from Eire had been known to beach there
rpose of minor trade with the local folk.

were a kind and generous lot. They bathed us
d us and asked nothing of us in return save our
nd our fellowship. They eyed our hounds with
, having never seen such tall dogs before. On the
ng of the eleventh day they sent us on our way with
enough to last us through our two-day journey to the

o it was that we went, with no premonition of what
s to come. The day passed uneventfully. When night
ll upon the earth, we again gathered dry wood and built
r fire high, to warm us and cheer us as we thought of
ur respective homelands with joyous anticipation.

Perhaps it was our fire which drew them, or the sound
of our laughter and song, for surely ours was a loud and
confident gathering. The clansmen in the village had not
sent us off without their own brand of home-brewed ale
to "warm the nights of the wanderers." We had all im-
bibed deeply, drinking from the skin flasks until they
hung flaccid and dry. We had even shared the brew with
the hounds, finding immense pleasure in seeing them stag-
ger in drunkenness.

We slept well and deeply. The warm and dreamless
sleep of the pleasantly sotted. When dawn colored the
sky, we did not heed it but rooted more deeply under the
blankets, which had been a gift from the villagers.

How long we lay there, oblivious to the change which
was taking place around us, I do not know. I remember
only that I was the first to awaken with a start. I sat bolt
upright, staring.

Our camp was surrounded by a dozen enormous, fair-
haired, bearded men who casually sat on their haunches
as they patiently waited for us to awaken. They were
dressed in tones of dun and gray, in rough wool and
leather and linen. They had set their huge painted shields
behind them, and each held, or balanced across his
thighs, a handsomely wrought short throwing javelin.
They were, in the main, young men. From the set of their
features, they might well all have been relatives. To a
man they were ruddy-faced, with sharp blue eyes and a
smirk of self-satisfaction upon their faces. One of them

Anger twitched in my palms, curling them into fists. "I
will follow the will of the Lord my God. It is He, not I,
who shall defy you."

He stared at me, measuring, nodding as he affirmed his
summation. "I see a man who follows his own will. Mark
me, Christian, Amorgin is right when he speaks of the
banshee wind. It lives within us all. It is best to face it,
lest it catch us unaware and sweep us away. In truth,
I see no passive lamb when I look upon you. There is
a lion living in your skin. Be wary. He will break free
someday. The question is: Will he eat you, or will he
eat your god?"

The sun climbed toward noon, then seemed to stand
exhausted in the sky, turning all the world to soft gold.
We moved slowly beneath it. We were not far from the
sea, yet the salt wind did not reach us. The world was
still, trembling with heat, silent save for the murmuring
conversation of insects within the low hills.

There had been a change in the land occurring grad-
ually over the past few days. Our hunger had dulled our
perception. We had failed to take note of it. The grasses
grew taller. The air bore no stink of carnage. In the furrows of the hills, birdsong filled the wood, and freshets
ran clean and cold so that we could drink our fill, and
did, until our bellies growled and our senses sparked with
gratitude.

It was beside such a freshet, in the shade of willows
with long leaves blistered with galls, that we paused to
rest. Like wild men, we plucked grasses and foraged for
edible roots and herbs. There were nettles growing along
the bank. We stripped the stinging, barbed skin away, ignoring our burning fingers, and sucked on pithy, tasteless
vegetable flesh while the hounds sniffed for their own sustenance and whimpered pitifully to themselves. Chewing
the unpalatable, fibrous nettle, I remembered the morning's words with the captain and found my eyes following
the dogs as I sadly wondered which one of them would be
candidate for the night's supper.

At what moment did we hear the sound of the pigs? It
seemed that we all froze at once, staring at one another
in hopeful disbelief. They came trotting and snorting,
snuffling and grunting down toward the freshet. The wind
must have been with us, for they evidently caught no

scent of men or dogs. They came. Not one. Not two. But an entire herd of them. Lean, long, wiry-haired, and totally oblivious to us.

I exhaled my disbelief in a sigh of gratitude. "Merciful God in Heaven . . ."

The hounds went stiff, heads up, suddenly salivating. Then, men and beasts together, in a howling, shouting explosion of joy, set upon the pigs at once. I was unarmed, so I could serve best as a foil, waving my arms as I confounded would-be escapees, grabbing potential runaways and holding them fast to the ground while my companions dispatched them readily, their eyes filled with visions of the evening's meal.

For two days we were content to remain on that blessed embankment, feasting off that afternoon's kill. On the second day, Amorgin found a honey tree not far from where we had first seen the pigs. Together we all went to the tree and built a fire and smoked the bees into a swarm of angry confusion which, at last, under Comla's guidance, gave us access to their treasure: a horde of liquid amber rich enough to satisfy us all to surfeit and beyond. Yet, before any of us had tasted it, Comla bid us hold.

"Wait," said he, holding out a massive chunk of dripping comb. "This we offer in sacrifice."

The others muttered their agreement, suddenly disturbed by the fact of their neglect. Other than occasional mumblings of gratitude, none of them had made a move to properly thank their gods for the blessing of the pork upon which we had all gorged ourselves. They had eaten and slept, and eaten and slept, and eaten again, with no thought save that of recovering their strength. I alone had spent the hours in silent prayers of thanksgiving, blessing God for his long-withheld benevolence to us.

So they set aside the honey and set about the task of building a new fire, a "god fire," gathering stones to make an altar before it. They went to the freshet and washed themselves, and each of them brought up a joint of pork and a generous wedge of his portion of the honey as they gathered before the fire, calling me out, insisting that I join with them.

"We must thank the gods," said the captain.

"There is but One God."

Amorgin growled with impatience and disgust. "Are'ya goin' to start that nonsense again?"

The captain fixed me[...] "We shall thank all of th[...] for, in truth, we cannot be[...] ing has come."

"It has come from the God[...] before none save Him."

"Then, you shall not partake of t[...]

"If that is the will of God, so be it.[...]

Amorgin's face went black with ang[...] gant, stubborn, insufferable little bastar[...] the wrath of the gods down upon us again[...]

He started toward me. From the look[...] knew that if he put his hands upon me, he w[...] to wring my head from my neck. The capta[...] out and caught his arm, restraining him. "Easy, [...] D[...] not waste your energy or your anger. The gods h[...]ve de[...] signed to smile upon us once again. Despite the Chr[...] tian."

Amorgin snatched his arm free. "Tell that to Flanná[...] he growled and spat viciously onto the ground at my f[...]

They made their sacrifice without me, and though my[...] mouth salivated with desire for my portion of the honey, I tasted none of it. The next morning, having devoured all but the hair and hide of the slaughtered hogs, we broke camp and moved on.

For nine days we walked across a land which no longer bore the stain of violence. In the nights we built our fires high, for no longer did we feel any threat or sense any hint of danger. Our snares captured fat rabbits, and in the streams we found fish which seemed to go out of their way to blunder into our rudely fashioned traps.

On the tenth day, as we made ready to set our snares for the evening meals, we came upon a shepherd girl. She stared at us with clear, curious eyes, and when the captain spoke to her, in her dialect, telling her of our hardships, she blinked and suggested that we walk a bit farther that day. She told us that just over the next hill was her village and, surely, her people would wish to hear our news and share with us the comforts of their hearth and board.

It was a tiny hamlet, a mere scattering of wattle-and-daub hovels; the homestead of an extended clan which was content to live upon the land with its cattle and hogs, tending its small flocks and keeping well out of the way looked at me, nudged the man next to him and, laughing, made a comment in a language which was totally foreign to me.

I instinctively sensed danger. Comla lay next to me, snoring sloppily. I jammed my elbow into his arm. He opened a bloodshot eye and muttered a resentful and sleeepy "What . . . ?"

There is a language transmitted in silence between men in times of trouble. I did not move or speak aloud, yet Comla clearly heard me. He sat upright, automatically drawing his knife.

I reached out and lay a warning hand firmly upon his arm. "Hold . . . and easy . . ."

His eyes widened, then narrowed with speculation as he surveyed the situation. "Vandals . . . or Goths . . . northmen of some sort . . ."

His words affirmed my fears. "What do they want of us?"

He did not reply. To my amazement, he spoke to the strangers in their own tongue.

The largest and oldest of the lot, evidently the patriarch of the pack, grunted and replied in what seemed an amiable tone.

Comla cursed. His face congested with anger.

"What did he say to you?"

"Just that he's our master now. That he'n his kin has broke off from the main ranks of their people. They've took a fancy to the land hereabouts and has set up a village not a half day's stroll to the north. Their women needs men's hands, but they are warriors and will not do a woman's work. So they've come huntin' for slaves. Seems we's their catch'a the mornin'."

The sound of his voice had roused the others. As Comla and I had done, they shifted in their bedding and then started up. Crimthann simply sat and stared, wide-eyed, his face white. The captain and Amorgin both rose to their feet, painfully sober.

The patriarch eyed them both, taking in their drawn weapons. His brow rose at the sight of Amorgin's short sword. He spoke.

Comla translated. "He says we're to put aside our weapons like obedient little boy'os. He'n his kin has brought leg irons for us. We're to put'm on and then we'll all march back to their village together, where we's to be presented as gifts to their wives'n daughters."

The captain took a step forward, his manner and bearing immediately identifying him as our leader. Like Comla, he also spoke the tongue of the barbarians. He used it to them now, curling his words downward with cold contempt.

Comla tensed beside me. "He's just accused the big boy'o of cowardice . . . said that only men of no honor would set upon others without givin'm a chance to stand in their own defense."

The barbarians exchanged knowing looks. Slowly the patriarch rose to his full height. He was a massive man, perhaps as old as forty, yet straight as a forest pine. He had unusually expressive pale-blue eyes which, perhaps in another situation, might have been considered handsome. His blond, red-tinged eyebrows shifted upon his wide brow. He raised his head and spoke to the captain with total disdain.

Again Comla translated. "He says that we're drunken fools and he would not waste a true man's honor upon us. He says that if we would dispute'm, he'll gladly demonstrate the true state of our value, which, he says, is about equal to that of our hounds . . . animals so useless that they do not even growl to warn their masters of impending danger."

I looked to the dogs. They still slept in a twitching, drunken stupor around the embers of the fire.

The captain flailed stern words back at the patriarch.

Comla winced. "He says that we are men of Eire and will not go willingly or easily into slavery."

The patriarch nodded. His kinsmen seemed pleased. They rose to stand beside their leader, testing the weight of their javelins.

Hesitantly, Crimthann got to his feet and wheezed weakly: "They's twelve to our five . . ."

"Four," corrected Amorgin with a leer. "The Christian's no man, even if he was armed . . ."

Somewhere within me, something had begun to bleed, to run cold with a flooding of anger which would not be contained. I rose to my feet, glaring at Amorgin. "Would you put me to the test again? Perhaps this time I shall smash your vicious jaw and not just your nose."

The others stared at me, shocked. Comla allowed himself the luxury of a titter at Amorgin's expense. I met the captain's eyes and was cut to the quick by their intensity.

"Has the lamb yielded to the lion, then? Will you stand with us?"

I did not flinch. "I will not be a slave again."

His head moved with grim assent.

"We's seamen, not warriors," reminded Comla, stiffly getting to his feet. "These men we face is hardened fighters, weaned on blood they is, suckled on it at their mother's teats. By the memory of the Red Branch Knights of the days'a glory . . . we's no match for'm."

Crimthann's face had gone from white to gray. He was having difficulty catching his breath. "No match . . ." he whispered.

Amorgin growled deep in his throat. "What words are these? By the gods of Eire, even the puke wants to fight'm!" He reached down and hefted his blanket, deftly whirling it around his left forearm, steeling himself for combat. "Stand tall, boy'os . . . by the grace'a the gods'a glory, we'll all live to see another sunrise as free men."

Fear came to live within us all at that moment. Yet, as we began to close ranks, facing the barbarians with steadfast belligerence, we followed Amorgin's example and wrapped our blankets around what would, in normal battle circumstances, have been our shield arms.

The northmen stared at us a moment, muttered amongst themselves, then, to our amazement, set aside their javelins and drew their knives. It was a statement of respect. They would face us in hand-to-hand combat. They would claim no advantage, save by their number. We had shown ourselves to be men of honor in their eyes.

What happened then still rises as a bloodied haunting with me. Comla had been right. We were no match for them. Crimthann fell first, gut-stabbed and screaming in terror like an incredulous child.

The barbarians were all around me when I saw Comla die. Two of them ripped him, back and front, so that he stood a moment, knowing Death before he fell. Then someone grabbed me. I felt the pressure of a great arm coming down across my throat. As has often happened in my life, I did not think. I reacted, bending over, catching my attacker off balance and pitching him over my head.

He was a large, tawny man, and for a moment he lay stunned, shaking his head.

Suddenly Amorgin was beside me, a bloodied knife in his left hand, his short sword in his right. "Well done, puke!" He thrust his sword into my hands, then bounded off to face his own destiny.

The sword was light within my hands. How perfectly its haft seeeemed to set within my palms. The weight of the weapon seemed an extension of my arm. I was light-headed. My arms swept the air before me with the blade, slicing, testing the heft of the weapon. How right it seemed to me in that moment. How infinitely good.

The man on the ground was regaining his senses. Barbarian. Slaver. Murderer. These were the words which twitched upon my tongue as I looked upon him. Behind my eyes I saw the faces of the dead. Flannán and Comla and Crimthann. Dubh and Draigenn. The Rigan and the sons of Sencha. I saw the miles and the years which separated me from my homeland, and saw the Briton shore receding from me across a sea of blood.

Within me there was a distant, rising thrum, a tightening, like a string being drawn taut and then released. And then broken as something seemed to explode within me. It was the flaming light of pure rage. It was pain. It was pleasure. It was the banshee wind roaring unbridled from out of an eternity of benighted canyons. It was a dragon within me, consuming my humanity and my faith and out of an eternity of benighted canyons. It was a dragon within me, consuming my humanity and my faith and my very soul.

I lifted the sword, swung it high, raging out at the barbarian as I charged him, intent upon granting him no mercy. I wanted his death more than I wanted my own life.

"Padraic!"

The call of that name brought a fraction of a second's pause. Who had called it? Who even knew of it? I had not heard it spoken since I had fled Eire. I used only my Roman name with the seamen, and they, disdaining that, called me simply "Christian."

I stood over the barbarian, my arms straining to gather the maximum force necessary to cleave his skull in two.

He stared up at me out of eyes which still refused to focus. He was obviously dizzy, disoriented.

I could smell blood rising in my nostrils. My flesh seemed melded to the sword.

But it never fell. In that moment I was struck mercilessly from behind with a blow so powerful that I fell forward, sprawling into the darkness of oblivion.

21

THE house was dark and dusty, with sunlight filtering in through breaks in the walls and thatching. Spiders spun their web high in the crudely cut rafters. In the shadows, a heavy-bodied woman worked at a loom, and a girl spun fluffs of carded wool into thread upon a drop-spindle. A man lounged upon a rope-strung pallet, humming idly to himself as he sharpened a skinning knife with dreamy concentration. After a while, satisfied with his work, he set the blade aside, stretched and yawned and, after mumbling a few words to the woman, rose, stretched again, took up the knife and ambled from the room through a hide door which led out into the sunlight.

I lay very still, aware of the fact that I shared my cot with another who lay moaning in troubled delirium beside me. I could feel the heat of his fever through the light piece of woolen cloth which covered us both. I must have moved then, for pain sparked at the back of my neck and head. I exhaled an inadvertent sigh of protest against it.

The girl rose and came to me, placing her palm across my forehead to check for fever. The thin, silky strands of her hair had been braided into plaits which hung limply over her narrow, bowed shoulders. She wore a plain, gray, sleeveless, ankle-length gown, tied at the back of her unnaturally blocky neck like a child's smock. She stared at me out of slanted, blank blue eyes which seemed completely without guile or malice or willingness to judge. Yet, somehow, she seemed to see clearly, directly, so that although she was little more than a girl, she seemed old beyond telling, as though she had somehow lived before and known too much of the world. Past. Present. Future. All were written on her slack-jawed little face.

And yet she was a child, blessed with an obscure innocence which would be hers until the ending of her days.
She was totally withdrawn into herself. She saw everything. She saw nothing.

The woman at the loom barked a reproach, and the
girl left me to return to her thread-making. The woman
rose then and came to me reluctantly, talking to herself
as one does when tending an unwanted chore. She looked
at me with shrewd, sharp eyes the color of burnt peat.
She lay a heavy, meaty palm upon my head, pressing,
deliberately reviving my pain.

I did not like her, or her touch, but when I tried to
move away from her I realized, for the first time, that my
hands and feet were bound and that a strong cord was
wrapped about my waist, holding me fast to the cot.

She felt me straining against my bonds and slapped
hard at my midsection until I lay back, glaring at her.
Muttering, she went to the door, pushed back the hide
covering, and shouted sourly to someone outside.

The man returned. The two spoke, snapping one another until the man grunted with annoyance and disappeared. He was back in a few moments. To my amazement, I was actually glad to see that he had Amorgin
with him.

He seemed little the worse for wear, with only a minor
gash across his forehead. Only when he smiled did I see
that he hd lost a tooth or two and that his mouth was
dark with dried blood, though there was little swelling.
He seemed in decent spirits as he came toward me, despite the leg irons which made a raw, bruising sound as
he walked across the earthen floor.

The man nudged him and Amorgin came close to me,
seating himself at the edge of the cot.

"I'm to talk sense to'ya," he said. "They've set me to
workin' the querm when I'm not tendin' the forge for the
smith. A captive there speaks a bit'a the tongue'a the
Gael. Between us, we's come to an understandin' of these
bastards' wants. Seems there was sickness here a time
back. They's short-handed. They needs men. The women
was more'n a bit'a upset with'm when they dragged us
back in less than top workin' order."

"Us . . . ?"

"You'n me and the captain here, though they half
killed'm tryin' to get the chains on'm. When he wakes

. . . if he wakes . . . gentle'm down, boy'o, for I've been made to know that though these bastards needs us, they'll not keep a sullen slave. They'd rather slit his throat and hunt down another."

My head was throbbing. I squinted through rising pain. "Slave . . ." I exhaled the word, unable to accept it.

Amorgin's hand lay upon my forearm with the weight of intended assurance. "Be a nice peaceable boy'o. Let'm heal your hurts. Don't give'm no trouble or none'a that arrogant lip'a yours. Soon enough they'll drop their guard and then we'll be off after the freedom bone faster'n fire flamin' in a grease pot!" He winked at me. "You did us proud back there, boy'o. Aye. You fought like a true son of Eire . . . for a puke, that is. Sure'n, though mind'ja I never thought to hear myself admittin' it . . . I'm thinkin' that your god was with'ya boy'o . . . aye . . . roarin' like a lion . . ."

I looked at him blankly. I had been a willing host to the banshee wind. It had eaten my faith. "Crimthann and Comla and Flannán are dead . . . for what purpose, Amorgin?"

He shrugged. "The gods don't need no purpose. They's gods. They sweeps a man's life as they will. Don't do no good to question. There's no answers. Not in all this world."

The captain slept for many hours. I feared for his life. His breathing was shallow, fitful. When I turned my head toward him, I could see the angular lines of his profile. Even in sleep there were seams of tension, dark groovings from nostril to jaw, from eye to cheekbone. His lips were swollen. His forehead was distended and humped with bruises. Blood had oozed from his ear and lay dried and scabbed at the back of his neck.

The woman came to us now and again, testing us for fever as impersonally as she would have tested loaves of bread for doneness. She muttered incessantly, and when she lay cool towels upon the captain's battered face, she did so with merciless thoroughness, pressing until he moaned. She would smile then, her short, thin lips cracking with pleasure.

The day lengthened. The light which shone through the walls and roof changed from gold to gray. The girl came with a pot of broth. She spoon-fed me wordlessly. When she had done with me, she turned to the captain. He could not eat. She brought a towel and laid it gently upon his brow. Unlike the woman, her touch was so light that he did not rouse at all but actually relaxed.

Then the man came, a surly-faced dullard. I was forced to relieve myself in a pan. Like the woman, he found pleasure in causing pain. He handled me roughly, cursing me the while. Then he turned his attentions to the captain, pulling back the woolen cover, laughing when he saw my reaction. The captain's chest and arms had been cruelly slashed and only haphazardly sewn. The man tested the woundings with quick, brutal little finger jabs, nodding as the captain exhaled in pain.

Later in the night, when the woman and man sucked air through open mouths and snored with total abandon upon their sleeping couch, the girl rose from her pallet, took warm water from the fire-pit cauldron and quietly, surreptitiously filled a basin with it. From within the folds of her sleeping gown, she took a tiny cloth bag and from it poured a few dried leaves, sprinkling them into the basin. These she crushed carefully, as though they were the most precious things in all the world. She crossed the room to us then, walking as silently as a house cat. Tenderly, she drew back the cover and began to bathe the captain's lacerations and bruises with her bare hands. When she had finished, she gestured for me to turn my head away so that she might tend my wound. I did as she wished. My head throbbed at the base of my skull from a bruise which seemed to house fire. Yet the girl's fingers, though they probed gently, brought no pain. She dipped her hand in the basin and lay her palm against the place of my injury, holding it there, pressing with such exquisite tenderness that the weight of her hand was no more than the weight of mist. When at last she withdrew and went back to her own pallet, she had freed me of pain. Gratefully, I closed my eyes and acceded to sleep.

I awoke to darkness. Pain had returned. I lay quietly on the cot, listening to the captain's even breathing, finding comfort in the fact that he seemed improved. Night lay thick within the room, palpable. Somewhere, high amidst the ill-made thatching, something moved, scurried. A rat? A scavenging nocturnal insect? Perhaps a serpent? The darkness of the room seemed to invade my senses.

I thought bleakly: Whatever is there, at least it is free of the twisting machinations of the Fates. It is bound only by the limitations of its own will.

My thoughts bled away into quiet desperation. I tried to pray. No words would form. Within me there was another bruise: the throbbing pain of bitterness and resentment. Memories of violence and degradation moved behind my eyes until the bile of anger soured my mouth. I sought refuge from my thoughts in sleep.

It came to me, drowning me in miles of falling darkness, in tides of black, stifling emptiness which promised nothing, prophesied nothing, and left me at peace within a tomb of my own desiring.

Then, in a sudden bright storm of dream, there was a voice. No. Not a voice. An awareness. A knowledge. A sense of precognition so intense that it was inscribed into my brain as clearly as letters newly carved in stone.

"Two months will you be with them."

I started into wakefulness, chastising myself. It had not been the Inner Vision. It had not been the Sight. Hope started to rise in me, but I would have none of it. Fool, I told myself, your Inner Vision and your Sight are naught but the prodding of despair.

"Christian . . . ?"

A wave of relief swept through me. The captain had spoken.

He exhaled wearily. "You spoke aloud in your sleep . . ."

"A dream woke me." I wondered if he knew where he was and would have asked him, but he interrupted with a question which gave me to know that he was cognizant of his whereabouts and of our situation.

"You said: freedom . . . mark me . . . in sixty days . . . as though a god spoke through you . . . your God . . . after all of this . . . ?"

His voice was too flat, too weighted with fever to be the voice of one in any way capable of rising to sarcasm. I replied evenly, suddenly cold as I spoke the truth to him. "I am no longer certain that I wish to follow my God . . . if He is God . . . if there are any gods at all . . ."

He drew in a rasp of breath. Because of his fever, his wrists had not been bound. He reached out to touch me. His hand lay heavily upon my forearm. "We will see . . . you and I . . . in sixty days . . ."

How empty I felt in that moment, as though my body were a shell encompassing nothing.

The captain's fingers curled about my wrist. For all of his hardness, he was a compassionate man. An older and wiser man than I. He sensed my despair and wished to ease it. "In sixty days . . ." he repeated. "We shall see . . . in sixty days . . ."

Time. I was bound in Time. In hours of endless work. The captain healed and grew well again. He did not speak to me of my dream. He thanked his gods for his return to health, and I stood aside balefully, thinking: There are no gods . . . there is no God . . .

The great querns turned, grinding out the hours, the days, the weeks. We grew strong again. Our barbarian captors fed us well and treated us civilly enough. They were a highly organized and religiously disciplined lot within their own ranks, save when they were drunk, which was often, or when they came to blows over their habitual gambling and gaming disputes.

The village, such as it was, had been built over the ruins of a small Gallic farming town which, in true barbarian style, they had coveted and then taken at will, killing or enslaving all those who dared to stand against them. Their settlement was now comfortably complete, moated against would-be takers, with circular or rectangular log houses, efficiently mud-plastered, with high, steep roofs and large spaces of open ground between each dwelling. There was a warm spring just outside the moat. The people, both men and women, though not at once, spent much time lounging in the mineral waters. There was a council house and, on appointed days, the men would gather there, fully armed, to settle legal squabbles or, if they were not of a mind to be lawful, to organize raiding parties—groups of skilled warriors who would then go out to scavenge and terrorize at will, bringing home slaves and cattle and whatever booty they could win as they reveled in the wake of the banshee wind.

As for me, the captain and I belonged to the bellicose couple in whose house we had awakened. We were repayment of a debt owed them by the patriarch of the tribe. Though we worked from dawn to dusk for them, assuming all of their daily chores, from tilling their meager fields to churning their butter to washing their laundry and the udder of their cow to currying their precious horse, they never ceased to grumble at us. Only from the girl, their daughter, was any kindness shown.

As the days sped away, we were given wood and thatching and pots of mud and were made to understand that we must build a slave house for ourselves. It was a custom of these people to provide private shelter for their slaves. So we set to the task and in time completed an adequate lean-to sort of affair, with room enough for ourselves, a few musty blankets, and our cookpot. As we worked, now and again Amorgin would find some excuse to saunter by. He never failed to send us a surreptitious, conspiratorial wink, as though to say: Make yourselves comfortable, boy'os, but do not forget that these bastards with whom we live is our masters . . . and that they's slain our companions and our hounds . . . do not forget . . . for sure and the promise of the freedom bone is sweet indeed.

It has been said that we are as seeds cast down into a benighted forest, knowing Darkness, ignorant of our dependence upon the Light. We are children of the earth, sending out our roots instinctively through black loam, holding fast to what we know, reaching for nourishment within it.

Above us, the great green living crowns of the trees draw into themselves the sustenance of Light. Below, untouched by sun or warmth, reacting to a need which is born in all of us, we begin to reach, to strain upward, twisting in blind aspiration toward an existence yet to be defined or even fully conceived. And when, at last, the Light is found, often it is shaded and the seedlings, weary, pause in their growth.

Some, by their own choosing, will no longer seek, no longer reach. The dark loam of life will be enough for them. They are content. Slowly, so slowly that they cannot even know it is happening, then turn back upon themselves, feeding upon a soil which cannot alone sustain them. Soon they begin to fade and fall away into their own shadows. Time will incorporate them back into the earth, and it shall be as though they had never been.

But the others are not content with loam and Darkness. Something still throbs within them, pulsing, reminding of dimensions yet unseen, unfelt, yet surely promised. They continue their growth upward out of the shadows until, at

last, the shadows fall behind. The Light of Life swells
within them, nourishing them so that they may stand tall
and strong against wind and storm, children of both
earth and sky—still reaching, ever reaching, knowing that
their purpose is yet to be fulfilled.

I was still a child of the earth, shadowed by my doubts,
harassed by memories of my own failures, bitter with resentment against the clouds which had risen to obliterate
the Light of faith within me.

The days continued to pass. I sought the tedium of a
routine which brought an exhaustion that was reward
enough for me. I slept well in the night. I did not dream.
Of God or gods. Of prophecies, of Vision. I was content
to wallow in the mire of self-pity, grateful for a bondage
which at least had brought to me a tenuous peace of mind.
Was I not well fed? Was I not sheltered against the elements? Was there not useful work for me to do? If I
thought of freedom or of the Briton shore, I presaged my
thoughts with a nondefinitive: yes . . . yes . . . someday
. . . somehow . . . and, like the poor, mind-blighted daughter of my masters, I was content to simply live from day
to day.

In this way the summer passed. Fall tread upon the
earth, leaching summer's green from the grasses, breathing
frost into the dawn. The trees began to shiver in winds
which smelled of rain. Daylight no longer lingered to
warm the lengthening nights.

The harvest was brought in and the barbarians set to
readying themselves for a great god feast. It seemed that
they were drunk much of the time, sotted with happiness
over the bountiful harvest, pleased with themselves and
their gods and even with their slaves. We were given extra
rations of both food and drink, and in the nights the sound
of drunken, contented slumber rose as one great heaving
snore from the village.

It was on such a night, in the heavy, black hours which
preceded the dawn, that we were awakened by Amorgin.

I should say that the captain was awakened, because
by the time I was roused by a painful jab to my side, he
had already worked free of his chain, a short hobble-link
which was attached to our leg irons each night so that our
masters would not have to fear our escape.

Amorgin had brought two strong-stemmed awls which
he had stolen from the smith. With them, a man might pry

open the links of chain which hobbled him. So he had done and, in a gesture of comradeship which I would not have expected from him, instead of bolting in pursuit of his own liberty, he had risked all and had come to us, wishing to share the freedom bone.

We did not speak. There was no need for words. I sat up and, holding the chain so that it would make no sound, held out my legs and watched as Amorgin inserted the awls into the links which had been fastened to my leg irons. Slowly, straining, perspiring profusely, he turned the awls against each other until the metal which bound them grudgingly yielded.

Quickly, carefully, we made our way out of the village. The moat presented no difficulty. It was guarded by only one man. He was alert only for the threat of men trying to steal their way in, not out. We climbed the enbankment and slid into the shallow water, slithering across it like water snakes, rousing no sound.

On the far side, once out of eyeshot of the sentry, we broke into a run. The miles slipped past us. When at last we stopped, brought short by the dawn, we took refuge atop a wooded knoll which gave us a wide overview of all the lands surrounding us. No one could approach us without our knowledge. Before they could present a threat, we would be fast and far away.

For a while we lay back, panting, breathing in the intoxicating wine of success. Then the captain turned to Amorgin and acknowledged the extent of his gratitude.

"We owe you our lives, man."

Amorgin grunted and nodded his rusty head, smiling with self-satisfaction. "And so'ya do." He looked at me. "You can think your god now."

The friendly gibe snagged in me, rousing no anger, only the cold truth which I spoke evenly. "I am a free man, by your grace, Amorgin. I thank you. My God has had nothing to do with it."

His brows rode out and away toward his hairline with surprise. "Ach! Am I hearin'ya right?"

I was aware of the captain's eyes upon me. I looked to him questioningly.

"Do you remember . . . ?" His voice was troubled. "Weeks ago . . . there was a dream which made you speak aloud in your sleep . . . in another voice than your own . . . a dream which promised freedom . . ."

"I remember. I spoke my hope and my frustrations."

"Do you not think that it was more than that?"

"I have spent too much of my life listening to dream voices which lead only to confusion . . . which set me upon paths that take me nowhere save into despair . . ."

The captain's eyes did not move from my face. "Do you know what day this is, Christian?"

"The first day of our freedom."

"Aye. And more. Since I first awakened to bondage, I have marked the days. I had no knowledge of Amorgin's plan to escape, nor had he knowledge of your dream. Yet he came to us. As your God foretold through you. 'Two months will you be with them.' Those were your words, boy. Two months. And tonight . . . the first night of our freedom . . . it is the sixtieth night . . ."

I stared. "Coincidence . . ."

"Or Vision?"

The world seemed suddenly bright and cold with accusation. Within me something was turning, scraping desperately at what had been, for these past few weeks, a pleasant and unchallenging sanctuary. Then it fell back, inward into a truth which devastated me.

Through all of the long years and across all of the long miles, the God of my fathers had been with me, directing my way through a morass of danger and duplicity which, surely, had it not been for His grace, would have consumed me. Yet the road had been so bloodied, so full of pitfalls, I had questioned it. I had doubted the way of it. I had balked again and again. Though God had saved me from the murderous hands of raiders not once, but thrice, I had turned against Him. Though His Power and His Holy Word had touched me upon the Mountain of Mists and within the court of the Ri Miliucc MacBuain, I had set my heart against Him. He had led me, through Vision, to a road which had taken me from bondage in Eire, and now, though the path was twisted and bloodied, I was a free man. As He had promised. Yet it had taken a pagan to jar me back into faith.

The captain leveled a meditative brow as he measured me. "I think I would know more about your god . . . I think . . . perhaps . . . he *is* a god worth knowing."

Amorgin was shocked to the very core of his being and beyond. "What!? The god'a pukes?"

The captain looked at him and smiled evenly. "Can you

not see it, Amorgin? You of the banshee wind . . . the Christian's god has worked his will through you. And any god who could mold you, the least likely to be molded, may well indeed by the supreme god of all the world."

Never again did I doubt the will of the Lord my God. Never again did I turn from the Light or the calling of voices within my dreams or from the mists of Vision. Yet I did continue to question. The way of His road was still unclear, multibranched, veiled with cloud. I followed uncertainly, desperately wanting to do His will. I know now that I tried too hard to understand. I know now that only a fool attempts to interpret the will of God.

It was soon winter. There were no ships to be had in any port, though we did find a peaceful harbor and sought work there as laborers so that we might earn passage money for our journey home.

The months passed slowly. We roomed together in a dismal little waterfront inn. In the nights, the captain asked me to tell him of the Lord my God. As my words brought the clarity and serenity of faith back to my heart, so also did they win the captain to Christ, even as they turned Amorgin from us in disdain. It was not long before he left us to follow the banshee wind, taking up with a band of traders of ill repute who were bound for the inland trade routes that led into the rich heartland of Galicia.

Slowly the spring came and, with it, word of a ship making ready to sail, not to Eire or to Briton, but to the coast of Italy and beyond. It would be a voyage of two years. The captain signed on, telling me that here was his chance to earn enough so that when he returned at last to Eire he would be able to once again become master of his own vessel.

And I?

"Wait," he advised. "Soon a ship will make ready to stand out for the Briton shore. You've enough saved to pay your passage."

"No." I stood beside him, looking into myself. "By my lack of faith, I have forfeited all right to pleasure. God's will be done. If He intended me to return to my people, the ship of my deliverance would be here. Now. But instead there is this . . . a ship which sails into the unknown. The Lord my God tests my faith. I shall not fail Him again. I shall follow where His providence shall lead me. If, eventually, this voyage shall lead me home, so be it. If not . . . I shall abide in His grace . . . without question . . ."

So it was that for two long years I was a seaman. With the captain, I came to know the waters of which Comla had spoken in the Long Ago. And when at last we put about for home, my thoughts were light and filled with hope and eagerness. For I had met many a tradesman who had been to Briton in the years since I had been away from it. They assured me that for all of the devastation of the coast, peace still reigned inland on the western shore.

Then, in the sullen blue waters off the coast of Gaul, I saw the Isle of Lérins. As I stared at it, the cold bite of disappointment shattered my mood of thanksgiving. My thoughts of home bled away.

I, son of arrogance and doubt and the banshee wind, had followed the path of God and it had led me here. To this bleak, bony, bramble- and viper-infested island. To this island of chaste and holy men. Though I did not wish it, the path of Destiny had brought me to this shore. I must do penance for my years of arrogance and doubt. To assure the leashing of the lion of violence which prowled my soul, I must forswear all further hope of joy within the world of men. I must become a priest. I must dedicate my life to God. This, I told myself, must surely be the will of the Lord.

22

"Brother Patricius!"

Time. Running back like the tide. Carrying my soul with it. Back through the years. Back across the miles.

"Brother Patricius! Can you not hear me?"

I started out of my reverie, blinking at the reality of a pinch-faced Brother Julian.

"Are you ill, brother?" he asked.

I turned away from him. I stood upon the cliffs at the edge of the sea and stared out at it. It was as calm as a lake. The summer sun pressed upon it, flattened it, caused the great brown hanks of kelp to rise and skein out across the surface like strands of hair. Mermaids' hair. Mercia's hair. The comparison depressed me. Again I turned, facing neither sea nor monk, but staring across the bleached and bony headlands, my hands tight around the dry, splintery haft of my scythe.

"God have mercy . . ." I did not intend to speak aloud, yet I did, making an imprecation of what should have been a prayer. "Am I never to forget? It has been four years since last I saw Eire . . . yet I am haunted . . ."

I turned my head to the sky. High above, miles above, the wind touched clouds of ice. It frayed them, bent them up until they stood against the sky like stallions running before the sun. Once again memory jabbed me. I saw the winter skies of Slemish. Saw the frost-burnt flanks of the great mountain. Saw Dubh seated beside me, wrapped in his disreputable lummon, his blue eyes bright as he pointed to the tribelands far below. As always happened when I thought of him, memory turned cruelly. I suddenly saw his face as it had been in death.

I closed my eyes against the unwelcome specter. "Christ! Why can I not forget?"

"Brother Patricius, you are unwell. Come inside. Perhaps the heat . . . ?"

"I am well enough," I replied and thought: God help me, I am dying.

The monk did not move. He stood beside me at the edge of the sea cliff, holding down his crude homespun robes which the wind seemed intent upon billowing. "We are concerned about you, brother. You are not yourself these past weeks." His voice held an edge of concern and of annoyance. "If you will not share your feelings with us, how can we help you?"

I did not look at him. I turned up my head so that I might stare at the sun. It had long since claimed the height of noon. It stood high above me, yellow as an egg yolk, with a nimbus of sea mist around it. When had I last turned my face up to such a sun? Long ago. As a boy upon the sea cliffs of Briton.

"Ten years . . ." I said. "God . . . can it have been ten years . . . ?"

"Since you last saw your homeland?"

I did not appreciate Brother Julian's perception. He was a tall, thin, gray-haired man who seemed to have come to his vocation so easily. I glared at him. "This is my homeland. I have made my home in Christ. A priest needs no roots, no ties save those which he finds within the mercy of God."

He stared at me. Like all of my fellow monks upon this dry little island off the coast of Gaul, he had grown used to my moods and my temper. But he had not grown patient with them. He folded his hands across his midsection and reminded me, pointedly: "You are not yet a priest, brother."

Sarcasm? Or merely a statement of fact. No. I was not yet a priest. I shivered with the frustration of that truth. "No. It has not been enough that I have dedicated my life to God, that I have served Him, that I have dug wells for Him, and planted vines, and sown seeds, and worked amidst the viper-infested shrubbery of this island so that the monastery may be raised for the greater Glory of His Name. It has not been enough that I proclaim the wonder of His promise with every brier and shrub which I tie and bring to burning, that I work until I can no longer tell the hour save by the tolling of the bells which call me to prayer. It is not enough . . . for you . . . for my superiors here . . . or for God Himself!"

He seemed to withdraw into himself, stunned by my fevered outburst. "Brother Patricius," he said after a moment of serious consideration, "why are you here?"

"Why . . . ?" The question turned in my gut and ached like a bruise. "But that is clear. I have given my life to God. As penance for the sin of doubt. As penance, brother."

He shook his head. "How can you know that He wants this of you?"

"It is His will."

My steadfastness annoyed him. "Someday, Brother Patricius, may the Lord grant me the ability to interpret His will as surely as you seem able to do. How can you be so certain . . . so absolute in your faith that this . . . this life you have chosen upon Lérins is right for you . . . right for God?"

I could feel the color draining from my face. "I am certain of nothing . . . except of this: God has touched my life. He has allowed me to experience His Power, His grace, His infinite mercy . . . and I have doubted Him . . . I have failed Him . . . again and again . . ."

Brother Julian sighed, obviously not satisfied. "Shall we pray together, brother?"

"No."

Silence for a moment, then another sigh. "Then I shall leave you to pray alone."

"Bless you." The words had been a facetious curse.

He could not help but feel the barb. He shook his head, ignoring it, forgiving me. "God be with you, brother." He turned and left me, going as silently as he had come, with the hem of his garb lightly crushing the leaves of the leathery shrubs as it brushed against them. They released their aromatic oils easily. The scent was strong and highly medicinal, the healing incense of the earth. Yet it did not heal me. I glared out across the sea. How blue it was. How still. It was a sight which should have brought to me a sense of peace, of equilibrium. Instead, it brought the aching, ill-defined tormenting dissatisfaction which had filled my days and nights and dreams ever since I had come to this holy place.

Suddenly filled with self-loathing, I fell to my knees. "God!" My words were loud. Fervent. "Hear me!" The litanies rose from my lips, from my heart, from my soul. The well-used, well-worn prayers of centuries. Then, when I was at last certain that Brother Julian was well beyond earshot, my own words: "Son who is the Sun, You nourish our souls and make men of us, not beasts. I have given my life to You. I ask only that You make of me a passive lamb, that You cleanse the wolf of confusion from my soul. Grant me peace!"

Did I expect a direct and instantaneous reply? Yes. I wanted that. A miraculous intervening force that would pour into me the healing grace of peace of mind and heart. But it did not come. The hot, dry hand of the sun was upon my back. It burned me. It caused sweat to bead upon my skin and to lake within the recesses of my garments. I rose to my feet, thoroughly distracted and angry. I stared back at my fellow monks. They bent to their work in the fields as easily and confidently as cattle bending to browse. I experienced a momentary loathing of them. How I envied them their contentment. How I despised myself for my lack of it.

Turning back toward the sea, I gripped my scythe and swung it high, hacking down with it into the woody trunk of a briery bush.

. . "Brother! You wield your scythe as a sword! Surely that shrub is not the reincarnation of Judas Iscariot!"

The cajoling voice of Brother Ignatius startled me. I turned toward him, resentful of his intrusion into my solitude.

He put up his small, work-toughened hands and shook his head with self-admonishment. "It is a fault of mine," he explained. "I fear that I am an inveterate eavesdropper. I do not mean to do it. My heart is totally contrite. My soul is consistently repentant. But my ears . . . they lead me astray."

"You heard my prayer?" His admission both embarrassed and angered me. "There must be a place in Heaven for sneaks, brother. God willing, it shall be apart from the rest of us."

He clucked his tongue at me. "Then surely I should be in Hell." He was a small man who tended to portliness despite his hours of hard work in the fields. Beneath his pointed chin was a smooth dewlap of fat. He had the dark, soulful eyes which were possessed by so many of the men of Gaul. Those eyes fixed me now. They were filled with a loving mockery which caused my temper to flare.

"Has Brother Julian sent you to me?"

"He worries about you."

"Does he? Well I am well enough. So leave me," I demanded of him. "I would be alone with my God."

"*Your* God? Is He yours alone?" Again he clucked his tongue. "Of course, of course," he said slowly, in the language of his people. "You are the brother who is without fault. I had forgotten. It is difficult to remember your state of perfection when you spark to anger as easily as a piece of kindling sparks to flame. Or is temper considered to be a Christian virtue these days?"

He knew how to shame me. He saw my discomfort and ready penitence. He lifted up his hands again, in a gesture which told me that he was not offended. "You pray for peace, my brother . . . a fair and wondrous grace . . . but has it not occurred to you that God's will is sometimes worked through the withholding of graces?"

He had come to stand close beside me. "Now, take peace," he said thoughtfully. "It is a splendid state of mind, no doubt. A vast and tranquil plain upon which man's soul may graze as a lamb on new grass. You pray for peace. You were a shepherd once. But God did not wish you to remain a guardian of lambs. Perhaps He has other plans for you? Peace . . . it has no spurs to prick a man to action. And you are a man of action. A most impatient young man. You condemn yourself for this. But sometimes God has need of impatient men. Who is to say what is His will? If your spirit is restless, my brother, why not listen to it? Perhaps it carries a message for you. Ask of the Lord."

"I ask. There is no reply. I am not worthy of a reply. Time and time again I have proven that."

His scant brows arched up and out. "But you are the young man who has claimed to have dreamt the dreams of holy Vision . . . to have witnessed the Power of God . . ."

I searched his eyes for the skepticism which Brother Julian had so freely shown to me. The monks of Lérins, though holy men, were also men of their times. They were quick to remind me that the Age of Miracles was past and that would-be seers must be thorough in the scrutiny of their dreams before ascribing them to the realm of Vision, holy or otherwise. They listened to my tales of "holy voices" graciously enough, but they were most reticent when it came to acknowledging their belief in them. Most often they would ask me to analyze the dreams. What had I eaten prior to my dreaming? Gas on the stomach had been known to raise up devils, as well as angels, from dreams. The monks were always ready to remind me that many a self-acclaimed prophet had witnessed his visions dissolve with the escaping of a belch. And what about my mattress? Had it been too hard or too soft? Or had I lain upon a cot or upon damp or stony ground? Were there secret fears or desirings which I dared not voice to myself save through my dreams? I must remember that during my days in Eire I had been a mere youth, an impressionable boy, and living with severely superstitious pagans. Dreams. A man must beware of his dreams lest, too late, he discover that he has been tricked into following the schemings of his own vanity or, worse, the machinations of the Evil One. The latter had surely come to dwell among them in our troubled times, planting the insidious seeds of doubt and confusion not only among the heathen barbarians, but among good Christians and even within the hearts and minds of those who governed the Church itself. Take heed, the monks warned me, of the example being set by such learned men as Pelagius who, even now, in the name of Christian wisdom, sought to defile the doctrine of the Church with an unspeakable heresy.

I had examined my dreams. Again and again. I had called upon the holy voices and the wondrous grace of peace which had been mine when faith had first come to me upon the Mountain of Mists. But God's grace does not come upon a man's command. It is a gift which is given in His good time and for His good purpose.

"I no longer dream dreams of holy Vision . . ." I said bleakly to Brother Ignatius. "I have proven myself unworthy of the grace which once granted an unblemished faith to me."

"Brother! Brother! There has been but one worthy man born in all this world! He now sits at the right hand of the Father. And did not even He feel the sting of mortal doubt as He hung upon the cross? Come, come. Would you put yourself above our Lord? You are young. Youth is not passive. Youth is quest and question. Such is the will of God. Life has been difficult for you. Cruel. Confusing. I do not find it surprising that you should be a bit befuddled by it all. But you must not scourge yourself so thoroughly. Flagellation can easily become yet another of the Devil's devices, a snare to trap us in the sin of our own pride. You have come to Lérins after many trials. You have made known your desire to stand with Christ. He does not expect you to be without doubt or sin. He asks only that you strive to rise above your mortal failings as you follow His Way. Do not forget, brother, that the saints were men like you and me. They were not born into any miraculous state of sanctification. They were men who sought God, who chose to defy Evil, who tried to transcend their own weaknesses in their desire to serve and to glorify their Creator."

"I am no saint, Brother Ignatius."

He laughed softly, obviously in agreement, then chided me: "He has worked in less likely clay than that which stands before me." He studied me for a moment. His chin burrowed into the dewlap of fat. He shook his head and smiled—the gentle, musing smile of one who wore his faith as securely as he wore his own skin. "We can be certain of one thing in this life, brother: that God wishes us to toil in His vineyard, to reap the harvest of His good earth, to share His love with our fellow men, and to walk the paths which He has laid for us long before we were ever born."

The words jabbed me with painful and unwelcome

memories. I stared at the monk, yet did not see him. Instead, I saw the great banquet hall. I heard the laughter of the women and the bells of the lampooner. I saw the face of the Ri Miliucc MacBuain and I heard the druid's voice: "The road has been laid . . . long before any of us were ever born. Send the boy away, my lord. Send the boy away." I shut my eyes. Blood seemed to well within them. I saw the dead of Eire: Dubh, Draigenn, Leborchom, the Rigan, the maid, the guardsman, the people and the sons of the Red Ri Sencha. I saw the barbarians of Gaul, and my dead comrades: Flannán and Crimthann and Comla.

"The road which I have followed has taken me through Hell," I said.

"And has brought you to Christ." He lay comforting fingers across my hands. "Blessed is the man who has seen the powers of Darkness and recognized them. Blessed is he who has embraced the Light. Your road has led you to Lérins. What more could any Father ask of His son?"

I opened my eyes and turned them toward the sea. "I don't know," I replied, weary to my very soul. "I don't know . . ."

It must have been a very small viper which struck me upon my heel. Brother Ignatius had left me to my thoughts and prayers. I had resumed my work as destroyer of brambles. The sun was high. My scythe rose and fell in a great, sighing, rhythmic arc. I was perspiring heavily. My feet had become so calloused that I did not feel the serpent's sting, only an itching, burning numbness which began to ascend upward from my heel.

I paused. Leaning against my scythe, I lifted my foot and rubbed it. It was sore to my touch. Leaning forward to examine it, I started at the sight of two tiny dark wounds, like twin fragments of pepper imbedded in my dusty flesh. I had been warned that the vipers of Lérins could be deadly. As I stared at the marks which the serpent's fangs had inflicted upon me, a wave of fear assaulted my senses. I saw myself, dead and pale, being lowered into the earth by my grieving fellow monks. I heard the Masses being offered for the repose of my soul. I saw Brother Ignatius, dewlap quivering, piously reminding the others that they should not mourn: "God has at last granted our brother the peace for which he has so long yearned." I saw myself ascending into Heaven. The clouds of God's domain parted, only to send out a shaft of lightning which flung me down into Purgatory and beyond.

The numbness crept higher. It burned in my calf. I broke into a cold sweat. A cramp gripped my belly. A result of the viper's sting? Or merely a spasm brought about by terror? I shall never know. I, who had faced the curses of a malevolent druid, who had spurned the threats of both Ri and Rigan, who had survived prolonged enslavement and imprisonment, and who had fought for my life against Gaelic raiders and the barbarians of Gaul, fainted dead away like a swooning schoolmaid.

I was very ill. But the viper had been very small. I shivered and sweated and gave all of my good brothers in Christ cause to worry. Yet, within the week, I was well on my way to recovery.

The abbot Honoratus came to sit with me. He brought books to me, and another letter from home. I had, during the past few years, corresponded with my family occasionally, telling them little about what my life had been, save that, by the grace of God, I had survived great hardships and that my intention was now to become a priest. My mother responded with jubilant letters. I learned that she, father, Grandfather Potitus, Romana, and Claudius' family had all safely excaped the raiders, thanks to Claudius, who had come down from the hills in time to see the dreaded brown sails rounding the headlands. He had warned our villa in time, though they had barely managed to escape inland before the barbarians struck at the shore. The servants who had died in the attack had evidently chosen to remain behind in order to hastily gather together their few most treasured possessions. They had not been hasty enough. I had witnessed their reward. Romana, unmarried still, now supervised a school and a home for orphans. Grandfather Potitus had died peacefully in his sleep only three months after I had been taken captive. Raiders had made life upon the western seacoast of Briton impossible. My family had completely abandoned the villa and had taken permanent residence and refuge within the townhouse at Bannavem Taburniae. My father was struggling to recoup the Patricius holdings and investments after many losses, so that the family would not drown in financial ruin as had so many of those around them. Claudius' father, Licinius, according to my mother, had spent the last years constructing some sort of stone fortress out of the ruins of his villa. He had dreams of raising and training an army there. It was a structure the likes of which no Christian Briton had ever seen before, based on a prototype which Licinius had seen when he had been a tradesman in the far eastern lands of the heathen. My mother frowned on his venture, and on the fact that so many of the young men were rallying to him. His daughter Clodia had been widowed after a brief marriage. She came often to visit with my parents, always ready to discuss her frequent correspondences with her brother Claudius, who had, long ago, journeyed to Rome in pursuit of his priestly calling. My mother's words laughed across the miles whenever she wrote of Claudius. Surely, except for me, had there ever been a more unexpected candidate for the priesthood? By claiming us as His own, my mother claimed that God had proven Himself to have an amazing sense of humor.

I stared at her familiar script, as though by focusing upon the written words I might somehow bring to life the flesh and blood and substance of the woman who had written them.

Honoratus, browned from the sun, with the compassion of his faith shining in his eyes, offered me water from an earthenware cup. "How long has it been since you were home, my son?" he asked.

"Nearly ten years now."

"Then you were only a boy when you left your family."

"I did not leave them. I was taken."

"And now, after so many years of hardship, have you no wish to return to your homeland? To embrace your loved ones? To show them the man you have become ... the man who would be a priest ... ?"

He had left the sentence unfinished, as though he wanted me to complete the thought. I looked up at him, not understanding his intent.

"I *shall* be a priest."

"If that is God's will."

"It must be His will."

"Must it?" His lids narrowed as he measured me. Finding the sum, he nodded. "Why, then, Brother

Patricius, do you find no happiness with us here upon Lérins? You say that God has touched your life. You say that you have offered up your soul to Him . . . and yet He strews your path with vipers, with years of bondage in a pagan land, with violence and bloodshed. Even here upon Lérins, you have said that His peace eludes you." He smiled. "Peace is a fragile blossom, my son. Those who seek it too diligently often crush it in the zealousness of their search. You must rest now. Sleep. Dream of home. We will talk later."

The days passed.

I rested. I slept. But I did not dream of home. I dreamt instead of my years of bondage in Eire. I dreamt of the ship which had carried me away from that cursed island. I dreamt of the scorched earth of a ravaged Gaul. I dreamt of pirates and barbarians and of the banshee wind which had led me to violence against them. I dreamt of the dream which had promised freedom to me, and of the dream voices which had come to me in Eire. They had sighed within me as weary waves upon a shore, as though somehow they had known that I would not heed them.

Why, then, had they risen and moved within me? Could there be a more unworthy vassal of the Lord in all of this world? Why should His Power have been revealed through me? Would a warrior choose a splintered, brittle piece of straw with which to prove his might against an enemy? Would a sculptor choose a crumbling block of rotted marble out of which to carve a work of lasting beauty?

No. God had not chosen me. He was chastising me.

As I slept upon my pallet within the monastery, I dreamt of the soul-ravaged young man who, after being released from bondage in Gaul, had chosen to sign himself away into two years of self-inflicted penance. He had turned his back upon all hope and joy and plans to return to his homeland. Let God be the wind which directed his destiny. Let God remind him of his failures and his doubts as he worked as a common seaman aboard a vessel bound for ports strewn across the length and breadth of the wide seas.

I dreamt of the brown sails which had filled with winds born out of Gaul and Italy and the islands of the Tyrrhene Sea. I dreamt of the guilt and dissatisfaction which had stalked me in a hundred ports. And within the dream, I heard the voices sighing, as constant as the wind that lived amidst the rigging of the ship.

I saw the mountains of Sardinia, where the women dyed fine wool and danced their ancient dances. I remembered the bone-dry hills of Corsica, beneath which the olive orchards filled the valleys like silver seas. I relived the days spent out upon the open waters beyond the Balearics as the ship tacked along the tip of the North African continent and then put about for home, sailing past the restless hills of Crete, upon the wine-dark waters of the Aegean. Homeward. And then, as surely as Odysseus was drawn by the siren's song, the voices began to rise within me. Calling me. Not homeward. But to islands off the coast of Gaul. Holy islands. And eventually to one island. The holy isle of Lérins.

I awoke.

The dream vanished. The room in which I lay was dark, small, soundless—the comfortless cell of a monk. I sat up on my pallet. Leaning back upon my arms, I stared around me and was overcome with the familiar acid of dissatisfaction and discontent. My eyes sought light within the darkness. There was none, only a vague suggestion of dun stone and the smell of dust and the scent of my own perspiration.

Why am I here?

To serve and to glorify the Lord your God.

Then why can He not grant me the peace of mind which should put me at my ease with Him? Why do I find no joy in my faith? No gratitude? Only anger and frustration!

Silence. From within me. From without.

Disconsolate, I lay back. Though I was still weak from the effects of the serpent's venom, another poison worked within me: my youth and virility harassed me like a devil twisting and dancing within my soul.

I closed my eyes. Colors and memories rose behind my lids: the yellow hills of Crete, the scent of round, flat breads baking on an open hearth while a woman bent over them. A young woman, clad in a dusty garb of white. Woman with skin as gold and shining as brass. Woman looking up at me from beneath dark lashes, her eyes measuring me, absorbing me, following me. Woman rising and seeking me out amidst the shadows of a merchant's stall. The noontime sun imperious above the earth. The merchantmen drawing together for a midday meal. The woman drawing back within the deserted shadows of the stall, urging me to follow her. Woman whispering, laughing softly, promising, offering until I turned away in shame. As I always turned away, though my body raged in anger at me, flailing me with memories of a pleasure which I had not known since that day, so long ago, in the Briton wood; a pleasure which, as an illustration of my total penitence, I had vowed to forswear for the remainder of my life.

I flung my arm across my eyes and pressed in upon them, calling for sleep again, determined to dream dreams which would cause no leavening within me. I dreamt of the soft greens of Eire, of unfolding miles of mauve hills and misted skies. I dreamt of shadows dancing sensuously upon a forest floor sheltered by the swaying, sighing crowns of great trees. I saw the face of a young girl with eyes as brown and warm as loam newly turned beneath the sun. I recalled the sweet, moist scent of her flesh, the pressure of her young body against my own, the soft yielding of her breasts against my palms, the searching flame of her kiss.

I opened my eyes. The colors vanished. The memories faded. Yet passion ached within me, ebbed slowly, gnawed persistently for fulfillment. I rose to my feet distraught. Slowly, I bent and prostrated myself upon the cool earthen floor. With my arms spread-eagled, I pressed my forehead against the ground. I began to pray aloud with a vehemence which trembled for control. At last my voice became a whisper. At length it was only a soft sigh in the darkness. I slept. Dreamless, black sleep as heavy as my doubts. As unfulfilling as my youth.

Three weeks passed before I was well enough to resume my duties. Though I walked with a pronounced limp, I did not inform the others that my ankle often swelled in the night and caused me great pain. I had come to believe that this was just punishment for my gross failings and my inexcusable confusion. I suffered in silence, content with my penance.

Nearly one month to the day after I was struck by the viper, still another serpent stung me. Praying as I worked, I had payed no heed to what might lie concealed in the shrubbery. I stared at the reptile as it vanished into the brambles. I lifted up my foot. There, on the already afflicted heel, I saw the unmistakable indentation of two little puncture wounds. This time I did not faint. I cursed, less at the serpent than at myself. I had been careless. I knew well what to expect for my reward.

I did not recover quickly. Even after my body seemed well, my right leg was numb to my knee and sore as a boil to my touch. For weeks I could not move my toes, and a faint, tingling sensation would march up and down my right arm and side like an army of invisible stinging ants.

Yet, improbable as it may seem, the serpents of the Lord had not finished with me. Despite the imprecations of my brothers in Christ, and despite their suggestions that I stay out of the fields since the serpents seemed to find me totally irresistible, I took up my scythe again. My only concession was to the leg bindings which Honoratus had insisted that we all wrap about our limbs.

It was nearly autumn and still very warm. The brambles were dried from months of heat. The seed heads of the grasses stuck to our robes and worked their way through the heavy fabric to pick our skins. One late afternoon, I felt my leg bindings coming loose. As I bent to refasten them, I was struck upon my left wrist by as fat and glassy-eyed a viper as any devil might conjure. We stared at each other, that viper and I. I knew that once again I must suffer the pain and illness which would soon inevitably descend upon me. Once again my fellow monks would be forced to waste their precious energies caring for me, a careless fool whose flesh no serpent seemed able to resist.

With pure and unholy wrath, I reached out with my bitten hand and grabbed the sluggish, shedding snake about its poisonous throat. I choked it until I had wrung it dry of life. Then, filled with the venom of my own anger, feeling the viper's milk beginning to work within my arm, I walked steadfastly to the cliff edge and brandished the dead reptile before God and the blue miles of ocean. With epithets which should have been unknown to a man who sought the priesthood, I hurled the viper into the sea.

"Mon Dieu!"

I wheeled to see Brother Ignatius staring at me. His

mouth was agape. His dewlap trembled. He pointed at me, stammering: "My brother, is it your wish to drive the snakes of Lérins into the sea singlehandedly? Surely that was the bravest act I have ever witnessed! So large a snake would surely have killed any of our older or frailer brothers had it stung them. But to reach out and grab it bare-handed? Would it not suffice to simply cut it in two with your scythe? Surely, you might have been bitten again."

"And so I have been." My tone was as venomous as the sting of the serpent. "And if God is truly merciful, which I have long ago begun to doubt, perhaps this sting shall be the end of me!"

It very nearly was. The viper had injected its venom deeply and copiously. They told me later that I lay in a coma for over a week. When at last I regained consciousness, I was spent and feverish and wearied to the point of death. Once again I felt the presence of the Dark Angel beside me. I smelled his breath and felt the weight of his shadow.

It took months for me to recover. Winter came. With it the wind and rain. My left arm remained useless, alive only to pain and constant recurring infection. I spent my time in study and meditation, stumbling over lessons in the Latin which I had failed to master as a boy, attempting to learn the language of Gaul and growing thoroughly frustrated by the subtle nuances and complicated grammar of the Gallic authors. Still, I read hungrily, determined to make up for my years as an errant student. Inspired by the Bible and the Testaments and by the writings of such as Cyprian, Augustine, and Irenaeus, time slipped away from me. At last my arm was healed, though it still pained me. I attempted to resume what duties I could, but soon it became obvious to me that my brothers in Christ were going out of their way to spare me.

When spring at last arrived, with wild flowers beginning their first tentative explosions of color upon the bony hillsides, the abbot Honoratus called me to him.

"I have made the necessary arrangements for your return to your family and homeland."

"I have made no request to leave Lérins."

"You have been gravely ill. I believe that a journey to your homeland will refresh you in both body and spirit.

Besides, I have heard that there are few serpents in Briton."

The barb had been gently spoken, meant to soothe, not to snag. Yet my temper was roused easily these days. I replied sharply: "I realize that I have been a trial to you. To all of you. But surely it would be against all odds for me to be struck again. It would be—"

"A distinct possibility." He finished the sentence for me. "I have been assured, brother, that if you are again stung by a serpent . . . your chances of survival are slim indeed."

"Then I shall die in the service of Christ."

He smiled and shook his head. "Your need to please God is most sincere. You feel that you have offended Him and now must make the ultimate restitution: the offering of yourself to Him through a life of total sacrifice. Most commendable. Yet I must remind you, brother, that a man must come to God out of love for Him, with supreme joy in his heart as well as a need to demonstrate humility through penance. You have been with us for nearly two years. Your faith is strong. But where is your joy in the Lord? Where is your love for Him?"

I opened my lips to protest. Truth closed them.

"You have told me that God's presence troubles your soul."

"Only because I would do His will and yet fail Him again and again."

He nodded introspectively. "When you first came to us, brother Patricius, you said to me that God had called you here. Is it not possible that you have misinterpreted His calling?"

The validity of the question disturbed me. I preferred to ignore it. "I shall be consecreated as His servant."

"Perhaps. In time. When it is certain that this is His will."

"It must be. Why else would He have touched my life?"

His eyes narrowed speculatively. After a moment he said decisively: "The Lord seeks those who rejoice in His name. He wished His sons and daughters to follow His Way with hosannas upon their lips. He desires no bitter, angry servants. Perhaps, through the serpent's sting, God is showing you that your destiny lies elsewhere, brother?"

The weight of my own failings settled upon me as a

dark and smothering cape. I moved my shoulders as
though I would shrug it off. It only settled more heavily
upon me. "God brought me here . . . to this holy
place . . ."

"As a seaman aboard a trading vessel?"

"Yes. Surely so."

He sighed. "Has it not occurred to you that there is
not a trading ship in this part of the world which does not,
sooner or later, wet its keel in the waters off Lérins on its
way to the ports of Gaul?"

"I have been called to be a priest!"

It was anger which he saw within my eyes. "Have
you?" He met the defiance which he saw upon my face
unflinchingly, reflecting out to me from his own eyes all
of the strength and assurance of a man who had long ago
made his peace with God.

As I looked at him, it was as though I gazed upon the
island of Lérins itself, for it was Honoratus who had
brought God to this little piece of earth where now the
Holy Spirit lived in the wind, and the wisdom of God
fell to nourish the land with life-giving rains, and Christ
lived and breathed within each of those who labored in
His name. Upon Lérins, though my restless spirit had not
been healed, I had found shelter from the storms which
had so cruelly buffeted my life.

"Do not send me from this refuge," I implored. "Let
me live here with God."

He was suddenly impatient with me. "God lives within
you, Magonus Sucatus Patricius. You must seek Him
within yourself. You cannot hide from Him within His
house."

He sat across from me behind a wide, roughly hewn
writing table. Resting his elbows upon it, he laced his
fingers together so that they formed a support for his
chin. He looked at me out of stern and knowing eyes.
"You have come to Lérins so that you might turn your
back upon a world which has brought violence to your
soul. You say that you wish to be a man of God. Yet you
refuse to allow God to enter the sacristy which you claim
to have laid for Him within your soul. In truth, brother, I
do not believe that you seek God at all. He has laid a
searing hand upon your life. I believe you have come
here to hide yourself away from Him. You say: 'I shall

be a priest for You! I shall suffer the life of a contemplative for You! So now leave me at peace! Let *my* will be done!' *Your* will, brother Patricius. Not the will of God. And these voices which you claim to have heard, I believe that they are the voices of your own desirings, born out of no holy source, but out of your own needs. In truth, you have made Lérins a refuge . . . so that you may be spared further testing by God."

The accusation appalled me. Truth is a cruel and often unwelcome blade. My temper flared against it. I rose to my feet and slammed my palms down against the table. "Testing! What do you know of testing? Look at you, dwelling within sanctified halls, with the blessings of Rome upon your head, with the sweat of your brow the only blood you shall most likely ever be asked to shed for Christ! Where are the scars of your testing? Shall I show you mine? For again and again I have been tested and found wanting. God touched my life upon the Mountain of Mists. Yet I could not make His voice heard within the ring fortress of the Ri Miliucc MacBuain. Nor could my knowledge of Him assuage the beast of my own rage in Gaul. Yes! I *have* come to Lérins to find refuge, for the hungry armies of men will not scourge this impoverished and pious little kingdom; they will leave us at peace as they seek power and pride in the world of men. Refuge? Oh, yes. I seek refuge. Have I not earned it? Will the testing never end for me?"

He studied me. Long and sadly. Then, softly: " 'Father . . . remove this cup from me . . . but yet not my will, but thine be done.' "

The words of Christ chastised me. My temper shriveled and grew sour within my mouth.

"The cup cannot be passed from us," said Honoratus. "The wine, though it be bitter, must be drunk."

BOOK V

FROM THE WESTERN SEA

> . . . and thus did they cry out with one mouth: "We ask thee, boy, come and walk among us once more."
>
> Saint Patrick—from his *Confession*

23

How can I tell you of my days in Briton?

Long days. Lingering days. Healing days. Warm days lenghthening into summer and then gentling—oh, have ever days been more gentle!—into an autumn which burnished the land and touched my heart with inner joy, saying to my soul: Forget the past! Dissect it from your memory! Is your homeland not serene? Have your prayers for peace not at last been answered? Honoratus was right. You were not destined to become a priest. God has brought you home. Here you are content. Here you belong. Here you are truly needed.

I was twenty-seven, no longer a slave or a seaman or a monk. I was a lord. My father had been suffering from a degenerative disease which his physician had been unable to cure or diagnose. My mother, afraid that she might be accused of attempting to turn me from my professed vocation, had chosen not to reveal this to me in her letters to Lérins. When I had arrived home, she had wept and proclaimed that my return was surely the will of God. I had been home a month before it became ap-

parent to us all that I must take the cloak of family re-
sponsibility from my father. At his request, I became
master of the Patricius estate and of our many holdings
and investments. My duties and obligations were many.
They filled each waking hour, leaving no time for morbid
reflection, for brooding over past failures and the muddied
implications of yesterday's dreams.

Ineed, as the months slipped away, it seemed that God
had, in His infinite wisdom, honed me for this purpose.
The years of hardship and discipline, coupled with my
studies upon Lérins, had prepared me to cope with my
new responsibilities. I warmed to them, rose eagerly to
the challenges of them, and was pleased to discover that
I had an innate talent for management.

Did I actually imagine that God had walled off west
Briton from the troubled world? Did I not recognize the
truth of the times in the tenuous economy of my homeland? Did I not see it in the atrophied lifestyle of my
people? No. Though the Age of Darkness threatened the
lingering season of my long-fought-for contentment as
surely and inevitably as Death stalked the flaming leaves
of the autumn forest, I would not see it. I had had enough
of Death, of pain, and of humiliation and deprivation. I
clung to my illusions of tranquillity. I convinced myself
that the turmoil of the world was far away from me. I
basked like a blind man in the ebbing warmth of summer and that last sweet autumn. I grew strong and well
again. At day's end, I greeted the night eagerly. A servant
would bring a flagon of hot, mulled wine to me. I would
savor it within the solitude of my room. I would offer up
prayers to God, thanking Him, blessing Him for having
at last delivered me into a life of contentment. My mind
numbed by the wine, I would fall gratefully into dark,
warm, dreamless sleep.

In this way the summer passed and the autumn came
and began to ripen. Looking back now, I find it difficult
to recognize myself in that studious, feverishly energetic
man who thought that he had cast off his yesterdays as
easily as a spider casts off its skeleton at the end of a
year's growth. Could I not have known that just as a
seedling lives encased within the tree forever, so does
Yesterday dwell as a touchstone within each man? The
boy I was, the youth I was, the man I was . . . these shall

dwell within me forever. They are the core of all that I am and of all that I shall ever be.

Winter came and, with it, the rain and mist and storms and seemingly endless hours in which there was little work to do and much time for reflection: of Now, of Yesterday, of Tomorrow.

In response to a growing and ill-defined restlessness, and in an attempt to escape the rising of questions and the stirrings of memory within me, I began to involve myself in the maintenance of my sister's orphanage. There are those who believe that it was Fate which called me there. Fate? Destiny? The hand of God? I know only that it was the first rising of the great comber which would soon sweep me up and away from my homeland forever.

But on the day I first saw my sister's orphanage, it was not Destiny which I smelled in the wind. It was the foul, sweet odor of soiled swaddling rags being boiled in cauldrons of soapy water. The orphanage itself was a rundown, ramshackle cluster of buildings situated downwind of the cattle yards at the eastern periphery of the town. It had been a livery stable once, housing the pleasure horses of the gentry. When the legions had been withdrawn, the hills and plain of west Briton had become the province of lawless men. The gentry had learned to seek their entertainment within the confines of the town. The stable had been abandoned for five years before Romana had purchased it.

"Surely you could have found more suitable housing," I accused my sister, observing the deplorable condition of the buildings, the scabby little expanse of meadow upon which children played and squabbled.

Romana had matured into a grim and uncompromisingly blunt woman. There was a proud, almost belligerent assurance about her. "This is not the first time that the Lord has seen fit to shelter His own within a stable. God has provided for us. Not well, I'll admit. But He *has* provided. You must understand, Magonus, that Briton has changed since you left us. These children, I'm afraid they are the refuse of the times. The people of Bannavem Taburniae feel little loyalty to them. They have come here, or been brought to me, from all parts of west Briton and beyond. My boys, some as young as five, have admittedly been thieves upon the hillsides. They have sold themselves and their sisters for bread. The girls, some mere babes of nine and ten, have been whores upon the roads and even within the town. I do not doubt for a moment that many a so-called Christian merchant or tradesman has lain with them and considered his coin and seed well spent."

Her voice had become as hard as granite, as cold and cutting as falling ice. "Many of the babies have been brought out to me secretly, in bloodied little bags, after their mothers failed in their attempts to strike them from their wombs. Six of my older girls are pregnant. They could find neither shelter nor pity within the town."

I looked off across the little meadow to where three young girls were standing over steaming cauldrons, stirring diapers with long wooden sticks. One of the girls—could she have been more than twelve?—was swollen with child. "The people of Bannavem Taburniae are Christians," I said. "If these children have needs, surely the townspeople are bound in Christ to fill them."

Her features tightened. "Are they? One would assume so. Yet, were it not for the charity of the few, we would all go hungry. By the grace of God, there are some who have not forgotten the true meaning of the faith. And by the grace of Licinius, my older girls have found employment as laundresses at his fortress. In the spring, he sends out his men to help us turn the fields and set them to seed."

"Licinius? Claudius' father?"

"God praise his name. And Clodia. You remember little Clodia? She comes often to help the girls with their sewing and cooking skills."

"But rumor has it that Licinius has become a madman, a pagan . . ."

"We do not speak of religion, he and I. I know that the elders disapprove of him. But they also disapprove of me, and of this place, reminding me again and again that half of my children never knew Christ's holy name before they came to me, that many of them are the spawn of barbarian rape. But I ask you, brother, as I ask them: Are they not children of God all the same? What shall I do? Turn them away in the name of Christ?"

"Surely the elders must—"

She cut my words with an angry, impatient sigh. "The elders! A huddling of fearful, impotent old men who re-

fuse to see the truth of the times! Do you not understand
why they repudiate Licinius? Because they fear him. Because as they cling to the old ways, Liciuius draws the
support of the young, leading them to hope in what he
calls the New Day. But will they listen to him? Will they
grant him the financial assistance he so sorely needs? Of
course not. Commitment terrifies them. Even to such a
cause as mine. They have actually told me that my
charges would be best 'left to God.' Our own parents,
Magonus, living in luxury, refer to my efforts as an em-
barrassment, as a wasted, ill-founded 'ever-sucking well of
charity.' God forgive them."

So I found my new commitment. Throughout the town,
rumor added a new name to its list of potentially mad citizens. Though my parents were definitely not pleased by
my new tack, I assured them that I would be prudent and
spend upon my new endeavor only that portion of the
family reserve which would be my legal inheritance. Despite the times, my family was wealthy. It seems that in
any age, despite wars and pestilence and famine, there is
always some sheltered nook or cove which manages to escape. For the time being, west Briton was that se-
questered harbor of Life-Goes-On. The aristocracy of
Bannavem Taburniae fattened and grew docile in its be-
calmed waters. Only the most cursory glance at my family's books revealed to me the extent of their success and
the minimal concern they had demonstrated toward charitable endeavors. With controlled anger and an undeniable
sense of shame, I began to fill the winter hours with plans
for the betterment of the lifestyle of my sister and her
orphans. As I worked for them, it seemed to me that God
had truly had a purpose when he brought me home from
Lérins.

An architect was employed to design the new buildings
which would house the children. Contractors were called
to discuss the cost of lumber and tiles. Then, later one
afternoon as I rode out to the orphanage, Destiny touched
me as I drew rein and found myself staring off toward the
low range of hills which lay betweeen Bannavem Taburniae
and the sea.

It was a cold, damp day. It had been my intention to
reach the orphan's home before dusk so that I might share
the evening meal with my sister while we went over the

architect's sketches for the new girls' quarters. Romana
had been most adamant in stating the specifications which
the structure must meet: A separate wing for the pregnant girls, adequate provision for privacy and the practice
of personal hygiene, and a chapel, no matter how small,
to serve as a much-needed spiritual retreat. I had tucked
the rolled parchments into my saddlebags and had been
anxious to show them to Romana. I knew that she would
be as pleased by the drawings and proposals as I had
been.

The land stretched upward after it left the town, sweeping and arching to the horizon like gentle swells upon a
summer sea. Gray beneath the shadow of the clouds, it
was farmland in the main. Spring would see broad seg-
ments of the fertile earth set to seed. A large portion of
the acreage belonged to my family. For this reason I had
been drawn by curiosity to pause. A small group of men,
clad in oiled hides against the threat of weather, was
marching and drilling in tight military precision across the
Patricius fields. I spurred my mount and rode out to discover the identity of the trespassers.

They were young men. Farmers' sons in the main. I
recognized several of them as apprentice tradesmen from
the town. Their leader, mounted upon a huge dun horse
with hoofs as wide as serving platters, came toward me.

"You distract my men." He was a stranger to me. His
voice was deep, heavily accented by some foreign tongue,
and had the bite of authority.

"And you trespass upon my lands." Even as I spoke,
the sound of the man's voice had snagged painfully into
my brain. I must have visibly reacted.

Destiny removed his stiff hide rain-headdress. He inclined his head deferentially. His hair was a ruddy yellow,
streaked with gray and brown. It was very long and
thick and had been plaited up around his wide head, in
the manner of the men of Eire. "You would be the lord
Patricius. The brother of Lady Romana. I am Llwyn,
from the northland beyond Dyfed, in the service of
Ceretic, lord of the clan Dumbarton, which now holds the
lands to the north and south of the great wall of Antoninus."

"Your tongue is scarred by the accent of the Gael."

He seemed pleased by my recognition. "You have a
discerning ear. I am Pict. But I was raised in fosterage

upon the Western Island, in the great northern reach of Ulster, in that eastern portion of the land known as Dalaradia. Do you know it?"

He had spoken in the language of the Gael. The sound of it caused the world to go white for me. Blinding, shattering light. I stared at him and could not determine whether I wished to flee from the sight of him or to strike him dead as he sat upon his horse. "You have no leave to trespass upon Patricius land." I would not speak to him in the language of Eire. I spoke my own native tongue, fighting for each word so that it might not betray my emotion.

"Your sister, the good and gracious Lady Romana, has given Licinius' men leave to use this field. I do so in his name."

The man had lapsed back into the language of Briton. He was civil. Totally pleasant. The whiteness began to fade for me. Mercifully, the world began to clear and grow calm, yet I felt weak, as a man must feel when a seizure has left him. My eyes followed the twisting plaits of the man's hair. I thought of the Ri and had to shake my head to jar it free of the unwanted memory. I stared at the stranger and informed him peremptorily: "Licinius has always kept a Christian house. His son, Claudius, is even now a priest in Rome. He does not deal with pagans."

The man Llwyn signed the cross. Emphatically. "I am baptized in the name of the most holy Trinity. I command Licinius' fortress whild he journeys north to counsel with the people of my tribeland. The Lady Romana will confirm this. Now, if you will excuse my impertinence, the hour grows late. I must insist that you leave us to our training. As I have said, your presence distracts my men."

"Men?" I appraised the motley ranks of would-be soldiers, remembering the many times I had heard my parents speak with infinite disdain of Licinius' attempts to raise what they dubiously referred to as an "army." Looking at the shabbily clad youths, I understood the why of their words. They seemed a frail and pathetic lot, indeed, when compared to the legions of Rome which I remembered from my boyhood. Llwyn's insistence that I leave my own lands did indeed sit as impertinence with me. I had no intention of yielding to him. With no attempt to veil my sarcasm, I said to him as I looked at his men: "If these are men, I am a maid."

Llwyn found no humor in my statement, nor had I intended any. He replaced his helmet, replying acidly: "I cannot speak for the fact of your manhood. But my men *are* men. Do not doubt that." His eyes had narrowed. All civility had vanished. They had become civet's eyes: shrewd, wary, measuring, and potentially deadly. "In the old and old and ancient days, our warriors went naked before their enemies. If the landed aristocracy of Bannavem Taburniae continues to grant Licinius no support, we may yet march naked again. But make no mistake, my lord Patricius, naked or clothed, we shall fight. We shall not be conquered again. Unlike the landed gentry and the learned gentlemen of the city council, we are not passive lambs who will hand over our birthright to any usurper who would forcefully press his will upon us. I cannot speak for you, lord, but Briton or Pict, we are men who have not forgotten that we are Celts . . . and that this land belonged to us before the name of the Caesars ever became a curse upon our world."

I, who had been enslaved by the Gael, felt no kinship with the ancient race. Like all members of the Romano-Briton aristocracy, I had been taught disdain of it. Celts? The blood of the race might flow in my veins, but I had been raised to feel alien from it. Celts lived in Eire, and in the land of the Picts, and in Dyfed and Cornwall, and across the Channel in motley tribes which were thoroughly ignorant of Christ and the ways of civilization. In Briton, the Celts had been vanquished and Romanized for over three hundred years. I thought of my experiences among the Gael and thanked God for that. Arrogantly, I said to the Pict, indicating the youths with a snap of my head: "Small men indeed when compared to the might of Rome."

"Rome . . . ?" His eyelids flickered as though insects had walked over them. His lashes, pale and stiff, rose and fell, then hovered to screen the fire of anger which sparked within his brown eyes. "So the hound still wears the collar of its master and begs to be leashed, even though the master had abandoned the kennel? Be advised, Lord Patricius, that the elders may now rule the council . . . but the men you see here . . . we are our own masters now."

His right hand went up and formed a fist across his heart. Again he inclined his head, with obviously feigned respect. Reining his big horse around, he turned his attention to his men. They went back about the business of training as though I did not exist.

Angered and humiliated, I wheeled my own mount back toward the orphanage. The little mare was lathered and bewildered when at last I leaped off of her back and, still holding the rein, confronted my sister.

"There was a pagan on the northwest pasture . . . drilling boys . . . contemptuously telling me that you had given him leave to trespass there."

"Llwyn? He is no pagan. He is a good and decent man, Licinius' right hand. He spoke the truth. I have given him leave to use the field at his discretion until seed is set in the spring."

"Good and decent Christian men do not train their brothers in the ways of war."

"Someone must train them."

Her reply stunned me. "Why? There is peace in west Briton."

"Is there? Perhaps for now. But for how much longer, brother? If, after so many years of suffering, you have found comfort in a world of your own peaceful illusions, peace be with you. As for me, I cannot forget the sight of the villa as it was when the raiders left it. God willing, I shall not look upon such a scene again. Our island is besieged, Magonus. Without protection, it can be only a matter of time before the tide of violence touches us again. Surely you must realize this."

"We need no pagan Celts masquerading as Christians to guard our homeland. Surely the elders, the councilmen, they have devised adequate protection against raiders."

"They have long ago come to a unanimous decision on that subject: Ignore the threat and God shall simply work a miracle and make it disappear."

My mind seemed to be expanding, reaching, grasping. "You cannot be telling me that, in all of the years since I was taken in the last raid, nothing has been done to prevent another attack."

"The town has been walled. Doorways have been narrowed. Street-facing windows have been barred. Family treasures have been secreted in underground vaults. All actions suggested not by the elders, but by Licinius. The

common people are rallying to him. Were it not for his
efforts, Bannavem Taburniae would be as vulnerable before the raiders as the villa was. Even as it stands now,
the peace which you so treasure could be shattered in a
moment by those who would, if we allow them, obliterate
the very name of God from the face of the earth. Come,
come, brother. Do not look so shattered. You have been
home now for several months. It is time you faced the
truth."

Like the mists of morning which are shredded by the
winds of a dawn which promises storm, so were my illusions and a sense of tranquillity tattered and torn away
from me. For the first time since my return to Briton, I
saw my homeland as it was, not as I wished it to be.

There were bars across the merchants' stalls. The roads
were rutted. The buildings within the forum were no
longer maintained. Lethargy lay upon the land like dod-
der. The town, like a blossom withering upon an up-
rooted vine, was succumbing to a slow, insidious decay. I
saw avarice and distrust and fear in the faces of my people. I began to listen to their dissatisfactions and gossip.
The gnawing worm of insecurity savored every bite which
it took from my confidence. Even at Mass I felt distracted, ill at ease, pursued by the specter of the new
age.

On a day streaked and sodden with rain, I went before
the elders of the council to respectfully state my fears to
them.

"Rumor has it that no plans have been made to protect
the town or its citizens in the event of a raid."

"Raid? The Scots have struck us once. Why should they
come again? Does lightning brand its mark into the same
tree twice?"

"In Eire, upon a mountain called Slemish, I learned
that if a tree stands vulnerable, it is struck often . . . until it is seared to the heartwood, until it blackens, until it
is rent, until it falls to the earth, where it is consumed by
decay."

If my statement sobered them, they showed no signs of
the sobering. They were men all advanced into middle
age and beyond. My youth and concern were to be pacified, not taken seriously.

"Bannavem Taburniae is not a tree upon a mountain."

"But it is a town which stands vulnerable."

"Ahh, but we have Licinius to protect us from the wrath of lightning. Surely you know Licinius?" They were smirking with amusement.

"I have not seen him since my homecoming. But yes, he was once a close and honored friend of my family."

"He has changed since those days."

"Has he?"

"Have you not heard the rumors about him?"

"I try not to take rumor to heart. It has a habit of gnawing at the edges of truth."

Learned eyebrows arched. "Licinius claims to have dreamt dreams of holy Vision."

"Blasphemous assertion!" The words snapped at me. "A man like that! As though the Spirit would speak through him!"

Anger had begun to ripen within me, slowly. "I remember that when I was a boy, Licinius was warning us of raiders. No one listened . . . to a man like that."

"Could we have known?"

"Licinius knew."

"Assumed."

"Correctly."

"The man was a merchant . . . had a number of ships . . . made his fortune on the seas . . . and not always honestly, we might add . . . did business with pagans wherever they'd have him. His captains told him of coastal raids. He got his news from them, not from any holy dreams."

"We should have listened."

"Perhaps, perhaps, but that is all in the past. The raiders have struck our portion of the coast once. They shall not come again."

"You cannot guarantee that."

"No. Nor can Licinius guarantee our safety. The man's gone mad. He's built himself a fortress. Taken him ten years. It stands out on a point of land, jutting into the sea. To frighten off the raiders. As though any structure would deter those sons of Hades."

"He is trying to raise an army."

"Oh, yes, and quite impressive it is too: at least thirty farm boys, with nearly half of them out of puberty. And Heaven only knows how many scythes and plow horses and, perhaps, even a few slingshots. And hay forks. We must not forget the hay forks."

"If he were properly financed . . ."

"By us? By the members of this council? Christian men finance a warmongering madman? It would be a sin against God."

"Then it is true?" I pressed. "You have made no provisions for the safety of this town?"

Hands went up tellingly. "God is with us."

"As He was with us on that day, eleven years ago, when the coastal villas were laid waste and I was taken as a slave to Eire?"

Eyes expanded vacuously. "As He was with us on the day which brought you safely home to us."

Shoulders shrugged. "And besides, the Scots are seasoned warriors. If they should decide to strike us, to come inland, do you honestly believe that Licinius' poor, misguided boys could keep them at bay? They would be slaughtered like so many unweaned lambs trying to stand firm against an army of wolves. No. No. The best manner of protection is to yield. Yield."

"To your own slaughter? By merciful God, the simplest of plans would suffice: lookouts posted along the coast, runners to give warning, hiding places determined for the women and children, our young men taught to bear arms effectively."

Silence. Total. Then. "When you were a monk upon the island of Lérins, did you and your fellows practice the art of combat so that you might assure your lives against violence by those who are, when all is said and done, only fulfilling the will of God? Can we, as followers of Christ, in the name of righteousness, raise our arms against our brothers?"

The question was as old as the catacombs. For a moment it brought me pause. Then the reply came, as sure and steadfast as the beat of my heart. "Lérins is a poor and bony island. There are no women or children upon it. Barbarians seek spoils and an outlet for their lust. They would find little to interest them upon Lérins. But there is wealth in Briton, and the precious blood of our families. I do not believe that God, who has granted us our faith, who has led me home after so many years of trial, has set these raiders to do *His* will. Rather, I believe that they work the will of Evil and the Powers of their own dark and bloodied gods. Can we, as followers of Christ, in the name of righteousness, not seek to protect our women and children from those who would rape, slaughter, or enslave them in the name of the Evil One? Perhaps God, in His infinite wisdom, has granted us the time to ready ourselves for the next onslaught? Perhaps, even now, He is speaking through us, warning us, advising us that if we are strong and ready, the raiders shall leave us at peace."

They were not impressed with my argument, and said so. "There has been no sign of raiders in this vicinity for eleven years."

"Then thank God for that blessing and look to the future. I have been a shepherd and I have learned this of the wolf: If he once preys upon a flock successfully, he will return to drink of its blood again. But if the rams and the dogs are alert and ready to fight him, the mactire will turn away and be content to keep to his forest. He will allow the flock to graze in peace."

"Wolves . . . rams . . . dogs . . . come, come, you do not dwell among the pagans of the Western Sea now. God has brought you home. Be content, my boy."

The words were so outrageous that I felt lightheaded. "Content? When at any moment I could once again be enslaved? Are you content? Do you not know that the common people mutter against you? There are factions developing in the town which could split the order of our society in two. The people fear for their lives. You, as their governors, must ease that fear, must bring to them a sense of security. If you do not, they shall seek it themselves without and despite you."

Learned heads went together. I was obviously making them grossly uncomfortable. At length, tolerantly: "We will study on your suggestions."

"We will read on the matter."

"We will consider the best course of action to take, if action is indeed indicated."

"And when will you decide?"

My impatience was not appreciated.

"In the Lord's good time. In the Lord's good time."

The Lord's good time slipped away. Days of it. I went to them again. I was told to be patient. To wait. They would summon me when they had made their decision. I agreed. But my soul had become restless. It ran with the mactire in my dreams.

I awakened one dawn to the bleak and howling cry of the wind. I rose, shivering, and looked out upon the growing day. Beyond the glass of my window, the inner courtyard was washed with a thin, metallic pink glow. The sky above was cloudless, yet somehow leached to gray. The wind filled it. Cried. Howled. The call of the wolf, of memory, of Yesterday. Slowly, hesitantly, I dressed. I knew where I must go.

The villa lay ahead. The slave Trimarinus pointed off to it. I had already seen it, sensed its presence in the very texture of the day. The wind still howled, bitter and pungent with the scent of the sea. Trimarinus pulled himself deep into his cloak as protection against its bite. He was my bodyguard, or so he thought. He carried a knife at his thigh and a short-sword at his belt. He had been a member of my parent's household since before my birth. Though he was loyal, the years had softened him, in flesh as well as spirit. I doubted that if we were beset by thieves he would have the will or the courage to use his weapons. Yet, when he had seen me preparing to leave the townhouse, he had followed, asking my destination. When I had told him, he had thrice crossed himself.

"The day," he had said, indicating the wind with an upward twisting of his head, "it bodes storm . . . the wind is from the west. A good day to take one's ease by the hearth fire. The villa . . . there is nothing there . . . only ruins."

"Enjoy the hearth fire for me then," I had said, swinging up into my saddle. "And do not inform my parents of where I have gone. I do not wish to worry them."

"But surely you do not intend to ride out alone?"

"I do."

"No, my lord, the hills and the coast, there are robbers dwelling there . . . men who would steal your horse and clothes and leave your corpse for crow meat." He had taken hold of my mount's bridle. "You shall not go," he informed me, assuming himself to be master of the situation. Our combined memories of my childhood granted him privilege with me. I would always be a boy to him.

His attitude had thoroughly vexed me. "I will ride where I will. I am master of the Patricius household now.

Have you not come to understand that yet, Trimarinus?"

"It is understood, lord." His broad face flushed. "But you shall not go alone. I will ride with you."

"I ask no man to risk his life so that mine might be kept secure."

"Would you command me to stay then? Knowing that I would be shamed?"

He had the knack of woman's wheedling. I was anxious to be on my way and in no mood to be patient with him. "Come on along then, but by your own wish, not at my command."

As we approached the villa, it seemed to me that the elements had made a combined and conscious effort to conceal its remains. Sand and earth had drifted to form dunes along the colonnades. The walls had collapsed. Lichens crusted them. Travelers had camped here, using the scarred remains of the walls as wind breaks. They had built careless fire pits of the remnants of my youth: chipped tiles, broken slabs from the once ornate columns, fractured pieces of pottery.

We dismounted. Trimarinus tended the horses while I went off to wander through the ruin alone. The wind followed me, echoed around and within me. It filled me with the desolation which comes to a man when he faces the distances which Time has placed between himself and his youth. He sees it all so clearly, yet it is remote from him, as though he trespasses into another world where the images are not born of thought or memory, but are as real as he is real. He sees them as they were, as they are, shut off from him forever in some mysterious, transparent room where they are lived continuously, over and over again, trapped in Time, eternal. He reaches out to them, to the youth he was, to the boy he was . . . and the boy pauses and stares back at him out of Time. He waves. He beckons. He calls on the wind, but there is no sound. The man cannot follow.

I walked slowly. Room by ruined room until, at last, I paused in the room where Destiny had found me.

"Are you not afraid to die, boy?"

I saw the face of the black beard. And Mercia. And the head of my slave Arnos impaled upon a spear. I saw the uplifted arm of the brown-eyed raider rise. I saw it fall and gasped, shocked by the fire of remembered pain, amazed that it could spark so real and true. My hand went up to my shoulder, and for a moment I thought I felt torn flesh and broken bone. The moment passed. There was only the slight rising of the old scar beneath my fingers. Yesterday slipped away. Relieved and suddenly weary, I turned and walked out into the wind, seeking the solace which men, from the beginning of Time, have sensed waiting for them at the edge of the sea.

Gray sea. Restless sea. Sea skimmed with foam churned up by the wind. Strands of kelp, ripped from the depths by the turbulence, veined the surface, skeining out like strands of hair. On a brighter day the sun would transpose the brown hanks of them to red. Red. Like Mercia's hair. Red. Like the hair of the Morrighan.

Within me there was a slow turning, a congealing of unwelcome memory. I looked out across the water and realized that there, beyond the miles, beyond the wind, lay Eire and Dalaradia and the ring fortress of the Ri Miliucc MacBuain. A heavy bank of cloud lay hulking in the far west. It would be the mother of the wind which presaged the storm that would soon touch the Briton shore. Now it lay over Eire. No doubt it was raining there. Snow would be falling on the heights of Slemish. Shepherds would be huddled within their meager shelters, their dogs tucking noses beneath tails as they sought warmth. Lights would be burning in the grianan of the Rigan Mercia. In the great hall of the Ri, the king's candle would be sparking and sputtering, straining for life above the ever-welling pool of molten wax which always threatened to drown it. Within the kennel, Bruthne would be seated before the oven, baking dog breads, stitching methodically upon tethers always in need of mending. Beyond the ramparts, the mactire would be lifting his voice in defiance of the storm, and somewhere within the great forests the allies of the Red Ri Sencha would be gathered within encampments, listening to the tales and the prophecies of seanachies and druids. And within the earth, water would be drip-dripping upon smooth stones which had known the weight of a young man as he had passed over them on his way to a secret Mass upon the slopes of Slemish. Slemish, the Mountain of Mists, shouldering up the sky, bearing the weight of the storm. Did the flame still burn upon it in the mountain glen? Above the clouds, did the stars still shine like druid's eyes—staring, unblinking, somehow accusing, watching me across the miles?

"Master? Are you ill?"

Trimarinus' question brought me gratefully out of my reverie.

"You have gone as pale as Death," he said.

"It could happen again."

"What, lord?"

"You were not here on the day of the raid?"

"My wife was in childbed. I was with her in the town, thanks be to God."

I turned and looked past him, back toward the villa, back eleven years. The wind made strange whisperings and moanings in the rent and blistered walls. It sent the sounds rushing, wailing. And then, for a moment, so bright and quick that I reached out to hold it, I saw a boy run out from the skeleton of the house.

The wind seemed to stop as the boy ran out across the fields. Across weeds and patches of the frost-burnt progeny of wild seeds. He ran inland toward the hills. Despite the chill of the day, he was dressed lightly in a simple white linen tunic. His unruly bronze-toned hair caught the light of the cold winter sun and warmed it. His stride was long and even, the light, reaching, earth-eating stride of the wolf. He looked back at me as he ran. One arm went up, beckoning me to follow.

"Padraic . . ." he cried. "Come on along, Padraic . . ."

He was Youth. He was Yesterday. He vanished with the rising of the wind and the shout of Trimarinus' voice.

"Look, master! Do you see it! The rabbit! Fleet as Time. Pity we weren't closer when it broke from the ruin. It would have made good roasting. But the warren may be close by. Let us go closer. With luck, we may be able to fetch home an evening's fresh supper."

I smiled, obliquely. "That is what I fear. That the raiders may think as you do. That they may decide to seek out our fat warren and carry off more gentle, passive rabbits to their heathen island."

It took him a moment to understand the meaning of my words, then he gasped and signed the cross, broadly, defensively. "You must not think such thoughts, master. You will bring the wrath of God upon us. Surely, the men who know, the councilmen, the elders, they say that the barbarians shall not come to this shore again."

Men will believe what they need to believe. For some there is no convincing. Ever. Until it is too late. I cast a questioning glance down the coast. "How far is this fortress which Licinius has built?"

"Only a mile from here. Near where his villa once stood. But no man rides there. Not without an invitation."

"When Licinius returns from the north, I shall ride there."

He was disturbed and made no attempt to hide the fact. "Be forewarned, master. There are those who say that Licinius has cast his lot with the Devil himself."

"The Devil dwells in Eire, Trimarinus, and with the barbarians in Gaul. I know. I have lived with him. And by the holy name of the most merciful God who has at last seen me safely to my homeland, I swear to you that I shall not live with him again. Such is not God's will for me." Why, in that moment, did I suddenly recall Brother Julian's words to me? "Someday, Brother Patricius, may the Lord grant me the ability to interpret his will as steadfastly as you seem able to do." How strained with facetiousness that good man's voice had been. The memory of it seemed to mock me, to send shadows rising within me.

"Come," I said impatiently to Trimarinus, "let us fetch the horses and return inland. I am cold."

Perhaps I should have waited for their summons, but when I arrived home from the villa there was a message waiting for me from Romana. The implications of its contents set a fire raging within me. I was awake most of the night. The next day, before I had even taken my morning meal, I dressed and went to the forum.

The council was in session, debating some obscure point of law concerning tradesmen and holy days and how goods should or should not be displayed on the eves of major feasts. I interrupted them. They were thoroughly annoyed.

"Can you not see that we are occupied with other matters? Important matters?"

"Yesterday I rode out to the coast. Everything is as it was. None of the villas have been reconstructed."

"The times, the times . . . they deprive us of our luxuries. Who can afford second homes these days?"

"Or the memories which haunt them? I do not think that the problem is one of economics. I think it simply illustrates the basic common sense of the people. The villas have not been rebuilt because, due to a lack of leadership on the part of the council, the people shun the coast because they fear the threat of raiders."

"Nonsense! It's the cost of living pure and simple. You were a seaman. You know how hazardous the trade routes are these days. Why, a man daren't risk the importation of precious building supplies . . . glass . . . tiles . . . fine wood . . . when he can't even guarantee a decent shipment of pepper for his own table! And wine from Gaul? One practically must offer up his children for sale if he expects to obtain anything that comes even close to pleasing the palate! And it's the same with olives from Greece. The quality is most distressing, and at that it costs nearly an arm and a leg for a mere keg, and I'll tell you this, for all of the cost, the flavor is not what it used to be."

I could have vomited upon them. "I care not a fig in Hades about wine or pepper or olives or the cost of living. You all look fat enough when I compare you to my sister's orphans."

There was a mass sucking in of breath. I did not wait for the exhalation of it.

"When I returned from the coast last night, my sister had sent a message to inform me that Licinius has returned from the north with military advisers from the lands beyond the Wall of Antoninus, Pictish tribesmen under the leadership of a Christian lord, one Ceretic of Dumbarton. It seems that I have been invited to meet with him and with his guests at his fortress."

The news obviously shocked them. "Surely you shall not go!"

"Surely I shall. Licinius has long supported my sister when no one in the town, save the priest on his meager income, would grant her more than the rags in their closets or the crumbs cast off by their house pets.

Knowing looks which I did not like passed through their scented, fastidiously well-robed ranks. "Your sister is one of the few persons of her station who does not consider the man mad."

"You should advise her, Magonus Sucatus Patricius, to remember the origins of her name. She is a patrician and should keep to her kind. Licinius may have married into the aristocracy, but he was low-born, the son of merchant-men and thieves. Since his widowing, he has obviously re-

verted to kind. Even his daughter, the pious widow
Clodia, lives away from him with her mother-in-law here
in the town."

The thought of Clodia warmed me. I saw her often
since I had taken an interest in my sister's orphanage. I
said impatiently to the councilmen: "The widow Clodia
lives apart from her father only because it is not suitable
for a woman to dwell in an armed camp of men."

They muttered. They had no wish to concede the point
to me. "These tribesmen from the north . . . what do you
think this means to us?"

"It means, gentlemen, that Licinius is beginning to sup-
plement his farm boys with warriors and to beat his
ploughshares into swords."

They bridled. "This is a Christian land. We will suffer
no barbarians among us! How dare the man dispute our
authority!"

"Someone must dare." I was thoroughly disgusted with
them. "All of these long, long eleven years . . . what have
you dared?"

They were offended. "We dare tell you, Magonus
Sucatus Patricius, that you are impertinent."

I could stomach no more of them. "And you, learned
gentlemen of the council, are a gathering of impotent,
hypocritical old fools!"

24

THE fortress had been constructed upon the very tip of the
peninsula. It faced outward into the sea, presenting no
point of vulnerability, offering no cove in which a boat or
curragh might be safely beached or anchored, and lifting
no section of cliff or wall which might be ascended by
anything more substantial than the mist. It was said that
on a clear day the guardsmen upon the parapets could
sight the distant peaks of Eire rising out of the Western
Sea. They could glimpse as far south as the rocky coast of
Cornwall and then turn to watch clouds forming over the
highlands of Dyfed in the country some called Wales.

Trimarinus signed the cross. "I tell you, master, there is
the stink of Hell about the place. You must go no farther.

There is still time to return to Bannavem Taburniae before nightfall."

The narrow, well-trod pathway to the fortress lay ahead of us; a dun, muddied ribbon running along the spine of the peninsula amidst furze and rain-slicked boulders. The winter sea whooshed and boiled black on either side, stirred to storm like a restless liquid within an enchanter's cauldron.

Trimarinus would have turned his blocky little gelding back toward the hills had I not reached out and caught his rein. I could see his face, a resentful shadow glaring balefully at me from within the protective cavern of his hooded goat's wool cloak.

"Forgive me, master. I am no coward. I only wish to prolong the grace of God which has blessed us since your homecoming."

I put a reassuring hand across his forearm. "And I thank you for that, old friend. But it is for the sake of God's grace that I ride here."

His features drew up into a knot. His eyes searched my face imploringly. "Look to the man's banner. It speaks the truth of him. The truth which you must heed."

I stared ahead toward the fortress. Blackened by three days of rain, it shone darkly against the leaden sky: a hulking stone and timber raven turning inward beneath its battlements against the breath of the approaching storm. A banner streamed out from the top of the great tower. It snapped defiantly in the wind. I could make out the blood-red background: a golden lion with a black wolf held broken in its jaws. The sight of it pleased me, set the fingers of excitement thrumming across the back of my neck.

"The golden lion of Briton breaks the back of the ravening black wolf of the Scots. It is a proclamation of defiance: a statement of Licinius' ambition to protect his homeland."

Trimarinus exhaled a vigorous, antagonistic sigh. Defiance . . . protection . . . proclaimed upon a banner the color of blood. It may be true enough, my lord, when you speak before the council and tell them that we Christian lambs must have a shepherd to guard us. But has Christ Jesus set a hungry lion to keep His sheep safe from wolves? Shall the likes of Licinius protect us or devour us? I see blood upon his banner, but where is the Cross?"

"The Cross, old friend, is bloodied and defiled across the length and breadth of Briton and the continent. I have borne witness to this. There is peace in west Briton now. But the enemy is all around us: north in Dyfed, south on the far shore of Cornwall, east in the camps of the Angels and Saxons and Jutes."

Again he signed the cross. Enormously. From the top of his head to his genitals. From shoulder to shoulder. A broad marking off against Evil. "God keep them content and forevermore away from us!'"

I swore an oath of intolerance. "How long must it be before Britons realize that the will of God is worked through men?"

The sky had begun to bleed rain. It pearled on the finely woven thick blue wool of my hooded cloak. My horse, a fine bay mare, scented storm in the growing onshore wind and shifted her weight restlessly. The air had grown quite cold, carrying with it the sting of sleet. The mare's nostrils expanded and contracted, giving off whirls of steam. I cast a glance at the lowering sky. With haste and luck, the shelter of the fortress could be reached before the full downpour of the squall broke upon us. Cursorily bidding Trimarinus to follow me, I gave the mare a sharp inward jab with my booted heels. She snorted and broke into a nervous trot.

The peninsula lay ahead, narrow as a blade. On either edge of it, sentries had suddenly loomed as shadows swathed in the clouds and frayed, wind-shattered spume of the crashing surf. They were well-armed and clothed against the weather. I saw the dark lines of muted tartan and knew that there were no farm boys here. A voice called out. It seemed disembodied by distance and wind and mist. I shouted out my name and was told to pass. I did so, noting that Trimarinus followed close behind.

The mare danced, whinnying and straining at the bit. She did not like the path onto which I urged her. She would have shied back from it had I not held her firm. The gatehouse lay ahead. In a few moments I was in the shadow of the great tower. Announcing my name to the guardsmen, I looked up, shielding my eyes from the rain which had begun to fall in long, stinging, silver lancets. The banner of Licinius was directly above me. Trimarinus had been correct. I could see no Cross upon it.

If there was the stink of Hell about the place, the scent of industry, discipline, cooking fires, and the falling rain masked it. Trimarinus was escorted off to a hot meal by a deferential young man who was polite enough to ignore his grumblings and mumblings. I was led up into the main hall by way of a narrow stone stairwell. It was a crude structure. The hall was a primitive, high-ceilinged, plank-floored expanse built directly over the stable. The smell of cattle and horses, of urine and dung and moldering straw, rose from below. No herbs had been strewn across the floor to mask the scent. No stalks of incense had been lighted. Yet, as I met the gaze of my host, the offensive smell of the room seemed to vanish.

Licinius stood across from me behind an acre of littered table. There were charts upon it, and maps, and a vast array of writing materials. Though the room was poorly lighted against the late-afternoon storm, I saw him clearly and felt the shock of recognition. I knew that he was two years past his fiftieth birthday, yet Time had marked him with no visible scars of aging. In a land ruled by right of power instead of by right of law or inheritance, this man would have been king. Power lived in him as surely as the vast and restless currents live within the sea. I could sense it in the room: a contagious surging of thought and impatient, virile flesh.

He came out to me from behind the barricade of his table. He clasped my forearms in greeting, and his strength affirmed itself in the hard, sure pressure of his palms against my skin. "I did not think you would come," he said. "The aristocrats of Bannavem Taburniae do not usually choose to travel about when the weather turns foul."

"Perhaps I have not been home long enough to have assumed their liabilities."

He liked what he had heard. "I doubt if you ever shared them, my boy," he said, nodding, pumping my arm enthusiastically. "By the sweet uncurdlable milk of holy Mother Mary, it is good to see you, Magonus. It brings memories of good times."

"For me, too." I began to speak of the days when his son Claudius and I had been as brothers.

His face went as cold and as blank as a stone. He waved me to silence. "Claudius is now a priest in Rome, the land of his mother's people. He has made himself a stranger to me and to his homeland."

A servant entered and relieved me of my rain-soaked
cloak. I thanked him. Licinius had released my arms. He
obviously had been disturbed by my mention of Claudius
and had no wish to discuss his son. He was staring at me,
measuring me, openly approving what he saw.

"You dress as a lord, Magonus. Since your return to
Briton, rumor has come to me saying that you manage
your estate and investments with the finesse of a man
twice your age. Yet of late you have disdained the 'wisdom' of the elders and have spoken on my behalf in the
council. Why?"

"I have come to doubt the wisdom of the elders."

His eyes narrowed. They moved over me scrupulously.
"You are as lean and as hard as a fighting man. And your
eyes . . . they fix me as surely and honestly as any blade.
Can it be true that you, whom I remember as the most ar-
rogant, outspoken, defiant little iconoclast in all of west
Briton, sought to live the life of a monk?"

"It is true."

He shook his head, accepting and disbelieving. "The
man in you won out, eh?"

"The man and the God. It seems that I was not made to
be a priest. But I am a Christian, Licinius."

"And is it as such that you have defended my name
against spurnings of the councilmen?"

"I have not so much spoken for you, I have spoken
against them. I have been twice enslaved, Licinius. I do not
believe that God would will me to bondage again, or that
He wishes His people to stand defenseless against those
who destroy them and make a mockery of His name."

His body tensed as though ready to spring. "Nor do I,
my boy! Nor do I." Beneath his heavy, simply cut garments, the muscles bunched and ran as though they sought
an escape from the skin which held them. His forehead
had knotted together like a swollen burl upon an oak. His
eyes, a paler blue than my own, had ignited with suppressed excitement. They seemed oddly phosphorescent,
as though lighted from within. They glared at me like
stones made momentarily luminescent by the washing of
blue light which is sometimes a gift of the summer sea.
"Years ago I warned them that they must unify . . . that
they must set up watchtowers along the coast . . . that
they must allow the young men to be trained to the
sword."

"I remember. I would have joined with you had the raiders not taken me."

"Would you, Magonus? Would you join with me now? Even though the elders contend that it is against the laws of God for a Christian to make war?"

"Is that your intention? To make war? Or to keep the peace?"

A laugh exploded out of him. His head swung back on his pillared neck. A maned lion's head, with the copper hair thick and coarse and the beard only begrudgingly tamed by clipping. One powerful arm swung forward as he jabbed an index finger at me. "That is exactly what the old, blind, constipated goats will not see. Peace cannot be merely wished for. It must be maintained and protected."

I noticed that he wore the heavy leather wrist guards of the skilled archer and hand-to-hand fighter. The metal studs which had been clamped into the side flashed in the dimly lighted room like cat's eyes.

"Is it any wonder that the youth of Briton grow restless? I tell you, Magonus, many a young man has turned in frustration from the Sacraments of holy Church. Many a once pious virgin lights candles, not to the God of our fathers, but to Sulis Minerva. The old dare not walk the streets, even to attend Mass, for fear of robbers. Lovers rarely venture into the privacy of the woods lest they be set upon by thieves and murderers. Because of the failure of the councilmen to govern, the people no longer mind the laws. They bow to the gods of the times, the petty and vicious little gods of self-interest and self-preservation."

Frustration twitched in the corners of his lips. "Sorry. I did not invite you here so that you might listen to me tirade. But merciful God, if someone does not step forward to unify the people, to govern them, to guarantee their security, I tell you, we need not wait for barbarian raiders to destroy us. We shall destroy ourselves."

The relentless tide of his words had battered me, pummeled me with the fists of growing excitement. "You speak my thoughts," I said.

His arms swung wide, a gesture of exasperation. "I must be speaking *somebody's* thoughts! Each week more young men come out to me. They offer to serve me. But, I ask you, am I Christ Jesus? Can I divide the loaves and the fishes to feed them all? Can I clothe them, or arm them, or hope to shelter them indefinitely? No. Not without the total

support of the people of this district. I must have grain and
fruit and cheeses and the thousand pounds of dried stuffs
which must be stored so that this fortress will stand in the
event of a siege."

"The common people support you."

"In the main. But there are isolated farmsteads and
hamlets which stand aloof, offering up words and nods of
approval but no more. And, after all, it is the gentry who
own the land, as you well know. And the gentry are ruled
by the dictates of the council, which refuses to dictate save
on all but the most petty and unimportant issues. We are
governed, Magonus, by those who either cannot, or will
not, govern. Yet I cannot help but ponder: for how long?"

The implication was clear. I allowed it to settle before
responding. "Why have you asked me to come here,
Licinius? Romana has informed me that you have other
guests. From north, beyond Dyfed."

I could not read the look which came to his features
then. Anger? Distrust? Annoyance? Perhaps all three.
"The councilmen have forced my hand, Magonus. I have
brought the Future with me from beyond the Wall of
Antoninus. You shall meet with him in good time. But for
now, I have invited you here so that I might settle certain
questions which plague me. Questions about you, concerning rumors which I have heard of you . . ." He allowed
the words to drift. Then, frowning intensely, he asked: "Is
it true that you believe in dreams, Magonus?"

"Dreams . . . ?" Even as I spoke, I felt the tightening of some unwelcome foreboding within my gut.

"Dreams!" He repeated impatiently. "The will of God
worked through Vision . . . through prophecy . . . behind a man's closed lids when he sleeps."

I nodded. "They say . . ."

"They! It is God's truth! I know. I have dreamt the
dreams of Vision and, by suffering sweet Jesus, I have
been as Noah with the ark: the butt of every joke. The
merriment of every scoundrel. It was dream and Vision
which have urged me to construct this fortress, after those
I have seen in the lands of the pagan Moors. For ten
years I have labored at it, forced to bring in labor from
abroad when I could not find enough local men who
would work for me. Eventually I succeeded in making
a pauper of myself, but not before the dream was fulfilled. It is Christ's holy truth that, if need arose, I could

shelter the entire bedamned population of Bannavem
Taburniae and all its surrounding farmsteads within
these walls. Oh, not in the style or comfort to which the
gentry are accustomed, but in safety. A handful of loyal,
well-trained men can hold these walls against an enemy
indefinitely. The common people are beginning to see the
wisdom of it. They feed me when the mood moves them.
God help me, some of them even write ballads about
me!" He paused and glared at me. "But to the gentry and
the members of the council . . . I am still a madman."
Again he paused. He seemed to be waiting, listening
for a sound from beyond the room. "There," he said,
straining to hear. "Did you hear it?"

There was no sound but the distant sound of the storm
beyond the walls, and the stirrings of men within the fortress, and of cattle and horses. Somewhere a dog barked
and a man laughed.

"Hear what?" I asked.

"Listen. Beyond the walls."

There was only the sound of the storm. I told him that.

"But that is exactly what you must hear. What they
must hear. Don't you see? Come. I will show you."

Night had fallen. The rain was beating upon the parapets as though it sought to pound them into oblivion. The
wind was up. The mists were down. The world was
black, held off somewhere beyond a caul of gray, wet,
roiling cloud. The stonework of the tower shone in the
darkness. Avalanches of rain sheeted down from the em-
brasures. The sea raged below, roaring, thundering. Enormous waves were rolling upon the coast, screaming as
they rose and fell, exploding upon the rocky shore of the
peninsula: pounding, crashing, shaking the very foundation of the fortress.

We had clothed ourselves against the weather in swaths
of oiled hides which we held over our heads. I thought I
heard Licinius laugh. The sound was drowned by the battling roar of the sea and the storm. We were alone. Licinius had dismissed the guardsmen, who stood their duty
even in fog or storm. I turned toward my host. He was
taller than I. Broader. I could see his beard and the arching hook of his wide nose shedding water as copiously as
the stonework. He lifted up his arms and let the rain
cape fall away. The forces of the night drenched him in

an instant. He put back his head and opened his mouth, drinking in the elements. This time I did hear him laugh. Clearly. Deeply.

For a moment I thought that the warning concerning him had been justified. He seemed mad. He did not even shiver with the chill of the icy rain or battering wind. He seemed impervious to it, a man carved from some rough and heavy-textured stone. Then he turned and looked at me, squinting through the gray-dark night and the beating rain. It was not madness which I saw in his face. It was the incredible intensity of resolve.

"Can you not see it? It is as though it displays itself for your benefit!"

"See . . . what . . .?"

"Power!" He was shouting to be heard above the storm and the sea. "The night displays it for you, Magonus! Power of storm and sea . . . with my fortress standing tall and firm against them. Power! This is what the elders see in me . . . and what terrifies them. The power of a tide which they cannot change. The power of the raging force of the New Day, a day which holds no place within its light for the weak or for the passive. A New Day which will unify the people of Briton under one banner. As in my dream."

"The banner of Licinius?"

"I do not know. Nor do I ask it." His head went back, mouth open to the rain. "God!" he cried, raising his arms again, turning slowly around and around. "God of power! God of all worlds since the beginning of Time!"

If supplication can be defiant, his words were so. If the Sight was truly mine, I should have seen. What he was. What he would be. What he must be. I felt the slow feeling of withdrawal which comes to a man when he senses the unknown. Premonition? Yes. It was that. I should have remembered it from Slemish. And from the court of the Ri.

Licinius came close to me, leaned toward me so that I could see the fire of purpose within his eyes. "God is with me in this venture, Magonus."

His certainty was devastating as he guided me across the tower and together we stood against the wind which whistled through the most western-facing embrasure. "Can you feel it? Can you smell it? The wind blows true. From across the miles. The smell of land, of the Western

Isle, blown to us out of the storm. On a clear day, from this height, a man can see it. And not a ship or raiding curragh can cross this land-locked bow without my knowledge. In the fog or rain, and even on nights of storm such as this, my men are with the sea birds in the cliffs and in the hollows of the inland hills. Waiting. Watching. Ready to report to me. To warn the people. I tell you, Magonus, such men and fortresses as mine shall keep us safe and strong. I have been to the north and I have seen what the people of Dumbarton have done under the leadership of their lord Ceretic. At Alcluith they have raised a fortress such as this. They have unified. They have marked the beginning of the New Day, of the drawing together of the Celts: from north beyond Dyfed, to the southernmost reach of Land's End, across the island to Londinium itself. Wherever we are beset, God has begun to bring our people together at last. He is raising an army of farmers and tarriers, of blowers of glass and smiths and bakers, of weavers and potters . . ."

He stopped speaking abruptly as his train of thought changed. When next he spoke, his voice was the shrill cry of a hawk soaring free on the wind. "I have joined ranks with Ceretic in the hope of the New Day. Now let the elders oppose me. Let them dare. Those self-righteous, supercilious, foolish little men! Do they honestly believe that Rome shall ever return to protect them? Do they honestly believe that if they ignore me long enough I shall cease to exist? Do they not know that I could take what I need from them now? With this?"

His right hand curled into a fist. Hard. Tight. Power shone on the wet musculature of his hand. "I have held back for the sake of their precious peace, for the sake of the traditions which they so cherish. I have held back because I have not, until now, been ready to move without fear of unleashing the beast of anarchy upon the land. But I ask you, Magonus, is the leash not rotting away of its own accord? And if I do not move soon, shall it not have developed a thousand heads, each with its own ambition, its own sense of direction; each with its own dream and purpose . . . not for the good of the whole, but for its own end? Then, surely, there will be war. Not brought to us by invaders. It will be a war waged between brothers. Class against class. Clan against clan. And once it begins, there shall never be peace upon the

land of Briton, not for a thousand years or for all Eternity.
We shall have consumed one another; and in the end,
when the barbarians at last invade us, there shall be none
to fight them . . . but barbarians."

The rain beat into my face. It stung my eyes. I could
not think. The worm of confusion turned within me, bit
into my belly and cramped there. I must have shivered,
for Licinius reached out and gripped my shoulder.

"Listen to me, tirading like a madman! I will talk you
to death out here in the rain if you don't stop me! Come
now, you've been patient long enough. We will go in
and share a hot meal together while we discuss this further. Then I shall tell you God's purpose for us."

"Us?"

"Of course! I knew it as soon as I returned from the
north and heard the rumors about you and your confrontation with the council. Why else do you imagine that
I have invited you here, save to confirm what must surely
be the will of the Lord? Can you not feel it, Magonus?
Do you imagine that God has sent you home to us from
the Western Isle after all of these years with no purpose
other than your own comfort in mind? No. *This* is the
purpose, my boy: our mutual destiny . . . our place together in the rising of the New Day."

We were to dine alone. The lord Ceretic and his kinsmen had gone out with Llwyn earlier in the day to survey
the countryside. The storm had caught them unprepared.
They had sent a rider to the fortress to advise Licinius
that they would be spending the night enjoying the hospitality of one of the inland farmsteads.

A table had been set for us in the main hall. There
was a joint of lamb, a platter of good, sweet, succulent
oysters, which are nowhere in the world so fine as they
are in my homeland, and small loaves of unleavened rye
bread which had been specially flavored with fragrant
herbs and aged cheeses. There were spiced eggs and limp,
peppery vegetables marinated in cider vinegar. To wash
all this down, there was a pitcher of the strong-smelling
barley ale for which Briton is famous, or perhaps I should
say infamous, throughout the civilized world. To finish
the meal, there were crumbly pasties made oily with fill-
ings of honey and crushed nut-meats.

"For one who worries about an empty larder, you dine well and royally," I said.

"For now," he agreed. "The farmers and the poor have been generous. It is the long term which causes me concern. Besides, this is unusually fine fare for me. It is a special meal, in honor of an old friend and a most welcome guest."

A hot bath and massage awaited us after we had come in out of the rain. Our appetites had been perked by the competent ministrations of the masseuse. Though no longer a girl, the woman was not unattractive. I had refused to strip naked before her. Licinius had teased me.

"So you *have* been a monk."

"For over two years I was upon the Isle of Lérins."

"Lérins? Within eyeshot of Gaul? With her sultry shores beckoning? No wonder you left the calling."

"It left me."

"Ahh."

"It would be more suitable, Licinius, if you had a man to tend your baths."

He shrugged. "Would you deprive this good woman of her livelihood?" He sighed with pleasure as her strong, sure hands kneaded the broad expanse of his back. "Tell my guest, woman, of how you came to your position here."

She did not look up at me as she spoke. She kept her head turned down to her work. "My brother and me's come here from our village. Upland it was. Near Viroconium. It's been two, perhaps three years now since we come. I don't like to speak on it. I'd six brothers then, when we lived in the village. A poor village it were and too far inland for Scot raiders to be concerned with. Yet one day they come, and they took what little we had, and they burned the village, and many a maid was mounted, and many a lad was slain. There was slaves took off from us, and the dead was so many they was like cobbles lying in the road. Now there's only my brother Gan'n me. When we heard of this place, we come to serve the lord who's not afraid to let all the world know that if the barbarians try to shaft him, they'll be getting some of his shaft back. And in kind."

Licinius rolled off of the table, nodding his satisfaction with her words as he stood beside her and wrapped a towel about his hips. "Do you imagine that there is peace and security within the town of Bannavem Taburniae, woman?"

"I think there is not. But here there's safety. With you. Within these walls. Aye."

His mood grew suddenly dark with introspection. "Does our Faith not teach us to be our brothers' keeper, Magonus? And have not the elders of this time abandoned their brothers?" He looked at me and his eyes were clear and challenging. "Is it not our Christian duty, Magonus, to protect our brethren?"

"As God gives us to protect them."

He laughed. Spontaneously. "And do you wonder if God has given this . . ." His arms went out to indicate the room and all which lay beyond it. "Or if it is merely the contrivance of an ambitious man?"

His tone was friendly, yet sharp with accusation. I replied, defensively: "I have been advised many times, by Christians and pagans alike, that God does indeed work His will through men. Yet men often misinterpret His will and attempt, not always consciously, to bend it to their own purpose. God knows, I have been guilty of that sin. I have come to know that a man must judge carefully . . . whether he is to be an instrument of God . . . or whether he has used God's name as a ruse and excuse to explain his own desires."

He nodded. "Were you as blunt when you were a slave to the pagan Scots?"

"I was."

"It is a miracle that they did not have you slain."

"They tried. More than once."

He was intrigued. "And you survived, with never a lesson learned?"

"I survived, by the grace of God, with many a lesson learned."

"And many an enemy amongst the Scots, I'd wager."

"Only three."

"In six years? Not a bad record."

I smiled wanly. "Two kings and a druid. Not exactly a good record, either."

His brow furrowed. "Since when do slaves keep such impressive company?"

"I did not choose it."

His eyes were measuring me. I could almost feel them walking over my skin like invisible antennae. "No . . . I daresay you did not . . ." He called for the garments which the masseuse had gathered up and held folded across her arm. "I believe that I was right about you, my boy," he said as the woman helped him to dress. "All the rumors . . . all the gossip . . . all of my daughter's exuberant opinions . . . I have weighed them against my memories of you. By the blood of the Cross, my boy, I like the sum. You shall be heir to all of this when I am dead. By God, it is the will of Destiny."

"Heir . . . ?"

He smiled at my obvious amazement and incredulity. "I am too hungry to discuss it now. Let the woman get on with your massage. Take your time. Allow her to pleasure you. I shall share my dream with you when you have finished and while we break bread together."

He started to leave the room. I could not lie still for the massage. I took up my clothes, hastily dressed, and followed him back to the main hall. He was already at the table, washing down a mouthful of spiced eggs with ale.

"Here. Eat!" he demanded. "Clodia arranged the menu when she learned that you had agreed to dine with me."

I seated myself numbly. "Your daughter is a most gracious and charitable lady." I felt the comment necessary, yet had no wish to discuss anything which might cause him to deviate from his statement concerning my place in his "destiny."

The knowing light of mirth sparkled in his eyes. "Clodia's charity to your sister's foundlings has been renowned . . . since your homecoming."

I stared at him. "And before, surely."

He looked to his trencher, speared a piece of lamb and put it to his lips. "Come, come, Magonus, surely you are aware of the fact that my daughter courts you?"

The admission was a revelation which I chose to ignore. "Why have you invited me here?"

"So that you might come to know your place within the rising of the New Day. I will speak honestly, Magonus. I am no longer young. Sometimes, I wake sweated in the night and I think: When I am dead, who will care for my men, for the farm boys who have sworn to serve me as though I were their king, for the Picts who have come, at the decree of their chieftain, to grant me aid? Shall my fortress be abandoned? Or shall it be taken over by the battling heads of my beast of anarchy? I have no sons, Magonus."

"Claudius . . ." I was sorry for having spoken the word before I was able to recall it.

He snarled. "I have sired a priest, not a man!" He shoved his trencher away from him and lay his hands, palms down, upon the table. "I have thought on this for many years without satisfaction, without solution. In my dreams I have seen a Briton which is fragmented, blood-ied, torn by the conflict of ambitious men. Vision? No. Warning."

He rose to his feet and stared at me. "Since your home-coming, the dreams have been of peace, not of blood. Seeing you now, the man you have become, I understand. You . . . high-born . . . respected by your peers and by the common people alike. We are the two faces of Briton, you and I. The high-born and the low. When we unite, together we shall persuade the people to stand with us against our common enemy. You are the first member of the aristocracy to openly speak against the council. I tell you, Magonus, it is indeed the beginning of the New Day."

He seated himself again. "Look back. Back three hun-dred years and beyond. Were we Britons not one people before we were conquered and taught to be Roman? When the Caesars first came to our shore, we gathered together upon the cliffs . . . men, women, children, we fought against them until the earth could drink no more of our blood. By God, Magonus, we were a proud race then and can be again. The blood of the ancient race still flows within us. It is rising now, all across Briton. The people will meld, Magonus, as surely as the house of Licinius and the house of Patricius shall meld when you and Clodia are wed."

I made a conscious effort to close my mouth as it fell into a gape.

He was infinitely pleased with himself. He leaned back in his chair and swung his legs up, crossing them at the ankles. "She's been in love with you since she was twelve. We've discussed it thoroughly. The Patricius name and resources bear much weight in this community. As my son-in-law, you would reflect back upon me the respect of your kinsmen, associates, and neighbors. You have an exceptional gift for management. I can use you to put the fear of God into my accountants. I'm afraid they are all thieves. I have little patience and less talent when it comes to keeping books, and they have found me out." He slapped his knees. "And you are young. And strong of will. You share my dreams and my fears. But most important of all, Magonus, you are a man whom others will follow. I saw that in you the moment I set eyes upon you. By God, my boy, you are the son I lost when Claudius left Briton to enter the priesthood."

I was not complimented. I was stunned and angry. "With what confidence you manipulate the lives of others! Marriage is a Sacrament, Licinius. It is not a maneuver."

He swung his legs down and leaned across the table toward me. "It is the plum in my pudding, Magonus. But if you would prefer it without the sweetening, so be it. I would have you as my ally under any circumstances." Mirth sparked in his eyes again. "Frankly, I did not think there was a bachelor in all of west Briton who would not be pleased by the prospect of marriage with my daughter."

I thought of Clodia, of brown eyes shining beneath dark lashes, of a dimpled smile, of a warm and silken arm threaded through my own. How many suitors did the woman have? And did I not irascibly, irrationally loathe them all? She was devout and generous, dedicated to my sister's orphans, who adored her for her beauty and her kindness. But then, everyone adored Clodia. She was God's smile upon the earth. It was with a bleak and bitter heart that I said to Licinius: "I cannot marry."

"You are betrothed to another?"

"I cannot marry."

His brow creased into a scrutinous furrowing which told me that the light of comprehension was beginning to flicker. "Have I misunderstood? Is it still your intention to someday become a celibate monk?"

"Such was not God's purpose for me."

"Then you are free to wed."

"No. Years ago . . . I made a vow . . ."

"To remain chaste forever? Even though you were not to become a priest? Who would hold you to such an impossible promise?"

"God will hold me to it."

My piety was not to be taken seriously. "Don't be a sanctimonious ass, Magonus! The Gospel clearly states that it is better for a man to marry than to burn. Are you telling me that you are not a man? Have the Scots or the monks of Lérins neutered you?"

"I am a man, Licinius. A man of my word."

"Clodia will not approve."

"I seek only God's approval."

"And how do you know that He would not grant it?"

"Impossible . . ."

"Is it? Have you asked the bishop?"

"There has been no reason . . ." The words trailed off as hope awakened within me, winged, beating for release and recognition. "Do you think . . . ?"

"When did you make this vow, Magonus? When you thought to become a priest?"

"Long before. As penance for past sins."

"Suffering Jesus! What sort of a sadist priest would assign such a grievous penance? A lifetime of chastity!"

"No priest. The penitent himself."

He was shocked. Silently, he appraised me. After a moment, he asked quietly: "Are you one of those men who seeks adversity, Magonus?"

"It has sought me."

"And are you not weary of it?"

"I am."

"Then grant your support to me, my boy. Stand with me as my son in the hope of the New Day. The people of Bannavem Taburniae must be protected by our alliance."

I was dizzied by confusion. I thought of Trimarinus, of the great, dark battlements of the fortress rising against sea and storm. I thought of the blood-red banner and heard myself say: "When the Cross stands over the lion, then I shall stand with you."

Licinius' brow furrowed as he sought my meaning. Then, understanding, he nodded vigorously. "It shall be done. The banners shall be resewn on the day when the bishop grants his blessing, on the day when your betrothal to Clodia is sealed."

The bargain was made in my heart. "On that day," I said, and wished it were tomorrow.

25

WE were to be married in the spring. My parents' complaints were mollified by the thought of grandchildren. They loved Clodia even though they did not approve of her father and considered the marriage to be below my station.

The spring came, and with it, one early dawn, I was awakened by the sound of Clodia's voice whispering to me from beyond my bedroom window. Wrapping the bed coverlet about myself, I crossed the room and peered out into the thinning darkness.

"Clodia . . . ?"

She "shh-ed" me to silence as I opened the window. "It's a miracle that I'm here. Hurry. Dress. And be silent about it."

"What is it? Has something happened?"

"Of course something has happened." There was the sting of impatience upon her whisper. "I've bribed one of my father's men to serve us as a bodyguard. We have the entire day to ourselves. So hurry and stop staring like an addlewit!"

She turned away and would not hear another word from me. I dressed and went out into the inner courtyard. She took my hands and reached up to place a light and hasty kiss of greeting upon my cheek.

"The horses are tethered on the street. I've brought the day's meal. Now, don't say another word lest you wake your wretched slave, Trimarinus, who will insist upon following us like some unwelcome shadow of judgment."

I looked back toward the gate. It was closed, with the bar and lock still in place. "How did you get into the courtyard?"

"I climbed the wall! Father's man hefted me up. How else could I wake you without rousing your entire household?"

I should not have been amazed. Clodia had been bright, impetuous, and willful as a child. She was even more so now.

"Hurry," she urged, tugging at my hands, attempting to lead me to the gate.

I resisted. "It is neither customary nor appropriate for us to be alone together before the wedding."

She stopped abruptly, suddenly rigid with anger. Even in the half-light of the morning, I saw her large dark eyes go round and hot with temper. She had inherited her mother's opulent Roman beauty and molten disposition. "What do I care for what is either customary or appropriate? We shall be husband and wife in two short weeks and we are practically strangers to one another. We have not had so much as an hour alone together since your homecoming. Merciful Heaven, have you been a party to the nonsensical tradition which would keep us apart? We are not children, you and I. I cannot speak for you, but I am a widow a good year removed from the giggling days of simpering virginity." Her whispers had risen and grown strained. She sighed and shook her head. "Have I awakened the man in you? Or is it the monk? If it is the latter, perhaps you had best go back to your bed."

We kept well away from the woods where robbers were known to dwell and, with Licinius' armed man to protect us against a chance meeting with thieves, we rode out across the hills and spent the morning simply dawdling, admiring the countryside, talking of days gone by, racing our horses whenever the mood moved us. The young guardsman kept his distance, riding slowly behind us as he blew lilting, merry tunes out of the hand-carved fife which was his prized possession.

It was not yet noon when we at last dismounted beside a small copse. The guardsman would have kept to himself, but Clodia insisted that he keep company with us and share our meal. He seemed embarrassed at first, but after several deep draughts of ale, he was content to eat with us and then lie back as he serenaded us with whatever tunes we would hear. He was an admirable musician. Clodia sang along with his melodies in as sweet a voice as I had ever heard. I listened, entranced, then joined in. We filled the copse with songs and laughter, and soon, as the sun lazily claimed the noon, the guardsman dozed, then awoke, flustered and scolding himself. Clodia and I slept then. Easily, deeply, while he played gently on his fife for us.

I awoke to the sound of his melodies. Distant sound. Slow, dreamy, blown from the far side of the hill. Clodia lay beside me, her head propped up on one hand, the other hand idly teasing a stalk of grass across my lips.

"We are alone," she said.

I pursed my lips against the tickling grass. "The fifeman?"

"He will not come to us until we call for him."

She leaned across me and kissed me. As a flower opens to the sun, so did her mouth open upon mine. Her hair had fallen loose. I could smell the delicate scent of the lavender which she had crushed and rubbed into the long, shining strands. I reached up and touched her hair, running it through my fingers like skeins of black silk.

She drew back from me for a moment. Her eyes searched my face. Then she smiled as no woman had ever smiled at me. Soft as dawn was that smile, warm as the fluid which protects the unborn child within its mother's womb, as filled with the promise of infinite love as is life itself when it is new and unblemished by the world. Her hands moved up and released the clasp which held her stolla. The cloth came away, fell softly against me as, in a moment, did she lie softly against me.

Our kiss was renewed. Slowly, the sure, rising heat of passion filled us both. There was no drawing back from it. No thought. No deliberation. There was only the pure, driving force of flame which impels a man and a woman to become one.

And so we would have been. Until, shivering at the moment of acceptance, she put back her head and whispered with the soft exhalation of a woman about to take life into herself: "Yes . . . now . . . forever . . . pledge your love to me now . . . now . . ."

Even as she yielded to me, so did my desire shrivel and grow cold. Her words had plunged me into the icy surf of memory. I stared at her and saw not Clodia, not my betrothed, but another woman: her face flushed with passion, her eyes as wide and vast and threatening as infinity. I saw the face of the Morrighan. I heard her voice. Her triumph.

"You are pledged to me . . . by blood and by body . . . you are pledged to me . . ."

Clodia had tensed and drawn back from me. "What is it?"

I sat up and put my face in my hands. "I don't know," I lied, wishing to escape the question. I was cold and shaken and ashamed.

I could hear the sighing of her garments as she clothed herself. "We will wait, then." There was no criticism in her voice. No rebuke. She reached out and touched my shoulders, tenderly. "I love you," she said. "My most precious monk. My would-be priest. If you fear that God is watching us, we shall wait until after the wedding."

Why did the words sting me so? I knew that she had not intended them to burn as acid. Yet they did. Would-be priest. Most precious monk. My mind was suddenly filled with memories of Lérins. Of stinging serpents and cold cells and harsh food. Of my brothers in Christ prostrate before God in endless prayers and devotions. Had I not thanked God a thousand times for having delivered me from that? Then, why did the memory, as it ebbed, make me wish to run after it, to draw it out of the past and into the reality of the present? It was as though a friend had called and then vanished, making a reply to him impossible. I felt battered and exhausted, drained to my very soul.

I looked at Clodia and smiled weakly. "Forgive me," I said. "I am a fool."

"Yes," she assented, cajoling lovingly. "You are."

The dream. It seems to me now, looking back, that half of my life has been dreams. But this dream. How can I explain it? As with the coming of the Power and the spirits of the Otherworld in the mountain glen, there are those who will believe and those who will not believe. There are many who would ascribe it to guilt or to subconscious wishes, or to gas upon the stomach, or the wild spinnings of a too-fertile imagination. At the time of my dreaming it, I would gladly have agreed with them. In truth, I denied its message. Never was a dream less welcome. Never has a dream so touched my soul.

It came to me innocently enough, through the fibers of memory as dreams often come. It was disembodied by Time and by sleep. Soft. Warm. Posing no threat to my rest. It recalled to me that night upon Slemish when Mercia and MacCairthinn had led me to the Mass being celebrated by Victoricus. I saw the secret passageway and heard the dripping of water and the scuffling of hurried steps along the ancient stones. I saw the hulking shoulders of the Mountain of Mists, and saw the stars whirling away forever across the black night sky of Eire. I saw the silent, anonymous figures walking across the dark hills. I saw the great billa, the holy tree, splayed out across the night. I saw the ruined stone. I saw the flame. The tiny flame. The insistent flame which Leborchom and I had kindled in the Long Ago.

"For what purpose . . . the years and the miles . . . the quest and the question . . . for what purpose?"

Who spoke? I do not know. Somehow the dream went very bright, and upon the darkness I saw Victoricus coming toward me. He held out his staff to me. I took it. Letters seemed to appear within his hands. Countless letters. So many that he could barely hold them all. He began to read. Yet it was not with his own voice. It was a sound such as I had never heard. It was the voice of no one man. It cried. It moaned. It wailed. It was the voice of all Eire.

"We are the voice of the Gael . . . from beside the Wood of Focluth . . . from the place where Dubh was born and from the place where he died . . . from the hills and moors and boglands . . . from the mountains and rivers of all Eire . . . we ask thee, boy, come and walk among us once more."

I awoke then. Instantly. I was shaking as though with fever. Every scar which the Gael had inflicted upon me ached as though freshly bruised and torn. I rose from my bed and walked out into the inner courtyard. The night was deep and cool and sweet with the scent of spring roses. I crossed myself as I drew in lungfuls of this treasured reality.

"Magonus . . . ?" My mother's voice. Light, treading lest she disturb the other members of the household. "You cried out in your sleep. Are you not well?"

"I am all right now," I assured her.

"Are you certain, dear? It's so close to the wedding. All of the plans are made. We can't have you sick now. Shall I call the physician?"

"It was only a dream that woke me."

"A bad dream?"

"A very bad dream."

"Groom's jitters," she said, with the certainty of all mothers when discussing such matters.

I though of Clodia lying soft and naked against me. I trembled with quick and aching desire for her. How could I not have taken her? I felt the hot blush of shame burn into my cheeks. Groom's jitters. Is that what had caused my withdrawal? Is that what had prompted the dream? Would my inner self run back away to slavery in Eire rather than face another episode of impotence with her?

By merciful God, I thought angrily, when next I lie with her I shall be her husband and she shall be my wife and never, ever, shall she have cause to accuse me of demonstrating "groom's jitters" again.

It seems to me now that a great sea was beginning to rise up around me. I was in the trough, shadowed by the rising walls of a Destiny which would soon lift me up and carry me away on a spuming crest which I could not control or deny. Yet in the trough the sea was calm. After so many years of storm, I cannot truly fault myself for trying to prolong it. I clung to it as tightly and possessively as a man who digs his toes into slipping sand, hopelessly attempting to stand against the tide.

With the dream, the tide had already turned for me. I should have known it on the day that Egan came.

"There is a visitor for you," my mother said and left me with him in the atrium.

He had not changed. He had merely lengthened. I said that to him, and laughed, for it was pure joy to look upon him.

His smile came slowly. It did not fully blossom. He stared at me out of that long, frail face, his eyes innocent, and said: "Padraic. It is true what they said of you in the town. You are a fair and fine lord, you are."

How easily the language of the Gael came back to me. How eagerly I went to the young man and embraced him. "You were . . . what? . . . seven years old when last I saw you? In the kennel of the Ri, a mere pup yourself. And how did you escape from there, young lad?"

"I did not escape, Lord Padraic. I was sent. With my hounds. And with the rath under constant attack by Sencha's raiders, in truth, glad I was to be away from it, even though the journey to Egypt was long and frightening for me. But the Lord has been with me. As you promised in the Long Ago."

Though he was as thin as a willow slip, there was a

hard, resilient handsomeness about his slender frame. As I gripped his shoulders, I nodded with approval of him, as though I were a parent and might take pride in him. "You would be . . . fifteen now?"

"I am that, lord."

"And am I to take it from your words that you have become a Christian?"

" 'Twas you gave me the Faith. So it is that I've sought you across the far miles, to thank you for the most precious gift that I shall ever receive in all my life . . . and to tell you that it is my intention to become a priest so that I may return to Eire to preach the Gospel to my people." He paused. He seemed embarrassed and more than a little sheepish. "I had hoped somehow that we might return together . . ."

I was astounded. I remembered the dream and put it from my mind. Surely this was merely the wildest coincidence. "How have you found me, Egan?"

"Oh and that is a long tale, it is. I thought you dead when I left Eire. In Egypt I was, at the harbor with my new master. There was a sea captain there from Eire. He was speaking to others about a boy he had once known, a young man. A Christian, Roman-born, from the isle of Briton. I overheard him as he talked. He said that the boy had been a slave to the Gael, and had escaped and had shipped with him. He said that the boy had brought him to faith in Christ, for the boy had the Sight and had foretold the future through his god and his dreams. So that very night I ran off from my Egyptian master and have followed wherever word has led me to you. Sure and the word has led me far indeed, Lord Padraic."

I stared at him, completely amazed. I noticed his clothes then. Not since my own days of flight and wandering had I seen the like. His garment was of the roughest wool, worn through at the elbows, ragged at the hemline. His sandals were patched. Strips of leather and rags had been wrapped about the soles to keep them in place.

"By the name of blessed Jesus, Egan, you look as though the rats have been at you. You can't wander about the town looking like this! Tomorrow we shall go to my tailor's. You may choose any fabric that pleases you, any combination of colors . . . even seven. Yes! Seven! Like a Gaelic Ri, eh?"

"I am no king, Lord Padraic, nor do I wish to dress as one."

"Perhaps not, but we can't have you attending my wedding looking like something the dogs have chewed on."

"Wedding?" He seemed disturbed. Confused. Lost.

"Indeed! Rejoice for me, boy! I am to marry in less than two weeks!"

"So and I shall, Lord Padraic, if it is God's will . . ."

I did not appreciate the bleakness of his tone. "Of course it is God's will. More than you know. Tell me, have you see the fortress of Licinius?"

"That and I have. Never have I seen the like outside the lands of the heathen Moors and Byzantine Greeks. It is all the talk of the common people. I walked from the harbor to see it for myself. Sure and it seemed a dark and evil place."

I attempted to pay no heed to the spark of annoyance his statement ignited within me. "I can assure you, Egan, that if there is anything 'dark' or 'evil' about the fortress, it is seen only by those narrow-minded souls who refuse to face the truth of the times. Licinius' fortress is the hope of Briton. His daughter is to be my bride."

His head went up as though I had dealt him a physical blow. "Then it is true what they say in the town: that you have allied yourself with the one who is called the salvation of the New Day. Beware, Lord Padraic. The common people call him savior. Sure and it is a blasphemy against the name of the Lord."

I was suddenly fiercely angry with him. "You know nothing of Briton, Egan! Would you, like the elders of our council, suggest that we turn up our throats in submission to the raiders of Eire? If you would, then it is not I who have taught you your faith."

My tone had been sharp. It had cut him. "You have taught me of the lamb of God who, by His sacrifice, has taken upon Himself the sins of all the world. Have you taught me incorrectly then?"

"If you have come away from my teaching believing that He went blind and dumb to His destiny, yes. Christ was no passive lamb trussed up by God and made ready for the slaughter. He sought His fate, called out to it. He is the Second Person of the most holy Trinity, Son of the God of Power and might, creator of all worlds since the beginning of Time. He is the God who touched my life in Eire so that I might now understand the threat given my homeland by the wolves of the Western Sea. With Him and with Licinius, I will stand against the barbarians to keep His holy word alive among my countrymen."

He seemed irritated. "Will you now? And whose faith shall you be keeping? Licinius' or Christ's? Begging your pardon, Lord Padraic, but I remember well how you taught me that someday the lamb would lie down with the lion. I do not remember you saying that the lamb would have to become a lion first."

My anger was completely routed by his words. He had spoken so quietly, with an almost tender persuasiveness.

"Have you not thought, Lord Padraic, that it would be better to transform the lion instead? With the word of God, I mean. Then the lambs of the world would have no need to fear."

Within me there was a quick flowering of memory: of Sencha lying forcefully spread-eagled while the Ri Miliucc MacBuain held up his severed manhood impaled upon a blade. "No power on earth could make lambs of the lions of Eire, my boy."

He cocked his head. "No power on earth," he agreed. "And no laws, either. For I have come to think that no law, no power, no matter how well intended, no matter how strong, can long stand righteous in the world of men. Because it *is* the world of men. Or have you forgotten the truth of The Way, Lord Padraic? Have you forgotten that it has been written that until all the world knows of God's love, until all Mankind bows to His decrees and to His laws, there shall always be lions and wolves to feast upon the lambs. Without Christ to guide us, to be sovereign king over us, surely there shall always be the sword."

I could not seem to catch my breath. Egan went on. A calm, sure, sweeping tide of soft words.

"Think of it, if you would. Remember back, if you would. The laws of Eire, surely in all the world there are no finer laws. And the Ris who govern Eire are good and just men. But they are men who, out of ignorance, worship gods which allow them to be manipulated by their own mortal weaknesses. Miliucc MacBuain was a good and kind lord once. Now he is damned. It need not have been, not if he had known and accepted Christ."

He smiled apologetically. "I know that I am not much of a man. But I shall return to my people. I shall bring to them the Gospel of my Lord Christ Jesus . . . to all of them . . . to houndsmen and millers and cooks and serving maids . . . to flaiths and druids and all who will listen . . . not to me, surely, but to the holy Word of God."

"They will have your head for your efforts."

He began to reply, then changed his mind. His face had flushed crimson. He looked down, away from me, shuffling his feet. "I think I must be going now."

"You have just arrived! You must rest . . . partake of the hospitality of my house . . . you must . . ."

"I must go, Lord Padraic. It seems I have made a mistake in coming at all. You are not the man I have sought these many years."

"Surely you did not expect to find me still a slave, a kennel hand?"

"No, lord, that and I did not. In truth, I did not know where or how I would find you. But in Eire, sure and you were a different man. The Lord's holy Spirit spoke through you. It touched all who knew you. Everywhere along the roads, you shared God's word with every man or woman, slave or free, so that we all knew that Christ was with you. That was why the druid feared you and, I think, why the Ri loved you."

"Love?" The premise was too ridiculous to consider.

"Did he not put you beside him at the banquet? Did he not take your word over the druid's? Did he not run the hounds across the hills with you, as though you were his equal? Aye, the son he never had."

I could not define the emotion which rose in me then. It confused me. I said, hastily: "I still bear the scars of the Ri Miliucc MacBuain's love. Thank you, Egan, I am content to do without it."

"The common people of Briton say that this man Licinius would also make a son of you. So you see? It is not unusual for men to love you. Perhaps they see in you what I can no longer see: God's strength and honest face."

I stared at him, unable to respond.

The flush of crimson had paled upon his face. His eyes moved from me and drifted across the sunny atrium with its mosaic floors, frescoed walls, and baseboards filigreed with gold. "It must be difficult to be a Christian in a place like this, knowing as you do how many poor and hungry souls there are in Eire, thirsting for the compassion of Lord Jesus."

How pitiful he seemed, a half-grown, half-starved, would-be apostle. If I had inspired the light of the fanatic to shine within his eyes, I felt deeply and sincerely repentant. "The thirst shall be filled, Egan. In God's time, by wandering monks and bishops, by the priests of holy Church. Not by you, boy."

He seemed infinitely sad. "But I shall become a priest, Lord Padraic. Holy Church must be made to know that God's time for Eire is now. Not tomorrow. Not when it shall be safer or more comfortable or more convenient. You once risked your life to speak of God within the hall of a pagan Ri. You brought the Light of God to Dalaradia. Can it be that the fire of your own faith has been extinguished?"

"It has been banked. Mercifully. God has at last granted me peace of mind and heart. For the first time since I was taken as a slave to Eire, I am content."

"Content!" The prickling of anger ran across his features. "Is that the goal for all of us now? Peace of mind? Contentment? While the world around us drowns in the fires of damnation?"

"I cannot save the world."

"No. When I look at you now, as you are, surely I know that you could not." He began to back away from me, bowing from his waist. "I am sorry to have troubled you, Lord Padraic. God's blessings on you."

"No. I will not allow you to leave. You will stay for my wedding."

He paused and straightened. I had commanded him. Hotly. Surely. The weight of the command had offended him. His brows knit together, then went wide. "I cannot stay for your wedding, lord. Sure and I would weep at the sight of it." He stiffened and stepped back from me. "I must go now," he said evenly "and yet I must also wonder: Why would the Lord God have brought you to the Gael? Why would He have touched you with a knowledge of His Power, with the Inner Vision and the wonder of His Word and Revelation, only to send you off . . ." His hands went out, palms up, fingers open to indicate the luxurious room. "To this . . ."

Had a week passed since Egan's visit? The day was warm and bright. The townhouse was in a turmoil, with cooks and seamstresses and tailors making pandemonium of my usually serene domain. My mother had worked herself into a state of hysteria, running about the house, sighing and mumbling to herself as she constantly found items which must be added to her list of things to be attended to before the wedding. I had not felt well since Egan's departure. I had treated him poorly and knew it. I had sought him in the town, but no one knew of his whereabouts. A general malaise settled upon me, precursor of the terrible illness which was soon to come. As yet there was no fever or nausea or pain, merely a constant depression, a nagging wound which I mistakenly took to be only dejection and remorse. I wished desperately to make amends to Egan, yet he was gone, as though he had never come to Briton at all.

I sat in my room, half dressed, staring out at the inner courtyard. My mother invaded my privacy with the brash, unthinking self-assurance of all mothers with their sons.

"Shall we have lamprey?"

I looked at her blankly. "Have it where?"

"At the marriage feast, of course. I know that it is bad for the digestion, but what will be thought of us if we do not serve it?"

My malaise had made me tolerant. I thought little about the fussings and preparations for the celebration of my marriage. That was woman's work and joy. I cared not for it, save that I would have my mother happy and content.

"Whatever pleases you," I told her.

"It is *your* wedding, Magonus."

"And *your* feast."

She exhaled her despair of me. "Men! What good are you in moments such as this? You care nothing for the finer things of life. The only thing which concerns you is that the nuptial vows be made quickly and that the marriage bed be clean and soft."

I smiled drolly. "A matter of masculine priorities." I leaned back in my chair and closed my eyes. The first washing of fever touched me then. I shook my head to free myself of it. "I do not care for lamprey. I would as soon not have it."

"But the guests shall think us peasants if we do not offer it!"

Impatience made me shout. "Then serve it and have done with it! Why ask me, if all you intend to do is tell me in the end?" I rose and went to fetch my clothes. I felt a sudden need to be out of the room and away from her presence.

"My," she rebuked me. "You are in a black mood." Her tone was flat and quivering with protest. "You've not been yourself, Magonus, ever since that ragged young man came."

I bent to lace my sandals. "Tell Trimarinus to ready my horse."

"You shall not ride out from the village alone!"

I straightened and shook my head with loving condescension. "It is amazing, is it not, that I have managed to survive all of these past years without a nursemaid?"

She frowned and harrumphed. "Not very well, I might add." Her brow came down as she squinted at me. "Do I see fever in your eyes, Magonus?"

"No, dear, only the need to be out of here for a while. My mare and I could both use a good cleansing workout. I shall ride out to the fortress. Last time I saw Licinius, I did not have a chance to finish looking over his books. His accountants have made a royal jumble of them—deliberately, to hide the discrepancies."

"You will take Trimarinus along?"

Why was it that her questions always sounded like commands? I gave her a brief and loving hug. "Yes, to please you, I shall take Trimarinus."

The day was fair. We reached the sea in good time and, riding out upon the headlands, sighted the peninsula. The fortress stood ahead. I pointed. "There. Look to the banner, Trimarinus. Do you see the Cross upon it?"

He twitched his shoulders begrudgingly. "I do."

"What do you say of Licinius now, old friend? Do you still believe him to be in league with the Devil?"

"I believe that Time will tell the truth of him."

The man was impossible. I told him so. Spurring the mare, I galloped on ahead of him, knowing all too well that he would follow in his own grumbling good time.

There was dust on the trail ahead, stirred by the passage of a group of mounted men. They were just ahead of me, making their way toward the fortress. There were, perhaps, twenty of them, with several rickety, heavily loaded carts, a string of nervous horses, and two mewling cows with udders so swollen that their teats leaked and nearly touched the earth.

It was a happy and raucous group. They lifted their voices in song. I saw Llwyn riding his huge dun horse at the head of the gathering. I caught up with him and slowed my mare to a trot. He was riding beside another man who was mounted upon a small, brown, lathered stallion. The man, a lean, powerful, hawk-faced fellow, was dressed, as was Llwyn, in bold tartan.

"Ahh, Lord Patricius." Llwyn seemed glad enough to see me. With obvious pride, he cocked his head to indicate the other man. "My cousin. Ceretic. Lord of Alcluith and the clan Dumbarton."

I lowered my head in a half-nod of deference, acknowledging the other's rank. "We meet at last. I have heard many good words of you from Licinius."

He had the dark good looks of the northern Celt; the natural arrogance and self-assurance of a man born to lead others. Yet, when he reached out and clasped my hand in ready greeting, I felt more than the strength and steadiness of a warrior. Instinctively, I withdrew my hand and rubbed it upon my thigh as though I had touched something unclean.

If he saw my reaction, he gave no hint of it. His tone was that of one who would be a friend, the very essence of congeniality as he indicated the carts and horses and cows with a backward twist of his head. "Not bad for a beginning, eh?"

"Bad?" Llwyn bantered. "It is the start of our independence, the first mark of our authority!"

I looked back, nodding. "How did all this come to be given? Surely the generous folk of Bannavem Taburniae had no hand in such a gift."

"Gift?" Llwyn turned the word, mockingly. "I suppose we could say that it was a gift . . . freely given, eh Ceretic?"

The other smiled. "Albeit reluctantly." To me he added: "The time for asking is over."

Understanding was beginning to dawn on me. It was not welcome. "You took all this . . . by force . . . ?"

"As was due us," replied Ceretic.

"Due you? From whom?"

"From those who would reap reward in time of stress, but withhold assistance in time of need." He drew in a breath and readjusted his weight upon his saddle. "As you know, Lord Patricius, Licinius sent for me to act as adviser. I've been through this all before when trying to gain sure footing in my own land, for my own tribe and stronghold. If the people are to be protected, they must grant their support. An army cannot be fed on good intentions. If the people are too stupid and selfish to see the truth, they must be made to see it. By force, if need be."

"And who determines the extent of the force?"

He saw my as-yet-to-be-defined disapproval and sought to make light of it before it clarified into open dissent. "We are all Christian men here, Lord Patricius. We share the same hope in the Resurrection. By the grace of our Lord Jesus Christ we are baptized in the name of the most holy Trinity. Any force that we shall exact shall be in the name of God and to assure His peace here in Briton."

Fever began to rise in me again at that moment. I suddenly felt distractingly weak. I could not fully react to his words. I could only measure them, sift them, wishing to find truth in them. I was unnaturally tired. I could not think clearly. Somewhere within me, around me, the thinnest rising of memory rose with the haunting whisper of the banshee wind. The stench of blood rose into my nostrils. I fought it away along with a nearly overwhelming desire to vomit. Sweat stung onto my forehead and I leaned forward, bracing my open palm against the mare's neck lest I fall in a faint from my saddle.

"You are ill, lord." Ceretic's statement was heavy with sincere concern.

I reached up to wipe my brow. The wave of nausea was passing. The dizziness had ebbed. "I have not felt quite myself for days now . . . forgive me. I think I shall ride ahead and beg a cool ale from Licinius. Perhaps that shall steady me."

"Aye. Do so. I shall send a man along to see you safely there." He called out to a shiny-faced youth who was taut with delight at being summmoned to follow the bidding of his lord. "Accompany Lord Patricius to the gatehouse."

"Aye." The word was a gulp of eagerness.

I had the distinct impression that if Ceretic had ordered the boy to leap to his death from the cliffs of the peninsula, he would have done so without question. And gladly.

The ale was cool. Licinius poured for us both. I seated myself at his table and drank deeply, gratefully. For a moment I was refreshed. Before me, strewn across the wood, was the usual clutter. Maps. Styluses. Ink pots. An uneven stack of parchments with a sheathed short-sword flung down across them to serve as a paperweight against the impetuous drafts which chilled the room and moved at will within it like ghosts. I put my hands around the thick-textured glass of ale and allowed the chilled liquid to cool my palms. As I lifted the glass and drank again, my eyes held upon the short-sword in its intricately worked leather scabbard. When next I spoke, my words startled me as much as they did Licinius.

"From which village did Ceretic and his men exact tribute?"

"Tribute?" The word offended him.

I wanted to apologize for its use. Yet, with my eyes still holding upon the sword, I asked harshly: "Is there a more suitable term?"

He cocked his head, trying to define my mood. Misunderstanding it, he shrugged, off-handedly amused. "I would say: fair share."

I had to force my eyes from the sword and, as I did, my head began to ache again, dully. I looked at Licinius. "Would you?"

"What else? The people of this district . . . they send out their young men . . . they praise the cause of the New Day . . . but they will contribute nothing to its maintenance."

"They? Which village?"

"Some petty farming town a few miles inland. It was not from Bannavem Taburniae."

"Yet."

He had been standing across from me, leaning casually back against the wall as he drank. My statement caused his brow to furrow. His lips worked to suppress his annoyance. "Of what do you accuse me, Magonus?"

I stared at him. The bright, stabbing light of a thousand disconnected memories flashed like some mad patchwork behind my eyes. I squinted. Reaching up with the thumb and index finger of my right hand, I pressed in upon my lids, trying to erase the vision. It blurred but did not disappear. Yet it refused to be clarified. It was color. It was light. No more than that. "I don't know . . ."

Licinius saw the illness growing in me and worried over it. "I will send for my physician . . ."

"No." The memories were fading. I waited for them to be gone before I opened my eyes. "I am better now. But this man . . . this Ceretic . . . he troubles me."

He put down his glass and came around the table to me. Seating himself on the arm of my chair, he put a paternal arm about my shoulder. "Ceretic and his clansmen intimidated a few fools. A lesson was needed and a lesson was learned. From this day forth, when I ask contributions from the populace, they will remember the weight of Ceretic's threats and be more considerate of the virtue of generosity. It is for their own benefit."

"And yours."

"Of course. I tell you, Magonus, Ceretic has made me see things in a different light. I have been too passive. You know how it is to the north of us . . . to the east . . . on the continent. And I know what I have seen in the tribelands of Dumbarton, at Ceretic's fortress at Alcluith. His leadership has won much for the people there."

"Security?"

"And respect. The people know that he is lord and that he shall protect them."

It was as though a hook were being dragged through the depths of my soul, drifting, snagging in memory, sending taut and trembling messages which I had no wish to transcribe.

"Is that what you would be to the people of Bannavem Taburniae, then? Lord protector and holy savior?"

He tensed and withdrew from me. "In the name of Christ, Magonus, what sort of sniveling piety is this? I sent Ceretic out to be an extension of my will. I asked him to avoid violence. If, confronted by the arrogant, selfish, short-sightedness of a few local officials, he found it necessary to bruise a few egos and batter a few heads, what matter? The New Day has dawned. The people must be made to understand that, for their own sake, they must yield."

"Or you shall break them?"

He was clearly angry with me. "I or the barbarians. I think we would both agree upon which is the preferable choice."

The hook freed itself of memory and drifted, carrying my thoughts with it. "Yes . . . we must stand united . . ."

"Well, then." He was not a man to savor anger. He released it. "Why do we exchange heated words? Let us instead drink a toast to the dawn of the New Day."

He poured ale for us again, filling our glasses until they foamed high. We raised our arms to offer the toast, but before it could be made, we heard the sound of quick, sure footsteps rising within the stairwell.

Ceretic, lord of Alcluith and the clan Dumbarton, entered the room without ceremony. He had bathed and clothed himself in fresh, dark garments. His hair had been freshly coifed in the manner of the Britons of old: worn long and pulled back from his forehead, with a lock of hair held high by a serpentine clip at the top of his head. By Roman standards, it would have been considered a woman's style, yet there was nothing feminine about the lord of Alcluith. He moved with a fluidity and aggressiveness which was forthrightly male. He crossed the room with the long, sure step of one who is familiar and comfortable with his surroundings. Reaching Licinius, he grasped his free arm in greeting as he proclaimed: "You should have ridden with us! You should have seen them cower and offer up all that they owned."

He turned to me and gave me an expansive nod of greeting. "I trust you are feeling better, Lord Patricius?"

I told him that I was, ignoring the thickening ache in my head.

Ceretic pumped my arm enthusiastically. "It is amazing what the threat of force can accomplish among cowards. But what is this? Do I interrupt a toast?"

"To the dawn of the New Day," affirmed Licinius. "Here. Hold. We shall drink together." He went to the stairwell and called down for another glass to be brought.

Ceretic was pleased. To me he said: "It was a clever ploy . . . sending a stranger, an emissary with a heavy hand . . . the fools will remember only the bruise of threat, but will not associate it directly with their lord. Yet, in the future, when he asks assistance from them . . . they will think carefully before they refuse."

"Did you work violence against our people, then?"

"No violence at all," he assured me. "It was not necessary. The visible threat of armed men was enough to convince them."

A young boy arrived with a glass, delivered it, bowed, and was off like a hart after the coin which Licinius flipped to him as reward.

Ceretic nodded with approval as the boy scampered off. "Offer a scamp like that gold and he'll follow you to Hell and back without so much as a whimper. I pay my own men a wage, a portion of whatever we take."

"Take?"

He replied enthusiastically. "I come from a poor land, Lord Patricius. We are surrounded by barbarians. The threat to us is severe. There is little sustenance. Occasionally, it is necessary for us to go out into the countryside and take what we need."

"From whom?"

He did not like the question. "From those who have disdained our protection."

Licinius handed Ceretic a brimming glass. "We must drink to the day when we shall be united . . . from Land's End to Alcluith and beyond . . . to the day when none shall refuse to support us . . . to the day when, in the name of Christ, we shall drive the barbarians back to their heathen lands so that Britons may once again live in peace and plenty."

Ceretic accepted the glass and lifted it high. "I shall drink to that, and deeply, and to the day when Christians, by the will of God, reach out across the Western Sea and strike just vengeance until that cursed isle runs with the blood of those who have harried and brutalized us for so long."

Again the hook snagged within me; tearing, rousing the beginning of an unwelcome and obscure vision. "Vengeance? In the name of God?"

Licinius reached out and brushed his glass forcefully against mine, "Drink, Magonus! To the hope of that sweet day!"

"And if the barbarians do not choose to be driven?"

Ceretic was downing his ale in great gulps. He paused, took the glass from his lips, and swallowed audibly as he wiped foam from his meticulously clipped mustache with his fingertips. His thick, black brows came together across the bridge of his nose as he stared at me with hard, unforgiving eyes. "Surely then, Lord Patricius, they shall be driven."

"By whom? I have joined with Licinius so that we might, through strength and purpose, hold the peace. The barbarians threaten us because they know that we are weak, incapable of defense. When they learn of our strength, of our willingness to stand against them, we shall have canceled their threat."

"Never." His eyes stripped me of my manhood and told me clearly that my words had reduced me to a child in his opinion.

"I have known good men among them," I said.

"Pagans?" He turned the word viciously.

"Only because they do not know the word of Christ."

The statement caused him to laugh. He turned to Licinius. "The man's a bloody monk!"

Licinius' tone was light with amusement. "Forgive him. He has been too long upon Lérins. He tends to lapse into fits of righteousness now and again, but usually he has a sound head on his shoulders." He smiled at me, disarmingly, or so he thought. "Come, come, Magonus, drink with us!"

I stared at him for a moment, then moved my glance to Ceretic. His eyes met mine. Unblinking. Serpent's eyes. As surely as a man sees his own image reflected out to him from a mirror, I saw what he was and raised my glass to him. "To the beast of anarchy," I said, and drank.

Licinius went taut. His anger toward me had returned. "What is this, Magonus?"

"Truth." I did not flinch. "Tell me, Licinius, if the lamb becomes the lion, shall he be more worthy of salvation than the wolf?"

Ceretic hissed annoyance. "Not only a monk . . . but a maker of riddles!"

Memories came to me then, clearly for the first time, on a tide of fever and nausea. It was as though I stood upon the deck of the little trading curragh. The world pitched and swayed beneath me as I spoke. "I have lived among the barbarians . . . in Eire and in Gaul . . . and I have learned this of them . . . that without the just and gentle wisdom of Christ to guide them, to shepherd them, their souls are free to run with the vagaries of every tide which would take them . . . to respond to every whim which would carry them. But there *are* good men among them, just men, men who would follow The Way if it were made known to them."

Ceretic exhaled a contemptuous snarl. "I care not for the souls of the barbarians."

"And what of your own soul? Can you, baptized in the name of the most holy Trinity, bend to expedience and not be broken by it?"

Ceretic shook his head. "Even God Almighty shall make allowances for the times."

"Shall He?"

Slowly, Licinius put down his glass of ale. He reached across the table to where his sword lay sheathed. There was the cold hiss of metal being drawn from a scabbard. He took the sword and held it out before me, blade down, haft held high.

"For now, Magonus, though surely Ceretic and I do not wish it . . . here is God's grace . . . here is the cross . . . here is the hope and the future of Briton . . ."

My eyes held on the blade, on the cold, gray glint of polished metal. For a moment, so brief that it was seen and gone in a mere rush of seconds, the room in which we stood grew dark and distant. Everything within it ceased to exist for me. Everything but the sword.

It was a cross. It was a great, towering, gleaming cross of silver; as heavy as the moon, as light as air, as luminous as storm clouds when the sun burns bright and hot behind them. It seemed to be held by no man. The tip of the blade was imbedded deeply into the polished wood of a massive table such as I had never before seen. A round table. A hundred men could have seated themselves around it. From the place where the sword stood in the wood, blood oozed and ran, as thick as the molten heart of the earth.

I shivered. I felt desperately ill. The vision was gone. I said weakly, remembering Egan's words to me: "When the lambs become lions, they shall not be content to allow their brothers to return to peaceful grazing once the wolves are slain and laid to rest. They shall become the predators of the New Day. And in time, they shall devour one another."

"Riddles again," drawled Ceretic.

Licinius grumbled and frowned. He slid the sword back into the scabbard. "What has come over you, Magonus? Your words make no sense to us. A man must do as he must do . . . to survive . . ." He flung the sword back onto the table, trying to be done with the impatience he was feeling toward me. "Both Ceretic and I share your wish for peace. But we must be willing to make concessions to the times. If we do not, there shall not be a Christian left alive to sing a psalm in all this world."

Behind my eyes, Mercia's face; devout and gentle Mercia, Rigan of Dalaradia, who had conspired against her lord to keep a fellow Christian alive. "I wonder . . ."

Licinius studied me a moment. He saw the illness in me. Again his anger ebbed. He came to me and put his wide, hard hand upon my shoulder. "You are no longer a monk dwelling in the peaceful realm of the comtemplative. You have chosen to live as a man in the world of men. By the blood of the Cross, my boy, the truth must be faced. If Christ's kingdom is ever to be secured in Briton, it can only be done through the threat and the power of the sword."

Pushing his hand away from me, I rose slowly from the table, my palms flat against the wood. "No." Though the word was spoken softly, it allowed no debate. I met Licinius' glance and held it, not defiantly, but with infinite sadness. There was a sound forming within me, murmuring for release, working upon my tongue. It was as it had been on that night so long ago upon the Mountain of Mists when I had spoken to Dubh and Darerca of the life of Christ. The words issued from my lips, but they were not mine.

"God's kingdom shall not be won through the sword. Wars cannot be fought in His name. Yet they shall be fought. Clan shall fight against clan. King shall war against king. Individuals shall be consumed by their own murderous pride and ambition. The blood of Man shall be the wine of Satan. The Lord of the Dead shall grow fat upon the decomposing flesh of the damned. We cannot humble ourselves before God as long as we insist that we are masters of our own destiny. We must yield or we shall be broken. You and Ceretic may well issue in the dawn of a New Day . . . but it shall not last. By your defiance and manipulation of the laws of righteouness, you have assured its inevitable destruction. Only when all men and all nations walk in The Way of God . . . only when men cease to make a mockery of their faith . . . only then shall there be no soil for the nourishment of

Evil . . . only then shall Satan shrivel like a malignant vine beneath the healing grace of the Son. Then . . . and only then . . . shall there be peace on earth."

He stared at me. Did he understand? Did he see the Spirit speaking in me, as Egan had seen it, as Darerca and Leborchom and the captain and so many of the people of Eire had seen it? Whatever it was that he saw, it grossly disturbed him.

He stalked belligerently away from me to the opposite side of his littered table. He seated himself heavily in his chair. "You *have* been too long upon Lérins, Magonus." He frowned deeply. "I have told you, as I have told Ceretic, that I have had a dream. A vision. Briton *shall* be united. I may not live to see it, but by all that is holy, I shall have been instrumental in bringing it to pass."

"May God have mercy on you, then. The dawn of your New Day shall rise . . . righteous . . . and flawed. And the king of your New Day shall be slain by forces which you will have set within his own seed. His sword shall rise from out of a great stone. And he shall rise with it, shining like the sun itself before he is eclipsed by shadow. His memory shall be bloodied, his unity shattered, the origin of his name forgotten. Briton shall be in darkness . . . because of what you have wrought in the dawning of your New Day . . ."

Once again the words had come through me. Alien. Unwelcome. They left me shivering with loneliness and cold despair. Like the druid Néladóir, I had seen beyond Tomorrow. Through mists. Through clouds. I had glimpsed what no living man had yet glimpsed. Shreds. Fragments. Colors. Truths. Then all were gone from me. No longer mine. No longer any man's.

Sweat stood out on my forehead. I had seen the future of Briton and somehow knew that I held no place within it. Licinius and Ceretic . . . the lions of the New Day . . . they would write as they must upon the pages of its destiny. And I? I must follow another road. One that had been laid for me long before I was ever born.

I shook the thought away. I was trembling, violently. Fever had risen to pound behind my eyes and within my ears. It filled my mouth and my nostrils with the taste of blood.

"Licinius . . . look at him . . . he is ill unto death . . ."

Ceretic was no longer mocking or contemptuous. He was genuinely concerned.

Licinius was on his feet and coming around the table toward me. "Ceretic is right. You tremble as though with palsy. No wonder you speak so strangely. It is the fever upon your tongue." He seemed to find comfort in this assessment of a situation which had come close to un-nerving him. "Come," he insisted. "Let me help you. I will call my physician. You must rest here awhile."

"No," I protested with upraised hands, backing away from him.

"It is nothing to be ashamed of, my boy. The best of men are stricken limp of limb and lame of brain every now and again." Still he advanced toward me. He was smiling, attempting to reassure me. "Come. I insist that you stay the night. It is the least that one ally can do for another."

I stepped back down into the stairwell. "I am not your ally, Licinius," I said quietly. "God help us both. I am your enemy."

26

"MAGONUS!"

Romana called to me. I chose not to hear. Beneath the linen of my bed sheets, I stirred in my sleep and dreamt that I was a boy again. The sun was high and I stood beneath it. Claudius stood beside me, tall and splendid in his red woolen cloak, with his sister on his arm—pudgy, dimpled, disarming little Clodia; Clodia the child and then, as can only happen in a dream, sud-denly a woman grown. She was smiling, the smile of one who holds a secret. She leaned toward her brother and began to whisper about it to him. He looked at me and laughed.

I ran away from them. Away across the inland hills, across a grassland made yellow by the sun, toward the woods where the world went dark and towered above me, filling me with the rising whisper of a wind which seemed to be summoning me on.

"Magonus!"

The dream has shattered. I sat up upon the narrow

bed and gazed up at my sister. The illness which had been working in me during these last few days had finally taken hold. I felt weak, disoriented, dizzy.

"There is someone to see you," she said.

"Did I not tell you? No one was to know of my whereabouts."

"Everyone knows where you are. Where else would they look for you? Considering the fact that you have put me out of my own room, you might at least be courteous enough to tell me what I am to say to them when they ask about you. It is your second day here. Mother and father are worried. Clodia is distraught. And now there is this young man, insisting that I allow him to care for you if you are ill, as you once cared for him."

I swung my legs over the edge of the bed. "Egan is here?"

"That is his name. He has been helping in return for bed and board. He has been with us for several days now, sleeping with the boys in their quarters. But really, Magonus, if you are ill, you must allow me to call a physician."

"No." I leaned forward, resting my elbows on my knees. I felt faint.

Romana exhaled a sigh which betrayed a mixture of concern and exasperation. "Magonus, you must let me call a physician. For the sake of Heaven, brother, it is but two days before the wedding!"

"There shall be no wedding."

I heard the sharp intake of her breath. "You cannot mean that!"

I lay back upon the bed. I do not remember if I replied to her or not.

A physician was brought out to me. And the priest. I were purged and sweated and prayed over. Strong herbs were burnt in the little low-ceilinged room so that their vapors might ease my breathing. I knew none of this. I only knew my dreams.

They spun out as skeins upon a weaver's spindle. Memories. Fears. Hopes. They were caught and thinned and fused by sleep and fever, then thickened by a prodding consciousness which would not allow me full rest.

I must tell you of these dreams. Without an understanding of them, you will have no knowledge of the

man I was about to become. It is written in the Bible that
God chooses his apostles and takes them to Himself,
branding them, though they often bolt at the thought of
the branding, searing His word as fire upon their tongues.
It is written that once the brand is felt and acknowledged, these men are never again their own. They are
God's men forevermore, following Him through their own
choice once He has shown them the road of His choosing.

There are dreams and there are dreams. I know. I
have dreamt them all. But the druids know, and the simple men of faith of all nations and creeds know, that there
are dreams which are not dreams. There are dreams
which are the substance of a world beyond this world,
dreams which transport us beyond our own understanding
of reality. They take us beyond Tomorrow. They take us
into Vision. They give to us a Sight which is not ours to
hold. They are dreams of Darkness and of Light. They
transform us or destroy us. Why? I do not know, save
to say that it is the work of Destiny, and that, perhaps,
for each man there comes a moment of choosing, of acknowledging, or of walking away upon his own road.

My dreams that night were ordinary dreams at first.
Then, subtly, they changed, like sheevras and specters
seeping up out of the Otherworld to merge with the mists
on the night of Samain. There was a wind rising, within me, around me, beyond me—I could not tell. There
were voices in the wind. No calming, peace-bringing, song-
singing voices. They were voices which stabbed me.
Voices which punctured me to my very heart. They cried
on the wind, they called, they taunted. They were neither
male nor female, adult, nor child; they were the sound of
the sea wind frenzied by storm; they were crows cawing
and wolves wailing in the great benighted forests of Eire.
They moaned like the lost souls of all the world: "For
what purpose . . .the miles and the years . . . the quest
and the question . . . for what purpose . . . ?"

Words formed then. Prodding out of time.

Egan's voice. "Why would the Lord God have brought
you to the Gael? Why would He have touched you with a
knowledge of His Power . . . only to send you off . . . to
this . . . ?"

Comla's voice. "Are'ya so sure, boy'o, that'ja have not
found a home among the Gael . . . ?"

The voice of the Ri, recalling prophecy. "Tell me, boy, when you came to Eire . . . was there a storm upon the sea . . . ?"

"No!" My own voice as I sat bolt upright on the bed. Sweating. Shivering. Staring straight into the face of Egan, who had been seated beside me through all of the long hours of my delirium.

"Tell them to stop," I demanded of him.

"Them . . . ? Who . . . ?"

"The voices." A fire burned in my belly and at the back of my head. I bent over and retched upon the floor.

Egan put his hands upon my shoulders. "You must rest and sleep, Lord Padraic. Sure now you are very ill."

"I cannot rest. I cannot sleep. They grant me no peace."

"They . . . ?"

"The voices. The memories. They come to me. They haunt me. They draw me back into Yesterday. God, Egan, what do they want of me?"

He eased me back upon my bed and began to massage my shoulders. "Rest now, brother of long ago. Ask of the Lord. He shall answer if an answer is what you're truly seeking."

Fever washed over me then, swept me away from Egan and the little room and the sweated linens of my bed. It swept me swiftly and mercilessly, as though I were a tiny stone caught in the suck of some relentless tide. It swept me up and placed me upon a distant mountain, upon Slemish, within the shadows of the glen. The billa was there. The ruined stone was there. The little fire burned, surely, steadily. A boy knelt before it. The boy was I.

He rose. I rose. Once again, as in the dream of so long ago, I stood within the wondrous crystal. I walked within it, within that great and gleaming clarity of stone. As in the Long Ago, each step I took revealed to me a new and awesome facet of the radiance which sparkled all around me. Ahead, there was a light, somehow rising, being born out of itself. As it took on substance, it revealed a central core: a towering three-trunked pillar of fire from which a corona emanated as though flaring out of the sun.

The Light turned. It twisted. From it came a sound, a roaring, a rising, not a voice, yet somehow, within me and all around me, it did speak. It made me know that I must prostrate myself before that Power which no mortal man has ever seen.

I fell upon the earth, if it was earth. I pressed my eyes against my hands. Then—was it within myself? No, it seemed beyond me, around me, beside me—I saw the figure of a man bent in prayer. He looked toward me. He spoke in the voice of a man: "Can it be that you do not know Me yet, Padraic? The years and the miles . . . the quest and the question . . . can you still imagine that they have been without purpose? Can you still doubt the way of your road?" He paused and smiled with the gentle sadness of one who had borne all of the sorrow of the world. "He that had laid down His life for thee, it is He that speaketh in thee."

A heavy dew had settled in the night. I awoke to hear it dripping from the roof tiles. It was almost dawn. The birds had begun to stir and chatter in the darkness of the trees and shrubs. I propped myself up onto my forearm and looked about the room. I felt light, clear-headed, amazingly hungry. The room had been cleansed. Egan slept like a faithful and fretful hound across the foot of my bed. I nudged him with my toes. He came wide awake immediately. Anxious, he leaned to touch my cheek.

"Praise God! Your fever has broken."

"I have had the strangest and the most wonderful of dreams, Egan."

I felt as filled with joy as a man who has sought a lifetime for a hidden pathway to some wondrous treasure. Then, in the very instant when he has given up all hope of finding it, there it is, laid out before him as clear and bright as a river shining in the sun. As I looked at Egan, the miracle occurred. It was a quiet miracle, surely nothing as awesome as the toppling of the heathen stone in the mountain glen. The likes of Moses or Joshua would not have been impressed. But it was a miracle. And it was mine.

I was awake. I had no fever. Yet, as I looked at Egan, it was as though I viewed him through some strange gauze: a mist, a veined and tendoned cloud, a webbing which set him far off from me. He spoke. I could not hear him. I reached out to him. I could not touch him. We were in two separate worlds, he and I.

In his world there was the rising murmur of the growing day. In mine there was the voice of the Gael: "We ask thee, boy, come and walk among us once more." I saw the dove then, waiting for me in the land to which she had flown, sheltering in the heartland of Eire while all around her the world was consumed by the battling forces of the beasts of anarchy, by the lions of the New Day. She would wait there, warmed by the fire which Leborchom and I had kindled in the Long Ago. She would wait. For me. For the Word of God. And in time, when the Age of Darkness had passed, when the shadowing flight of ravens was no longer welcome in the world, she would be safe and strong and ready to fly out across the sea again, to heal the scars of the world, to raise her joyous song of hope for all Mankind. Slowly, beyond the vision, I heard her voice. It was the voice of Light. It was the voice of Life. It was the Source of all sound. "It is I who arm you . . . so that toward the rising and the setting of the sun men may know that there is none beside me. I am the Lord . . ."

As quickly as a page is turned, the vision was gone. Hesitantly, I reached out and touched Egan. There was no gauze, no mist, no cloud, only a man and a youth together in the growing light of the New Day.

"Your face, Lord Padraic . . ." Egan's eyes were round with wonder. "You've seen the dragons . . ."

"Dragons?"

"Aye, Don't you remember them? The dragon Future. The dragon Unknown."

Memory sparked. A memory which brought no pain, no remorse. I saw a small, frail boy of seven trembling with fear. I smelled the good sweet smell of hay and sleeping pups. I saw a tiny rush lizard etched like an animated shadow against the rough board walls of a kennel stall. I saw myself, holding the boy against his fears, sustaining him with my faith in the Lord my God. And now he sustained me, and the faith of my fathers belonged to us both.

I looked at him and smiled, accepting the memory and the truth; acknowledging them to be forevermore a part of myself. "It seems, Egan, that the dragons stand upon a road which insists upon bending back upon itself."

"To Eire?" The word was so full of tremulous hope that it almost drowned itself.

"To Eire."

"But my Lord Padraic has no wish to return there."

"Perhaps, after all has been said and done, Egan, it does not matter what I wish. The road bends back despite me. I think it is time for me to follow it."

He was trembling with incredulous elation. "The druids do say, Lord Padraic, that the roads have been laid for us . . . long before we are ever born . . . and that, somehow, the future of all Mankind is written in its past."

I rose from the bed and crossed the room. The door opened easily, effortlessly. The warmth of the growing day washed over me. I could see the land of Briton stretching away, rising gently to the hills which stood between Bannavem Taburniae and the sea. There was a soft wind stirring. It carried with it the scent of the sea, and of a distant island. I thought of the druid Néladóir, of his warnings spoken in the brightly lighted hall of the Ri Miliucc MacBuain. I thought of the Mountain of Mists and of the small, tender flame burning in the mountain glen. I thought of Miliucc's obsidian eyes alive with the reflected flickering of his own hearth fire as he recounted prophecy to me.

Flames and divinations. Druids and kings. Somehow, the will of God had called me to them and now was summoning me back again. I shivered. Not with chill. Not with fear of apprehension. With release and with acquiescence.

"Will you face the dragons with me, Egan?"

"Aye, lord, and that I will."

"We will have to study first, you know? Long and hard and for many a year. We will have to arm ourselves as priests with the blessings of holy Church and with the wisdom of the prophets. We will have to be as wise and as wary as any of the druids if we are to bring the Lord Jesus into the den of the mactire."

"The Lord God will make us so." He came to stand beside me. "Look, Lord Padraic, the sun is rising quickly now."

He had turned to face it. I closed my eyes. I did not have to look toward it to see it. It was rising within me, as it has risen within men of faith since the beginning of the world; vast beyond the dimensions of Man's imaginings, a beacon of Light raised against the Darkness of infinity. The heat of it seemed to be reaching across Time to touch me, to encompass me, to bathe me in its essence. It was Life and I stood beneath it. It was Life and it burned within me.

Egan walked out of the house and paused to draw in deep, deliberate breaths of the morning. "Sure and it shall be a fine new day, Lord Padraic."

The long hours of my illness had left me weak, yet I followed Egan and stood beside him. Together we turned and watched the rising of the sun. It touched the land with light, pushing the shadows westward before it, westward across the land and hills and Western Sea. Westward to Eire, following the flight of ravens to where the dove had flown and now waited, at the end of that long and torturous road which had been laid for me long before I had ever been born. Or perhaps, perhaps it did not end in Eire at all, but only just began there? Only God and His dragons could answer that for me.

I put my arm about Egan's slim shoulder. "The road will be long for us, my boy."

He smiled, undaunted and eager. "The road is always long, Lord Padraic, when it is leading a man home."

AUTHOR'S NOTES

This book is a novel. Yet it is a tapestry woven of history. Wherever possible, I have spun the tale within the framework of fact. Saint Patrick's youth is viewed through the mists of antiquity, obscured by the roiling, silent fog of centuries. The date and place of his birth are disputed. The year in which he was taken as a slave to Ireland is debated. To date, no records exist which can affirm Patrick's ordination as a priest, much less his confirmation as a bishop. We cannot pinpoint the year in which he ultimately returned to the isle of the Gael as a missionary. We have, when all is said and done and all of the theories are arrayed before us, only Patrick's words and the many myths with which the story-tellers have clouded the truth.

Fifth-century Britain and Ireland offer today's researcher all of the enigmas of the Dark Ages. Here and there a bit of history shines brightly, but the rest is shrouded, smudged, open to doubt, speculation, and the wild spinnings of the imagination. Remember, if you would, that Patrick lived approximately one hundred years *before* King Arthur, in an even mistier age than that which would later give to us the heroic tale of Beowolf. It was an age in which the dogma of the Church was challenged, an age in which men believed that dragons stalked the earth, a time in which sorcerers and "devils" manipulated the lives of kings and common folk alike. Britain had not yet known castles of feudal lords or Norman conquests. The British race, as we know it today, was yet to be born. Roman influence upon the island nations of the Western Sea had been shattered. Barbarians were sweeping across the Continent to claim their place on the eastern shore of Britain. Raiders from Ireland, then called Scotia, were bringing the realities of carnage and murder to the peaceful Christian communities along the western shore. From the north, Pictish tribesmen were seeking to forcefully retake the lands south of the walls of Antoninus and Hadrain. In A.D. 409, the last of the Roman legions were withdrawn from Britain. The Age of Darkness descended.

Saint Patrick lived in a world that was witnessing the

collapse of the institutions of civilized man. It was a world that cleft the ancient roots of countless peoples; that questioned the validity of old gods while, in some sectors, pagan philosophy was being strengthened and revitalized in direct opposition to the values and morality of the God of Constantine.

It was in such a sector of the war-wearied earth that Patrick lived, labored, and ultimately dedicated his life to the God of his fathers. Within his lifetime, he brought the Light of Christ to the people of Ireland. He brought to the proud Gaelic Celts the written word; the alphabet, with which he helped them to set down for posterity their wondrous sagas and their incomparable Brehon Laws. Because of Patrick, despite the Reformation, the history of the ancient Irish has been preserved. Because of Patrick, when the Black Death and the Age of Darkness decimated Europe, Irish monks and scholars kept the candles of culture and enlightenment burning. Yet, what does the world today know of Patrick? Not even his true name. Much of the history that has come down to us concerning him is, in truth, obviously legend. Conversely, we must not fail to recognize the fact that much of the legend may well be history.

We see the saint in plaster and marble, it stained glass, and—God save us—even in plastic. We see him as an old man, tonsured, arrayed in the vestments of a bishop. He is reputed to have driven the snakes of Ireland into the sea and to have taught the Irish people of the holy Trinity by illustrating its facets with the lowly three-leafed shamrock. Yet Venerable Bede has written that Ireland, since its earliest occupation by man, has been free of serpents. And Patrick, not once in any of his writings, has made mention of the shamrock. But traditions persist— and, I believe, not without reason. Their roots lie in the loam of truth, and this much we do know of Saint Patrick: He was a youth of sixteen when he first came to Ireland as a beardless, skull-shorn slave who had been "beaten to the point of death" by his captors. He was brought to them as an atheist, not as a man of faith. Patrick, before he could change the ways of the Gael, had first to be changed by them.

Who was this youth who found the God of his fathers, not in his Christian homeland, but high on a wild, brooding mountain in a pagan land? Who was this Patrick who claims to have witnessed, against his will, miracles and holy visions which called him to fulfill a task which he abhorred? Who was this arrogant, virile, charismatic young man who loathed the posturing intellectuals of Gaul and who openly defied druids and kings and the gods of the Otherworld?

I have sought to discover this.

I have drawn the tale from many sources, some of the most noteworthy being: Patrick's own *Confession*, his *Letter to the Soldiers of Coroticus*, from his magnificent prayer *The Lorica*, and from Paul Gallico's remarkable biography of the saint, *The Steadfast Man*. The descriptions of the people and lifestyle of the ancient Irish have been made possible, in the main, by P. W. Joyce's *A Social History of Ancient Ireland* (Vols. I & II), Maire and Liam dePaor's *Early Christian Ireland*, and by such of the old tales as *The Hound of Ulster* and *Da Derga's Hostel*.

Why have I told the tale as I have told it?

In my attempt to capture the mood of a fifth-century narrative, I have chosen to capitalize many words that are usually begun in lowercase. For example: spirit, power, darkness, light, force, good, evil. Whenever I have used them interchangeably with the words "holy Spirit," "God," "Satan," or "Christ," they are capitalized. In keeping with Celtic and Greco-Roman tradition, I have also capitalized the words "death," "fate," and "destiny" whenever they are meant to be understood as "the Fates," the dark angel "Death," or the god-figure "Destiny."

When I have written of "the Otherworld" or "the Long Ago," I am referring to them as specific places. I have done the same when I have capitalized "Time," "Tomorrow," "Yesterday," or "Unknown." As far as the characters within the novel are concerned, these words are often used in reference to specific, albeit mystical, places to which they believe a man or woman might actually travel if circumstances would allow.

I have capitalized the terms "Sight," "the Inner Vision," and "the Inner Eye" in an effort to differentiate the mystic from the commonplace, as well as to follow the well-worn path of tradition which usually finds them capitalized in the old tales and sagas.

As to the spelling of place names and Irish characters

in the novel, I believe that a note here is necessary just in case any Celtic scholars have read this far and have, out of pure and justified frustration, ground their teeth into their gums. Even the most cursory research into ancient Gaelic culture reveals as many diverse spellings for the various kings and gods and locales of old Ireland as there are shamrocks growing wild on that island. So, after much consideration, I have chosen my spellings from those least likely to mind-boggle non-Gaelic speaking readers. Irish is not a phonetic tongue, and I wanted my readers to be able to experience the lovely music of its sound. So, I have usually chosen the spellings most easily read by non-Irish speaking readers. For example, "Slemish" is the modern, Anglicized spelling of "Sliabh Mis," and comes close to duplicating those soft Gaelic words which, in English, freely translate into "The Mountain of Mists." The spelling of the name of the Ri Miliucc appears in the old texts as "Miliucc Moccu Buain." In the more modern references, it is "Milchu MacBuain." Since "Moccu" is merely another spelling of the Gaelic "Mac" (son of), for the sake of consistency I preferred to use the modern and more familiar spelling. However, no matter how many times I read the name "Milchu," it kept rolling off my tongue as "milk you" and totally distracted me from the proud, star-crossed personality I was attempting to describe. After much consideration, I decided to combine the two renderings of the name. So it is that the reader has been given "Miliucc MacBuain." As to the spelling of the name of "Padraic," it is, and was, the Irish spelling. "Patrick" is the Anglicized version and, to my ear at least, has a harder and less pleasant sound than the original spelling.

For those who found their eyebrows arching when, quoting from Saint Patrick's *Confession*, I stated that the man was the grandson of a priest, mark this: Though celibacy for the clergy was mandatory in Spain since the Council of Elvira in the year A.D. 305, it was not until the eleventh century, six hundred years after Patrick's death, that it became mandatory in the Western Church at the Roman Synod of 1074 under Pope Gregory VII.

As to the characters within the novel, Padraic, his parents and grandfather, the Ri Miliucc MacBuain, that giant MacCairthinn, the captain of the Irish curragh, the abbott Honoratus of Lérins, and Ceretic of Dumbarton are all

actual historic personages. Padraic's dreams and visions
are, in the main, his own and are well described in his
Confession. In the *Confession,* Patrick speaks of Victoricus coming to him in a dream, bearing "letters" from
the Irish. Though the man is presented as holy vision, the
name and the person seem real and remembered; so I
have placed him at the Mass held upon the Mountain of
Mists. The lands around that mountain, Slemish (or
Sliabh Mis, as it was called in Patrick's day), are still
known as Dal Buain and, for centuries, seanachies pep-
pered their tales with the "curses" Patrick was said to
have rained down upon that ancient lord's head. Though
not recorded in the *Confession,* it is evident in the old
tales that the Ri Miliucc MacBuain had a great effect
upon Patrick's life. He was his master for six years. There
was a tight and lasting emotional bond between them.
When the saint eventually returned as a bishop to Ireland,
he set out to meet with the Ri. Miliucc MacBuain chose
to commit suicide by self-immolation rather than face
Patrick again. Why? The ancient tales and chronicles give
us this: "Then Patrick stood still on the southern side of
Slemish—there stands a cross in that place—and he saw
the fire from afar. He was silent for the space of two or
three hours except for sighing and groaning. Then he
said, 'I know not, God knows. Yonder Miliucc's house is
on fire. He is burning himself lest he believe in the Eternal God at the end of his life. Upon him lies a curse:
of him shall be neither King nor crown prince and in
bondage will his offspring and his seed abide forever, and
his soul shall not come out of hell up to doom after
doom."

Many a historian has wondered if Patrick had not some
special skill and fearlessness with the great, tall Irish wolf
dogs, and if this skill did not eventually win him his passage to freedom aboard an Irish trading vessel. From his
Confession, we know that he, an escaped slave, did have
some barterable skill with which, after walking two hundred miles, he offered to "pay for my passage" with the
Irish traders who did, indeed, have aboard their ship a
cargo of hounds. So I have taken the liberty of assuming
that he might well have spent some time as a houndsman
or kennel hand during his six years in bondage within the
truath of the Ri Miliucc MacBuain.

Patrick's adventures with the pirates and the barbarians

in Gaul happened much as they are recounted in this
novel. The vision of "freedom in sixty days" is presented
as Patrick recalled it in his *Confession*.

Saint Patrick and the nonexistent snakes of Ireland
have become hopelessly enmeshed in tradition. Why?
Some have wondered if the serpents are not merely sym-
bolic of the old gods. Perhaps. Yet many a scholar has
surmised that the saint may have spent time upon the
little isle of Lérins off the coast of France. There is a
monastery there. In Patrick's time it was still under con-
struction, and its abbot, Honoratus, was winning a reputation for driving its booming population of vipers into the
sea. No doubt his stalwart monks assisted him. Perhaps
one young man more than the others? Patrick does not
tell us. That Patrick did indeed wander "through Gaul
and Italy and the islands of the Tyrrhene Sea" after his
phenomenal escape from his second enslavement, this we
know. It is not improbable or unreasonable to assume his
encounters with the serpents of that isle, as I have presented them, beyond credibility. Several years ago, as an
employee of the Los Angeles Zoo, I knew an animal
keeper who was bitten three times in one year by the
same viper. He survived all three snake bites, even though
he was allergic to the antivenin.

Patrick's toppling of the standing stone in the mountain
glen is based upon the many legends which speak of
Patrick's destruction of the great "wailing" stone, Crom
Cruach, a megalithic idol which stood out upon the plain
of Magh Slecht.

Claudius, though fictitious, has been drawn from that
unnamed friend of Patrick, so dear to his heart and thoroughly incorporated into the memories of his youth, who,
in later years, betrayed him when his ministry to Ireland
was in question.

Patrick does not claim to have been virgin when he
came to the priesthood. Indeed, his strong views concerning the value of the state of chastity seem to indicate un-
happy experiences in the opposite realm. Women followed
him eagerly and were many of his first converts. It is not
unreasonable to assume that during his youth, as a young
man returned home after years of suffering and humiliation, he might have known and loved a woman such as
Clodia.

Licinius is representative of the first Briton warlords

who began to assert their dominance soon after the ebb of
Roman rule; lords who sometimes dared to dream of a
unified Briton, a dream that would come to fruition and
shatter with King Arthur. Ceretic, known to Roman his-
torians as Coroticus, was, in fact, lord of Alcluith, Fort of
the Britons, in the land of the Picts known to us today as
Scotland. The ruins of that fortress, Castle Rock, can be
seen in Dumbarton. When Patrick served as a bishop in
Ireland, Ceretic sent his murderous "Christian" raiders
against the Irish shore, plundering and slaughtering in the
newly established Christian communities. His eventual
confrontation with Patrick was inevitable. It is immortalized in one of the few documents known to have been
written by the saint's own hand, his *Letter to the Soldiers
of Coroticus.*

Because of the man that Patrick the boy became, he
must have known a Leborchom, a Dubh, a Darerca, and
certainly at least one Amorgin. Because of the content of
The Lorica, and for the sake of intrigue, romance, and
adventure, I have blessed the Rí Miliucc MacBuain with
Mercia, blighted him with the druid Néladóir, and beset
him with the Rigan Cairenn and the Red Rí Sencha.

The scene in the mystical wood with the whore Morrighan is pure invention: allegory. But it has not been
written casually, or without purpose. Patrick, in his *Confession,* alluded to a "sin" committed in his youth, a sin
which haunted him all of his life and nearly cost him his
mission to Ireland. Whatever its nature, Patrick was never
fully able to forgive himself for its commission. To further
the telling of the story, I have drawn up out of the grab
bag of fifth-century Celtic myth, magic, and symbolism
and have come up, not accidentally, with the Morrighan.
Patrick believed implicitly in the power of sorcery, the
"evil spells" of women, and begged God in *The Lorica* to
keep him protected against "all knowledge which is forbidden the human soul."

The Morrighan is more than a mere member of the
mighty clan of Irish earth goddesses. She is the war fury,
the Phantom Queen, the portent of death to be found in
battle. Celtic mythology finds her bathing the extremities
of those whose death in battle has been preordained. Sexual union with her was believed to assure victory in battle. So I have conjured the scene in the wood.

The wild boar figures prominently as a source of magic

and power in much of Celtic mythology. Maponos is an ancient British god of the hunt. In the novel, Padraic is challenged by the boar, wins the challenge and, though he knows it not, gains the Power. He is called Maponos by the Morrighan, for he is indeed a hunter, a young man blindly seeking himself and his destiny. He bathes in the magical, sulphurous waters of the stream which has been borne up out of the Otherworld, lies with the Morrighan and thus insures his victory in his lifetime battle against the forces of Darkness and Evil. The three red-hooded crows are yet another facet of the Morrighan legend, a triplification of the Phantom Queen herself. In the Ancient World, the crow or raven was the symbol of battle and its accompanying slaughter. Irish legends speak of The Three Morrighans: Badhbh, the Raven; Nemhain, the Frenzy; and Macha, namesake of no less than three of Ireland's most powerful warrior queens. So I have placed the Feathered Furies beside the Morrighan. I have shown them leading Padraic toward the west because it was in this direction his destiny lay . . . in the land of his enemies, the pagan Scots known to us today as Irishmen.

Joan Lesley Hamilton
Fawnskin, California